Praise for the novels of Candace Camp

"Alex and Sabrina are a charming pair."
—*BookPage* on *His Sinful Touch*

"Fun…frothy…entertaining."
—*Smart Bitches, Trashy Books* on *His Wicked Charm*

"Those who have not discovered Camp's Mad Morelands are in for a treat… Camp is a consummate storyteller whose well-crafted prose and believable characterization ensure that this intriguing mystery…will utterly enchant readers."
—*RT Book Reviews* on *His Sinful Touch*

"From its delicious beginning to its satisfying ending, Camp's delectable [story] offers a double helping of romance."
—*Booklist* on *Mesmerized*

"[A] beautifully written charmer."
—*Publishers Weekly* on *The Marriage Wager*

"A smart, fun-filled romp." —*Publishers Weekly* on *Impetuous*

"A clever mystery adds intrigue to this lively and gently humorous tale, which simmers with well-handled sexual tension."
—*Library Journal* on *A Dangerous Man*

"Delightful." —*Publishers Weekly* on *The Wedding Challenge*

"A truly enjoyable read." —*Publishers Weekly* on *Mesmerized*

Also by Candace Camp

CANDACE CAMP

AN
AFFAIR
AT
STONECLIFFE

HQN

ISBN-13: 978-1-335-51307-6

An Affair at Stonecliffe

Copyright © 2022 by Candace Camp
and Anastasia Camp Hopcus

Recycling programs
for this product may
not exist in your area.

This is a work of fiction. Names, characters, places and incidents are either the product of the author's imagination or are used fictitiously. Any resemblance to actual persons, living or dead, businesses, companies, events or locales is entirely coincidental.

For questions and comments about the quality of this book, please contact us at CustomerService@Harlequin.com.

HQN
22 Adelaide St. West, 41st Floor
Toronto, Ontario M5H 4E3, Canada
www.Harlequin.com

Printed in U.S.A.

For Kat Tolle

AN
AFFAIR
AT
STONECLIFFE

PROLOGUE

NOELLE GAZED DOWN at the sleeping baby. How were they to live?

At first she had been too numb to think, moving through the past few days in a dazed state, unable to believe that this was real. Adam was too young, too full of life to die. Why had he been so reckless? And why, dear God, *why* had she argued with him that night?

She shivered. Their home was still and silent, empty of his laughter, his words, even his scowls or curses when his work went badly. Noelle wished she could return to her earlier befogged state. But this morning, as she had stood at his graveside, the Paris sky fittingly gray and drizzling, her heart had accepted what her mind refused to the past three days. Never again would she see her husband's smile or feel the touch of his lips on hers.

But she could not allow herself to sink into a morass of grief. She had a baby to care for. As she watched her child sleep, a fierce surge of protectiveness rose in her. She must face the harsh truths, the bitter reality, for Gil's sake. There was no one to solve her problems—or even to give her advice.

Adam's artist friends? His models? They were all as penniless as she was. Her father was far away in Oxford, and in any case, he was an impoverished academic who could barely manage to support himself. Even less likely to help was Adam's aristocratic father, who had been so opposed to Adam marrying "beneath him" that he cut his son out of his life.

Noelle glanced around their flat, forcing herself to take stock of her situation. There was no money here. Noelle had used the pittance she had stashed away just to pay for Adam's burial and the small headstone—and oh, how it hurt that a man of his artistry should have so little to mark his passing! The butcher refused to sell anything to her until she paid their bill. The wine merchant was already dunning them—that was what set off her argument with Adam and sent him storming out into the night. The flat itself was paid only through the end of the next week, and their landlord was a hard man who would not care that he was tossing a widow and a fatherless baby into the street.

It was enough to make her dissolve into sobs, but Noelle had cried so much the last few days that she was utterly drained of tears, and in any case, it would do no good. Crying never solved anything. She must think of what to do. Madame Bissonet would take her back at the millinery where Noelle had worked before Gil was born. Noelle had been a good clerk as well as an excellent model for Madame's hats, not to mention the added benefit of being able to converse with English customers.

But how was she to work there—or anywhere—with a small baby? She could hardly carry an infant about the showroom with her or take time from making bonnets to feed and tend to him. Even if she could find a way to do so, the money she could earn would be very little. They had always lived on the stipend Adam's family sent him despite his estrangement from them. Noelle's salary had merely helped make ends meet when Adam's extravagant spending sent them into dun territory. It wouldn't be enough to live on. And she had no hope that the Rutherfords would continue to provide Adam's much-disliked widow any aid after his death.

She could sell Adam's work. She looked across the room to where his easel stood by the window. Finished paintings crowded all around it—the fruit of his genius, the rich glimpses into his soul—some dark and stormy, others visions of stunning beauty, and all of them compelling. It made her heart ache to think of letting them go, but she would have to try to sell at least some of them. That would bring in enough to live for a while, but he had been able to sell too few of them in the past for her to think she would be able to reap any great sums. They were worth far more to her than they ever would be to someone else.

Noelle turned away, going to the alcove that served as their bedroom, and began to take off the black dress she had worn to Adam's funeral. Adam would have hated that; he had always said she was suited only for color. She had but one black dress. It was old and uncomfortably tight across her breasts, so full now since the baby was born. Tossing it onto the bed, she pulled on the bright silk wrapper Adam had bought her. It was far too extravagant, as were so many of the things that he bought, but it was soft and comfortably loose, and it made her feel closer to Adam.

Taking an ornate box from the dresser, she sat down on the bed and opened it. The jewelry Adam had bought her was the most valuable asset she possessed. She began to pull out the pieces, laying them out on the bed beside her. The diamond earrings Adam had given her when Gil was born. Gold bangles. An enameled brooch. A jeweled hairpin that looked like a dragonfly. Pendants, earrings. That foolish narrow ruby-and-diamond tiara that Noelle would never attend anything formal enough to wear.

Indeed, she would never wear most of them. She had protested time and again that Adam spent too much on jewels and clothes for her; it would have been far more useful for him to pay the rent. But Adam was the son of an earl, and he'd never completely adjusted to his new financial circumstances. He would complain about his lack of funds and call the monthly payment he received from England "blood money." He would make periodic vows to follow a budget. But then he would see something he wanted, and he would buy it on the spot, without regard to the price.

That first bracelet he'd given her, she had promptly handed back to him, saying heatedly that she was not the sort of girl to accept such a present from a man. She smiled to herself, stroking her finger over the delicate chain of sapphire flowers. Adam had kept it and presented it to her again after they married, smiling in that irresistible, mischievous way of his and saying he believed she could accept it now.

Noelle swallowed the lump in her throat and fastened the bracelet on her wrist, holding her arm out to admire it. She pulled out the matching necklace that he'd given her on their first anniversary. Going to the mirror, she fastened it around her neck. She smoothed her finger over the delicate stones, remembering the way he looked as he gave it to her. Tears welled in her eyes.

A thunderous knock sounded at the door, breaking

into her reverie. Whirling, she ran for the door in the futile hope she might keep the visitor from waking the baby. But, naturally, Gil began to howl, his tiny face screwing up and turning red. In exasperation, she flung the door open.

A tall, lean man stood outside her door, his strong-boned face set in a stony expression and his eyes the cold gray of a winter storm. His brown hair had no silver to it, but his fierceness gave him an authority that his age, and even his obvious peerage, didn't.

Noelle took an instinctive step back. The man's eyes flicked down her and beyond to the cradle. "I believe your child is crying."

"Not until you started banging on the door." Her temper flashed at his tone. Turning, Noelle scooped Gil up and held him against her chest, murmuring soothing noises. When she pivoted back to the door, she saw that the man had walked into the room uninvited and closed the door behind him. He stood there silently, his coolly assessing gaze roaming over the small living quarters.

His eyes fell on the unmade bed, the contents of the jewelry box spread across it, and his lips lifted in a sneer. "Sorry to disturb you. I can see that you are deep in…um, *sorrow*."

His tone gave a sarcastic twist to the words that made them sting and brought a flush of embarrassment to Noelle's cheeks even as they angered her. "Who are you? What do you want?"

Suspicion of the man's identity was already tickling at the back of her mind. English, aristocratic, contemptuous…and surely she had seen a charcoal drawing of this man among Adam's sketches.

"I am Carlisle Thorne. I am a friend of the Rutherford family."

"I see." Adam had spoken of him several times. Though not related to Adam by blood, Thorne had been the earl's ward. He had lived with Adam's family for some time and had been something of an older brother to him. When Adam first mentioned him, it had been with affection, but after their marriage, his references to the man had turned bitter. Adam had believed Thorne would intercede with his father, but instead he had, like the earl, opposed the marriage.

Noelle remembered well the letter Adam had received from Carlisle Thorne. He'd torn it up and flung it on the ground, but Noelle had pieced it together and read it: *It is entirely understandable, even expected, that you should dally with the lasses while you are at university, but it is out of the question for a man of your heritage to marry one of these common girls.*

It had only exposed the man's arrogance and narrow mind, but the words had made Noelle feel ashamed. Even now, she could remember the pang of hurt, assuaged only partially by Adam's fierce denouncement of Thorne.

It was not surprising that this icy man was the author of that missive. She felt sure his opinion of her had not changed. Certainly, she had no liking for him. But still, she could not help but feel a quiver of hope. Thorne had been something of an emissary between Adam's father and his renounced son in the past; the earl had sent Adam his monthly stipend through Thorne. If the earl had sent Thorne himself to pay a visit, surely that meant he would help his son's widow and child, no matter what he thought of Noelle herself.

Thorne's gaze went to the bundle in Noelle's arms. Gil had once again fallen asleep against her chest. Thorne shifted awkwardly, tilting his head to look at the baby's face. "Is this…"

"Yes. This is Gil. Adam's son."

He gave a short nod and turned away. For a moment Noelle thought he was about to simply walk out the door, but then he swiveled back to face her. "I am here to return Adam to his family."

"Return him to his family! They would not accept Adam when he was alive, but now that my husband has died, they want his body?" Noelle flared. "It's a trifle late, isn't it?"

His eyes darkened and for the first time it was fire, not ice, that flared from them. "I am well aware that I did not arrive in time to save Adam from the disastrous consequences of his marriage to you."

Noelle drew in a sharp breath, shocked. "Are you implying that *I* harmed Adam?"

"I am implying nothing. I am saying plainly what we both know—if he had not run off with you, Adam would be alive today." His words pierced her, and Noelle could say nothing as he continued, "I will regret to my dying day that I did not keep him out of your clutches. But I am not too late to save his son."

Tears sprang into her eyes, and Noelle turned away to hide them from him. She laid Gil back in his little bed, buying herself time to force down the pain and anger that threatened to swamp her. She hated this arrogant man. But she had to think of her son. She must take care of him, and Carlisle Thorne was the only person who might do that. If he was offering to provide support for Adam's baby, then she must accept it, no matter how humiliating, no matter how much it galled her.

Not looking at him, carefully keeping her voice drained of emotion, she said, "And how do you propose to do that?"

"Ah. Yes. Now we are at the heart of the matter, aren't we? No need for any pretense; you are ready to bargain. What is your price?"

"My price?" She turned to face him, confused. Was she supposed to figure out how much it would cost to raise her child? And what an odd way to put it. "I—I'm not sure—"

"You must have a number in mind. What will you take to give me Adam's son?"

Noelle stared at him, stunned. "You want to *buy* my baby?"

"If you want to call it that." He frowned. "Did you expect me to hand over a pile of banknotes and leave him here with you? To let the earl's grandson be raised in…" he gestured vaguely around the apartment "…in this? In the sort of life you will lead? No. I can assure you I will not. The earl is his legal guardian, as you must know. The child will be earl one day, and he shall be raised at Stonecliffe, just as Adam was, in the care of his grandmother and grandfather. *You* will take the money and be on your way. A thousand pounds."

"No," Noelle said weakly. She was too shocked to put her thoughts into order. He could not really expect her to sell him her child.

His mouth tightened. "Two thousand, then. You'll have money, your jewelry, your clothes, and you won't have the burden of a child. Even a woman of your face and form would find it difficult to attract a protector with a baby in tow. Here." He reached inside his jacket to pull out a small pouch. "I haven't that much in coin with me. I will have to visit the bank. But here is a deposit on that." He tossed the pouch down on the table. "I'll return tomorrow for the boy."

With that, he turned and left the room as abruptly as he'd entered it. All the air in the room seemed to be sucked out with him. Noelle could hardly breathe. Her heart hammered, and she stared at the pouch as if it were a snake. Thorne thought she would sell Gil to him.

No, he wasn't Gil to that man. He had called him *the boy. The baby. Adam's son.* He'd never once said his name. As if Gil were a thing, a possession that belonged to the Rutherfords. Anger surged in her, breaking her paralysis. Noelle picked up the small leather pouch and hurled it at the door. It hit with a satisfying thud and fell to the floor, spilling a few gold coins. If only she'd been quick enough of mind to have hurled it at *him* as he left.

The noise jarred Gil awake again, and he began to whimper. She picked him up and tried to soothe him, but it was difficult with her own feelings jumping about so. Carlisle Thorne was a rigid, uncaring, ignorant bully. How dare he intimate that she was the sort of woman who would find a "protector" now! That she would become some man's mistress!

Without knowing her, he had judged and condemned her from the very beginning for the crime of loving a man above her station. He labeled her "common" because her father was a teacher instead of a peer. Her father was a respected scholar, a learned, thoughtful man to whom other academics turned with their questions. He was a man superior in manner, mind, soul, and every other way to someone like Carlisle Thorne.

Gil was both hungry and wet. As she tended to his needs, her anger drained away. She nursed him, rocking, and considered what she would do and say when she faced Thorne tomorrow. Her desire was to throw the coin purse in his face as she screamed invectives at him. But that would serve little purpose and would only confirm his low opinion of her.

Instead, she should be as icy as he was, hand him back his money and order the horrible man to leave. She would make it clear that she would never think of handing her son over to him or the earl to raise. He would be furious. She was certain he was unaccustomed to being denied. It made her stomach clench to think of confronting him. He was a frightening man—his size, his implacable face, his cold, gray eyes. But she would do so because she had to. She stroked her finger over Gil's soft cheek, smiling down at him. She would do anything for Gil.

But what, she wondered uneasily, would Thorne do when she refused him? What if he decided to simply take the baby from her? What if, when she told him no, he snatched Gil from her arms and strode off? Her insides churned at the thought. She couldn't stop him; even a mother spurred by terror and rage could not match his strength. Surely a gentleman would not resort to such a thing. But then, she would never have imagined that a gentleman would try to buy her baby.

She tried to remember what Adam had said about Carlisle Thorne. He'd termed the man "like a brother" to him, though he was no relation, but bitterly added that Thorne was more his father's son than Adam himself.

Sometimes when he was in his cups, Adam called Thorne dictatorial, straitlaced, unfeeling, a traitor. He even intimated darkly that Carlisle was probably glad to have Adam out of the earl's life so that he could be the man's son. Noelle had dismissed much of what he said as exaggeration, born from his hurt at the man's abandonment of him. After all, Adam also told her smiling stories about this time or that when Carlisle pulled him out of some fix or other.

But now, having met Carlisle, Noelle thought perhaps Adam had not been harsh enough in his assessment. Thorne was more than unfeeling; he was cruel. No man of any sensitivity would want to take a child from his mother or tell a grieving widow that she was responsible for her husband's death. He obviously despised her. She could well believe that he was capable of stealing Gil from her.

Even if he did not snatch the baby right out of her arms, there was the very real possibility that the earl would go to court to take Gil legally. Thorne had said that Adam's father was the child's legal guardian, and Noelle was well aware that women had few rights in this world. Her father was a freethinker, very interested in the rights of individuals, including women. When she had told him she wanted to marry Adam, he had said acerbically that as soon as a woman married, she ceased to exist in the eyes of British law. She could not own property. She was subject to her husband's authority. She had no recourse if he beat her.

A widow did have some stature. She could, at least, own property. But Noelle suspected it could very well be true that she could not hold legal guardianship of her child. Thorne had seemed quite confident in his statement, and she was not naive enough to believe a court would favor her claim over that of a nobleman. She had seen too many instances of young "gentlemen" at Oxford slipping out of any consequences for their behavior simply because their fathers were men of importance.

She stood up and paced the room, her nerves jumping. It wouldn't be enough to refuse to give Thorne her child. She had to make sure Gil was out of the man's reach. She didn't know where she would go or how she would live, but it was clear that she had to leave. Now.

He would be pounding on her door again tomorrow, and she needed to get as far away as she could before he went looking for her. Laying Gil down on the bed to coo and kick, she began to gather up clothes. She could take only the barest essentials. Everything would have to fit in a bag she could carry, for she could not haul around a trunk.

She grabbed a sack from Adam's studio. She felt a pang at leaving his paintings, but she must. She stuffed a dress and undergarments into the bag, as well as clothes and nappies for the baby. Wrapping up a hunk of cheese and some bread in a napkin, she tossed that in, as well. What else? The jewels. She must take those; they were her only source of money. Noelle scooped them up, adding the necklace and bracelet she wore.

Last, she made sure Gil was dry and dressed warmly, then found the plainest dress she owned and her sturdiest boots and put them on. She tied on her cloak and covered her golden hair with a scoop-brimmed bonnet that partially shielded her face. She must look as nondescript as possible.

She wasn't sure where she would go—Italy, or perhaps Prussia. Thank heavens her father had insisted on her learning Latin, French, and Italian, calling them the languages of beauty and learning. Latin would do her little good, but the other two would stand her in good stead. She had studied German, as well, simply because she was adept at languages. Those would open up most of Europe to her.

She knew Thorne would try to find her. Where would he expect her to go? Home, she imagined, back to England, to her father. He would look for a coach going north. So she would go in any other direction. Perhaps she would travel south to Nice or Marseilles; there, she could catch a boat to any number of places. Italy, perhaps. Her friend Yvette and Yvette's husband, Henri, a sculptor, had moved to Florence a few months ago so that he could hone his craft in the city of Michelangelo. They would take Noelle in, give her a little time to decide exactly what to do.

The important thing was to travel quickly. Thorne could catch up easily if she was on a lumbering public coach. Even worse, she doubted there was one leaving this late; it was already dusk. The fastest way would be to hire a post chaise. She could leave almost immediately. And she felt sure one of Adam's friends would do her the favor of making the transaction so that the innkeeper would not see a very identifiable young woman with a small baby.

Even if he managed to find the inn where she rented the vehicle, she would be hours ahead of him, probably more. The only problem with her plan was the expense of hiring a post chaise. She would have to sell some of her jewelry. Opening the small sack, she studied the pieces. Which should she sell? She had long thought

Adam bought her too much jewelry. Now, it seemed far too little.

Worse, it was evening, and all the shops where she could sell it would be closed. Her eyes slid over to the pouch of gold coins. But, no, she couldn't take the money he had tossed at her in exchange for Gil. It would be stealing. Besides, the thought of even touching that money was abhorrent. She refused to do anything that indebted her to Carlisle Thorne.

But she must think of Gil. She had to take care of him, had to get away from Thorne as far and fast as she could. Perhaps she should put her pride aside. For a moment, she hung there in indecision. Then she grabbed the pouch and dropped it into the pocket of her skirt. She would pay the man back, every cent. She swore it.

Wrapping Gil up in his blanket, she tucked him into the crook of her elbow and picked up her bag. With a single glance back at the home she and Adam had shared for two years, she slipped down the staircase and out into the dark night.

CHAPTER ONE

Five Years Later

"I'VE FOUND HER, SIR."

At his employee's words, Carlisle Thorne straightened in his chair. When the butler had announced that Diggs was here, Carlisle had expected nothing but a routine report of lack of success. Carlisle's pulse picked up, but he pushed down the hope rising in him. After all, Diggs had found the woman before, only for her to slip away. "Where?"

Diggs's usually dour face creased in a rare smile. "Here in London, sir."

Carlisle stood up. "Are you certain?"

"As certain as I can be. Her hair's brown now, and she looks thinner, but I saw her myself. It's hard to mistake those eyes, sir."

"Yes." Those eyes—large and a distinctive vibrant blue, outrageously lovely. It had been the first thing he'd noticed about her…before his gaze dropped to her blatant display of jewelry and complete lack of mourning.

"And she has a boy with her, sir, just about the right age."

"Thank God," Carlisle murmured. That had always been his secret fear, that somewhere in her travels, Noelle would decide Adam's son was too much trouble and simply leave him behind. "Well...it appears she has finally made a mistake."

"Yes, sir. I guess she got too confident. Figured you'd stopped looking for her."

In the chair across from Carlisle, Nathan Dunbridge snorted. "Clearly doesn't know you, then, Carlisle."

"True, sir." Diggs nodded toward Carlisle's friend and offered, amazingly, a full-fledged grin. Nathan had that effect on people. More soberly, Diggs turned back to Carlisle. "She's working in a millinery shop. Madame Bissonet's. Popular place, from the looks of it. I checked the owner's background; it's the same person she worked for in Paris. Before..."

Before this whole mad pursuit began. Before Adam died. Carlisle shoved that thought aside, as well. "Have you discovered where she lives?"

"Yes, sir." Diggs nodded, coloring a little. That was where they had slipped up two years ago and lost her. "I followed her to her home myself. Both places will be easy enough to catch her. No back doors at either one. I can follow her home again tonight, take a man with me, bring her to you."

"No. I don't want the boy frightened. It's better if I go to her. Let's do it tomorrow morning at the shop. She'll be more amenable to reason there, not as likely to create a scene. Continue to follow her, but for God's sake, don't let her see your man. She's crafty; she might notice. I don't want anything that could make her bolt."

They made arrangements for the time and place, and Diggs left. Carlisle looked over at his friend, who had been following their conversation with great interest.

"Looks as though you've finally got her in your net," Nathan said cheerfully. "How long has it been now?

Four years? Your worrying has certainly added four years of gray to your hair."

"Five. I wasn't quite thirty when all this started. And I would refer to my hair as having a stately silver at the temples. Salt and pepper, if you want to be thoroughly pedestrian."

"Being thoroughly pedestrian is ever my goal in life."

"I'm not counting any victory until Adam's son is back at Stonecliffe." Carlisle's expression turned grim. "That blasted woman's eluded me at every turn. I underestimated her before—I won't make that mistake again." He sighed and sank back down into his chair. "One of the countless mistakes I've made. I bungled it from the start."

"Understandable. Adam had just died; you were grief-stricken."

"Yes." Thorne leaned his head back against the tall chair and closed his eyes, recalling the moment. "I was grieving for Adam, bitterly regretting…oh, everything, right from the start. Why did I pick that time to say, 'He's a man now, he'll have to learn for himself'? I should have gone to Oxford as soon as he wrote that he was going to marry her. I could have made him see reason. Instead, I merely dashed off a letter."

"You couldn't have known Adam was actually serious that time. He was always off on one thing or another, and in weeks…even days, he would drop it entirely and be off on something else. How were you to know he would take it into his head to elope with her to Paris? Hard as it is for you to believe, you aren't omniscient…or omnipotent."

"I should have guessed he'd do something like that. He was bloody impulsive, still young and easily seduced. If I'd gone to Oxford and seen her, I'd have realized how dangerous she was. As soon as she opened the door in Paris, I understood why Adam had been ensnared by her. He loved beauty above all else. The lad didn't have a chance." Carlisle sighed. "I should have gone with him to talk to the earl again. I could have made Adam agree to wait a reasonable period, and that woman would have been off after some more lucrative prey. But I had things to do in the city, and I was…well, I was tired of having to intervene, I suppose."

"As well you should have been. It was wrong for you to always be placed in that position."

Carlisle gave a dismissive half shrug. "I was the one who put myself there. But I couldn't have chosen a worse time to decide to let the earl and Adam manage it on their own." He looked down for a moment, adjusting his cuffs. "And then…to have finally persuaded the earl to mend things between them, only to have Adam die before I could even write him." Carlisle shook his head. "I wasn't thinking straight after that. And when I saw her standing there with not a trace of mourning, all bedecked in her jewels—she'd been gloating over them; I could see them spread out on the bed—I was blind with fury."

"Of course you were."

"All I could think of was getting Adam's baby away from her and back to the countess. But I was stupid to toss down that coin purse. It was a foolish, dramatic gesture. I didn't realize she was clever. I thought she would jump at the chance to have the money and be free of the impediment of a child so she could pursue a new victim. But she obviously knew she would have an easier and more luxurious life at Stonecliffe, as the mother of the future earl."

"Seems extraordinary behavior to me. Why didn't she simply turn down your offer? Bargain for a healthy allowance to bring up the child—what is his name again?"

"Gilbert, according to the birth records. She called him Gil—sounds like a stable lad."

"Gilbert, then—if she wanted to keep Gilbert, why not ask for money for his benefit? Or return to Stonecliffe to live with him?"

"I don't know." Carlisle sighed. "I've wondered about it thousands of times. I assumed at first it was a ploy to get more money from me. I thought I would receive a letter from her suggesting different terms. When she didn't write, I decided she hoped to go to court and persuade it to establish her as the boy's guardian instead of the earl. I could have told her that was ludicrous, but she probably knows nothing of the law. When Drewsbury died, I thought she'd come sweeping in then, swanning about as the mother of the new earl, and take up residence at the London house."

"Perhaps she didn't know he'd died," Nathan offered. "Maybe she found out, and that's why she came back to London."

"I suppose. She's certainly avoided England before. But then why hasn't she come to me and announced herself?"

"I think we can safely assume that the woman wants to avoid you."

Carlisle let out a little grunt, half humor, half frustration. "I'd say so, since she's given me the slip four times now. But why not go to the countess? No one could be kinder than Lady Drewsbury. Or the earl's man of business? His attorney?"

"I've no idea. Maybe she doesn't like the look of the man." Nathan shrugged.

"That's a ridiculous reason not to talk to a solicitor." Carlisle snorted. "No one in their right mind would do such a thing."

"Hah! I can't stand to see my attorney—he looks more suited to be an undertaker than a man of business. Ghastly pale and all skin and bones." Nathan gave a theatrical shudder. "Besides, you have said many times that this woman obviously isn't in her right mind."

"That's true." Carlisle allowed. "She has done absolutely nothing sensible—just continued to run like a thief all over Europe, adopting disguises. Perhaps she's mad. Or maybe she does it to make me suffer. God knows, she has succeeded." He jumped up and began to pace. "When I think of Adam's son being brought up this way, dragged about all over, and God knows what she's been doing to support them—bloody hell." Carlisle broke off and swung around to face Nathan, his face set and gray eyes hard as stone. "But all that's done now. I've got her—and this time, by God, that woman will not get away from me."

NOELLE HELD GIL'S hand as they walked along the street. It was a misty morning, the air damp and cool upon her cheeks, but at least it was not foggy as it had been the last few days. She disliked the fog that crept and concealed, closing around her like spiderwebs. It was a fanciful comparison, and Noelle was rarely fanciful anymore, but it was a very real and practical problem: the fog made it difficult to see and it muffled sounds.

Anyone could be following her. Someone might be lurking unseen in a doorway.

Other people doubtless did not think of it that way, but they hadn't lived the last five years looking over their shoulders. She tightened her grip on Gil's hand. He responded, "Ow! Maman!"

"Désolé," Noelle responded, loosening her grip. She continued to speak French with her son, as well as with Madame Bissonet, even though both of them also spoke English. With customers or shop people, she used English, though she gave a soft French accent to her words. Their clientele seemed to feel there was a certain cachet in buying a hat from a Frenchwoman, and it suited Noelle to add another layer to her disguise.

Like the mousy brown wig over her own short blond curls. Or the drab dress in a rust-brown shade that complemented neither her skin nor her figure. Once she had adopted a limp and a cane, but that had been only for a journey; it was all too likely she would forget to limp, or use the wrong leg, if she had to keep it up for an extended period of time. She was considering, however, wearing spectacles, as she had once before. Her eyes were the most difficult feature to hide.

Noelle hadn't wanted to return to England. It had been over a year since the last time Carlisle Thorne's hired men had tried to kidnap Gil, enough to make her hope he might have given up. But she couldn't allow herself to trust that feeling. The man was a bulldog of an adversary—relentless, determined. Wherever she went, whatever name or disguise she adopted, he found her. Eight times she had had to abandon their life and run again.

He found her first only a few months after she fled

Paris. He hired a detective who had doggedly made his way through the artistic community there, paying for the names and location of every friend she and Adam had. It didn't take him long to reach Yvette and Henri, though fortunately word had made its way through the ranks of artists as soon as he started searching in Florence, and Noelle had escaped in time.

She realized then that she must never again go to someone she knew. She couldn't go to her father, knowing that he would be the most likely person for Carlisle to suspect of sheltering her, and after fleeing Florence, she had faced the fact that she would probably never be able to see him again. She never even wrote to her father unless she was on the verge of leaving a town, afraid Carlisle might discover where her letter had come from. Her father had been dead a year before Noelle had by chance discovered it.

Thorne found her again a year after she fled Florence, and that time she escaped only because a neighbor told her that a strange man had knocked at Noelle's door and when the neighbor popped her head out suspiciously to ask what he wanted, he hadn't answered, just hurried away. It had been enough to make Noelle pack her clothes, grab Gil, and run.

There had been other times and other places. In Brussels, Noelle had spotted a distinctly brutish man loitering around the house where she worked; in Rome, she had realized she was being followed. Another man approached her on a street in Madrid, saying her name and reaching inside his jacket. She'd flung the basket of vegetables she'd been carrying into his face and ran.

There were other, more terrifying incidents. In Barcelona, a man came up beside them and grabbed Noelle by the arm, spinning her around and flinging her to the ground. Gil, bless him, only three years old, had screamed like a banshee and attacked the man, hitting him about the knees with his wooden toy. Their attacker picked up the wildly struggling boy, but Noelle, still on the ground, managed to wrap her arms around the man's legs and hold on frantically while Gil struggled and screamed. They delayed the attacker long enough for the butcher next door to come running to their aid, cleaver in hand, at which point the kidnapper dropped Gil and took to his heels.

In Bern, there had been an attack in a park where Noelle was sitting on a bench, knitting, while Gil played. She'd jumped up and shoved her knitting needles into the man's side as he picked up Gil, and they managed to escape again. That was a year and a half ago. Since then they had been safe, but Noelle was too wise to trust in that. She must keep up the careful habits she had acquired over the years.

She never stayed in one place long. She changed the color of her hair many times. At first, she dyed it black, but after that she cut her own hair short and wore wigs of varying colors, often covering her head with a cap. She kept her wardrobe small—easy enough, considering the state of her finances—so that she could pack and flee at a moment's notice.

Staying unnoticed was her primary goal, so she wore dresses of drab colors that did not suit her. In public, she kept her face sober and unsmiling, leaching the vivacity from her looks, and she spoke quietly and only as much as was necessary. She lowered her gaze and sought the shadows. Only with Gil and an occasional friend was she herself.

Most of all, she was ever vigilant. Wherever she lived or worked, she first made a plan of escape. She impressed upon Gil the need to not speak to strangers, to immediately come to her if anyone tried to ask him questions or to entice him to go with them. And though she tried not to look at people directly, her eyes were always searching the area around her, alert to any quick, untoward movement.

Two months ago, however, she had broken her most cardinal rule: never return to England. She had worried over the decision. It was dangerous to come so near Carlisle Thorne. There had been no attempts for some time now, but she was certain Thorne was still looking for her, and the chance of her being recognized was far greater in London.

Though she had grown up quietly in Oxford and had not even been in London before she and Adam eloped, she had been considered something of a beauty by the university lads. No one but Adam had ever managed to breach her wall of polite disinterest, but a number of the students had tried. And doubtless her elopement with Adam had been the subject of gossip for months there, giving her further notoriety. And those idle, wealthy young gentlemen gravitated to the high life of London after they left school.

Perhaps the odds were small that she might run into one those young men in the city, but gentlemen did sometimes escort their wives, mothers, or sisters when they were out shopping for hats, and some even went into shops themselves seeking some gift for a wife or mistress. No matter how small, any chance of being discovered was too much.

So when Madame Bissonet decided to open another

shop in London and asked Noelle to help her, she had at first refused. But Lisette Bissonet was Noelle's friend as well as employer, and she was most persuasive, not to mention persistent. Lisette needed her help; it would be so much easier if she had someone she trusted who spoke English to hire employees and do paperwork, to bargain and lease and do all the things that opening a business in London involved.

Though Lisette did not mention or even hint at it, Noelle knew how much she owed Lisette. She let Noelle bring Gil with her to the store as long as he played quietly in the back. She let Noelle leave the shop to care for Gil when he was sick. She paid Noelle a little more than the others, as well as allowing her to design and trim hats on her own time, which Lisette would then buy from her to sell at the store.

Noelle's future at the shop in England would be better than in Paris. In a few months, after the place was established, Lisette would return to her main store and workshop in France and Noelle would become the manager of the London shop. She would be in charge and draw a larger salary. Not only that, she would have the use of the flat above the store, where Lisette now resided. It was nothing grand, but it was far more pleasant and roomy than the cramped quarters Noelle could normally afford to rent. Gil would even have a small bedroom of his own, and the place was well lit, with windows in every room.

The factor that weighed most heavily with Noelle was Gil himself. She glanced down at her son now and smiled. With his mother's blond curls and blue eyes and Adam's smile, Gil was a sunny, sturdy, intelligent child.

And he deserved more, so much more, than Noelle had been able to give him.

The money she could earn at the sort of work open to her was hardly enough to live on, and their frequent travels required even more money. She had had to sell several of the jewels Adam had given her in order to send back the money she had taken from Mr. Thorne. But she could not have lived with herself if she had not returned it. It was one thing to use his gold to get away, to keep her son free, but it would have been wrong to keep it. The rest of the jewelry had gone bit by bit, helping them to escape, providing medicine when Gil fell sick, supplementing the income she made from the sort of work she could do while also taking care of a baby.

She could have had an easier life, certainly, if she had accepted the help of the men who offered it, but she knew the return she would have to make for such help, and she could not do that. Noelle had managed to scrape by. She had done the best she could for Gil, but she knew that it had not been the life he should have had.

Like her, Gil didn't have many clothes. He'd lived in cramped quarters all his life; he'd often been left in the care of another woman while Noelle went to work. There had been times when both he and Noelle had gone hungry or huddled together under all the blankets they had, still shivering, because their tiny flat had no heat.

He should have grown up in luxury as the grandson of an earl. He should have a soft bed and nice clothes and enough to eat. He should have countless toys and books. A pony to ride and grooms to teach him. A tutor and someday an education at Eton and Oxford. A hundred things that Noelle could never supply. Worry and guilt ate at her—had she done the wrong thing by keeping Gil with her? Should she have let Thorne take him from her, no matter how much it hurt? Had it been sheer selfishness on her part to keep Gil?

No, surely not. He had been just a babe; he had needed his mother more than he needed any of those other things. It would have been cruel to turn him over to that cold man, to allow Gil to be raised by the very parents who had cut off their own son. She had done the right thing for him despite all the hardships. Noelle clung to that thought.

But if she could give him more—a better place to live, more of the comforts of life—then she must do it. The position Lisette offered gave her just that. More, it allowed Gil the opportunity to live in the country that was his homeland, to know England and Englishmen. She wasn't stupid; she knew that one day Gil would inherit the earldom, as Adam would have when his father died. He would become important and wealthy. She must do what she could to prepare him; she didn't want him to feel like a foreigner among his own people.

So in the end she agreed to move to London and help Lisette set up the shop. She would stay for at least three months, until Lisette returned to France. After that, she would decide whether to stay here and run the shop or to retreat to France.

So far, it had been going well. Gil seemed happy. He always enjoyed the excitement of a new place, the challenge of a different language, but it seemed to her that he especially enjoyed it here, pleased to add new words, new accents, to the proper English he had learned from his mother. He listened, entranced, to the Scottish widow who lived next to them and was soon salting his words with "wee" this and "auld" that, just as he memorized and repeated the cries of the street vendors.

Nothing had happened to alarm Noelle. She'd seen no one she recognized. The women who entered the shop had no interest in her other than to ask her about a hat. She and Gil walked to and from the shop to their small room every day without incident. The butcher's assistant tried to flirt with her, and a stranger had tried to start up a conversation on the street, his intentions obvious, but she stopped each man with a stony look, and they left her alone.

She kept a careful eye on the street outside the shop window and had come to recognize those who were regulars along it, who lived or worked nearby or delivered to the shops. No one had been loitering about on the street or watching the shop with unusual interest.

Only one man had come into the store to buy a hat. He asked Noelle to model it and smiled as he studied her, which made her uncomfortable, but he said nothing untoward and bought the hat, giving them a delivery address. Noelle watched him after he left the store. He strolled lazily along, studying the wares in the window of the jewelry store, then entering a tobacco shop, and she was reassured that he was merely a shopper.

The other day Noelle had felt a prickling across the back of her neck, the uneasy feeling of being watched. She'd stopped in front of a window, casually glancing back, but she saw no one who suspiciously came to a halt, as well, or ducked into a doorway. She continued to keep an eye out, making an unnecessary visit to the chemist shop, just to see if anyone behind her had chosen to linger nearby.

There had been no one. She was being overanxious.

She could not go running just because she had felt un-easy one day. But since then, she had kept a sharper eye out than before. Gil, beside her, showed no such uneasi-ness. He walked along, sometimes taking a skipping step or jumping across a puddle, chattering all the while.

Noelle unlocked the store, then cast one last look all around the street. There was nothing but the usual early morning contingent of shop owners opening their stores and vendors trundling along, calling out their wares. She opened the door and slipped inside, heading to the back to hang up her bonnet. The place was empty but for her. Lisette, upstairs, was a late riser, and so Noelle was usually the one to open the store.

Two more workers entered as Noelle went about making sure everything was in order, the displays set properly, taking a bonnet that had not sold well and placing it in another area where it would catch more no-tice. Nan, who worked in the front with Noelle, helped, and the other girl, Kate, went back to the workroom. Gil followed Kate to the back, where he usually spent his days playing quietly and doing little tasks for Li-sette and Kate, bringing them ribbons and decorations or retrieving something they dropped.

It was a slow morning with only a few customers. Lisette came downstairs and after greetings, took up her favorite spot in the workroom and began to create. Noelle spent her time working on the books, a task she was training to take over when Lisette returned to France. Nan loitered at the window, watching people go by and commenting on them.

"Oh, my, would you look at that? That's a beauty of a carriage. Hope they're coming here; it looks like they're plump in the pocket."

Noelle, having finished the books, strolled over to look. It was, indeed, a lovely brougham, glossy black and fitted with brass hardware, curtains drawn across the window. A man opened the door and stepped out. He was dressed in a jacket and trousers such as any working man might wear, with a soft cap on his head—not at all the sort to be getting out of an expensive vehicle.

Any sort of oddity always caught Noelle's attention, so she continued to watch as the man stood to the side, holding the door open for the gentleman climbing out after him. That one suited the carriage very well. He was dressed in black with a snowy white cravat meticulously arranged at his neck and an equally elegant hat on his head. The two men started forward, and Noelle drew in a sharp breath.

She didn't know the working man, but the gentleman was Carlisle Thorne.

CHAPTER TWO

NOELLE STOOD PARALYZED for an instant as her nightmare came to life before her eyes. Coming to her senses, she spun around and ran toward the back, calling over her shoulder, "He'll ask for me. Tell him I haven't come in yet. Delay him."

Leaving Nan staring after her in astonishment, Noelle hurried into the workroom, calling Gil's name. He turned, eyes wide at the tone of urgency in her voice, and ran to join her. She didn't pause to grab her bonnet or even to glance at Lisette and Kate, just took Gil's hand and hastened up the wooden stairs. Behind her, Lisette exclaimed in French. Lisette would realize what had happened and do her best to help. Noelle heard the tinkling of the bell above the door in front as she hurried past the door of Lisette's flat.

A small door at the end of the hallway opened onto a narrow staircase half a flight up to the attic storage room on the top floor. The storage room was not as wide as the rooms beneath it, and the set of windows on the rear wall looked down on an empty strip of the flat roof that covered Lisette's living quarters below. Noelle ran to the windows and shoved one of them up, then climbed through it. Carefully, she lowered herself down as far as she could, then dropped lightly onto the roof beneath her. Behind her, Gil scrambled down like a monkey, and she caught him as he jumped the last few feet.

The shop abutted the buildings on either side, and it was easy enough to step over the low parapet onto the roof of the adjoining building, and from there to the next one. They hurried to the last building, where Noelle lifted a flat panel. A set of servants' stairs from the building's former life as a residence led down to the street.

Noelle had plotted out and practiced the entire route to make certain escape was possible from the shop, which had no back door. Since she had planned to soon be both living and working there, she knew she must have a ready way out of the building, and Lisette, the only one who knew Noelle's history, had been happy to agree to that condition.

At the bottom of the stairs, Noelle cautiously opened the door onto the side street and peered out. Seeing nothing suspicious, she and Gil slipped out and walked swiftly down the street. They were almost to the end of the block when she heard a shout behind her. She risked a glimpse back and saw Thorne's companion running toward her. She took to her heels. Darting across the street, she and Gil continued to run.

Though she knew it cost her time, Noelle couldn't resist glancing back to locate her pursuer. Thorne had joined the man and was closing in on Noelle. Her pace was greatly slowed by Gil's short legs, and he was tiring. If she picked him up and carried him, though, she would herself be far slower. In any case, there was no way she could outrun Thorne.

Her only advantage was that she was familiar with the area. She turned right at the next street and ran for the alleyway she knew lay between two buildings. It was a risk, a place where she could easily be trapped, but she also knew that the drapers and other stores used the alley for deliveries of supplies in the morning. More than that, she knew the draper's apprentice, who usually spent much of the morning carrying supplies and goods in and out to a cart in the alley. She dodged around a cart and between two men carrying bags into another shop. And there, thank heavens, was Micah, pulling a long bolt of cloth out of a cart. He had the back door of the store propped open.

Micah turned, and his eyes widened at the sight of Noelle and Gil running toward him. His gaze shifted to the men behind her, gaining ground. Noelle had no breath to speak, could only send Micah a pleading look as she darted through the open door. But he was quick to understand and kicked the prop from the door, then stood in front of the entrance, blocking it with the long bolt cloth in his arms. "Help! Thieves!"

Noelle hurried away from the growing clamor outside the rear door and made her way past startled workers and customers to walk out the front door. A hack was unloading a passenger across the street, and she ran to it. She rarely if ever took a hack because of the expense, but she had to get away from here quickly.

The hack driver frowned down at her suspiciously, and she pulled out her purse, jiggling it, and he nodded. She climbed in, and they started off slowly. Gil bounced on the seat, excited at the new experience. Noelle kept an eye on the door of the draper's shop, but did not see Thorne storming out before the carriage turned the corner and the shop was out of sight. She ran a hand over

Gil's hair and settled back in the seat, curling her arm around his shoulders.

"Will the bad men find us?" he asked.

"No, we slipped away. Don't worry. Even if they found us, they wouldn't hurt you. Remember what I told you."

"Yes." He nodded, his eyes solemn, but then he grinned. "We beat 'em, didn't we? I like running over the roofs."

"Yes, that was fun," Noelle lied. Gil was resilient. Noelle could only hope that the excitement remained with him more than the fear.

Gil turned to look out the window, getting up on his knees to see better. Noelle considered her situation. She wanted to simply rush to the nearest inn and take the first mail coach leaving for anywhere. But she must go home first. She had to get the money she had stored there, and it would be good to grab a few clothes and Gil's favorite toy, as well. She had eluded Thorne; they weren't following her. It would be safe, surely, to return to their flat and get their things before they sought a coach out of town.

She told the driver to let her off at Golden Square. The hack ride had gotten her away quickly, but Noelle didn't want to waste her money. Nor did she want the man to know her address. Given Thorne's tenacity, he might be able to locate the right vehicle and question the driver.

They walked from the square to their home, Noelle keeping up as brisk a pace as Gil could manage. The streets grew more narrow and twisting, the buildings more dilapidated, as they went into the St. Giles area.

Their pace was slowed by having to wend their way through the jumble of people and around piles of refuse.

She turned onto a small street that led to the little lane where her home lay. It was a quieter street and somewhat cleaner, as it still housed many of the French émigrés who had settled there in the years after the revolution in their country. Nor was it as riddled with thieves and prostitutes as the rest of Seven Dials. Still, Noelle had been eagerly awaiting the day when she could leave the area and move into the living quarters atop the store.

Out of an abundance of caution, she stopped and peered down the lane to the house where she rented a room. It was so narrow it was more an alley than a street, and it ended just past her home, giving her no chance of escape. Had she been choosing a place to live for longer than a couple of months, she would not have chosen this location, even if it did offer cleaner, quieter accommodations than the area around it.

Little sun reached the tunnellike walkway, making it perpetually gloomy, but it was light enough to see that there was no one loitering in the lane. Letting out a relieved breath, she hurried toward her door. Just as she reached it, the door swung open and Carlisle Thorne stepped out.

"Really? Did you think I wouldn't have found out where you live, as well?" he said, closing the door behind him.

Noelle jumped back and grabbed Gil's arm, whirling to run away again, but the exit to the street was blocked by Thorne's companion. She was trapped. Why, oh why, hadn't she thought of this? She remembered that uneasy feeling she'd had the other day; clearly, someone had been following her, even if she hadn't been able to spot him.

It had been foolish to come home, but she couldn't waste time on regrets now. She backed up almost to the wall, pulling Gil behind her to provide what little protection she could. Reaching into her pocket, she pulled out the sharp shears she always carried, pointing the tool at her enemy.

Thorne's eyebrows sailed upward. "Are you mad?"

"Don't touch him!" Noelle imbued her voice with all the menace she could muster, given her vulnerable position. She could never hope to defeat two able-bodied men. But she was determined not to let Gil go without a fight.

The man loped down the lane toward them, but Thorne held out a hand, halting him. Calmly, he said to Noelle, "Do you intend to stab me in front of your son? Surely you cannot actually believe that I would harm Adam's son."

"I won't give him up." She stopped, perilously close to tears. She could not allow this man to see any weakness. Swallowing hard, she continued, "You cannot have him. He may be Adam's son, but he doesn't belong to *you*. He is all the world to me, and I will not let you—" Her voice broke on the words.

"Don't you hurt her!" Gil shouted, popping out from behind Noelle's skirts. He was pale, but he planted himself beside her pugnaciously, his little hands curled into fists. "Leave my *maman* alone!"

Thorne looked down at the boy, his face softening, and he smiled faintly—an expression Noelle had never thought to see on his face. "Well, we have a fighter here, I see."

Startling Noelle, the tall man squatted down so that he was on a level with the boy. "You're a brave young man. That's good. You're like your father."

"You know my father?" Curiosity crept into Gil's voice.

"I did, yes. And your grandfather and grandmother. Your grandmother would like very much to see you."

"My grandmother?" Gil asked wonderingly.

"Stop it," Noelle snapped. "Stop trying to manipulate him. Gil, get back. Stay behind me."

Thorne let out an exaggerated sigh and stood up. "I am only trying to show the boy that there is more in the world than this." He glanced around him with the sneer Noelle remembered so well, taking in the discolored and chipped plaster, the peeling paint, the cramped walkway. "Is this really how you intend Adam's son to be raised? In this…squalor and filth?" His gaze went back to Gil, and he told him gravely, "I have no intention of hurting your mother. Or you. You needn't be afraid. I was a good friend of your father's. My name is Carlisle Thorne." He held out his hand to the boy, man-to-man.

Gil stretched out his hand to the man. Noelle sucked in a harsh breath and dropped her shears to grab the back of Gil's shirt. But Thorne did not jerk Gil away as she feared, merely shook the boy's hand and stepped back.

Gil turned his face up to Noelle, smiling as he repeated, "Carlisle Thorne, Maman."

"Yes, I see."

Thorne's eyes dropped to the ground, where the scissors lay. "I fear you've lost your weapon, ma'am."

Noelle gazed back at him stonily. "No doubt it amuses you greatly to rip a child from his mother." She bent down and picked up the shears. "We both know you can overpower me. And stabbing you would only land me in jail, where I cannot do anything to get him back." She dropped the scissors into her pocket, her voice hard as she went on, "But I won't stop fighting, I promise you that. I will take you to court. Yes, yes, I know." She waved away his words as he started to speak. "You are rich and powerful and a man. The courts will side with you, obviously. But how will you like all your peers learning how you have hounded us, trapped us? How you tore him from my hand? Because I will tell them. I will make sure everyone knows what sort of man—"

"For pity's sake, cease this drivel." Thorne's voice was crisp and as filled with contempt as his eyes. "You're frightening the boy."

"*I* am frightening him?" Noelle repeated in astonishment. "You chase us through the streets and accuse *me* of scaring Gil?"

"I chased you because you ran," he retorted. "If you had simply stayed there instead of haring off—"

"Stayed there so you could grab Gil?"

"Madam… I can assure you, whatever fevered tales you have concocted in your head, I am not intent on 'grabbing' your son. I merely want to discuss the situation and come to an agreement on his future."

Noelle let out a dismissive sound. "You still believe I would bargain with you over him?"

"I hoped you had acquired more sense." Thorne broke off, visibly reining in his anger. "I would like to talk to you. That is all. Will you agree to sit down and discuss it with me like rational people? Just you and I. Diggs could look after Gi—"

"You think I would put Gil in the care of your man? I am not so gullible. He stays with me."

"Perhaps we could go inside and sit down." He turned toward the house.

"No." She wasn't about to let this man sneer at her humble little room. Nor did she intend to let herself be enclosed in a small room with these two men, where no one could witness what they did.

"My carriage..." Thorne offered, gesturing toward the entrance of the lane. "It's only a few streets away."

She scowled. Even less would she agree to getting into a vehicle with him to be driven off to God knows where. "Don't be absurd."

"For pity's sake...then where? What place would satisfy your particular requirements?"

"It would have to be in public, in full view of others."

"Must we stand on the streets of Seven Dials?" he asked sarcastically. "Or would a more salubrious place do? A park, perhaps. We could at least sit down."

Noelle considered it. It was a good suggestion, a place where Gil could play far enough away to not hear them—he was right, it was better that Gil not hear the sort of thing this man was sure to say to her—yet she could keep a careful eye on him. She gave a nod, adding, "Alone, without your henchman."

She expected a biting remark or an argument, but he said only, "Very well." He motioned to the other man. "Diggs, bring the carriage closer. We're going to St. James Park." Thorne turned to Gil, saying, "You can feed the ducks."

"No." Noelle disliked his dictatorial manner, but there were several reasons, as well, that it wasn't a good choice. "St. James is too far; Gil is tired."

"That's why we'll take the carriage."

"I told you, I am not getting into a carriage with you."

"Bloody he—" He cut off his words with a glance at the child, and continued in a growl, "What is wrong with you, woman? What do you think will happen if you get into my carriage? I can assure you, I have no designs on your virtue."

"I didn't think you did. But I've had ample experience with your methods."

For a moment, she thought he was going to explode, but he bit it back. "I will hire you a hack, and I will follow you. Will that be suitable?"

She wanted to protest. It seemed somehow that giving in to him on anything was a step closer to defeat. But then Gil put his hand into hers and said, "I'd like to feed the ducks."

"Very well."

They did as he suggested, and a few minutes later Gil was happily tossing bread—bought by Diggs—to the ducks while Noelle found herself in the bizarre situation of sitting on a park bench beside the man who had terrorized her for years. Noelle presumed that Thorne was presenting this picture of reason and calm because he didn't want to incur Gil's animosity. Or perhaps he wanted to keep her from spreading the tale of his many attempted abductions. She suspected he planned to offer her better terms for selling her child.

But what would he do when she refused? Would he then simply take Gil? She would be unable to stop him. Panic welled in her, but she fought it down, clenching her hands tightly together on her lap. She could not let him see her fear. She had learned over the years that weakness was the surest way to encourage any man.

Thorne said nothing, studying her for a long moment. Noelle knew she must take the initiative. "I don't know what you think this will achieve."

"A truce, perhaps." His voice was light, but his gray eyes watched her intently.

"I will not sell you my son now any more than I would have five years ago."

"I never proposed *purchasing* him. I offered to lift a burden from you."

"Gil was not—and never will be—a burden to me. I will not give him up to you."

"I'm not asking you to give him up," he snapped. Drawing a breath, he went on, "He was a baby then; it would have made little difference whether you or another woman took care of him. But I would never think of 'ripping' him away from you, as you so dramatically put it. Whatever my opinion of you, he is attached to you and would suffer from the loss. I have no desire to hurt Adam's son. I am merely offering Gilbert the life he should have. The one you have stolen from him, I might add."

"That *I* have stolen?"

"What else would you call whisking him away to endure a life of poverty and squalor, bounding about from town to town like a rubber ball? Having no *place* in the world! Raising him among the lowest sort of humanity, exposing him to God knows what experiences." Red stained Thorne's cheekbones as his voice turned louder, sharper.

Tears sprang unbidden into Noelle's eyes at his harsh description of the life she had given her son, but she blinked them away. "It was *you* who forced him into a life on the run. If you had not hounded us from place to place—"

"I did not *hound* you. Yes, I looked for Adam's son. I wanted to talk to you, to see him, to—damn it!" He broke off and jumped to his feet, saying tightly, "I swore I would not do this." He paced a few steps away then swung around and returned, his voice once more calm. "I have no interest in exchanging recriminations. I want to talk about the present possibilities. Whatever arrangement we make would, naturally, include you, as well."

"And what would that arrangement be?" Noelle had little hope it would be anything she could accept.

"Providing for Gilbert's welfare and education. Making sure he is housed and clothed in the state to which he is entitled. He is the Earl of Drewsbury; he should be raised as—"

"The earl!" Noelle repeated, surprised.

"Yes, of course. When his father died, Gilbert became the heir to the earldom. I am sure you must realize that."

"The heir, yes. Someday he'll be the earl, but he's just a boy now. Adam's father—"

"Lord Drewsbury died two years ago," Thorne said bluntly. "Even though Adam's son is a minor and I have been named his guardian, the title is his, as is the estate. The boy should live there. He should get to know his people and form friendships with his peers. He should have servants. He should have decent clothes and food. Learn how to ride. He speaks well enough." There was a hint of surprise in his voice that grated on Noelle. "But he needs to know so much more to take his place in society. He must learn how to be a gentleman."

"I wouldn't want him to learn how to be a gentleman

like you," Noelle shot back. But in truth, his words hit too close to her own worries that she had deprived her son of the things he should have.

"Would you rather the child have no idea how to act, what to say, how to look? That he be an outsider in the world he must enter? He needs to learn about his property, how to manage his affairs, how to handle his money. Good Gad, would you have him go into that world like a lamb to be shorn by mountebanks and sharps, to fall into the clutches of some adventuress—" Thorne cut off his words and looked away.

Noelle supposed it was an improvement that he at least stopped short of saying an adventuress like her. He was right about all those things. She didn't want Gil to be tossed into a world that would look down its nose at him, that would decry his lack of sophistication. It hurt to think that her beloved child might turn into one of those arrogant young men, viewing the world through the narrow lens of aristocracy, but if he also had her leavening influence, surely that would not happen. His father, after all, had not been the arrogant, dictatorial snob Carlisle Thorne was. "What is it you want me to do?"

Triumph lit his eyes. "I want your son to come home. For you and Gilbert to live at Stonecliffe. There is the house in London, but I think you and he both would be happier in the country. Where you can, um, adjust more gradually to the change in circumstances."

"Where I will not embarrass you with my lack of breeding, you mean."

"I didn't say that." But the flush along his cheekbones told her that was exactly what he meant. "The country is a better place for a boy—there's much more for him to do, more freedom to move about. You would have an ample allowance, to use as you please."

He would, of course, think it was the money that concerned her. It was, she thought, a clear indication of Mr. Thorne's nature. The offer sounded idyllic, everything that she could dream of. But could she trust him? Why, after all this time, was he so willing to let her live with Gil at the estate? So reasonable, even generous? Was it that in such an isolated place, it would be easier to get rid of her without anyone noticing? She suspected that Thorne would like to, but was he that wicked?

She thought about the ruffians he had hired over the years and their attacks. She thought about the ice in Thorne's gaze and his contempt for her. Yes, perhaps he could despise her that much. More prosaically, he might hope that she would grow so bored in the country that she would return to London, leaving Gil behind. Or that he could set himself so firmly into Gil's life, maneuver into his affections so well, that as time passed, he could separate Gil from her.

Seeing her reluctance, Thorne went on, "The countess, Adam's mother, usually resides at Stonecliffe. If the estate seems too…large, too overwhelming, the countess could continue to manage the household. Or help you to do so."

"I believe I am capable of handling even so grand a thing as the Rutherford household." His low opinion of her angered Noelle. "I don't need Adam's mother looking over my shoulder."

"Lady Drewsbury is a kind and generous lady," he retorted stiffly. "She wants only to see her grandson. She would not criticize or judge you."

"Would you be there?"

"Sometimes. I have my own house, but I visit the estate frequently; I manage it for Gilbert. I am his guardian, and I have a certain responsibility to see to his care. I realize that's not an ideal situation for either of us, but I think we could manage it. Or, if you feel you must live in the city, there is the town house." He went on impatiently, "Why are you so reluctant? I would think you would be glad to have the opportunity to live a life of ease and comfort. To have your son live that sort of life."

"Because I don't trust you!" Noelle burst out, jumping to her feet.

"What the devil do you think I'm going to do? I am offering you a lovely home, clothes, ample spending money, an elevated station in life. In what way am I making you suffer?"

"I don't know what you're doing! That's the problem. Why are you offering me all this? Why have you changed? You've tried to wrest Gil from me since he was an infant, and now suddenly you're talking about treating me as if…as if I were someone else. Someone you didn't despise. Someone you didn't accuse of killing Adam."

"I didn't—"

"You did," she retorted firmly.

"Well, yes, but it—blast it, why does it matter what I thought five years ago? It isn't as if we are going to be thrown together constantly. I can assure you that I would treat you with the courtesy and respect due to Gil's mother."

"Oh. As you have these past few years."

"I am quite capable of keeping up a social pretense."

"Of lying, you mean."

His eyes turned even stormier. "I give you my word that I will be polite and reasonable."

"Your word?" Noelle let out a short, humorless laugh. "Why would I take your word for it?"

"Why?" He gaped at her. "Because it's my *word*. As a gentleman." His astonishment gave way to affront. "Perhaps the men you are accustomed to are without honor, but I am not. I have never lied to you."

That was true enough. He had been open about his dislike of her and his determination to raise Gil. Still… she was wary of living in any house under his control. The servants would be his; they would do as he told them. She could easily be trapped there, unable to leave. And, while a gentleman's word might bind him if given to another of his station, that didn't mean he would consider any promise given to an inferior like her as inviolable.

"Think of your son," he went on, seizing on her hesitation. "Think of the things he will be deprived of if you continue to live this way. He deserves to have a family, don't you think? To know his grandmother. The countess was devastated by Adam's death; she has yearned all these years to see her grandson. Isn't it only right that she should be given the chance to know him? Love him? Is it fair to withhold a grandmother's love from him?"

His words pierced Noelle's heart. Little as she trusted Thorne, she did want those things for Gil. She would do him a great disservice to keep him from them. She thought of Gil playing on the estate, watched over and cared for by everyone around. He could have a dog. Perhaps even a doting grandmother—she could not trust this man's description of the countess, but how could any grandmother not love Gil? Most of all, Gil would have peace and security.

Truth be told, that seemed a wonderful future to

Noelle, as well—no more fear, no more looking over her shoulder, no more trying to eke out a living. She could have all the time she wanted to be with her son, watching him grow and learn. It seemed like heaven… providing Thorne kept his word. But why would he not? It would cost him little to house and feed Noelle, and as long as she was allowed to be with Gil, he could be assured that she wouldn't take Gil away.

She must consider, too, what Thorne would do if she refused him. If she would not do as he wished, would he see taking Gil by force as his only recourse? It was clear he was accustomed to getting what he wanted. He might be willing to gain access to Gil by this easier method, but if he didn't, it wouldn't stop him. It was far more likely that he would abduct Gil right now if she refused his offer. "I… I need time to think about it."

Now it was Thorne whose brow furrowed with suspicion. "Time you will use to whisk him away again?"

"No. If you are not threatening to steal him, I have no reason to run."

He looked at her thoughtfully. "So…it is a question of trust."

"Yes, I suppose it is," Noelle agreed.

"I have no reason to accept your word."

"I have no reason to trust yours."

He gazed at her for another long moment, then said, "I have little choice here. If you will not take him and run—"

"I promise you I will not."

"Then I give you my word I shall not try to take him from you." He paused. "But I promise you also, if you break your word, if you run, I will hunt you down to the ends of the earth."

Noelle had no doubt of that.

CHAPTER THREE

"DO YOU TRUST HER?" Diggs asked as they watched the hack drive away with Noelle and her son inside.

"Hardly. But what choice do I have?" Carlisle pointed out. "Keep an eye on her. Not you; she'll recognize you. She's proven to be more resourceful than I ever imagined."

"Aye, she's slippery, that one."

"Indeed. Even if she doesn't run off, at least your man will be close enough to help them if she runs into trouble walking through that wretched place." Seven Dials. His jaw clenched at the thought of Adam's son living there, even if that street was on the slightly less squalid side of the area. "Daytime should be sufficient. I would think she has enough sense to keep her door locked and not venture out in that area after dark."

"I'll see to it, sir. I've got a lad who can look scruffy enough to pass in St. Giles. And we've got a good spot to watch the shop from a distance."

"To watch the front door, you mean."

"Aye, sir, I'm sorry. I would have sworn there was no back way out."

"There wasn't. I'd like to know how she worked it."

"Had to have some way through the other buildings. Or across the roofs, maybe."

"Well, as long as she doesn't feel threatened, I doubt

she'll go to such extremes. You keep watch on her. I'm going to Stonecliffe to inform the countess we've located her grandson." He hadn't sent word yesterday to Lady Drewsbury because he feared his blasted quarry would slip through his hands again. He wouldn't set the countess up for disappointment. Of course, that could still happen. Noelle—he could not think of her as Lady Rutherford—hadn't yet agreed to his offer. Still, she was considering it; he had seen that in her eyes. Carlisle couldn't hold back such important news from Adam's mother.

The past five years had been unremitting misery for the countess. With Carlisle's help, Lady Adeline had worked on her husband to take Adam back into the family. She'd been looking forward with delight to seeing her son again and holding her grandchild. Then her dream had come crashing down. Adam was gone, the baby missing. Lady Drewsbury spent the next year in deep mourning, not leaving the estate—indeed, rarely even leaving the house. Even though she had gradually come back to life, she still dressed in black, and the sparkle in her eyes was gone. Carlisle hated to see Lady Adeline so sad, so drained of life, and it was all the worse knowing that it was his own clumsy handling of the matter that had kept her from knowing her grandchild.

Lady Drewsbury was the most important person in the world to Carlisle; she had taken him in as a ten-year-old child, assuaging his grief over losing his father and treating Carlisle as if he were her own offspring. She was, in fact, more a mother to him than his own, who had been all too willing to release her child into the care of another so she could return to the lights of London. He was not alone in his regard for the countess. Charming as well as softhearted, she was easy to confide in and swift to offer a comforting word, and if anyone could prevail on that stubborn witch Noelle to accept his offer, it would be Lady Adeline.

The Rutherford estate was in Kent, and Carlisle's horse was swift. He reached the house before dark. Not wanting to leave the countess all alone after the late earl's death, Carlisle had spent the last few years at Stonecliffe as much as he had at his own estate. It was in many ways more his home anyway, having spent so much of his childhood and adolescence there. The footman greeted him with pleasure but without surprise, and Carlisle went into the sitting room unannounced.

Adeline was seated by the window to catch the dying rays of sunshine as she stitched at her needlepoint.

"You should have lit a lamp, my lady," Carlisle said, and the countess glanced up, a smile spreading across her face.

"Carlisle, love!" She pushed aside the embroidery and came forward, holding out her hands. "How nice to see you home again! I thought you would be in London for several more weeks."

"I had meant to stay, but the house is much too lonely without you." He bowed and took her hands in his.

"Oh, posh." Her eyes narrowed as she looked up at him. "Carlisle...what is it? You know something!"

"How do you do that?" He steered her back toward the chair; she would need a seat after his news. "I could never hide anything from you."

"Of course not. Now tell me." Her face tightened. "Is it bad?"

"No. Not at all. I have found Adam's widow."

Adeline drew in her breath sharply and sank down

onto her chair. She raised her hand to her chest. "And Adam's son?"

"He is with her."

Her hands flew to her mouth as tears filled her eyes. "Oh, Carlisle…this is so—I hadn't given up hope, of course, because I knew you would persist until you found him. But, oh! To actually hear it, to know…" She swallowed. "Sit down and tell me all about it. What happened? What is he like—did you see him?"

He took a seat on a nearby ottoman. "He's a grand boy. Sturdy. Blond hair, blue eyes. He looks much like Adam when he was young, though his hair is lighter."

Tears welled in her eyes again, spilling over onto her cheeks, but she wiped them away impatiently. "Go on. He's well?"

"Yes, he seems so. Brave little thing. He popped out, bold as brass, and told me not to scare his mother."

She smiled. "Yes, that sounds just like Adam. Did you? Frighten her, I mean?"

"I didn't intend to, I assure you. I only wanted to talk to her. But she took off, scampering across the rooftops, apparently, just to avoid me."

"The rooftops!" Adeline stared. "With the boy along?"

"Yes. I'm beginning to think she's half-mad."

"Oh, Carlisle, what should we do? Is she dangerous? Might she hurt Gilbert?"

"No, no," Carlisle said quickly. "Not at all. If anything, she clings to him too tightly. She grabbed him and held him back when he started toward me. She kept an eye on him the whole time we were talking, as if he might run away. She spoke rationally enough, but she was tense and on edge. She accused me of trying to abduct him! She wouldn't talk to me inside the store or her home; we had to be in the public eye. She wouldn't even get into my carriage."

The countess's eyebrows shot up. "But why?"

"I've no idea. I ask you…do I look like an ogre? Like someone who would kidnap a child?"

"No, dear, of course not." Adeline smiled and reached out to pat his knee. "You are always a complete gentleman. But she doesn't know that. You *are* somewhat imposing. Your stature. Your station in life. The high standards you hold. I can imagine that someone unused to being around gentlemen might be intimidated. And your first meeting was unfortunate."

"I know." Carlisle groaned. "I bollixed it up. I wasn't thinking straight. I was too blunt. Too quick."

"Whatever else she may be, she is a mother. No mother would be willing to hand over her child like that, just for money."

"I am less sure of Noelle's motherly love than you." Carlisle smiled at her. "You tend to color other people's actions with your own virtues. But you're right. I should have been more subtle. I should have waited, brought her back here and let her get bored and decide to leave on her own. But still… I don't know why that would warrant her being afraid of me. I only tried to give her money." He thought of the wariness, even fear, in Noelle's eyes. It made him feel unaccountably guilty. "I wouldn't have taken the boy from her by force. Or harmed her. You know I would never hurt a woman."

"I know you wouldn't. But perhaps she has been around other men who would."

Carlisle glanced at her, startled. "I hadn't thought…" The idea of a man hitting Noelle—hitting any woman, of course, no matter how bloody infuriating she was—

made his skin crawl, but he knew the countess might be right. "Not Adam."

"No, not Adam. But Thomas told me what sort of woman she was before she met Adam."

"He did?" Carlisle shot her a look of surprise. The earl always shielded his wife from anything sordid or low.

"Not in so many words." Adeline's smile mingled fondness with exasperation. "But I am not quite so naive as the men of my family like to believe. I was able to gather that he meant she was one of the women who offer their 'favors' to the young men in Oxford. And since Adam's death, given the sort of places you've found her, well, she wouldn't have met many gentlemen."

Carlisle nodded. He hadn't told the countess all the details of the areas Adam's son had lived in, or the vast number of times Noelle had dragged the boy from one place to another. It would have worried the countess needlessly. But Carlisle was aware of just what low types of men Noelle would have encountered. "So perhaps it's not me, but men in general that she fears. That might explain…"

"Explain what, dear?"

"What? Oh, nothing." He had never revealed to the countess his fears about Noelle becoming a rich man's mistress; it was much too shocking and would only agitate her for no reason. "Just…um, it would explain why she is so skittish and distrustful, I suppose."

"Will she bring Gilbert home?" Lady Adeline's voice caught in her throat.

"If I have anything to say about it, she will," Carlisle replied grimly.

"Well, I do hope you won't scowl at her that way,

my dear," Adeline said lightly. "If you turned that face to me, I might flee."

"No one could look at you with anything other than affection. But I assure you that I will not scowl. I will be agreeable, whatever I may think. She promised not to run again if I promised not to grab the boy from her. It was an easy enough vow since I had no intention of doing so."

"Of course you would not."

"However, she seems to think I would, so perhaps she'll keep her word. I'm keeping an eye on her, just in case she's lying."

"I must go to London." The countess stood up. "I have to see my grandson. I'll speak to her, mother to mother."

Carlisle rose, too. "I'm certain you would have more success than I, though I hate the notion of you having to plead and placate her."

"I will do anything." Adeline's usually gentle voice was like iron. "Whatever you think of her, whatever I think of her, whatever she's done or been, I *will* be her friend."

"I know. And whatever it takes, I will bring you your grandson."

"Pray excuse me. I must set my maid to packing my things. I want to leave right away."

"Now?" Carlisle asked in surprise. "But, Lady Adeline, surely—"

"No." She shook her head firmly. "I will take only a few necessities. My maid can pack the rest and follow us tomorrow. I cannot sit here patiently waiting while my grandson is in London. Even if we don't arrive until midnight, I must go."

"Of course. I'll have a fresh team harnessed."

As it turned out, they managed to roll into London before midnight, but it was nevertheless late, and after a hastily prepared supper, Lady Drewsbury went to bed. Carlisle, however, was too restless to sleep. He strolled down the hall into a front-facing room that had once been the countess's informal sitting room. Little furniture remained, the focus of the room being the multitude of paintings and sketches that covered the walls. It was the gallery of one artist, and it never failed to touch Carlisle with equal parts admiration and sorrow.

He had always known that Adam was exceptionally talented; he'd tried to explain to the earl that his son was not meant to run an estate but to create beauty. Five years ago, Carlisle had not come back from Paris with Adam's son, but he had brought his artwork. The earl refused to look at the paintings; Drewsbury viewed Adam's art as an enemy. But Carlisle had created this room for the countess. And himself.

He strolled around the gallery, going from piece to piece, ending, as he often did, at the unhung canvases stacked against the wall. Adam's wife was the subject of all of them. Carlisle could not bring himself to throw out any of Adam's work, but to hang that woman's picture felt too much like a betrayal. Adam had captured Noelle in every medium: rich oils, precise pen-and-ink, or pencil, dreamy watercolors. And in each one, she was utterly lovely. Carlisle pulled out one and set it against the wall to study it.

It was the best of them all. Noelle was seated, facing away, wearing that colorful dressing gown she had had on when Carlisle met her. One sleeve of the gown had slid down, revealing her bare white shoulder and much of her back. Her golden hair was up, but pinned messily, strands slipping from their moorings, and she was looking back over her shoulder, smiling in a way that was somehow both mischievous and sweet, as if she shared a delicious secret with the viewer.

Her dark blue eyes were lambent, her skin so velvety he could almost feel it beneath his fingers. There was an intimacy to the portrait that made one feel like an intruder and yet, at the same time, beckoned him to come closer. It was almost impossible not to feel a stirring of desire, just as he had that first instant he saw her standing in the Paris apartment, jewels glittering around her slender white throat. He'd been stabbed then by guilt, just as he was every time he looked at this portrait. Adam's widow. Carlisle's enemy.

He hated to look at it but could not keep himself from drawing it out now and again. It was like ripping off a scab: painful yet somehow irresistible, reminding him of his loss, his failure—not just to Adam, but to Adam's son and the countess.

Studying the painting, Carlisle thought of the woman he had met today. Her face was thinner now, the fresh, apple-cheeked beauty whittled away by the years into something stronger, fiercer…and yet all the more desirable for it. She disguised herself in drab clothes and darkened hair, but nothing could dim those luminous eyes or blur the elegant structure of her face. She was still utterly beautiful.

He disliked her. Disliked everything about her—her stubbornness; her impulsive, foolish flight from place to place; her complete lack of consideration for her child's grandparents, not to mention a deplorable lack of concern for her own son's comfort and safety. It still made his blood simmer to think of the taunting way she'd sent him back the purse of money she'd stolen—shoving it in his face that she had outmaneuvered him. That she'd found other avenues of support.

But standing there in that wretched lane, looking at her, Carlisle felt the same traitorous leap of desire that he had the moment he first saw her. Fortunately, he was also a man who could control his baser impulses. He was a man of thought, not impulse and passion. She was lovely, yes, but so were other women—women who did not thwart him at every turn. And though he could not deny a certain grudging respect for her abilities and her persistence in eluding him for so long, he didn't mistake those qualities for virtues. He preferred women of wit and honor.

If Noelle was wary of him, he was even more doubtful of her. He would be polite to her as he'd promised; he would give her what she wanted in exchange for the countess getting back her grandson. But he would be watchful. He did not trust her. Unlike Adam, he would not fall under her spell.

"It sounds to me as if he's being very—oh, what is the word?—*tres raissonable*." Business had been slow today, so Lisette and Noelle had retreated to a table in the back room to work and brush up on Lisette's English—though this morning Noelle suspected the woman's purpose was more learning gossip than the English language. Though she was Noelle's employer, Lisette had always been warm and kind to her. Only a few years older than Noelle herself, she had, over the past year, become Noelle's friend, as well.

"Reasonable," Noelle translated.

"Yes. I knew it was something close."

"I suppose he is being reasonable," Noelle admitted.

"Generous, even. To live a life of luxury. To be with your son." Lisette looked down at the cluster of wooden cherries she was attaching to a straw hat and made a little moue, dark eyes twinkling. "Instead of doing this? It seems an easy choice."

"If I could trust him. Which I do not." Noelle picked up a slender blue feather and tested it against another hat. "Why, after all these years, is he suddenly so generous, as you said? Before now, the men he sent attacked us."

Lisette shrugged. "Perhaps he admits defeat."

"But he'd already won. I walked right into his clutches. I couldn't have stopped him from taking Gil."

"You said he does not want to disturb Gil," the other woman offered, looking across the room to where Gil played on the stairs. "It would be, um, not comfortable to raise a boy who hated him."

"You're right. It would be much easier to take in both of us and worm his way into Gil's affections…and then, 'oh, my, the boy's mother dies.'"

"Noelle!" Lisette leaned forward, keeping her voice low. "Do you mean—you think he will kill you?"

"I'm not sure. He certainly despises me enough. And he considers me far beneath him, some inferior being. To him it might be nothing more than putting down a horse." She tilted her head to the side, considering. "Come to think of it, it might be far less. Englishmen do love their horses."

Lisette chuckled, as Noelle had intended, but said seriously, "*Oui*. Noblemen are not to be trusted."

Noelle had wondered more than once what story lay behind Lisette's distrust of the aristocracy, but Lisette had never raised the subject, and Noelle felt it would be presumptuous to ask.

"He is a handsome man." Lisette sighed. "It is too bad he is a scoundrel."

"You think he's handsome?" Noelle asked.

"You do not?"

Noelle frowned. "I've only seen him twice, but his face is so stern and his eyes so cold."

"Ah. Well, he smiled when he came into the store, you see, so perhaps he looked different. He is a well set-up gentleman and pleasant…well, at least until he—how you say—ran into the back, um…." She clapped her hands together and made an explosive noise with her mouth. "Like this."

"Exploded?"

"*Oui*. Just so." Lisette nodded. "Then he was stern, as you say." She pulled another face. In the store, she always adopted a solemn demeanor, wearing her dark hair in a conservative knot atop her head and dressing in rather somber clothes. But in private, Lisette had an expressive face and was prone to laughter and lively conversation.

Noelle glanced over at Gil and saw that he had turned toward them at the sounds Lisette made and was watching them with interest. He said, "Are you talking about Carlisle Thorne?"

"Ah, you recognized him!" Lisette laughed and lifted her chin, pulling her face into a haughty, frowning expression.

Gil laughed and hopped off the last three stairs in one bound, running over to them. He leaned against the table, examining the ribbons and various ornaments before them. "He smiled at me, though." He turned his face up to his mother a little questioningly.

"Yes, of course. He likes you, I'm sure."

"I liked the ducks. Can we go back?"

"Yes, we will one afternoon." Noelle bent over and kissed the top of his head. "Now, run and get me some lavender ribbon, love, one thinner than this."

The flow of customers picked up later in the afternoon, and Noelle returned to the showroom. Near the end of the day, a carriage pulled up in front, and a liveried footman jumped down to open the door for the woman inside. He hurried, too, to open the door of the shop, and for an instant Noelle thought he was about to announce the arrival of their customer in solemn tones.

The woman who entered paused and glanced curiously around the store. She was small, almost fragile in appearance, the look heightened by the full mourning in which she was dressed. Her face was softly pretty, with fine lines of age at the corners of her pale blue eyes and her mouth. Her dress and pelisse, though plain and black, were finely made, as was the elegant onyx mourning jewelry at her throat and ears. Clearly she was the type of important customer with whom Noelle always dealt.

"Welcome to our shop, madam." Noelle stepped forward to greet her. There was something vaguely familiar about the woman, and Noelle cudgeled her mind, trying to remember if the lady was someone she should know. She hadn't been in this shop before now, Noelle was certain of that, but perhaps she had seen her in Paris or earlier in her life, in Oxford. "May I help you?"

The woman, who had been staring intently at Lisette and the other clerk, now fixed her gaze on Noelle. "Yes, I, perhaps you can. I—I'd like to look at that hat." She gestured toward the stand at the farthest end of the counter, a small chip straw hat that was at odds with both the woman's age and her mourning.

"Of course." Noelle smiled politely and walked with her to the other side of the room. There was something distinctly peculiar about this woman, and Noelle's suspicions, always on the alert, were now fully aroused.

When they reached the jaunty little straw hat, the woman turned to her, her cheeks coloring. "I'm sorry. I'm afraid I am here on false pretenses."

In that instant, Noelle knew who the woman was and where she had seen not her, but a sketch of her, drawn six years ago by the woman's son. "Lady Drewsbury."

"Yes. Please…" The small woman took Noelle's arm, as if she feared Noelle might walk away. "I don't want to bother you or cause you any trouble." She glanced toward Lisette and the other salesgirl, both watching curiously, then turned back to Noelle. "But I so much wish to talk to you. I can wait in my carriage and we can talk when you, uh, when you can." It was clear she hadn't the faintest idea what the rules of employment might be.

Noelle's heart welled with pity for the woman. Adam had always spoken with love of his mother, never blaming her for the rift between him and his family, and whatever resentment Noelle might have felt for his mother for following her husband's wishes melted now in the face of Lady Drewsbury's obvious anxiety, hope, and sadness. Noelle thought of Gil and how she would feel if she had lost him.

"We can talk now if you wish." Noelle glanced toward the back room, then faced Adam's mother. "We can—would you—would you like to meet your grandson?"

CHAPTER FOUR

LADY DREWSBURY'S EYES filled with tears, yet her face shone with joy. "Yes. Oh, yes."

Noelle ushered her past the others, sending Lisette a meaningful glance. Lisette nodded and motioned for the worker in the back to join them up front. Noelle led the older woman through the low door and down the single step into the workroom, filled with the daily clutter of decorating bonnets.

Noelle suspected that Lady Drewsbury had never entered this sort of room, but the woman didn't even glance around. Her eyes went straight to Gil, who was kneeling on a stool, chalk in hand, drawing on a small board of slate. He looked up at their entrance and smiled, saying, "Maman," and proceeded to spout French.

"English this time, love," Noelle said. "I want you to meet someone."

Gil hopped off his stool, his interested gaze on the older woman, and he came forward, wiping the chalk from his fingers on his trousers.

"Lady Drewsbury, I'd like you to meet my son, Gil. Gil, please, say hello to, um—" She hesitated, not sure how an aristocratic woman like the countess should be introduced to her grandson.

But Lady Adeline resolved the problem by squatting down to the boy's level and saying, "Hello. I am your grandmother."

"My grandmother!" He turned toward Noelle, wonder dawning on his face. *"Ma bonne-maman?"*

"Yes, dear. She is your grandmama and she came to see you."

Gil turned back to Lady Drewsbury, peering up into her face in sudden concern. "Don't cry, Grandmama. Aren't you happy?"

"Yes, oh, yes, I am very happy. But sometimes I cry when I am happy."

"Really? I don't. I laugh when I'm happy." He demonstrated, throwing back his head and guffawing, hands on his stomach, in perfect imitation of their landlord in Paris.

Lady Drewsbury chuckled. "Often I laugh, too."

"You want to see my drawing?" Gil reached out to tug at her sleeve.

"Gil, don't," Noelle rushed to say, but he had already smeared a chalky residue across the black fabric. "I'm sorry, ma'am."

"No, it's fine," Lady Drewsbury assured Noelle, the smile on her face verifying her words. "It's wonderful." She stood up, taking the hand Gil offered. "I should very much like to see your drawing."

Noelle looked on in some bemusement as this woman, dressed in silks and lace, sat down upon a stool beside Gil to comment on his drawing, then followed him about the room as he showed her all the delights of the workroom. Heedless of the bits of ribbon and feathers her trailing skirts gathered across the floor, she exclaimed with pleasure over the miniature bluebird and the peacock feathers as if they were the grandest diamonds.

"And, look!" Gil hauled out his basket of bits and pieces of things he'd collected to glue onto a thin piece of board. "It's a castle, see? It's not done yet."

"Oh, yes, I can see that you are still working on it. But it's lovely." She traced a finger over the large outer circle made of blue ribbon. "Is this the moat?"

"Yes!" He beamed at her understanding.

Noelle, watching them, had to swallow against the lump that rose in her throat, and she blinked back tears. Excusing herself, though neither of the other two took much notice of her leaving, she went back into the showroom. There was no chance that Lady Drewsbury would abscond with Gil since there wasn't an outside door, and she thought Gil and his grandmother deserved some time alone.

Her chest ached as she thought of the years her son had missed with his grandmother and the longing she had seen in the lady's eyes. Noelle could not help but feel guilty for keeping Gil away from Lady Drewsbury all this time.

If only Carlisle Thorne had not stood in the way, the past few years could have been so different. If it had been only his grandmother, Noelle could have gone to this gentle woman, could have asked for her help. Surely a woman with such kind eyes would have taken them in, would not have been so cruel as to rob Noelle of her child. Being a mother, she would have understood… wouldn't she?

But it had been Carlisle Thorne with whom she dealt. And while the earl was alive, Lady Drewsbury would have had no power; it would have been Adam's father's decision. And he was such a hard-hearted man he had cut all ties with his own son because Adam dared to love someone of whom the earl did not approve. He would have acted no differently than Thorne—chasing Noelle and Gil across the Continent, time after time trying to take Gil from her. They had not cared about the pain they would inflict on Adam's son and widow in their pursuit.

But the earl was gone now. Thorne claimed he would not separate Noelle from Gil. Could it all be different? Could Noelle trust her years-long enemy to keep his word?

She looked over at the sound of the countess's footsteps as the older woman entered the room. Lady Drewsbury looked years younger than she had when she entered. "Lady Rutherford…"

How strange it felt to hear herself called that name. She had always been a plain "Mrs. Rutherford" to herself and the world. "Yes?"

"I wanted to ask… I know how…strained things have been the past few years."

That was one way of putting it.

"But I hoped that we might move forward from that. That perhaps you and I could be friends. Or, if not that, at least we could not be enemies. I would never hurt that child nor allow anyone else to. Please believe me."

"I can see that you care for him," Noelle admitted cautiously.

"I thought, tomorrow being Sunday, that you would be free and that perhaps you and Gilbert could come to the house for dinner. Or just for tea," she added, watching Noelle's guarded face. "So that we might all get to know one another better."

"'All?'"

"Yes, Carlisle will be there, I'm sure," Lady Adeline answered, obviously guessing the meaning behind Noelle's question. "I know that Carlisle behaved badly when you first met him. But that is not like him; he is a good man. He was just so distraught about Adam and so concerned for Gilbert. He has no children, and he didn't understand what he was asking of a mother."

Noelle crossed her arms. "I think he understood what he was asking quite well, and I understood what he thought of me."

Lady Adeline's cheeks turned a trifle pink, telling Noelle that the other woman knew Thorne's views as well as Noelle herself did. Indeed, it was more likely than not that Adam's mother believed the same thing about Noelle. The difference was simply that she wanted to see her grandson enough that she would ignore her feelings toward Noelle.

"Carlisle understands that he was wrong," Lady Drewsbury said. "He has sworn to me that he will be pleasant. And he would not break his word to me."

Noelle doubted the man's capacity for being pleasant, but she agreed that Thorne was the sort who would not break a promise to a peer, least of all to this gentle lady.

"Please," Lady Adeline pressed. "I think Gil would enjoy it."

Noelle knew that, too, was true. She nodded, giving in. "Yes. We shall come tomorrow for tea."

THE FOLLOWING AFTERNOON, standing in front of the Rutherford house, Noelle regretted her decision. The house was no grander than any of the others along the street. But all the homes were imposing and the effect of them

together in a row was even more so. Built of red brick
with white stone cornices and decorations, the town
house was relatively narrow, but it made up for that lack
of width by rising four stories tall. Several steps led up
to the glossy black door.

Gil's hand tightened in hers as he stared up in awe.
"Maman…"

"Yes, I know. It's quite large." Their own rooms
would have fit inside it many times over—indeed, this
house would have swallowed the entire store several
times over. Why had she been so foolish as to agree
to this?

It wasn't that Noelle was unaccustomed to wealthy
people. She had met many young noblemen who were
attending Oxford, and she dealt daily with wealthy and
titled women in the course of selling hats. Her own
manners and speech were equal to any peer's and her
education probably exceeded the countess's. After her
mother died at Noelle's birth, she was raised by an in-
tellectual father with modern notions of equality and
fairness. Noelle did not hold herself inferior to anyone
in Adam's family. Indeed, that attitude had more than
once gotten her into trouble in her various positions of
employment.

But there was something entirely different about entering their world, standing before their opulence and
feeling the weight of centuries of privilege and power.
Though she could not believe that Adam's sweet-faced
mother planned to capture her and wrest her son away,
Noelle could not quite suppress an atavistic fear of being
trapped inside, surrounded by enemies.

She was not about to let her son see her trepidation,
however. Nor would she let anyone see that she was in-

timidated, least of all Mr. Thorne. Giving Gil's hand a reassuring squeeze, she marched up the steps and rapped the large brass ring against the door.

"Look. A lion." Gil stared in fascination at the large door knocker in the shape of a lion's head.

There was cause for more wonderment when the front door was quickly opened by a footman dressed in livery. The footman, stiff with dignity, could not quite hide a small smile as he looked down at Gil. "Master Gilbert. Welcome home." Gil goggled at him, but the man did not wait for an answer, simply bowed politely. "Ma'am. Lady Drewsbury awaits you in the drawing room."

Noelle managed not to gaze around the entry in awe, though she was sorely tempted. The floor, patterned in large black and white squares of marble, was worth studying in itself, let alone the nearby statue or the table bearing a large vase painted in a Greek style and holding a mass of red roses. She followed the doorman to the drawing room.

As they stepped inside, Noelle made a quick survey of the room, checking for possible dangers and exits, as she always did. The countess rose from a chair and came forward, her face a mixture of joy and anxiety. Behind her, standing by the mantel, stiff and expressionless, was Carlisle Thorne and another gentleman, the only person in the room who looked at ease.

"Lady Rutherford. And Gil." The countess reached down to stroke a hand lightly over Gil's head. "I'm so happy to see you. Please, come in. You already know Mr. Thorne."

"Ma'am." Thorne bowed briefly toward Noelle and offered Gil a much more open smile. "Gilbert."

"Hullo!" Gil dropped Noelle's hand and walked over to Thorne, hand extended, clearly happy to repeat the adultlike handshake of two days earlier. "Are we going to feed the ducks today?"

Thorne obliged the boy with a handshake. "No, not today, I'm afraid. Another time."

"When?" Gil was not one to be easily put off.

"I don't know. Whenever your mother permits." Thorne looked over at Noelle.

Noelle's lips twitched with irritation. The man had neatly trapped her. If she refused another visit to the park with Thorne, she would be the one Gil blamed. She was saved from having to make an answer because the countess intervened, continuing her introductions. "I don't believe you know Mr. Dunbridge, who was kind enough to join us for tea. Though, I suspect, his eagerness had more to do with the hopes that my niece might be with me." She cast a twinkling glance at the man. "Unfortunately, Annabeth is with her grandmother in Bath."

"Nonsense, Countess," Dunbridge replied smoothly. "Your charms are more than enough to bring me here anytime. I am pleased to make your acquaintance, Lady Rutherford." Dunbridge made a more elegant bow to Noelle than Thorne had.

They sat down to a stilted conversation, as Noelle had expected. It was a difficult proposition to chat with strangers, especially given the animosity between her and Mr. Thorne. But Lady Drewsbury and Mr. Dunbridge did their best to keep the conversation going. They traversed every possible avenue concerning the weather, the season, and the city of London. There were pitfalls at seemingly every turn—the past, Adam—even mention of various foreign cities brought up an awkward, painful silence and sent them groping for another thread of conversation.

Happily, Mr. Dunbridge finally touched on the subject of art, and they were able to talk about various paintings, sculpture, and artists the rest of the way through tea. Thorne and his friend got into a lively (and obviously oft-repeated) discussion of the merits of the Dutch painters and the Renaissance Italians. When Noelle came down on the same side as Carlisle, he gave her a surprised look. She wasn't sure whether he was taken aback by the fact that she had agreed with him or that she was knowledgeable about the subject.

Gil, having long since finished his cakes and growing increasingly bored with the adult conversation, began to fidget. Noelle glanced at him, not sure how much longer he could stay on his best behavior. She should leave; the last thing she wanted was for Mr. Thorne to say her son was ill-bred. "Perhaps…"

Before she could suggest they depart, Thorne said to Gil, "Why don't I show you some of your father's toys? I'm sure we can find something to entertain you."

A frisson of alarm shot through Noelle, but before she could protest, Gil was on his feet. "Papa? Really? His toys are here?"

"Yes." Thorne stood up and reached down to take the boy's hand. "Your papa used to live here when he was a boy like you."

"No. Wait." Noelle rose, her stomach icy. What if Thorne planned to whisk Gil away and into a waiting carriage? What if this visit had been a ruse to trap her in the house and lure Gil away?

"You, too, Mama." Gil held out his other hand to

her. "We can see Papa's toys." He looked up at Carlisle. "Can Mama come, too?"

"Yes, certainly," Thorne said easily, shooting Noelle a sardonic look that told her he knew exactly what she was thinking. "Your mother is always welcome in this house."

Noelle went up the stairs with Gil between her and Carlisle, holding each one's hand. When they reached the landing halfway up, Gil jumped up the last step with both feet. As he often did that, Noelle responded in her customary way by lifting him up as he jumped. To her surprise, on the other side of the boy, Thorne did the same. With the man's added strength transporting him higher than usual, Gil let out a laugh of delight.

"Again!" Gil cried, so they repeated the action at the top of the stairs, this time with a trifle better co-ordination.

Noelle glanced over at Thorne. He seemed an entirely different man at the moment, his implacable visage softened, his gray eyes warm as he smiled down at Gil. She realized that Lisette had been right; he was a handsome man—and younger than his usual sternness made him seem. She had no doubt that he truly did like Gil. Maybe she could trust him.

He raised his head, his gaze meeting hers, and the smile fell away. She was reminded that he just as surely did not like her. Perhaps she could rely on him with Gil, but when it came to herself, she would be a fool to trust him.

They continued to the next floor, repeating Gil's game on the way up to the nursery. It occurred to Noelle that if Adam had lived, the two of them would have done this together often, and the thought made

Noelle's chest ache. Her grief over Adam had burned off long ago; she no longer missed him every day. But now and then, such as this moment, the thought of him twisted her heart.

The next floor was obviously not in use, containing only the nursery, schoolroom, and a couple of smaller bedchambers, and the place had a dark, cramped look. But Thorne pulled back the heavy curtains in the schoolroom, and the room was flooded with light. Gil was enchanted by the child-sized table and chairs and immediately bounced over to sit in one of them.

"They fit me." He swiveled his head, looking all around the room, and his gaze fell on the low bookshelves against one wall. "Look!" He shot out of the chair and dropped down on his knees in front of the shelves. "Mama, look at all these books."

"Yes, I see them. They're lovely." The ache in Noelle's heart grew as she thought of her father's house, where books were crammed into every nook and cranny and a child could read to her heart's content. But books were expensive and heavy to carry around with them from place to place, and she and Gil had only two, a Bible and a well-worn book of folktales.

"Are they stories? Like our book?" He grabbed one volume by the spine, then thought of his manners and turned to Thorne. "Can I look at them?"

"May I," Noelle corrected gently.

"May I look at them?"

"Yes, of course. But I can assure you that book is dull." Carlisle crouched down beside him, running his fingers along the spines, then pulled out a volume and showed it to Gil. "I think you'll like this one better. It was one of your father's favorites. I used to read it to him when he was your age." He laid the book open on the table. "Would you like me to read it to you?"

"Yes, please." Gil nodded his head decisively and plopped down in the chair. Thorne, on one knee beside him, began to read.

Noelle watched them, Carlisle's dark head bent close to Gil's shining golden curls. Whatever the man thought of her, the important thing was how he felt about Gil. With Gil, with the countess and his friend Dunbridge—well, really, she supposed it was with anyone except her—Carlisle Thorne was pleasant. She thought of the affection in his eyes when he spoke to the countess, the way he smiled at Gil. She could not believe that was deception, a play acted out for her benefit.

She thought of everything Thorne could give her son. If the man truthfully was willing to let her live with Gil...well, that would be quite wonderful. However much it might hurt to give in to her enemy, the thought of having as much time with her son as she liked, freed of worry about him being taken from her, was tantalizing. She and Gil could have a true home. She could stay in one place, no longer looking over her shoulder for the villain who pursued her.

The only problem, of course, was that she would be in the very lair of the villain who pursued her. How could she trust Carlisle Thorne after all the times he'd sent ruffians who had chased her like a hound after a rabbit, intent on snatching her child from her?

Perhaps Carlisle saw his offer to her as a form of payment—like his first attempt to buy her baby—a life of comfort for her in exchange for Gil. It rankled that if she took him up on it, he would assume he was right about her, that she had agreed because she wanted the luxury. But, in truth, what did it matter what Carlisle Thorne believed? It was Gil who was important.

She was tempted to say yes, but Noelle was too experienced, too cautious, to act so impulsively. And so, when Thorne had finished the story, she said, "Thank you for showing Gil this, but we should leave now."

"But we aren't through yet." Gil jumped up. He cast a forlorn look down at the book and faced his mother, setting his chin stubbornly. "I don't want to go."

"I'm sorry, love, but we must." Noelle prayed her son would not choose this moment, in front of this man, to turn disobedient.

To Noelle's surprise, Thorne intervened. "You must do as your mother says. Here." He closed the book and extended it to the boy. "Why don't you take this with you?"

"Really?" Gil's face lit up, and he reached out eagerly to take the book. "Can I, truly? I mean, may I?"

"Yes, of course. It was your father's."

"Thank you." Gil executed a courteous bow, as Noelle had taught him to do. "I want to show Grandmama." He trotted out of the room, cradling the battered book.

A small knot formed in Noelle's chest as she followed Gil. He was skipping down the hall ahead of her, already looking at home. Noelle felt as if she were being swept along by an increasingly swift current, with Gil now joining the countess's gentle pressure and Carlisle's hard determination. No, she definitely would not consent today. She must think it over in quiet solitude. However easy the path seemed to be, she had to be certain.

Thorne and the countess insisted on having the carriage brought round to take them home, and Thorne politely escorted them to the vehicle. Gil scrambled up, grinning broadly. Thorne turned to Noelle to offer her a hand up and said stiltedly, "Thank you for coming today. It has made Lady Drewsbury very happy." He hesitated, then went on in a constrained voice, "I—Gilbert is—you have raised him well."

Noelle, taken aback by his grudging compliment, wasn't sure whether to feel gratified or indignant. In an equally formal voice, she thanked him and stepped up into the vehicle. She ignored his proffered hand, reaching for the door frame, but he deftly intercepted, taking her hand in his, and she was forced to close her fingers around his, accepting the little boost. She wore no gloves—another sign of her lack of ladylike status, for she wasted no money on any gloves but those for warmth—and she felt his flesh against hers, warm and strong, and her stomach fluttered.

He closed the door, and the carriage rattled away. Across from her, Gil alternated between bouncing on the cushioned seat and peering out the window, talking all the while about Mr. Thorne and the book, his grandmother, the wonderful cakes, the cunning little chairs and table, and the delightful number of stairs one could jump up and down.

Noelle leaned back, listening to her son's chatter, and let the tension seep out of her. The cushioned seat was luxuriously soft, just like the graceful chairs inside the mansion and the rugs into which one's feet sank. It would be easy to sink into this plush life in the same way. And that was exactly why she had to get back into her home, her life, to think without the tempting distractions.

Could she trust Carlisle Thorne? He had been polite, and she thought of the way he had knelt beside

Gil, reading, altering his voice for each different character and imbuing it with tension as the wicked troll approached. She thought of Gil's laughter and his wide-eyed attention, of the way he had edged closer to Thorne as the troll in the story stalked his prey.

She thought of the man's compliment to her as he handed her into the carriage. She was almost sure he meant it—it had sounded too much as though it were torn out of him to be a deception. Indeed, she was not certain that Mr. Thorne *had* any deceptive ability. He had been quite straightforward in his dislike of her and his intentions toward Gil. He had pursued her openly, his attempts to abduct Gil relentless, but also quite open. He was, she thought, a man of force, not stealth.

She spent the evening thinking about the matter; she talked it over with Lisette the next day. All the while Noelle worked, she thought about it. Indeed, she could not seem to occupy her brain with anything else.

As they walked home after the shop closed, Noelle was still sunk in thought. Gil roamed forward and back to her. Noelle no longer worried about someone snatching him away. She was well aware that Thorne's man followed them home from the store every evening, which alleviated the danger of walking through the disreputable area.

As they made their way deeper into Seven Dials, a drunk staggered out of a tavern and stumbled over Gil, then cursed the boy roundly for getting in his way. Noelle grabbed Gil's hand and went around the man, who continued to hurl imprecations at them. He lurched forward, and though he was too drunk to accomplish anything other than falling to his knees, Noelle cast a glance behind her to reassure herself that Thorne's man was there. Less than a block behind them, their follower gave himself away by immediately whipping around and developing a sudden interest in the wall beside him. It was a different man than usual, and he wasn't as good at his task as the short man who usually trailed them.

For a few moments after that unsettling encounter, Gil was quieter, staying close to her side, but he soon began to chatter about the book Thorne had given him. Noelle had read one of the stories to him last night, and he was looking forward to another one this evening. "Mr. Thorne is nice," Gil said, pulling free from her hand to jump over a puddle. "He said I could call him Uncle Carlisle. He said there are horses on my 'state. Is that true? What's a 'state?"

"Estate," Noelle corrected. "It's a…a piece of land. I imagine there are horses."

"I'd like to have a horse." Gil galloped in place.

Noelle's heart contracted inside her chest as a sudden realization hit her: She was terrified that Gil would be weaned away from her, pulled bit by bit into the world of Thorne and the countess, the world his father had grown up in. There would be a governess, a tutor, then an education at Eton and Oxford. He would view Noelle more and more from a distance, becoming more like them and less like her until he was separated from her by his own choosing. What if Gil came to view his lowborn mother as Thorne did, an embarrassment and a scandal?

There was a wrench of pain at what might lie before her, and at the same time she felt small and shamed by the thought that she was holding back her son from the life he deserved, the world in which he belonged, simply because she did not belong there, too.

Gil frowned at her. "Maman? What is it?" He came back to her. "Are you sick?"

"No." Just sick at heart. Noelle forced a smile. "I was…thinking we might go see Lady Drewsbury to-morrow."

"Grandmama?"

"Yes. Grandmama." She braced herself internally. "Perhaps…perhaps we might stay with her for a while."

He let out a hoot and bounded away again. Through the shimmer of tears, Noelle watched him jump about. There was the sound of running footsteps, and Noelle half turned to see Thorne's man running toward Gil. Alarm shot through her. What had the man seen? She instinctively moved toward her son.

The man ran past her, roughly shoving her aside. She staggered and fell as the man wrapped one long arm around Gil's waist, lifting the boy up, and charged off down the street, Gil tucked under his arm. Noelle shrieked, rage and fury shooting her forward. Thorne's man wasn't rescuing Gil—he was kidnapping him!

"Stop! Let go of him!" She ran after them. Gil was kicking and screaming, which slowed the man down a little, and Noelle ran with desperation spurring her. Even so, the kidnapper was too strong, too fast, and she would never have caught him if a dog hadn't charged out into the street, lured by the shrieks and excitement. Thorne's man stumbled over the animal and fell to the ground.

He lost his tight grip on Gil, and Gil, bless him, came up twisting and kicking. The man kicked at the dog, and it let out a pained yelp as it skidded away. But the animal jumped up with a snarl and returned to the fray. He leaped at the kidnapper, grabbing his arm between his teeth, and Gil was knocked free, rolling across the cobblestones. The man struggled to get to his feet, still grappling with the dog, but before he could stand, a man with a crutch, presumably the dog's owner, slammed his crutch into the fellow, cursing.

Noelle reached Gil and pulled him up. Casting a glance back at the rapidly developing melee, she grabbed her son's hand and raced away.

Thorne had lied to her! Bitter bile rose in her throat. Everything yesterday had been a lie. All his words meant nothing. He had sought only to lure her into relaxing her guard so that he could send his man after Gil.

Every curse she knew ran through her mind. How could she have been so naive as to think she might trust him, to believe that he would keep his word? She should have known better. She *had* known better. She had gone against her instincts, let herself be seduced by the thought of peace and safety.

Noelle glanced back over her shoulder. No one was pursuing them. She slowed to a walk. She was panting, and beside her, Gil was limping. She stopped and knelt to examine him. His cheek was scratched, and his right hand and leg were scraped, but nothing seemed to be broken. She brushed the dirt from him and rose to her feet.

There wasn't time to tend to his scrapes and bruises. They had to hurry. They had lost the man for the moment, but Carlisle Thorne knew where she lived. The kidnapper didn't need to follow her; he could go straight to her house.

"Come, Gil." She took his hand. "I know you're tired, but we must hurry."

"Who was that man? Why—why did he grab me?"

Gil's voice trembled, and that made her almost choke with fury. For an instant, Noelle wished that Carlisle Thorne were here, so that she could fly at him, hitting, kicking, and clawing, for hurting her son.

"I don't know, sweetheart." Technically, that was true; she didn't know the man's name. And she must not set Gil against his grandmother and Mr. Thorne, the only people in the world he had besides her. "But there's no time for talking. We have to get home and pack." It was a risk to go there; Thorne could have also sent a man to their house. But she must retrieve her small hoard of money or she had no chance.

"Are we going to Grandmama's?" His voice lightened.

"No, pet. Not today."

"Then where are we going?" Once more, tears hovered in his voice.

"I don't know that either. All I know is that we must run away."

Again.

CHAPTER FIVE

To Noelle's relief, there was no sign of anyone watching their home. Hurrying inside, she lit a rushlight against the gloom and stuffed their belongings into a couple of sacks. Within minutes, they slipped out the door and back down the street, Noelle carrying the sacks and Gil toting the book Carlisle Thorne had given him. It irked her to keep anything belonging to that man, but she couldn't deny Gil that little bit to hold on to.

Her mind had been busy as she threw their things together, and by the time they left Seven Dials, Noelle had formed the rudiments of a plan. Keeping a sharp lookout all around her as they walked, she returned to the millinery shop. It was a risk, for Madame Bissonet's would be one of the first places they would look when they found she was not home, but she needed the help of her friend to accomplish her plans. Surely Gil's would-be abductor would first search in Seven Dials—once he got free of the feisty dog and his owner.

Dusk was turning to darkness, and Noelle stayed in the shadows nearest the buildings. When they reached their destination, she stepped into the shelter of a recessed doorway across the street and carefully surveyed the area. There was no sign of anyone watching the shop.

She ran across the street and hammered at the door.

There was a glow behind the windows on the upper floor, so Lisette was still awake. When she did not cease knocking, the window above the door was flung open and Lisette leaned out, glowering. "Who is—Noelle!"

Lisette's expression changed from irritation to alarm, and within moments she was down the stairs and unlocking the shop's door to let them in. Lisette's eyes were full of questions, but she held off while Noelle fed her tired son and put him to bed on a pallet in Lisette's bedroom. Then she pounced. "*Mon Dieu*, Noelle, what has happened? Are you running away again? I thought—"

"Yes, I thought differently, too." Noelle told Lisette what had happened to them on the walk home. "Will you help me?"

"But of course," Lisette answered instantly. "Would you like to stay here? You do not need to come into the shop, and they have no right to search my home."

"I don't believe they'd go so far as to invade your home," Noelle agreed. "But I cannot remain in London."

"You'll need to disguise yourself," Lisette said. "You can borrow some of my clothes. And your hair…" She tilted her head consideringly. "We could make it black. I have some black walnut powder."

"No. I'm wearing one of my wigs." Noelle reached up and unpinned the false hair, revealing her own golden blond curls, cut short for ease in wearing the wigs. She set aside the carefully braided arrangement of hair and combed her fingers through her tresses. "I shall stay with this for the moment. And thank you for the offer of clothes, as well, but I don't intend to conceal my identity. My plan, you see, is to lure Thorne's men out of London. With your help, if you will give it."

"Oui, bien sur." Lisette's eyes sparkled. "What are we going to do?"

Noelle explained her plan, which met with Lisette's enthusiastic approval. She finished prosaically, "But for now we must catch a few hours of sleep. There's an early morning coach that leaves from the Running Hare, but it's not until almost dawn."

"You've already inquired?" Lisette asked in surprise.

"The first day I was here," Noelle replied matter-of-factly.

"It is so sad." Lisette frowned in sympathy. "To always think of how to escape."

"The alternative is worse." Noelle shrugged. "I was beginning to think I could stop, but…"

"This man, this Monsieur Thorne, is a monster," Lisette said. "I shall like very much to fool him."

Noelle could not sleep. She had not thought she could, but at least Lisette and Gil were able to get some rest. Rising before dawn, the three of them ate a sparse breakfast of oatcakes and tea. After Lisette had opened the front door and carefully checked the street, Noelle and Gil walked to the Running Hare and bought a ticket to Dover for the two of them.

Her bonnet covered up her blond hair, but she made no effort to hide her face. She hoped the agent would remember her and Gil. Taking a seat, she waited for the horn to sound, announcing the departure. This was the most dangerous time. At any moment, one of Thorne's men could walk into the inn, looking for her.

As she watched, Lisette entered the room and bought a ticket. A short time later the coachman blew the horn, and the travelers crowded into the coach. She and Lisette did not speak to each other, but they managed to seat themselves beside each other in the coach, Gil in between them. They were all crushed in together, as was usual with the stagecoaches. Noelle was wedged against a large man who smelled of onions and sweat, and her knees knocked against those of the young man across from her. The young man tried several times to catch her eye, and the fellow beside her fell asleep and began to snore loudly.

Noelle ignored them both, too caught up in her own anxiety to care. The slow-moving public coach was a danger. If Thorne and his men acted quickly, it would not take them long to catch up with her. This was the likeliest vehicle for her to have taken, being the first one out at dawn and heading in the direction he would doubtless assume she would take.

She could not help but worry that her plan was a mistake. Perhaps she should have fled in the other direction, taken a coach to Liverpool or York instead of this craftier scheme. The plan would do her no good if he found her before the first stage stop. Her hands were clenched on her bag, her stomach roiling, and over the noise of the heavy vehicle, she strained her ears for the sound of rapid hoofbeats, a man's voice calling the coachman to halt.

If she could just get to the first stop…if her scheme worked…she might be able to completely elude him. It all depended on the amount of time it took for the would-be abductor to notify his employer of her escape. He had failed at his mission, so it would not be something he rushed to tell. He would surely have run about trying to find her himself before he admitted he'd lost Gil.

When he could no longer conceal his mistake, she

doubted that he would go to Thorne. A "gentleman" wouldn't soil his hands by dealing directly with a kidnapper. No, it would be Thorne's man Diggs who had actually hired the ruffians who pursued her, and the would-be kidnapper would go to him to confess. Diggs would be no more eager than his employee to tell Thorne of his failure. He might send out his men to scour the streets before he confessed that he had bungled the job. It could be midmorning before Thorne even knew they were missing.

She had no doubt that Mr. Thorne would send men after her. Indeed, it was possible Diggs might have ordered that himself before he told his employer of their failure. But she would have several hours' head start, and even though a man on horseback would be faster than the heavy coach, he couldn't race after her without exhausting his horse. And she doubted that the scum Diggs hired would be excellent horsemen.

No, it would work. It *had* to work.

Noelle glanced down at her son. He had begun chatting with Lisette a few minutes ago, and they continued to talk with the natural ease of longtime friendship. For her part, Noelle had carefully ignored Gil after they had settled into the coach so that it would seem he was with Lisette rather than her, and none of her fellow passengers would see anything amiss when he disembarked with Lisette.

A quick look around assured her that everyone else in the vehicle was asleep, talking to someone, or looking out the window. Noelle bent down and whispered in Gil's ear. "Remember that you're to leave with Lisette. I will return soon."

He looked up at her solemnly and nodded. She could

see the fear in his eyes, and it was all she could do not to hug him to her. But that might draw attention. She reached down between them and took his hand, hidden by her skirts.

When they rolled into the first stop to change horses, Lisette left the carriage, Gil's hand in hers. The two of them would board the first coach back to London—they ran frequently along this short route to the city—and Lisette would hide Gil in her quarters above the shop while Noelle led her pursuers astray.

With any luck, Thorne's men would not catch up to this coach before it reached Dover, and she would be able to also disembark at one of the stops before that and take a circuitous route back to London. Then she and Gil would truly flee the country. Perhaps they would go to Scotland and then across to Norway. She wished she had enough money to buy tickets to Canada; surely there she could lose Thorne for good.

Noelle watched Lisette and Gil walk away, struggling to keep the tears from coming. She had never parted from Gil like this. She had left him with another woman when she went to work, but that had been only for a few hours and she had not been far from him if he needed her. But now he would be in London, and she would be far away, trying to elude her enemy. She felt as if her heart was being pulled from her body with each step her son took.

But that didn't matter. What mattered was that he would be out of Thorne's clutches. Even if Thorne caught up with her, he wouldn't have Gil.

She settled back in her seat and closed her eyes, feigning sleep as a new passenger climbed on board and dropped into the seat beside her. A few minutes later, the horn blew, and the coach pulled out of the yard.

CARLISLE THORNE FELT uncharacteristically optimistic this morning. Across the breakfast table from him, the countess smiled and echoed his thoughts. "I think she's going to come around, don't you, dear?"

"I am hopeful," he responded. However optimistic he was, where Noelle Rutherford was concerned, he couldn't be confident. "She seems to be considering the idea."

"I thought so, too." The countess nodded. "She's… well, she isn't what I expected."

"No?" Carlisle buttered his toast. He found he had little desire to dissect the woman with the countess— or anyone else, for that matter. In truth, he didn't want to think about Noelle Rutherford at all. It brought up the most unsettling feelings in him—guilt and sorrow and even some bizarre impulse to help her. She was too thin, her eyes too shadowed, her posture too tense. And why did she continue to look at him in that wary way, as if he was about to pounce on her?

"No," Adeline replied decisively. "I thought she would be… I don't know, flamboyant, I suppose. But she was rather reserved, wasn't she? And the way she spoke, her manners—if I didn't know better, I would have thought she was brought up a lady. Wasn't it surprising how much she knew about art? I suppose one would pick up that sort of thing around Adam." She paused. "Though I must say, I was around the boy for twenty years, and I don't know those painters and sculptors. You and she left me quite in the dark half the time."

"Yes, I was struck by that, as well." Carlisle went on, "I think she will not be an embarrassment to you."

"No—though I don't care about that. She could drop all her H's and eat with a knife, and I wouldn't mind, as long as Adam's son is here. However, I do think I must order some dresses made for her. And clothes for Gilbert, as well, of course."

"Whatever you like." Carlisle smiled at Adeline. In the past he would have hated for Adeline to get her hopes up. But they were so close to the end now. Even though Noelle had not agreed, he was positive she was moving in that direction. He had seen the defiance and determination in her eyes change to yearning, even hope. He couldn't understand what held her back— other than that rock-hard stubbornness of hers—but he knew her resistance was weakening.

He was content to wait, at least for the moment. His fears about Adam's son were, if not gone, somewhat lessened. With Diggs's man trailing them in and out of the wretched area in which they lived, Carlisle could trust in the boy's safety. And whatever he had thought of Noelle, it was clear she loved Gilbert and took care of him the best she could. Adam's son seemed a happy, healthy child, and if he was not clothed or fed or housed as he should be, that situation was only temporary.

Carlisle excused himself, leaving the countess happily immersed in plans for new wardrobes, and went to his office. He found himself restless, though, his mind straying back to Noelle. Perhaps he should talk to her again. He could drop into the millinery on the pretext of buying a hat for the countess. He could, in fact, buy a hat for Noelle herself; certainly she could use one besides that plain, dark, deep-brimmed bonnet that effectively hid her face. He wondered, if he did so, whether she would wear it or throw it down and crush it beneath her heel.

His thoughts were interrupted by the butler announcing a visitor. Diggs walked in, the look on his face so tight, even worried, that Carlisle stood up in alarm. "What's happened?"

"She's gone, sir."

Carlisle stared at him, the man's words so far from his expectations that he could barely absorb them. "What?" Now anger flooded in, sweeping away his shock. "She's run away again?"

"I'm afraid so. Her flat is empty—there are a few things lying about, but not much. She's packed and gone."

"How the devil did this happen? You were supposed to be keeping an eye on her."

"Yes, sir, I know." Diggs lowered his gaze, his expression a mixture of shame and fury. "I had my best man watching her. But yesterday…um, he didn't follow her home."

"What?"

"It's inexcusable, I know, sir. He is usually so good—but he says yesterday afternoon, he started feeling drowsy, and the next thing he knew, he's sitting there, head on the table, and it's night."

Carlisle stared. "He fell asleep on his watch?"

Diggs squirmed. "Like I said, he's my best man; it's not like him. But he uses the tavern across the street from the millinery. The owner lets him sit at the window all day for a little fee. And he buys a pint now and then so he doesn't look so obvious."

"So he passed out drunk."

"Or someone could have dropped something in his drink when he wasn't looking."

"You think he was drugged? By her?" Carlisle began to pace.

Diggs shrugged. "I've got no proof…but, yes, that's what I think."

"Damn it!" Carlisle slammed his fist down on his desk. "How could I have been so blind? I thought—" He shook his head impatiently. "She played me for a fool yet again."

Noelle had planned it from the first. One didn't just happen to change one's mind and flee on the same evening the man assigned to her had drunk himself unconscious. No, it had to have been carefully executed; she would have had to make arrangements to acquire the drug—as well as find the man to put it in the drink for her, for she couldn't possibly have gotten close enough to Diggs's man without him recognizing her.

Her behavior Sunday had been an act. She had pretended to consider his offer to assuage his suspicions and buy herself time. And he'd been gullible enough to believe her. He'd even felt sympathy for her. Worse, he'd encouraged the countess to hope. Carlisle wanted to smash his fist through something.

But he pulled his temper back under control. He had to act, not storm about. "How long has she been gone? Did your man even think to look for her?"

"Yes, sir. Dawkins went straight to her place as soon as he came to. But it was late by then, and he was hesitant to knock on her door; his orders were to not let her know he was following her. So he waited for her to come out this morning. When she didn't, he checked and found her flat was empty."

"It was a trifle late to worry about revealing his presence if she knew him well enough to drug him," Carlisle said scathingly.

"He—I think he was scared, sir, because he'd failed to do his job. He was groggy, and he thought he'd drunk too much ale and simply fallen asleep. It wasn't until he talked to me that he realized he'd probably been drugged. I raked him over the coals for it, and I'll let him go as soon as I get back."

Carlisle sighed and waved away the idea. "No. He's hardly the only person Noelle Rutherford has given the slip. If he's your best man, as you say, we need him out looking for her."

"Yes, sir. I've set all my men on it. Dawkins asked her neighbors, but nobody saw her leave. They're a closemouthed lot there, of course, but he offered money and still nobody knew anything. My men are checking inns to see if she took a coach out. We started with the ones closest to her place, but she could have gone farther out to catch one, just to throw us off."

"She would," Carlisle said with bitterness. "She's always two steps ahead. What about the shop? Did you look there?"

"Aye. I did that myself, sir, first thing. That fancy French woman told me she'd not come in this morning. Seemed right put out, too—she started spouting French and waving her arms about."

Carlisle nodded. "Of course. The shop would be too obvious. She'll run for the Continent again, no doubt. Dover's the likeliest port. I don't think she'd have the means to hire a carriage, so she'll take the stage. She knows I'll come after her; her only advantage is time. That means she'll leave as early as she can. Find me the inns most convenient to her with the earliest routes this morning." He paused and let out a sigh. "Or yesterday evening. God help us if she was able to catch a mail coach last night."

He spent the next hour pacing his office and thinking dark thoughts. When Diggs returned with the names of three likely inns, Carlisle tapped one decisively. "The Running Hare. It's the earliest, even if it is a little farther away. And no doubt she found a bit of amusement in the name."

Carlisle's mouth twisted at his words. He was beginning to understand the woman better now. Despite her straightforward manner, Noelle was adept at deception. She'd played the role perfectly. He would have been suspicious if she had immediately agreed to his bargain. Instead, she'd refused at first, then gradually appeared to give way, leading him on while she made her plans to escape. She was more than clever or shrewd. She was fierce. Determined. And she despised him. It was clear now that reason stood no chance against that deep well of hatred inside her.

"We'll get 'em back," Diggs assured him. "I'll go after them."

"No," Carlisle replied grimly. "Send some men after her on the other routes, just to make sure. But *I'm* going to the Running Hare. I'll be damned if I let her get away again. I intend to deal with her myself."

CHAPTER SIX

DIGGS HURRIED OFF to do as he bid, and Carlisle sent word to the coachman to bring his light traveling carriage around to the front. Noelle might have time on her side, but his advantage was speed. The passenger coach would be slow; it wasn't one of the speedy mail coaches. His pair of grays was fast, and his traveling coach light. He wouldn't require the number of stops the public vehicle would, and he had the money to change out horses along the way. He had to catch her at Dover, if not earlier. If he let her board a ship to the Continent, he'd completely lose them again.

Going into his office, he pulled a pouch of coins from the safe; there was no telling what sort of problem he might encounter with that blasted woman. It took only a few bob at the Running Hare to get the stage agent to tell him that an attractive woman with a young boy had indeed boarded the earliest stage to Dover this morning. Carlisle hastened back to the carriage, telling his coachman, "Spring 'em, Morton."

His driver was skillful and his team swift, and they made excellent time. He wasted no time at his stops, pausing only long enough to change out the horses and let the coachman grab a drink and a bite to eat.

Still, they had not yet caught up with the coach late that afternoon, and Carlisle was beginning to fear she would reach Dover, where it would be far harder to find her. They came upon a coach stopped at an inn, and his heart leaped inside his chest, but it turned out to be a coach traveling the opposite direction. They pressed on, and it was dusk when they sighted a stagecoach lumbering along the turnpike in front of them.

Morton slapped the reins and soon caught up with the other vehicle, waving to the driver to pull to the side. With a shrug, the driver complied, and the heavy coach rolled to a stop. As soon as his carriage stopped in front of the stagecoach, Carlisle jumped down.

The driver leaned over and called down, "'Ere! Wot's goin' on?"

Carlisle ignored him as he jerked open the door of the coach. A large number of people filled the seats, and they all turned to look at him in astonishment. But it took only a quick glance to see that Gilbert and his mother were not among them.

Carlisle let out a soft curse and swung the door shut. He turned to the driver, who was climbing stiffly down from his high perch. "I'm looking for a woman."

The heavyset driver let out a bark of laughter. "Ain't we all, mister?"

"Is this the early coach from the Running Hare?"

"Aye." The coachman stretched, looking not at all displeased at being stopped.

"There was a woman who got on it. With a child. She's about this tall. Brown hair, blue eyes, trim figure. Dressed in drab clothing." Carlisle pulled out a few silver coins, and the coachman looked more interested.

"Aye, there was a woman like that. But she got off in Maidstone."

"The devil." Carlisle clenched his jaw. The wretched

woman had outwitted him yet again. She must have realized he would chase the coach down, so she had hopped off early. She could be anywhere by now.

The coachman went on cheerfully, "Weren't no lad with her, though."

"What?" That answer brought him up short. "No boy? It couldn't have been the same woman."

"A prime article in bad clothes?"

"She is attractive, yes, but…"

"I saw her." The coach's guard spoke up. "I didn't see her hair 'neath her bonnet, but she had a face like an angel. And she had a little one with her. I saw him when she got on."

"Well, she didn't have one when she got off," the driver retorted.

The other man tilted his head, considering. "Mayhap you're right. I saw her walking away, but I don't think the lad was with her."

Good God, what had she done with Gilbert? Carlisle blindly shoved a few coins at the guard and strode back to his carriage. The one thing Carlisle had been certain of was that Noelle loved Gilbert. Had that all been an act, as well? No. His mind recoiled from the thought. But, blast it, if she had not abandoned the boy, where the hell was he?

Carlisle had thought that he could not be any more furious at Noelle, but he found now that his anger could reach new heights. Frustration and anger boiled in him as he directed Morton to drive back to Maidstone. How many stagecoaches passed in and out of that town? She could have gone in any direction.

Still, he must start somewhere. Logically, she would have taken the first coach to come through the town.

Her aim was apparently not to go any certain place, but simply to cover her trail. There was more than one inn in Maidstone, but fortunately at the second one he tried, the ostlers remembered Noelle. It was lucky for him, he reflected, that no bonnet or drab clothes could make Noelle a woman whom men did not notice. A few coins in the hands of the grooms bought him the information that, two hours ago, she had taken a coach to Brighton by way of Tunbridge Wells.

He doubted that either place was Noelle's ultimate destination. She would have chosen that coach because from it, she could again go anywhere. Was her plan to double back to pick up Gilbert from wherever she had stashed him? Had she simply left him alone at some stage stop along the way?

Carlisle ground his teeth in fury. She wasn't fit to raise Gilbert—dragging him all over, keeping him from his family and his rightful place in the world, denying him the comforts and joys he should have. When he found Noelle, he'd have the boy's whereabouts from her, no matter what it took. And after that, he'd make sure Gilbert was never again out of his sight. Noelle had accused him of attempting to take her son away from her. Well, this time he bloody well was.

At first, he decided not to inquire at the stop that the coach would have made between Maidstone and Tunbridge Wells. That would eat up precious time, and he had much ground to catch up. There seemed little chance she would have gotten off at such a small place, where there would be no other stage passing through for at least a day. But he decided he could not ignore the station. Noelle was wily enough to count on such an assumption on his part and leave the coach early, then turn in yet another direction or take some other mode of transportation. There could be someone helping her; someone could have waited for her at that stage stop. Perhaps she was involved with a man. There had been no sign of that, but she was capable enough to have kept his presence secret.

His mood was dark as his carriage rolled into the inn and stopped. He descended from the vehicle. At that moment a woman stepped out of the inn's door, silhouetted against the light inside. Carlisle stopped short. He could not see the woman's face, but he knew her immediately. Noelle.

She whirled and darted back inside. Carlisle started after her.

CARLISLE THORNE! Could nothing stop this man?

Noelle had expected he would discover what coach she had taken out of London. He was too clever, too determined, not to do that. But she'd presumed he would send his men after her, not pursue her himself, and she'd hoped whoever pursued her would ride straight to Dover, where he would conduct a fruitless search for her throughout the city, while she left the coach early and caught a stagecoach going somewhere else—it didn't matter where, as long as it was away from Thorne and his men.

When they had stopped to rest in Maidstone, she'd slipped away to another, smaller inn, where she had the good luck to find a coach traveling to Brighton. She could disembark in Tunbridge Wells and make her way back to London to get Gil.

But then her luck had changed. The coach broke a wheel and had to be pulled to the nearest way station to be repaired. Noelle had been waiting ever since. Then, like a nightmare, Carlisle Thorne had stepped out of his carriage.

He was the most persistent, infuriating man Noelle had ever met. Since Gil was not with her, she didn't feel the sort of fear she had in the past. But there was no way she was going to just stand around and let him find her. Noelle darted past a startled maid, and went barreling into the next room, which turned out to be the kitchen. She ran through it and out the back door into the dark night. Behind her she could hear a shriek and a crash, and she knew that Thorne must be on her heels. She didn't dare glance back. Even with the moonlight, it was difficult to see the narrow path ahead.

A low stone wall appeared, and, lifting her skirts, she jumped over it, running on. She was, she realized, in a graveyard, and she had to slow down to avoid monuments and tombstones. Carlisle yelled her name, and a moment later she heard a thud, followed by a curse. With bitter satisfaction, she hoped he had run into one of the gravestones. Maybe he'd twisted an ankle.

Of course, he had not. She heard his running footsteps on the dirt path, drawing nearer and nearer. She ran through the lych-gate ahead and into the grassy churchyard itself. The church loomed up ahead and she had a desperate thought of running into it and calling for sanctuary. It wouldn't matter, though—there was no sanctuary from someone like Carlisle Thorne.

Her lungs were heaving, her breath coming in hard pants. She felt as if her heart was about to burst in her chest. He was so close she could hear his rasping breath. Her toe caught an exposed tree root, and she went down. Thorne grabbed her before she could hit the ground, pulling her back against him, but she kicked out at him, and, overbalanced, they both tumbled to the ground.

Thorne twisted as they fell, which cushioned her own fall. His arms were like an iron cage around her, but she fought, squirming and kicking and hitting him with her fists, struggling to get away. They rolled across the ground in an almost silent struggle, broken only by their panting breaths.

He straddled her, pinning her to the ground with the full weight of his body. Noelle pushed up in a vain attempt to dislodge him. She was suddenly very aware of their position. His body was pressed into hers. She was surrounded by his heat, the scent of him in her nostrils, mingling with the smell of earth and crushed grass, his breath rasping in her ear.

Thorne, too, must have realized how suggestive their position was, for he scrambled off and jumped to his feet. Reaching down, he dragged her up. "What have you done with Gilbert? Where is he?"

She lifted her chin and glared up into his face without speaking. He might have captured her, but she wasn't about to weakly acquiesce. She was, in any case, too breathless to say anything.

When she gave no reply, he let out a growl of frustration "Tell me, damn it, tell me what you did with Gilbert."

"And if I don't? What do you intend to do—beat it out of me?"

"It's bloody tempting," he retorted. "But I have never hit a woman and don't plan to start now. What I *will* do is haul you into court. I am the boy's guardian, and I think any judge would agree that it is I who have Gilbert's best interests at heart, not a woman who refuses to let him live a decent life. A woman who breaks her word at every turn." He dropped her arm, almost flinging it away. His eyes blazed; even in the darkness, she could see the fury in his face. "You promised me, damn it. You swore you would not run."

"And *you* promised not to attack us!"

"Attack you! What did you expect me to do? Stand still while you spirited Adam's son away?"

"No, you did exactly what I *should* have expected from you! I was a fool to believe you, to let myself fall into your trap."

"Trap? A comfortable home, a good life for you and your son, is a trap? Good God, woman, you are the most bullheaded, foolish...*suspicious* woman I have ever met!"

"As well I should be!" Noelle shot back. "After the way you've hounded me across Europe, all the times you've tried to abduct Gil. I *was* foolish, believing your promises, trusting you. Thank God I woke up in time to get him away from you."

"You're blaming *me* for you scarpering off?"

"Yes! You lied to me. All that pleasant talk, the kindness of the countess, the pretty pictures you painted of the life ahead for Gil and me, the way you oozed yourself into Gil's favor, promising him horses and books..."

"What's wrong with that? That's the life the boy should have!"

"It was all talk, that's what's wrong—all pretense to lull me into letting down my guard, making it easy for you to grab Gil."

"Grab Gil—sweet Jesus, are you back to that? I have never tried to abduct Gil! I would never—"

"You did! In Bern. In Barcelona. Or any of the many

other times you've cornered us. You did it just yesterday!"

"Bern!" He gaped at her. "Barcelona? What the devil are you talking about? I've never even been in Barcelona."

"Not you in person. A 'gentleman' wouldn't dirty his hands like that. It was the man you hired, just like it was your man yesterday."

"My man…" The anger in his face changed to bewilderment. He frowned, giving her a long look of consideration. "Perhaps you ought to tell me exactly what happened yesterday."

"He didn't tell you? I suppose he wouldn't want to report his failure. He followed us home from work, as always, and when we were almost there, he charged in, knocked me aside, and scooped up Gil."

"Noelle." Oddly, he had called her by her name for the first time, Noelle noted. His voice was measured and quiet in a way that raised the hairs on the back of her neck. "My man didn't follow you yesterday. In Bern, you were gone by the time Diggs arrived to deliver my letter. I never even knew you were in Barcelona."

Noelle stared at him, her legs suddenly weak beneath her.

"Noelle!" Carlisle jumped forward, wrapping an arm around her waist to hold her up. She sagged against him, her ears ringing, and he scooped her up, carrying her over to a bench. "Sit down. Lower your head."

She started to protest, but his hand was firm on the back of her head, pushing it down. She took a breath and the dizziness receded. Noelle straightened. Thorne sat beside her, watching her intently.

"Tell me exactly what happened in Bern and Barcelona," he said.

Shakily, Noelle ran her hands across her face, as if she could bring her thoughts into order by doing so. "It was, um, three years ago. Barcelona, I mean. A man came up and knocked me down."

"He *hit* you?"

"No, it was more that he grabbed my arm and threw me to the ground, but Gil created quite a fuss, and the butcher came to our aid. In Bern we were in a park, but I saw him coming that time, and I was able to stab him before he got to Gil."

"Stab him?" Carlisle's eyebrows soared.

"I was knitting."

"I suppose I'm lucky to have escaped a maiming at your hands," he said dryly. "Go on. What happened yesterday?"

"He was following us, as I said. I looked back and saw him. It wasn't the man you usually have trailing us, and I thought how he wasn't as good as the shorter one because he was too obvious. Then Gil began to jump about. He was excited because I'd told him—well, it doesn't matter. Suddenly the man darted in, shoved me aside, and grabbed Gil. He ran up the street." She let out a shaky breath, remembering. "I couldn't have caught him. Thank God for that dog. And the man who hit him with his crutch."

A faint smile touched Thorne's lips. "A dog. A man on a crutch. A butcher. You certainly have an interesting set of champions."

"Yes. Well." She tried to muster up a faint smile. "Not exactly the life of a lady." She linked her hands in her lap, turning her gaze down to them. She felt as if the world had tumbled down around her. "You didn't send them? Truly?"

"I did not." Thorne leaned forward and gazed squarely into her face. "I swear to you, on my life, on the life of the countess, on anything you want, that I have *never* sent anyone to wrest Gil from you. Yes, I searched for you all these years, but only because I wanted to persuade you to come home, to take up life at Stonecliffe with the countess. *Both* you and Gilbert. I would not have torn Adam's son from you. I wouldn't have done that to any mother. However overbearing I may be, I am not entirely hard-hearted."

Noelle felt her resistance slipping away. She wanted to believe him. She wanted to let go of her burden, hand it off to someone else. But how could she put her trust in this man? Her enemy.

"Think about it," he went on reasonably. "Why would I have tried to kidnap Gil yesterday? You were considering my proposal, I know you were. It was the sensible course. All I had to do was wait until you agreed. I had no reason to take Gil. You cannot really think Lady Drewsbury was in on some nefarious plot. How the devil would I have explained it to her when I showed up with Gil by himself? Why would I have frightened the boy like that when I could get what I wanted so much more easily?"

A new fear rushed through Noelle, and she shivered, her hands trembling. Embarrassed, she clasped her hands together. The last person she wanted to see her weak was Carlisle Thorne. For five years he had been her bête noire, the man who haunted her dreams.

He could be lying. He could be the unprincipled, untrustworthy man she had been certain he was yesterday evening. But it was true that it made no sense for him to attempt an abduction yesterday. He was about to get what he wanted. He didn't need to tear Gil away.

If Thorne was determined to separate Noelle from Gil, it would be more logical to do as she had been thinking yesterday—wean Gil away from her, offer him the advantages of wealth and power, pull him into the world of the entitled, until Gil no longer belonged to her. It was also true that the man yesterday was not the one who had followed her before. She thought of the years behind her. "But…if it was not you who tried to abduct Gil, that means…"

He nodded. "That someone else is after you."

CHAPTER SEVEN

"WE'RE GOING TO get Gilbert." Thorne took her by the arm again, though without his former iron grip, and pulled her to her feet. Setting off toward the inn, he went on, "But you two are not returning to that squalid room."

"You're putting yourself in charge, I see," Noelle said dryly.

"And you, needless to say, are automatically opposed to doing anything I suggest."

Noelle didn't point out that his statement had not exactly been a suggestion. She was too tired, too much in shock, to decide anything herself. It would be a wonderful relief to, for once, turn the problem over to someone else. She shook her head. "No. I'm not opposed to that."

Carlisle glanced at her. "The first thing we are going to do is get some food into you. And brandy. You need to rest. Clearly you're not yourself if you're agreeing with me."

"I'm fine," she began.

"No." He raised an admonitory finger. "I am in charge now, remember?"

His hand was firm beneath her arm, and Noelle realized that she was leaning against it more as they walked. He was right; she was dead tired. She had been unable to sleep much the night before, and now the energy that had kept her going was draining away along with her fear. She must not let herself depend too much on Carlisle Thorne. Perhaps he was not her enemy, but neither was he her friend. She had to remember that. But right now, she hadn't the strength.

They walked in silence for a while as they took the road to the inn, skirting the graveyard. After a moment, Thorne said in a low voice, "I am sorry that you have lived in fear of me for so long." Noelle glanced up at him in surprise. She could see only the side of his face, for he steadfastly kept his gaze straight ahead. "I am not—I never sought to harm you or Gil. It never occurred to me that you might be running from my men because you were frightened. That you thought I was going to steal your son from you."

"I can't imagine why I would have thought such a thing," Noelle retorted sarcastically.

He whipped his head toward her, scowling. "I didn't try to steal him! Or buy him. I—" He bit off his words and took a breath, once again looking away from her. "I realize that I was…rude to you when we met."

"That's one way to describe it." She noticed that he had not said he was wrong, only that he had been impolite.

His lips twitched in irritation, but he said only, "I regret very much that I gave you the impression I wanted to take your son from you. I hope you will accept my apology."

"I do." His words could not wipe away what he had said and done that night; he thought no more highly of her now than he had then. But what else could she do but accept his apology? It was something, at least, that he was resolved to be polite. She must get along with him. If there was danger to Gil from someone else, she would need all the protection she could find. She had no illusions that she could shield her son from harm as well as a man of Thorne's power and wealth could. If it meant Gil's safety, she would get along with the Devil himself.

When they reached the inn, they were quickly ushered into a private room with a small, welcoming fire, and brandy was brought in short order, confirming Noelle's opinion of how much more a man of influence could do than she could. She was grateful for that influence, though, as she sank onto a chair by the low fire. She was exhausted, every part of her aching. Somewhere in her mad dash through the cemetery, she had lost her shawl, and the evening chill of the churchyard seemed to have seeped into her very bones. Huddling in on herself, she leaned closer to the warmth.

"Here." She looked up and saw Carlisle looming over her, holding a glass in one hand. His brows rushed together, and he reached toward her shoulder with his free hand. "What—" Noelle instinctively shrank back from his touch, and he dropped his hand, saying gruffly, "Was your dress always ripped there?"

"I don't know." Noelle hadn't looked in a mirror since she'd changed disguises earlier. "It probably happened when we were fighting in the graveyard."

"I didn't mean—it was not purposeful. I…" His voice trailed off.

Noelle almost smiled. Clearly this man was dreadful at apologies. In truth, she thought he had been trying to protect her during their tumble. She remembered the way he had twisted as they hit the ground so that he had taken the brunt of the fall. Still, she was not inclined to try to soothe his guilt. Whatever he thought, whatever the truth was, his pursuit had terrified her for years.

Thorne thrust the glass at her. "Here. Drink this. You'll feel better."

The brandy burned a path from her mouth to her stomach, making her gasp, but she had to admit that it revived her a little. He told her to take another drink in that same irritating tone of command, and she did so. She hoped he wouldn't become accustomed to such obedience from her. She had no intention of supplying it.

"Good." He sat down in the chair across from her. "Now...we need to talk. First we must get Gilbert—where the devil is he?"

"With Lisette." At his blank expression, Noelle added, "The woman who owns the shop."

"He's *there*? All this time, he's been snug in the millinery store?"

"Yes. Lisette boarded the coach, as well, and at the first stop she and Gil got off and returned to London." Noelle straightened suddenly, panic sweeping through her. "Gil—" Her stomach twisted. "He has no one to protect him but Lisette." She stood up. "We must go. We have to get back to London right now."

"There's no need to panic." Thorne rose, reaching out to take her arms. "Gilbert *does* have protection. I left Diggs himself watching the millinery store on the off chance that you might come back there. He doesn't know that Gil is inside, but he or one of his men will be there twenty-four hours a day until I tell him otherwise. They would stop anyone leaving the shop with your son. We shall go to the shop and get him as soon as we reach London. Then I plan to take you, the boy, and the countess to the country. It will be far easier for me to keep an eye on you at Stonecliffe."

Normally Noelle would have protested the way he was making plans for her and Gil without asking, but right now she was happy to let him take charge. For the first time ever, she didn't have to plan, didn't have to be strong. She could let go and place it all in someone else's hands.

Thorne went on. "I will set Diggs onto investigating these attacks. I'm sorry, but I think we need to talk about them again. Were the earlier assaults done by the same man as yesterday?"

She shook her head. "No. It was a different man each time. I had the impression that they were hired ruffians, not the actual person who wanted Gil."

"You didn't recognize any of them?"

"I'd never seen any of them before." Noelle described the attackers as best she could. "I'm sorry. Each time it happened so suddenly, and all I was thinking of was saving Gil."

"I'll have Diggs look for the man from yesterday, but I think our best hope is to approach it from the other end. Who hired these men? And why? You assumed I was behind the attacks, so you believed the target was your son. But it seems more likely that they were after you, not Gilbert."

"Me?" Noelle gaped at him. The man's dislike of her was leading him down the wrong path. "There's no reason for anyone to attack me. No one hates me that much…except you, of course."

He ignored her words. "Gilbert is only a child. An adult is far likelier to have enemies."

"That man yesterday was clearly after Gil. He merely pushed me aside."

"What would be a better way to hurt you than to take your son? What better lure to bring you back."

"Back to whom? What are you talking about?"

"A jealous man."

"There are no jealous men in my life. This is nonsense."

"A woman who looks like you? You expect me to believe there are no former lovers? A protector who didn't want you to leave? A man upset because you favored someone else?"

Noelle jumped to her feet. "A protector! You're saying that I have been some man's mistress? Bought and paid for?"

He rose, too, saying impatiently, "There is no need to pretend with me; I don't care what you have done or who you've been with. I know—"

"You don't *know* anything about me or what I've done."

"Blast it, I am trying to find out who has been doing these things, and if you lie to me, you tie my hands. You're a desirable woman. After Adam died, you had to live. Much as I hate the thought of Adam's son being brought up in such an environment, I understand."

"You understand?" Noelle asked bitingly. "But naturally you do, being such a superior being. You *understand* that a pretty woman is automatically licentious. You *understand* that if men desire a woman, then *she* must be a hussy. Unless, of course, that woman is an aristocrat. A common girl, however, is an entirely different matter."

A flush rose up Thorne's neck. "It has nothing to

do with your class. I don't care if you were a chimney sweep's daughter. I assumed it because you lured a naive boy into marrying you."

"Naive." Noelle scoffed. "You think Adam was some innocent lamb without knowledge of the world or women? You think at twenty, he was untouched?"

Thorne grimaced. "I know Adam sowed his wild oats."

"Which is fine, since he is a man," Noelle interjected.

Thorne ignored her. "But he had no experience of the world, no understanding of the ways an adventuress could lure him in. He was gullible."

"Adam was far less gullible than you, if that is what you believe. I am not some siren who worked her wicked wiles on young men. I didn't meet Adam at a tavern or bordello or whatever lurid thing you've conjured up. He courted me in my father's house because he respected me. You see, *Adam* judged people by how they acted, not by who their ancestors were. Adam loved me, and I loved him. *He* was the one who persuaded *me* to marry."

"I did not—" Thorne began.

"Let me finish." Noelle's eyes flashed. "It is none of your business, and you will, I'm sure, believe what you want. But the truth—if you have any care for a minor thing like that—is that I have never been with anyone other than Adam nor have I ever sought the protection of any man. As for how I lived after Adam died—I worked. I worked as hard as I could, wherever I could. I sold the jewelry Adam gave me. I sold my wedding ring." Tears clogged her voice for a moment, but she plowed ahead. "I am well aware that men like you think everyone else is dirt beneath their feet, but the fact that I'm not highborn doesn't make me without morals. It's clear you have no respect for me, but you might have a bit of respect for Adam." She turned and walked toward the door.

"Noelle—I mean, my lady…" Thorne started after her.

She turned to face him. "I'm not *your* lady. And don't worry, I'm not running away. I know that I must deal with you for Gil's sake. But I do not have to sit here and listen to your insults. I'll wait for you in the carriage."

CHAPTER EIGHT

THEY DROVE THROUGH the night, arriving in London the next morning. The trip passed in icy silence, with Noelle pretending to sleep most of the time. They went straight to the millinery, and Noelle led Carlisle up to Lisette's rooms. Lisette answered the door a narrow crack, then swung it wide when she saw Noelle. Her eyes went to Carlisle Thorne, looming behind Noelle, and she started to slam the door shut, but Noelle put a hand on the door, stopping her.

"No, it's all right. I'm fine. We aren't—well, it's a long story, but Mr. Thorne and I have reached an agreement."

Lisette's eyebrows soared, but after a long, searching look at Noelle, she stepped back, admitting them. Gil came tearing out of the back room, shouting, "Maman!" His first words were a rapid spate of French as he flung his arms around his mother. Seeing Thorne, he grinned with apparent delight and switched to English. "Tante Lisette said you wouldn't be back today." He gave a little bow to Thorne. "Did you go to see Mr. Thorne, Mama? Are we going home now?"

"Yes—to a new home," Noelle answered. "You remember we talked about staying with the countess for a bit?"

"We're going to visit Grandmama?"

"Yes, and all of us will go to the house I told you about," Carlisle put in. "The one in the country."

"With horses?" The boy's eyes lit up, and he whirled and ran back into the bedroom.

Lisette pulled Noelle aside, whispering, "Are you all right? Is he forcing you to go?"

"I promise you, everything's fine—well, not fine, but it turns out Mr. Thorne wasn't the one chasing me all this time."

"Then who was it?" Lisette goggled at her. "Why?"

"I don't know. It's a dreadful puzzle, but Mr. Thorne will be able to protect Gil better than I could on my own."

At that moment Gil bounced back into the room, a small sack slung over his shoulder and carrying two books in his arms, and announced, "I'm ready."

"You took the book with you, I see," Carlisle commented.

"Yes. Mama said we must take only what's most important."

Thorne smiled in that way that had surprised Noelle each of the few times she'd seen it: a brief tilt up at the corners of his lips that somehow changed his whole face. "Shall I carry it for you?"

Gil nodded and handed over the books, taking the man's hand as he usually did Noelle's. "Grandmama will be surprised to see me, won't she?"

Noelle's eyes misted, her heart aching in a strange mingling of sorrow and happiness.

"Yes. She will be delighted," Carlisle was saying as they started toward the door.

"Maman?" Gil looked over his shoulder questioningly.

Noelle swallowed. "Yes, dear, I'm coming." She turned back to Lisette. "I promise I will write you as soon as we are settled and explain everything. I am sorry to leave the shop so suddenly, but I have to keep Gil safe."

Lisette shrugged in a Gallic way. "I will simply have to stay here a bit longer than I planned. It's of no concern. It is you I worry about. Are you sure you will be safe with that man? He is so grim."

"He is an arrogant, narrow-minded, humorless prig, but I no longer believe he will harm me, and he has the wealth and power to protect Gil far better than I can." Noelle smiled at her friend and turned away. If only she felt as confident as she sounded.

WHEN THE THREE of them walked into the drawing room, the countess sprang up from her seat and started forward, arms extended. "Gil! Little love."

Gil went to her without hesitation, letting her enfold him in her arms. Noelle felt a tug at her heart. How easily he accepted these people; he wanted a family.

The man Noelle had met on their previous visit to the countess stood beside the mantel. "Good to see you back."

"Nathan." Carlisle smiled. "Bit early for you, isn't it?"

"I fear I quite imposed on Nathan's kind nature by asking him to call on me."

"It was no imposition at all," Nathan said, smiling fondly at Lady Drewsbury. "I am always happy to chat with you."

"Dear boy." The countess smiled and patted his arm, then turned to Noelle, still standing in the doorway. "Do come in, dear. I'm so glad to see you." Her voice was smooth, lacking any hint of reproach, even though she must have been alarmed.

"I am sorry that we gave you any worry," Noelle said with complete honesty, walking up to the woman. "I—" She hesitated, glancing at Mr. Dunbridge.

"Don't hesitate to speak in front of Nathan," the countess assured her. "He is practically a member of the family; he knows all our secrets." She took Noelle's arm, leading her toward the small couch. "I hope that nothing I said upset you."

"No, it was a…a misunderstanding."

"A misunderstanding?"

"Yes," Carlisle put in. "We'll discuss it in a moment. But I think young Gilbert might like to play in the nursery." He looked over at Gil, smiling, and lifted his brows at the boy. "And perhaps some biscuits and milk might be in order?"

"Yes!" Gil trotted over.

Noelle half rose, casting a worried glance at her son. It made her stomach dance to let him out of her sight in this place, among these people. But Thorne was right to want Gil out of earshot for this discussion. She sank back down in her seat.

Carlisle waited until Gil left the room with a sturdy footman before he turned back to the others. "Lady Rutherford has been under the impression that I tried to kidnap Gil," Carlisle began bluntly.

"What?" Adeline and Nathan gaped at him.

Carlisle explained to them what had happened and what he had learned, his story punctuated here and there by a gasp from the countess or a "Good Gad!" from his friend.

"What will you do, Carlisle?" the countess asked when he finished.

"Take all of you to Stonecliffe, to begin with," Thorne replied. "You'd best set the servants to packing, my lady. I'd like to leave this afternoon."

"But, Carlisle dear, what about the clothes for Noelle and Gilbert? Couldn't we at least stay long enough to buy fabric? There's a seamstress in the village who could make adequate day dresses if we had the material. Surely we would be safe enough here in this house, at least for a bit."

"Yes, you'd be safe *here*. But you can't go jaunting about the city with an attacker on the loose."

"Gil can stay in the house, surrounded by our people," Adeline suggested.

Noelle didn't like the sound of that. The last thing she wanted was to be separated from her son. And she hated the thought of accepting handouts from the countess. It was already galling enough that they would be living on her charity. "Really, ma'am, you needn't…it's very generous of you, but—"

"Generous?" Adeline dismissed the notion with a flick of her wrist. "It's Gilbert's money, after all, and he has more than enough for new clothes. Isn't that right, Carlisle?"

"Yes, of course. Both of you should have proper clothes." Carlisle turned his shrewd gaze on Noelle. "Think how it would look if we had the Drewsbury heir and his mother running about in rags."

"Carlisle!" Adeline scolded. "What a thing to say." She turned to Noelle. "I'm sure he didn't mean…um…"

Noelle knew he'd meant exactly what he'd said. She and Gil would be an embarrassment to the family dressed in their cheap clothing. And somehow the thought that Thorne would buy the clothes for that reason, not out of pity or kindness, made her more willing to take the gifts. "Pray, don't worry, ma'am. I don't take anything Mr. Thorne says for truth."

She ignored the countess's soaring eyebrows and the chuckle from Thorne's friend Nathan as she stared back at Carlisle with a cool gaze to match his own.

"Buying clothes is not the problem," Carlisle snapped. "The problem is *you* putting yourself out in the street where this ruffian can attack you."

"What? I don't understand." The countess looked over at Noelle. "I thought it was Gilbert who was in danger."

"Gil *is* the one in danger." Noelle glared at Carlisle. "Mr. Thorne has it fixed in his head that I was the object of the attack."

"Bloody hell—I beg your pardon, ma'am." He nodded to the countess. Noelle noticed he didn't apologize to her for his language, just turned back to glower at her. "I cannot understand why you are so eager to put yourself in danger."

Noelle hadn't intended to go shopping. She didn't even want to, but now she was determined to do so. "I'm not. But I won't cower inside the house because you have decided that my son's attempted kidnapping was an attack on me."

"I'm sure not," Carlisle retorted. "That would make too much sense."

"Carlisle, dear, don't be rude." The countess rose and patted his arm. "I can see that you are in a bother about it, but you mustn't fret. We shall be perfectly safe in the carriage. The coachman and the footman will be with us."

"Anders and Jackson aren't enough," Carlisle said, but his expression showed that he was relenting. He sighed. "I'll go with you."

Noelle smothered a smile at the martyred look on Carlisle's face. It was almost enough to make her mellow a bit toward him. Almost.

"No need to sacrifice yourself." Nathan Dunbridge spoke up. "I shall be happy to escort the ladies in your stead." He smiled and bowed to the countess and Noelle. "I'll be the envy of all in the company of two such beautiful women."

To NOELLE'S SURPRISE, the expedition turned out to be enjoyable. It had been a very long time since she had gone shopping for pleasure. The countess was a pleasant companion, lightly chatting about this or that and displaying no disapproval of Noelle or her unfashionable attire, and Nathan Dunbridge proved to be a far more amiable escort than Mr. Thorne.

He was as charming as he was handsome. He was amusingly, unobjectionably flirtatious, not only with Lady Drewsbury and Noelle but with every other woman, from an acquaintance they met on the street to the flower girl on the corner (from whom he gallantly bought a posy for each of his companions). Noelle found herself chatting and smiling in an easy way she rarely did anymore.

Noelle was stunned by the quantity of Adeline's purchases. "But, Lady Drewsbury, this is too much. You have bought so many things, I'll never be able to wear half of them."

"You'll need a good deal more than just day dresses. Even living in the country as we do, one has assemblies and dinners and dances."

"Indeed, ma'am," Nathan said. "I am your nearest neighbor, and I'm sure I will have a party to welcome you. It will be a reward for visiting my dreary lawyer." He proceeded to entertain them with a description of his last visit to the solemn young solicitor. The man was urging him to sell some of his property. "Thompkins is correct, of course; the manor is under far too much debt, but Grandmother's ghost would haunt me the rest of my life if I sold it," Nathan added in a far more lighthearted tone than Noelle could imagine in the same situation.

In the face of Lady Drewsbury's insistence, Noelle accepted the clothes, but when Lady Drewsbury had the carriage stop at her own modiste's for even more frocks, she pulled Adeline to the side and said, "Please, you need not do all these things for me. You needn't try to pamper or persuade me. I am doing this for Gil's sake, not for any sort of payment."

The countess looked taken aback. "Of course not, dear. I'm not trying to bribe you, only to give you some of the things you should have had all this time. I—" She took Noelle's hand, tears shining in her eyes. "My son loved you, and the only thing I can do for him now is take care of his wife. I was so wrong before. I didn't want to go against my husband. I was sure I could persuade the earl to welcome Adam back into the family. I did, with Carlisle's help, but it was too late by then. Adam was gone. And I had given up my last few moments with my son because I chose the easier path. I will always regret that."

Noelle felt her years-long resentment of Lady

Drewsbury melting into sympathy. She squeezed Adeline's hand. "Adam loved you very much. He never spoke of you with aught but affection. I know he didn't blame you."

"Thank you." Adeline smiled, blinking away her tears. "I cannot change what is past. But I can—and I will—take good care of those who are left to me. Carlisle and Gil…and you. You are Adam's wife, and you are family to me."

CHAPTER NINE

WHEN THEY RETURNED from shopping, the countess went upstairs to rest and Noelle left to check on Gil. Carlisle turned to Nathan. "You deserve a drink after enduring a shopping trip. Let's go to my study." When they had settled down in the study, drinks in hand, Carlisle said, "Truly, I appreciate your doing that."

"It was no chore," his friend replied lightly. "I quite enjoyed their company." He paused, taking a sip, then went on carefully, "Lady Rutherford is...not what I expected."

"No, she's not," Carlisle agreed. "It may just be that the woman is an excellent liar, but...damn it, Nathan, I think I may have mucked up everything entirely. The woman despises me, and she's Gilbert's mother."

"I'm sure she will grow to like you when she's been around you awhile."

"I doubt it. She thinks I'm a sanctimonious, rigid, overbearing snob." Carlisle sighed. "And I don't know. Maybe she's right."

Nathan's eyebrows went up. "You? What are you talking about?"

"I wanted information about these attacks that happened to them previously, but I managed to offend her... again. I must protect her and Gil, and I need to know who might have a grudge against her. It seems more likely to me that these men are trying to harm her, not Gil. He's just a boy."

"A boy for whom you would pay a ransom."

"I thought of that. But how would anyone have even known he's related to me? They've been on the run since he was born, living under false names, changing their appearance. But Noelle—she's a woman whom no man would let go of easily."

"I suppose." Nathan studied his friend's face. "Certainly, you were determined to track her down."

"Of course. Because she had Gil. I hope you aren't implying that *I* have any feelings for her." A persistent stab of lust was *not* having feelings for her. "Noelle is the bane of my existence. The thing is, I asked her about her former lovers. Who had been her protector since Adam died. She denied that anyone had. She claims that she has been working all this time to support them. Doing menial tasks."

"Well, her attire would be proof of that. And you did find her working in a shop."

"I know." Carlisle set his drink aside. "If any man was providing for her, he certainly was doing a poor job of it. She's too thin and tired. And I cannot help but think—what if I have misjudged her all these years? What if she is telling the truth and she wasn't an adventuress who tricked Adam into a disastrous marriage? She says Adam courted her in her parlor and that he was the one pushing to marry, which would be just like him. Adam was always impulsive and emotional. The nature of an artist, I guess. I have never really understood it."

"Because you are a rational fellow; you think things through." Nathan paused, then said, "You weren't the only one who believed that of her. I envisioned her that way, too."

"Yes, because I told you so."

"And you believed it because the earl told you."

"Yes. I never questioned it. He hired a Bow Street runner to look into it, but perhaps the investigator told his client what he knew the client wanted to hear. Or Lord Drewsbury might have colored the man's findings to fit his beliefs. He was furious at Adam's defiance. I think he believed Adam married the worst sort of woman he could just to spite him."

"Which is also something Adam might have done."

"Yes. But I didn't look into it. I judged her without a shred of evidence. And, yes, if I consider it honestly, I was more inclined to believe it because she wasn't genteel. Not one of 'us.' I should have gone to Oxford to talk to Adam myself. I should have met her."

"Stop flogging yourself because you didn't run to Adam's aid. You're not everyone's protector."

"But I should have been *her* protector, not the bane of her existence."

"Well, now you are," Nathan said. "I know you, and no one could be safer anywhere than at Stonecliffe under your watch."

"I'll make sure of that," Carlisle said grimly.

"I would go with you except my mother has demanded that I stay here through her next ball. I have no idea why since I am of no use at all in planning a party, but I cannot refuse. She would cry, and…"

"And you would feel guilty and give in. You never have been able to withstand a woman's tears. Too bad I can't give you some of my rigid, overbearing ways." Carlisle's lips quirked up at the corner.

Nathan snorted. "As if you ever turned down one of Lady Drewsbury's requests."

"Well, who *could* refuse Lady Drewsbury?"

"True," Nathan admitted. "But my point is that after I see my mother through her party, I will go back to the manor. I'll be only a few miles away, and I will help you any way I can."

"Thank you. I don't want to put you to the trouble, but I admit I will be happy for another set of eyes and ears there."

"Trust me, you won't put me to any trouble. *That* will be taken care of by Mr. Thompkins."

"Who?"

"My solicitor. My very wise, very cautious, very punctilious solicitor."

"Ah, yes. The one who reminds you of an undertaker. Even so, I think wisdom and caution are considered traits to look for in a solicitor, no matter their pallor."

"I suppose they are. I just wish he didn't always tell me something I don't want to hear…such as how much marrying an heiress would help my finances." Nathan sighed and looked down at his drink, swirling it around in its glass. "It's especially irksome since the only woman I want is even more penniless than I."

"I know."

"And she loves another."

"I should think Annabeth is over Sloane by now."

"Perhaps. But she certainly hasn't transferred her affections to me. Am I a fool, Carlisle, to keep on waiting?"

Carlisle shrugged. "I'm not the person to ask. I'm not the kind of man who falls head over heels in love. Indeed, apparently I am terrible with women."

Nathan chuckled, shrugging off his mood. "Don't worry. You can win Lady Rutherford over. Apologize, and she'll come around." He added warningly, "But don't try to explain why; you'll only dig yourself a deeper hole. Trust me."

"I am well aware of that; I was trapped in that quicksand last night." He sighed. "Of course I will apologize. But somehow I think that Noelle and I are not destined to become friends."

After Nathan left, Carlisle went in search of Noelle. It was better to take his medicine now than wait, letting her dislike of him grow. He found her in the gallery where Adam's paintings hung. And, curse his luck, she was looking at the paintings of her that Carlisle had obviously set aside.

She glanced back at the sound of his entrance. "I see that I have been consigned to the dustbin." Her tone was light, even faintly amused, but Carlisle knew better than to believe for even a second that she felt no resentment.

"No. That's not—" What the devil could he say? There was no denying his exclusion. He could feel a flush of embarrassment spreading across his cheeks. Clasping his hands behind his back, he said stiffly, "I apologize. I, um, assumed things I shouldn't. And, um…" *Don't try to explain.* Nathan's advice sounded in his brain. "I judged you without any real evidence. I am sorry. I hope you will forgive me." *There. It's done.* Carlisle let out a sigh of relief. It was easy to apologize for little things, but it was damnably hard when the matter went deep.

Clearly he had surprised her, but after a moment, Noelle said, "I appreciate your apology. It would be easier if we could maintain civility between us." After that statement, which was almost ponderous enough to have come from Carlisle himself, she nodded to him and started toward the door.

"Wait," he said quickly, stretching a hand toward her, then letting it fall. "I wanted to speak to you for a couple of other reasons. I'm not sure how to, um…broach it, but while I believe you had no protector, there must have been men that made unwanted advances. I think they might be a good place to start in the search for who has been after you."

The silence was icy and Carlisle had to restrain himself from fidgeting.

"I don't believe that any of this is about me." Noelle's tone was crisp, but not hostile, and he relaxed a bit. "However, I want to assist in finding Gil's attackers in any way I can. There are a few men I have rejected. I will write down their names for you. The sooner you find that they are not after me, the sooner you will begin searching more fruitful avenues of inquiry. What was the second thing you wanted to ask?"

With her tone already cold, Carlisle wished he could think of anything other than his original query. But his mind was suddenly blank. And he couldn't just turn on his heel and leave. "I, er… I haven't given you any pin money."

"Pin money?" Noelle repeated blankly.

"Yes. I realized that I hadn't provided you with any sort of personal allowance."

Noelle stiffened. "After all you said to me, you have the audacity to offer me money? I can see how very sincere your apology was. You still believe that I can be bought."

"No. That's not it at all. It has nothing to do with—"

Carlisle sighed. Was every interaction they had going to end in an argument? "I'm not trying to buy you. I'm talking about living expenses."

"What living expenses? Gil and I will have a place to live and food to eat. You're already going to get an absurdly large bill for the clothes Lady Drewsbury bought for me—which I will repay."

Carlisle set his jaw. Perhaps she wasn't as immoral as he thought, but she was certainly as irritating. "That's absurd. I don't want reimbursement. And how, I'd like to know, do you think you would get the money to do so? Do you plan to sell hats out of Stonecliffe?"

"I don't know how I will." Noelle clenched her fists. "But I shall. I repaid you the first time, didn't I?"

"The money you stole from me? Yes, you were quick enough to toss that back in my face. And I must say, it was a remarkably foolish thing to give up that money just to jab at me."

"I didn't do it to 'jab' at you. I did it because I'm not a thief!"

"Oh, for pity's sake." He swung away, then back. "You are the most stiff-necked, unreasonable woman I have ever had the misfortune to meet. This is a senseless argument. First, I don't give a damn about the money. Second, it's not mine. The expenses for this house, your clothes, all of it, come from your son's estate, which I believe Lady Drewsbury already pointed out to you. And third, I'm not talking about food or rent, just personal money for you to spend as you wish. On ribbons or trinkets or whatever you want. Here." Thorne grabbed her wrist and, pulling a small pouch from an inner pocket of his jacket, he shoved it into her palm.

"Take it. And *do not* give this one back to me." Letting go of her wrist, he turned and strode out the door.

THEY SET OUT for Stonecliffe the following afternoon. Gil bounced from one side of the carriage to the other, trying to take in everything at once. The countess was happy to answer Gil's endless questions, and Thorne had chosen to ride his horse instead of sitting in the carriage with them. He said he did so because he wanted another person besides the groom and driver to guard the carriage. Noelle suspected that he simply didn't want to have to be polite to Noelle for the length of the trip.

Which suited her. The less she saw of him, the better—not, of course, that she didn't see him. She couldn't help but look at him as he rode on her side of the carriage. She had to admit he cut a fine figure on horseback. Boots and the trim cut of riding clothes suited him. He was very powerful and very male astride the large gray stallion, controlling it easily with his thighs. Something stirred deep within her, a tickle long since dead.

Carlisle glanced over, and Noelle turned her head away, embarrassed that he had caught her studying him. At least he couldn't know about the wayward sensation that had darted through her, that sudden awareness of him as a man rather than an enemy. He probably assumed she was plotting against him.

She glanced back out the window and found that he was now watching her. Raising her eyebrows, she met his stare, and after a moment, it was he who looked away. He put his heels to his mount and rode forward.

"Carlisle will take care of everything." Adeline nod-

ded toward Thorne, following Noelle's eyes. "You and
Gil won't be in any danger. Once Carlisle sets his mind
to something, there's no stopping him. He'll find out
who it is and put an end to it, I'm sure."

It must be nice to feel so secure, so certain of another
person that one could just turn her troubles over to him
and know it would be resolved. Unlike the countess,
Noelle was well aware that the only person she could
trust to take care of her and Gil was herself. "I know
Mr. Thorne will do his best to protect Gil."

"He's always been like that," the countess went on.
"From the moment he came to us."

Curious, Noelle said, "How did he, um, 'come to you'?"

"It was after his father died. His father, Horace, was
good friends with my husband, Thomas. Horace died
young, and he had named Thomas as Carlisle's guardian. Carlisle must have been ten. Adam was only three,
younger than the age Gilbert is now."

"His mother was—she'd passed on, as well?"

"No. Belinda is still alive. But she…well, mother-
ing is not her foremost skill. Mind you, I'm not saying
anything against Belinda; I'm sure she loves Carlisle.
But she is interested in politics and the government and
that sort of thing." Adeline waved a hand vaguely. "But
when she married Mr. Halder, who is of like mind, the
earl suggested that Carlisle might like to live with us
for a while."

"His mother gave him up?" Noelle's eyes widened.
Thorne's belief that Noelle would simply hand Gilbert
over to him made more sense now.

"Yes. One has to give her credit. She could have
kept Carlisle with her—after all, they had servants and
Carlisle had a tutor to look after him, and giving him

to us lowered her in some people's eyes. But she knew Carlisle was lonely, and would be much happier here with us. I don't think it was an *easy* decision for her. She did come to see Carlisle, and he went to visit her now and then, but…" Her voice trailed off doubtfully.

"I see. It's no wonder that Mr. Thorne is so fond of you."

Adeline smiled. "He loved Thomas, as well. Thomas was a good man." She leaned closer, gazing earnestly into Noelle's eyes. "I realize Thomas may have seemed…unkind to Adam."

Noelle could think of a few other things to call the earl, but she said nothing. It was clear that the countess wanted her to think well of everyone.

"Thomas was very unhappy over the separation," the countess went on. "He missed Adam, but he was just so stubborn that he wouldn't give in. Adam was the same; well, you know that, I'm sure."

Noelle smiled faintly. "Yes, I seem to recall that."

"They had harsh words and said things they should not have, but neither of them would be the one to capitulate. It was an awful time. Thank heavens Carlisle sent Adam that monthly stipend. I was going to, you see, but my pin money wouldn't have been enough to live on."

"Mr. Thorne supported Adam out of his own pocket? I thought it was Lord Drewsbury."

"No, Thomas was certain Adam would come back if he cut him off entirely. But Carlisle knew my son better than that. Carlisle was like an older brother to him. Always rescuing him from some scrape or other." Tears glittered in her eyes.

Noelle had trouble reconciling her own view of this stern, arrogant man with Lady Drewsbury's image of a loving and generous Carlisle Thorne. But she had seen him be good to Gil and the countess; clearly he was a different person with those he loved. It was doubtful that *she* would ever experience that with him, though.

Lady Drewsbury blinked back the tears in her eyes, and looked out the window. "We've reached the village. We're almost home."

They rattled through a small, sleepy-looking village, and before long, the carriage turned into a tree-lined lane. Stonecliffe loomed up before them, massive and dark. Two wings on either side extended forward from the main building, and a stone wall ran between them at the front to form an enclosed courtyard. No wonder Thorne had said they would be safer here. The place looked like a fortress.

"Don't worry, you'll get used to it," Adeline said with a little laugh. "Stonecliffe is formidable when you first see it. But once you've lived here a bit, it's quite beautiful."

Carlisle handed his horse over to a welcoming groom and came to the carriage to open the door and give the countess a hand down. He would have done the same for Noelle if she had extended her hand to him, but she did not. Cocking an eyebrow at her, he put his hand under her arm anyway to steady her. Mortifyingly, her foot slid on the little pebbles of the driveway, and she might have fallen had Carlisle not dug his fingers into her arm, keeping her upright.

He held her arm a moment longer, leaning in to murmur, "Careful. Sometimes it's good to accept a little assistance."

She sent him a quelling glance, rather spoiled, she suspected, by the fact that her cheeks were red with embarrassment. He released her arm and looked beyond her to Gil, who was standing in the doorway of the carriage, staring wide-eyed at the huge house before them.

"It's all right, Gilbert, you'll be quite safe here." Carlisle lifted the boy down. "I'll make sure of it."

"I know," Gil replied, looking up at him. "You're Carlisle Thorne."

"Yes. I am," Thorne responded, looking bemused.

"That's what Maman told me," Gil explained. "If something bad happens, I'm to tell them that they must take me to you. You wouldn't like it if anyone hurt me."

Thorne cast a quick glance at Noelle, but said only, "And your mother is correct."

"Come, dear." Adeline took Gil's hand and started into the house. "Let's go explore your new home."

CHAPTER TEN

THE INTERIOR OF the house was as imposing as the outside, with a cold marble sweeping staircase and portraits of long-dead ancestors sternly looking down on any who entered. Gil had a set of rooms for himself and his future governess, with a place in between filled with toys and books. Noelle's own bedroom was even larger than the one she had had in the house in London and beautifully decorated, with a view to the lovely garden below. One could not ask for anything more comfortable and spacious, but she knew it would take her some time to get used to living in such luxury.

Any degree of uneasiness was well worth it, though, for the amount of time she had with her son. Except for his naps and his daily lessons in riding—for Carlisle had made good on his promise of horses—she was free to be with Gil all she wanted. The two of them explored the gigantic house together, finding assembly rooms, a ballroom, two dining rooms, bedrooms, sitting and drawing rooms, cloakrooms, a smoking room, a study that was obviously Carlisle's domain, and several other rooms whose purpose Noelle could not even guess. And that was with one whole wing of the house closed off because it was unused.

But the crown jewel of Stonecliffe was the magnificent library, which she and Gil located on their second day. Though *library* seemed far too negligible a word for a room that had taken Noelle's breath away.

The ceiling soared high above her head, for the library rose two floors, with a winding staircase up to a second level of bookshelves running around three sides of the room. The other long wall held a bank of windows that let in a flood of natural light, and a grand chandelier hung from the high ceiling.

There were comfortable chairs for reading, as well as a table, and a rolling ladder to climb up to the highest books.

Noelle's heart lifted in her chest. Gil let out a delighted cry and ran about the place, climbing the ladder, twirling the globe, racing up to the railed second-floor gallery. Noelle simply stood and gazed about her in delighted wonder. This, she knew, would be her favorite room.

She saw little of Carlisle except at teatime and dinner, and he remained as aloof and formal as ever. Though there were only the three of them, they ate in the large formal dining room, huddled together at one end of the long, polished table. Carlisle exchanged a few stilted comments with Noelle about the food, and the remainder of the meal consisted of a disjointed blend of two separate conversations. One was between Noelle and Adeline about Gil and the other was between Carlisle and the countess about various people in their common acquaintance, with the countess offering occasional asides to Noelle in explanation.

It was not that Carlisle was rude or pointedly excluded Noelle. It was simply clear that he regarded her as an outsider—and one with whom he had little interest in developing a friendship. Noelle would have been hurt…if she had had any interest in talking to him.

She didn't, of course. There was no need to be friends with the man. It was just that, well, living in the same household would be easier if they were at least friendlier acquaintances. Over the passage of time, Noelle's attitude toward Thorne had been shifting. It was difficult to continue to be suspicious of his motive—what did she imagine he was going to do? He had obtained what he wanted: Gil's presence in the house.

He was good with Gil, patiently answering Gil's hundreds of questions and explaining how things worked. He gave Gil a pony, and more importantly, he spent part of every afternoon helping the head groom to teach Gil to ride. It warmed Noelle's heart to see the two of them returning from the stables, Gil riding on Thorne's shoulders or skipping along at his side, chattering. Gil, at least, felt no uncertainty about Carlisle.

Gil and Noelle often went walking in the garden, with Gil collecting various "treasures" along the way. He loved the little pond where the golden fish swam, and the quiet, peaceful spot was Noelle's favorite on the grounds, as well. One afternoon, when they turned the corner to go to the pond, Noelle saw that Carlisle was sitting on the wrought iron bench beside it.

Noelle came to a stop and was about to turn back, but Gil tore off down the path, shouting Carlisle's name. Noelle called after him, "No, wait, Gil, you mustn't bother Mr. Thorne."

However, by the time she had gathered her skirts and started after him, Gil was already talking to the man, pulling out his day's treasures. She was certain a man like Carlisle would have no interest in the things.

They weren't worth any money and that seemed to be the thing he held most sacred. But to her surprise, Carlisle shifted to more closely inspect the marble, bluebell, and oddly shaped rock Gil had found earlier. Gil leaned trustingly against Carlisle's leg as he chattered.

"I'm sorry for intruding on you," Noelle apologized.

Carlisle turned his head and smiled at her as he rose politely to his feet, and her heart skipped in her chest. Good Lord, but the man had a smile! It was a wonder he didn't use it to his advantage more. His face lost its implacable lines, his cool gray eyes turning welcoming and those stern lips curving in a way that made her nerves dance. Flustered, Noelle was suddenly aware that her hair must be wild after the walk, for she had forgotten to take a hat, and she was probably red in the face, as well. What in the world was wrong with her? As if it mattered if Carlisle Thorne thought her unkempt.

"It's no intrusion," Thorne told her. "I enjoy Gilbert's company." He turned toward Gil. "I used to pick up things around the estate. Odd rocks like these."

"Really?" Gil's face turned up to him in pleased surprise.

"Yes, indeed. My father was fond of gardens and I suppose I inherited an interest in digging around in the dirt, as well. I had a collection on a shelf in my room."

"Can I see it?"

"I'm afraid it's not there anymore."

"Why? What happened to them?" Gil frowned in concern.

"I don't know. Somewhere along the way I lost track of them." Carlisle smiled slightly at Gil's astounded look. "I know, it's difficult to understand. But sometimes when you grow up you…" He shrugged. "Lose things. Perhaps they're in the attic. We'll ask Bennett."

"He'll know." Gil held the butler in high regard. He ran over to the pond and peered into it. "I like the fish."

"I do, too. We had a pond like that at my home when I was your age. My father and I built it—though I suspect I was of little help." He smiled faintly, as if at some pleasant memory.

"Where's your father?" Gil asked. "Can I meet him?"

"I'm sorry. I wish you could. I think you'd like him. But I'm afraid he passed many years ago."

"Really?" Gil's eyes grew round. "My papa did, too. I don't remember him. I was just a baby." He squatted down to study the fish. "Are these the same fish? I like that color—like fire."

"It is a lovely color," Carlisle agreed. "And, yes, these are the same fish. They live a very long time. We brought them to the pond in a barrel of water." He gave a little chuckle, his face softening further. "I stood in the wagon to make sure the barrel didn't tip over."

Noelle smiled to herself at the image of a young Carlisle—his face no doubt set in a serious, determined expression, standing in a wagon, holding on to the barrel. "It was good of Lord Drewsbury to let you do that."

"Yes. He was very kind to me." He looked at her. "I wish you had had a chance to see that side of him."

Gil jumped to his feet, seemingly having had enough of the fish. "I want to show Grandmama my things." He darted down the path toward the house.

Noelle knew she should follow her son, not linger here. Carlisle would think she wanted to stay, to talk. Which, perversely, she did. But he would think it too bold of her. She turned to go.

"Noelle, wait." She turned back. Carlisle took a step toward her. He hesitated, then jammed his hands in his pockets and finally said, "I wanted to ask you…what Gilbert said when we arrived—that you had told him he would be safe with me…did you say that recently?"

"No. I told him as soon as he was old enough to remember and understand what he should do."

"But why?" He frowned. "Why would you tell him he would be safe with the man you believed was trying to kidnap him?"

"He would have been safe, wouldn't he?" She raised her eyebrows in question.

"Yes, of course. But you were afraid of me. You did your best to escape me every time. How could Gilbert believe I wouldn't hurt him when you were always running from the men you thought were sent by me?"

Noelle shrugged. "I didn't tell him *you* were behind the pursuit. Gil was young enough he didn't need an explanation. He just knew that bad men were chasing us."

"But why? When you hated and feared me? I would have thought…"

"I had to be realistic. I had to take care of my child. However I felt, whatever you did, I never believed you meant Gil harm. I didn't even believe that your intent was to harm me; I was simply the impediment in your way. And if…" Her voice caught, and she turned away, walking over to look into the pond. "If you had managed to steal Gil away, I knew how little likelihood there was that I could get him back. If anything happened to me, if he was suddenly alone in the world, I wanted him to be able to tell people where they should take him. Your name, I thought, gave him the best chance."

"I'm sorry." Thorne took an unconscious step closer,

his hand reaching toward her before he pulled it back. A flush rose up his neck. "I am so very sorry that I frightened you. I was clumsy and angry and filled with grief and guilt when I met you. But I didn't mean to threaten you or make you fear me. I hope you believe that. I hope that you will come to not fear me. I would never have hurt you. I will never hurt you. And I won't let anyone else do so either. I promise."

Something fluttered inside her chest, warming her even as it made her breathless. It would be so easy to put herself in his hands, to give over her worries and fears, knowing that his solidity and strength, his dogged persistence, his commitment to her was as real and firm as it was to Adam's mother and son. She wanted to believe him. She ached to trust him. But did she dare? What would happen if she let down her defenses?

Noelle let out a shaky breath. "I know." The certainty hardened within her. "I believe you."

That transforming smile broke across his face again. "Thank you."

And something, she wasn't sure what, but something vital, passed between them.

CHAPTER ELEVEN

THE FIRST TWO weeks at Stonecliffe, Noelle was busy adjusting to life on the grand estate. She learned the layout of the house and the names of all the staff. She and Lady Drewsbury interviewed prospective governesses. The butler gave her lessons on navigating the ton. Noelle spent what seemed to her an inordinate amount of time with Lady Drewsbury and the village seamstress discussing styles and trying on dresses in their various stages of production. The rest of her time she spent with her son.

After the governess came, however, Noelle had less time with Gil. He had lessons in the morning and continued his riding practice with Carlisle every afternoon, venturing out gradually into the surrounding park with Carlisle and the head groom riding on either side of him. Noelle enjoyed visiting with Lady Drewsbury, and reading was always a delight, but before long a life of utter leisure began to pall on her. She was accustomed to working all day, and she began to grow bored. Then she hit on the idea of organizing the library.

Though the room was obviously kept scrupulously clean, all sorts of books, from novels to advice on farming, were scattered across the shelves, and in a library this size, it was challenging to find what you were looking for. Cataloging and arranging the books in some sort of order would not only give her something to do, but would be useful, as well.

Noelle began by making an inventory of the books. Armed with paper and pencil, she climbed up the ladder and started her list. It was there that Carlisle found her one day, standing at the top of the bookcase, scribbling down information.

"Noelle?"

She was so accustomed to the utter silence of the library that she jumped, dropping her pencil. "Blast!" She turned and nodded to him in greeting. "Carlisle."

"I beg your pardon. I didn't mean to frighten you." He was staring at her in some amazement. "I, uh—what are you doing?"

Noelle started back down the ladder. "This library is absolutely chaotic. I have also never encountered anyone else in here—I presume no one must use it?"

He smiled faintly. "I use it, but I usually come in the evening, and I know where my favorites are. Are you looking for something in particular? Perhaps I can point you in the right direction. Mrs. Radcliffe's novels are over there." He reached out to help her down.

"Ah, I see," Noelle said dryly. "The sort of inconsequential books that I would be capable of reading."

A flush started along his cheekbones. "No. I didn't mean that. It's just—well, I know the countess enjoys them, and I also thought—"

"That being a female, that was what I would want."

"I beg your pardon." His voice iced over. "I did not mean to offend. I was attempting to be helpful. And what I was going to say was that I also thought that

The Mysteries of Udolpho was quite enjoyable when I read it."

"Oh." Noelle wasn't sure quite how to respond. She had trouble picturing a buttoned-up man like Carlisle enjoying such fanciful novels, much less admitting it. Though, she had to admit, she really didn't know much about him personally. Softening her tone, she went on, "Then perhaps we have both misjudged the other."

"It seems to happen rather often." His mouth quirked up on one side. And was that actually a hint of amusement in his eyes?

"I thank you for your help, but I discovered Mrs. Radcliffe's books a few days ago, and I have already read them."

"I see."

"For now, I am content with reading Petrarch's *Lives*."

"Petrar—" he blurted, his eyes widening, but he was quick to turn his words into clearing his throat. "Of course."

She let out a little laugh, her eyes dancing. "Really, Mr. Thorne… I think you might need to adjust your expectations a bit."

"I did not mean—that is to say, women are not usually…their education is…"

"Inferior? Inadequate?" She raised an eyebrow, but then took pity on his floundering. "You are right. Women's education is too often considered unnecessary and unimportant. Fortunately, my father was a different sort of man. He was a scholar and advanced in his views. He knew that my mind was as capable as those of the young men he taught at Oxford—frankly, more so in most cases. I received a better-than-adequate education from him, and I often helped him with research. Unfortunately, there was only so much I could do in that regard, as I could not enter the library at the school. Perhaps that is why your library took my breath away." She smiled, gesturing at the stuffed shelves of books around them.

"It has a great many books," Carlisle agreed, looking relieved to find the conversation now on common ground. "But you are right; they are in a sad jumble."

"That is why I thought I might catalog them. If you don't mind, that is." Noelle suddenly thought that perhaps she had presumed too much.

"Of course I don't mind," he replied in an astonished tone. "And it is *your* library in any case, not mine."

"I know. I just…it's difficult for me to feel quite at home here."

He moved closer, his brows drawing together. "I hope no one was rude to you or unkind."

"No," Noelle assured him, both surprised and pleased at his concern. "It is just…different. I'm sure I will become accustomed to the, um, dignity of the house."

"You mean the heavy-handed display of grandeur and wealth?" He smiled.

"Yes." She was struck again by what a wonderful smile Carlisle had.

"But are you sure you want to shoulder the task?" He glanced around the room. "Organizing this place could take years."

"Yes. But it will be years before Gil is grown."

"Still, it's a great deal of work. I wouldn't want you to feel that you must do anything."

"Are you trying to tell me that this isn't what a lady should do?"

"No, not at all." He sighed. "I have an extraordinary talent to phrase things poorly with you. I don't want you to feel that you must work, must do something to...to pay us back. Or make yourself acceptable."

"Oh." Noelle tilted her head to the side, considering. "I hadn't thought of that, really. The thing is, I'm not very good at just sitting around. This gives me something to do. Besides..." She smiled wryly. "This place disturbs my sense of order. My fingers fairly itch to arrange things."

"Then I will only thank you and say it is very generous." Carlisle cast a look around the large room. He crossed his arms, lingering despite his obvious discomfort. After a moment, he said, "I apologize for implying that you would only be interested in the Radcliffe books."

"Thank you."

"It isn't just the Radcliffe remarks, though. If it was only that, it would be a rather simple apology. It's the things I've said to you too many times. The meaning behind my words. I am deeply sorry that I've wounded you." He cleared his throat. "More than once."

"What you said didn't matter." No, it was what he *thought* that hurt. But she would not let him see that.

"It *did* matter. Because it hurt you. Because I was wrong to assume—well...the things I believed."

"You apologized. I accepted it."

"That may be. But I don't imagine you've forgiven me. I haven't forgiven myself. Seeing you the past two weeks, seeing your love for your son, your kindness to the countess, your grace and intelligence... I realize how very wrong I was." Carlisle broke off, swinging away and pacing a few steps before turning back to her. "I know you will not believe it, but I am not someone who looks down on others, who assumes the worst about a person without knowing them. At least, I normally am not. I will admit I am stubborn and probably dictatorial, as well; I am accustomed to having my way, and I don't enjoy being thwarted. I am proud of my family, but I am proud because of my ancestors' character, their honor and honesty and courage, not because of a happenstance of birth. I try to be just and fair with everyone I meet."

"So it is just me in particular?" Noelle teased, her playful tone taking the sting out of her words.

"You are particularly skilled at annoyance, I will admit," he responded with a little grin. "But none of this was your fault. I made any number of mistakes, not the least of which was blaming you for the schism in my family. You weren't responsible for Adam's volatility or Lord Drewsbury's stubbornness. For my own failure to intervene."

Noelle would have liked to hold on to her anger and hurt; they had been her support for many years now. However, she could not help but feel touched by Carlisle's words. "You couldn't have changed it. You say it wasn't my fault that Adam and his father quarreled. Well, neither was it yours, any more than saving the situation was your burden." Noelle couldn't help but think how Carlisle's smile had grown increasingly pleasing to her over the passing weeks, how very nice his lips were. She realized she wanted to move closer to him, to make his smile linger and grow.

Carlisle took a step toward her, his voice softer, lower. "I do not want there to be any enmity between us."

"Nor do I." She felt a trifle breathless. There was a warmth in his eyes, a look that made her insides tremble.

"Somehow I always seem to say the wrong thing when I am around you. I sound stiff and priggish even to myself," Carlisle went on. "And I cannot pay you a compliment without it coming out all wrong."

"You've paid me a compliment?" Noelle replied, smiling up at him, her eyes dancing with amusement. Good heavens, was she flirting with Carlisle Thorne? Her nerves were suddenly singing through her body.

"I've tried." The corner of his mouth quirked up, and he shifted subtly closer. "I fear I haven't succeeded."

"Perhaps you should try again." Yes, she was flirting with this dour man. Even more strangely, he was flirting back. It was mad; it was exciting.

"Perhaps I should." He reached out to touch one of her curls.

So lost was she in his eyes, his hand near her cheek, that it took a few seconds for the sound of hurrying footsteps to register. Noelle and Carlisle sprang apart, staring at each other for a long, stunned moment before turning hastily away. Noelle smoothed her hair and skirts, her pulse all the while beating rapidly. The steps sounded like the countess's, though far more rapid than her usual pace; Noelle dreaded what Adeline might see in her face.

However, as it turned out, the countess was clearly in too great a panic to notice anything odd about the scene.

She rushed into the room, breathless, cheeks flushed. "Carlisle! Oh, Carlisle, the most dreadful thing!"

Noelle's heart leaped into her throat. *Gil! Something had happened to Gil.* She started forward, but Carlisle, with his long stride, reached the countess first. "What is it? What's happened?"

"My mother is coming to visit!"

CHAPTER TWELVE

NOELLE STARED AT Adeline blankly. Surely she had heard that wrong. Carlisle, however, seemed to find nothing odd in the countess's statement. He merely let out a soft oath and reached out to take the older woman's arm and turn her toward a chair. "When is Lady Lockwood arriving?"

"That's the most awful part," Adeline responded. "This afternoon!" She brandished the piece of paper in her hand. "Her letter says she's leaving this morning." Her voice was almost a wail as she dropped down into the seat Carlisle offered. "What am I to do? Why couldn't she have at least given me a little notice? Waited a day or two for me to receive her letter? But then she wouldn't be as likely to catch something I've left undone."

"Or give you a chance to flee," Carlisle added. "Perhaps she won't reach the house today. You know how she stops every few miles."

Adeline gave him a skeptical look. "Don't try to give me false hope; not even my mother could take more than a day to get here from London."

"At least you'll get to see Annabeth—I assume Lady Lockwood is dragging her along, too."

"Of course she is," the countess said darkly. "She has to have someone to abuse on the trip. And since my sister married and moved out, poor Annabeth is her only victim. Thankfully, Nathan is escorting them. Perhaps he can sweeten Mother's disposition." Her tone was doubtful.

"Is she bringing her dog?" Carlisle asked, his voice switching from calm reason to a note of alarm.

"You know she is. She never goes anywhere without that little smushed-faced beast. He will chew on the legs of my Chippendale chest and soil every rug in the house."

"Not to mention bite my ankles," Carlisle added.

"And screech like a flock of distressed geese every time a servant enters the room. Bennett will probably offer his resignation."

She heaved a sigh and turned toward Noelle. "I'm sorry. You must think me a terrible wretch to bewail my mother's visit."

"I could never think that of you, ma'am. I am sorry that you are in such anxiety."

"Lady Lockwood is..." Carlisle cleared his throat. "Well, she is, um, a force."

"You needn't be polite, dear," Adeline told him. "Noelle will find out soon enough what Mother is like." She sighed and rose to her feet. "Well, I mustn't sit about indulging in nerves. I have to do what I can to get the house in order before she arrives."

Since the house was always in perfect order, Noelle wasn't sure what had to be done, but she said, "Please allow me to help you."

"You're a jewel, dear." Adeline smiled. "I will be most happy for your help."

THERE WAS A flurry of activity all over the house, with maids scurrying about making up Lady Lockwood's preferred suite of rooms, wiping away any possible dust in the rest of the already pristine house.

Noelle donned a cap and apron and joined in the cleaning. The maids were shocked, but Noelle didn't mind the work. At least it gave her body something to do as her mind circled endlessly around that moment in the library when Carlisle had tenderly touched her hair—and how she had wanted him to sweep her up in his arms and kiss her.

It seemed unfathomable that the stiff and formal man would have done such an impulsive thing as kiss her, but she could not stop herself from daydreaming that he might have if it hadn't been for the countess's untimely entrance. Even if he hadn't been about to kiss her, he had most certainly been flirting with her. Noelle was not that far removed from her courting years; she recognized the undercurrents, the tones, the smiles and bright glances.

While Noelle dusted everything in sight in the entryway and drawing room, the countess spent much of her time arranging the multitude of flowers she ordered brought in by the gardeners. Adeline stepped back, surveying her work critically. "Do you think it's grand enough? Mother does love a show of flowers."

"It looks grand enough for Buckingham Palace," Noelle assured her. "I hate to see you so nervous. Surely your mother is coming to see you, not a vase of flowers."

Adeline gave her a pitying glance. "You don't know my mother. She's not coming to see me. She's coming to see *you*."

"Me?"

"Yes, of course." Adeline's voice lowered as she went

on earnestly, "Please, don't let anything she might say upset you. She can be, well... I would say she doesn't mean to be rude, but I fear that isn't always true. She's old-fashioned and a bit high in the instep. She was once introduced to the queen of France."

"Marie Antoinette?" Noelle's eyebrows shot up.

"The same. Mother's very proud of that, and she has a sense of...of..." The countess frowned, clearly searching for words.

"You're saying that she will be haughty. That she will treat me as an inferior." When Adeline nodded, looking troubled, Noelle gave her a reassuring smile. Clearly a good part of Adeline's anxiety about her mother's arrival was because she feared Lady Lockwood would insult Noelle. "I promise I shall not take anything she says to heart. I am well acquainted with people who hold themselves superior to me."

Adeline gave her a wry smile. "To be fair, she holds herself superior to everyone."

"I've never met a queen, but I am accustomed to dealing with aristocrats. I not only withstood their arrogance, but I usually wound up selling them a hat."

Only an hour later, a carriage pulled up in front of the house, and Adeline, along with Noelle and Carlisle, went out to greet the arriving guests.

Noelle watched with interest as the occupants emerged from the vehicle. The first person to descend was Nathan, his face stamped with relief. He held up a hand to a young woman who carried a small bundle in her arms. The bundle began to squirm, and Noelle realized that this must be Lady Lockwood's infamous dog. Writhing madly, the animal managed to jump from the woman's arms with no apparent harm and tore across the courtyard, emitting the strangest sound, almost like a screaming asthmatic child. Noelle now understood why Adeline had compared it to a flock of geese. Carlisle sighed and looked down at the dog as it attacked his boot.

"No! Petunia!" The woman ran to them. "Carlisle, I'm so sorry." She snatched up the squirming dog.

"No need to apologize," he told her with a warm smile. "I am well acquainted with our Petunia. No doubt we'll miss her when she's gone. How soon do you think that might be?"

"Never," Adeline said darkly. "I'm convinced that animal is immortal. Annabeth, dearest." She stepped forward to hug the young woman, protesting dog and all.

Petunia was barrel-chested and short-legged like a bulldog, but smaller and with golden fur. She had large black eyes, a very short black snout, and a curly tail like a pig. Judging by the rolls of fat on her body, she must eat like one, as well.

The woman, on the other hand, had a heart-shaped face, a warm smile, and green eyes that twinkled with humor. Adeline released her niece and introduced her to Noelle. Annabeth, her eyes now tinged with curiosity and a certain reserve, held out her hand to Noelle. The countess's niece was not ready to accept her just yet, but she was not, Noelle thought, antagonistic.

Before Noelle could utter a greeting, there was a loud rap from the direction of the carriage and a sharp, "Annabeth! Come here! What are you doing, hanging about over there? You know I need your assistance."

"I'm sorry, Grandmother," Annabeth replied with

an ease that hinted at many repetitions. "I had to catch Petunia." She returned to the carriage.

Nathan, standing beside the vehicle with his hand up to help Lady Lockwood step down, said with strained patience, "Lady Lockwood, please, allow me to assist you. I assure you that I am quite capable."

Lady Lockwood barely spared him a glance. "Nonsense. Annabeth knows exactly how to do it. Besides, after that jarring ride, I expect I'll require both of you."

Nathan's smile grew even more fixed. Annabeth, holding the dog in a firm grip with one arm, arrived at the steps. Her grandmother planted one hand on her shoulder and stepped down, using the cane to support her on the other side. The slender Annabeth must be sturdier than she looked; Lady Lockwood was a large woman. Nathan put his hand beneath her elbow to steady her.

After this lengthy process, Lady Lockwood shook out her skirts, adjusted her hat, and strode forward with little sign of frailty, using her cane more for emphasis than support. She was a formidable sight, dressed all in purple, her bodice fitted and her full skirts hooped to the sides in the style of the past century. Her iron gray hair was unpowdered, but it was done up in an elaborate tower reminiscent of the same period, and atop it was perched a wide-brimmed hat decorated with an array of ribbons and feathers.

She marched majestically up to the countess, holding out her hand. For one wild moment, Noelle thought Lady Lockwood expected Adeline to kneel and kiss her ring, but Adeline only took it, saying, "Mother, welcome to Stonecliffe. I am so glad…" Her voice trailed off.

"Carlisle." The lady gave her hand in the same regal

way to Thorne. "You ought to do something about that road. It's nothing but ruts and potholes. I'm sure I must have a bruised liver."

"I'm sorry, my lady, but I fear I have little control over the king's roads," Carlisle returned. "I hope the drive to the house was smooth, however."

She retorted with only a *hmph* and swung back to her daughter. "Now, show me this girl."

As if Noelle wasn't standing three feet away from her.

"Yes, of course." Adeline turned toward Noelle. "Mother, this is—"

"I am Noelle Rutherford, Adam's widow," Noelle said, stepping forward boldly. It was a bit rude to introduce oneself, but she was not about to let this woman cow her.

"Well." The older woman's eyebrows rose.

"Yes," Adeline said before her mother could respond. "Noelle, please allow me to introduce my mother, Lady Lockwood."

"Indeed." Lady Lockwood lifted her chin and sent a cool, assessing gaze down Noelle.

Noelle made a curtsy that was enough to be respectful of the woman's age and rank but showed no sign of subservience. Noelle suspected that it would be a mistake to let Lady Lockwood think she was awed by her.

"It's a pleasure to meet you, ma'am," Noelle lied. "My husband spoke of you often." That was another bouncer, as she could not remember Adam mentioning the woman. She was counting, however, on the fact that he had never told her anything disparaging about the woman, either, which led Noelle to suspect that Adam might have been a favorite of Lady Lockwood's.

It seemed she was correct, for Lady Lockwood's brows and chin lowered a bit, and she said only, "Hm. I knew Adam would marry a beauty." With a sniff, she stalked past them into the house.

Beside Noelle, Adeline's shoulders relaxed, and she gave Noelle a hopeful smile before she followed her mother into the house. Carlisle sent Noelle a sardonic look and murmured, "First test passed."

Lady Lockwood and Annabeth, still carrying the dog, disappeared up the stairs with Adeline. Carlisle turned to a frazzled-looking Nathan. "I take it that it was a difficult journey."

"That woman could drive a saint to murder." Nathan blew out a long breath and followed Carlisle and Noelle into the entry hall. "If it wasn't the road, it was the heat—when *she* was the one who insisted on keeping the windows shut against the dust! Or the unsatisfactory service at any of the three—three, mind you!—inns at which she insisted on stopping. And that little beast put teeth marks in my new Hobys." He gazed mournfully down at his boots. "I just got them last week."

Carlisle chuckled. "That's why I always wear an old pair of boots around that hellhound."

Nathan sent him a fulminating look. "You might at least have the decency to pretend not to be amused." He turned to Noelle. "I must say, you handled her brilliantly."

"Yes, it was clever to bring up Adam," Carlisle agreed. "If there is anyone whom Lady Lockwood loved, it was Adam."

"I don't know how Annabeth puts up with her," Nathan grumbled.

"I suppose because she must," Carlisle said.

Noelle was grateful for Lady Drewsbury's lessons in their familial relationships, or else she would have been at sea in their conversation. Annabeth's mother, Martha, Lady Drewsbury's sister, had been left penniless on her husband's death, throwing both her and Annabeth onto the charity of Lady Lockwood. Martha had remarried and escaped her mother's dominion, but Annabeth had remained with her grandmother.

"She could go to her mother's house," Nathan protested. "Surely living with her stepfather cannot be as bad as living with Lady Lockwood."

"Lady Drewsbury would welcome Annabeth, as well," Carlisle added. "But you can imagine how well either of those would sit with Lady Lockwood, and she rules that family with an iron hand. Even Lord Lockwood is terrified of her."

Nathan's snort indicated his opinion of Lady Lockwood's nephew, who now held the title. "Yes, I suppose we must be grateful that Annabeth's grandmother lets her off the leash once or twice a year to visit Lady Drewsbury."

"Stay and have tea with us," Carlisle told his friend. "Or I can fortify you with something a bit stronger."

"Good Gad, no. I'm going to press on to the manor. I have things to do—see my attorney, talk to the estate manager…um, and other things."

"Ah, yes. Duty calls," Carlisle said dryly. "Especially when Lady Lockwood is here. You know your invitation is always open—the more targets Lady Lockwood has, the less pain each recipient endures."

Nathan sighed. "Yes, I know. The only redeeming feature of today's journey was knowing that poking at me saved Annabeth a few jabs. I'll come tomorrow for tea, if you like."

As Nathan turned to go back to the waiting carriage, Carlisle said, "Take one of my horses instead of that coach. It'll help blow away your irritations."

"Thank you. I'll send one of my grooms back with your horse." Nathan grinned. "It will be a relief not to get back in that vehicle. Lady Lockwood wouldn't have so rough a ride if she would buy a better-sprung carriage."

There was the sound of voices and the thud of Lady Lockwood's cane behind them, and they turned to see Lady Lockwood descending the staircase, the little dog running around her skirts. Noelle tensed, expecting at any moment for Petunia to trip up Lady Lockwood and send her tumbling down the steps. Adeline fluttered along beside her mother, and Annabeth brought up the rear of the procession, carrying a shawl and a bag, as well as an embroidery hoop.

"I must say, Adeline, it's a bit late to be having tea," Lady Lockwood announced in ringing tones. "I'm famished."

"I wasn't sure when to expect you." The pleasant tone of Adeline's voice was strained. "And then you wished to go to your chambers first."

"Naturally. One must freshen up after a long journey." They turned at the landing and the older woman's eyes fell on Carlisle and Noelle standing in the hall below them. "Ah, there you are," she said as if she had been searching for them.

She continued downward at a regal pace, but Petunia, spotting her prey, launched herself down the steps. Carlisle ignored the dog's frantic attack on his feet and moved to the bottom of the staircase to offer Lady Lockwood his arm.

She took a strong grip on him, saying, "At least your mother drilled good manners into you, however unreliable she was."

The countess closed her eyes, one hand going to her temple. It wasn't the last time Noelle would see her make that gesture. Lady Lockwood kept the company on alert throughout tea; one never knew when she was going to send a barb or a pointed question winging one's way. Carlisle deflected her comments with the ease of long practice. Adeline grimly endured her mother's conversation, her smile turning more and more wooden as teatime wore on. Annabeth said little, probably grateful that a new set of victims kept Lady Lockwood's attention off her. She spent most of her time hurrying over to pick up Petunia, who lost interest in Carlisle's boots and took to gnawing on the legs of various pieces of furniture.

Most of Lady Lockwood's questions were addressed to Noelle. With long experience at dealing with wealthy and demanding customers, Noelle kept her annoyance leashed and answered the woman with the same polite firmness with which she had addressed her earlier. In the end, Lady Lockwood, after a long, considering look, said, "Well, at least you're presentable."

"Mother!" Adeline blushed.

Noelle, however, didn't care about the old woman's casual insult. What mattered was that it appeared the woman would not engage in any social campaign against Noelle or harangue poor Lady Drewsbury about her— at least not any more than she already did. Noelle suspected that with Lady Lockwood, equal acidity was the best one could hope for.

"Well, Adeline?" Lady Lockwood said as tea drew to a close. "Where is this boy?"

"Gil?" Adeline asked, tensing.

"Yes, of course, Gil—a dreadfully common name; you must call him Gilbert. He is the reason I came all this way. One might think that my daughter would have presented my great-grandchild to me when he first arrived in London." She fixed a beady gaze on Adeline.

"I fear I am the reason for that," Carlisle interjected smoothly. "I thought it was most important to settle Gil in here at the Hall. Introduce him to everyone gradually, so that he isn't overwhelmed."

Lady Lockwood transferred her steely gaze to him. "*I* am not everyone, my boy. And I must remind you that you are not even his relative."

"True," he said equably. "I am his guardian."

Lady Lockwood waved a dismissive hand. "It's all water under the bridge now; no use in talking about it. However, having learned of his presence in your *letter*, Adeline, I came posthaste to see him, and I cannot but wonder why I have not yet met him."

"He has been upstairs in the schoolroom." Adeline clasped her hands tightly in her lap.

Like Noelle, Adeline must fear what harmful thing Lady Lockwood might say to Gilbert. However, Noelle knew that Lady Lockwood was right. She must meet him. And there was no reason antagonizing the woman over the matter, so Noelle said, "I sent word to Miss Abernathy to bring Gilbert down to meet you after tea. They should be here soon."

Adeline's mother gave Noelle another assessing look,

then nodded and rapped her cane against the floor. "Quite proper."

At that moment there was a stir as Carlisle pointed out that Petunia was sniffing around the leg of Lady Lockwood's chair in a suspicious manner, causing both Adeline and Lady Lockwood to exclaim and Annabeth to leap up and whisk the dog out of the room. A short but acrimonious exchange followed between Adeline and her mother over the danger Petunia presented to the home's prized Persian rugs. By the time peace was restored and Petunia was back, taking a nap after her exertions, the governess appeared in the doorway, Gil by her side.

"Gil, darling." Adeline smiled and held out her arms, and Gil trotted over to hug her.

"Mother, I want to introduce your great-grandson, Gilbert. Gil, this is Lady Lockwood, my mother."

Gil turned and gazed at the older woman in awe, taking in her cane and towering hair. Noelle tensed, ready to intervene, but Lady Lockwood, after studying Gil as intently as he did her, nodded and smiled for the first time Noelle had seen. "Gilbert. You look just as your father did."

Gil, recovering his manners, executed a perfect bow. "Pleased to meet you, ma'am."

"Come here, boy, and let me look at you."

Gil went forward without hesitation. She took his chin between her fingers and searched his face as if looking for secrets. Gil blinked in surprise, but his attention was too riveted on Lady Lockwood's hair to care about the inspection. He pointed to the glittering diamond ornament stuck in her curls. "You have a bird in your hair." He smiled. "I like it."

"Thank you." Were those tears in Lady Lockwood's eyes? If so, they were gone too quickly to tell. "You are very like Adam."

Petunia came awake with a start and jumped up, letting out one of her peculiar versions of a bark. Gil spun around at the noise. "A dog! You have a dog!" He turned back to Lady Lockwood, his esteem for her obviously rising even higher. "Can I pat him?"

Adeline let out a squeak of alarm and reached out, and Noelle took a step forward, but Petunia recognized a playmate when she saw one, and she made no attempt to bite Gil, but began to twirl and wag her little piglet tail so hard her whole back end shook. Gil burst into laughter and pounced on her, rubbing Petunia enthusiastically as she wriggled and licked his face.

Noelle looked over at Adeline, and the two women smiled. Gilbert had clearly won over the formidable Lady Lockwood.

LADY LOCKWOOD'S APPARENT approval of her great-grandson did nothing to sweeten the dowager's temper. Noelle suspected that the woman purposely tossed the household into a turmoil because she was bored. The maids scurried to do her bidding. Annabeth helped her in and out of her chair and up and down the stairs, carrying Lady Lockwood's shawl in case she grew cold, a pouch containing handkerchiefs, digestive pastilles for her stomach complaints, lozenges for her throat, lavender for a headache, and a bottle of hartshorn for emergencies—though as best Noelle could tell, Lady Lockwood was in amazingly good health, ate like a trencherman, and never exhibited the slightest indication she might faint.

The dog was the greatest interruption to peace. She barked at the maids and nipped the ankles of every man she saw; with the exception of Gil, Petunia seemed to have a particular dislike of males. Everyone breathed a sigh of relief in the afternoons when Lady Lockwood went upstairs for her daily nap, taking Petunia with her.

Nathan faithfully kept to his promise to visit the following day, though Noelle noticed that he and Carlisle quickly took shelter in Carlisle's office with a decanter of whiskey. Carlisle apparently found a great many matters that needed to be tended to outside the house, and his rides with Gil became longer. Noelle also slipped away at the first opportunity to work in the library, though she felt a trifle guilty at leaving Lady Drewsbury and Annabeth to deal with Lady Lockwood on their own.

Unfortunately, the time alone gave Noelle too much chance to think, and being in the library made her recall all too clearly that moment when Carlisle had reached out to touch her hair, his stern face softening, his eyes going to her mouth. She remembered the heat that arose in her, the quickening of her breath, the hunger to feel his lips on hers. It was foolish to think about that moment. Nothing would come of it. She didn't *want* anything to come of it. Did she?

There was no denying that she was attracted to the man. There was a strength to Carlisle that was compelling even when she defied it. And when he smiled… ah, when he smiled, a different man shone through— the man who was so good with Gil, the one who loved the countess. And the few times when that warmth was turned on her, she went a little weak at the knees.

But she knew that though he might desire her, he was

too controlled, too logical, to give in to whatever impulse he might feel. He didn't act on what he wanted; he acted on what he thought. And an affair between them was, above all else, foolish.

Distracted from her work by her thoughts, Noelle often found herself simply staring out the window. On the upper floor of the library, she had a sweeping view of not only the gardens below, but the countryside beyond, as well.

Today, as she gazed aimlessly out the window, her attention was caught by a movement in the distance, and she moved closer to the glass. A man was riding at full gallop toward the house. The horse soared over a low hedge and thundered on.

Noelle's stomach clenched. She knew that horse. She knew that man. Carlisle was bent over the horse's neck, his arm curved around a bundle on the saddle before him. Everything inside her turned to ice as Noelle realized that the bundle he carried was Gil.

CHAPTER THIRTEEN

NOELLE WHIRLED AND ran down the spiral staircase and started down the long corridor to the central portion of the house. Oh, God, why was this house so huge?

"Noelle?" She heard Adeline's puzzled voice as she ran past the sitting room. "Noelle? What's wrong? Where are you going?"

"It's Gil!" Noelle shouted, though she didn't pause. She tore through the conservatory and burst out the door into the garden. She rushed down the steps, turning left along the path leading to the stable yard. When she reached the edge of the garden, she could once again see Carlisle on his mount, now hurtling across the wide green expanse of the park. He had one arm hooked around Gil's waist, holding the boy tightly against him. Gil clutched Carlisle's protective arm with both hands, his eyes wide, hair flying. Beyond them, she could see the groom trotting along, leading Gil's pony.

She arrived at the stables just as Carlisle pulled the horse to a stop. Tossing the reins to a groom, he swung off, Gil in his arms.

"What happened?" Noelle cried out. "Is he all right? Did he fall?"

"He's fine," Carlisle said.

"Maman!" Gil leaped into her arms, making her stagger, and Carlisle jumped to catch her arm to steady her.

Noelle hugged Gil close, then pulled back to check him for injuries, sweeping her hand over his head and arms. "What happened? Are you hurt?"

"Someone fired at us," Carlisle said tersely as he steered her toward the house.

"What?" Noelle gaped at him. There was no need to ask if he was serious. Carlisle's jaw was set, his gray eyes fierce.

"A bad man shot at us," Gil told her, his hold on her beginning to relax, though he still kept one fist curled tightly into her dress.

"Probably a poacher," Carlisle interjected. "Just an accident. I'll send the gamekeeper out."

"A poacher?" Noelle asked skeptically. Everything inside her wanted to flee, to take Gil and run for safety.

"Yes." Carlisle's voice was firm and he cast a significant glance at Gil. "Nothing to be concerned about."

He didn't want to frighten Gil. Noelle nodded, relieved that he wasn't dismissing the incident.

"There was a bang, and then I was on the ground and Uncle Carlisle grabbed me, like this." Gil, obviously growing more comfortable by the moment, demonstrated, reaching down to scoop up an invisible person and yank him back against his chest. "Uncle Carlisle said a bad word."

Noelle hid a smile as Carlisle admitted, "It's true. And it was quite wrong of me."

"And we got back on Samson, and Samson *ran*." Gil's eyes were bright with excitement now as his fear left him. "We went over a hedge like we were flying. But I wasn't scared, was I?" He turned toward Carlisle for confirmation.

"Not a bit," Carlisle agreed. "You were most brave. And very good—you did just as I said and hung on."

"Can we do it again?"

"Get shot at? I think not."

"No." Gil let out a giggle. "I mean, jump like that. On the horse. Can I do that? Will you teach me?"

"Yes, when you're older."

"Look! There's Grandmama!" Gil spotted the countess, pale as death, waiting for them at the edge of the garden. "I must tell Grandmama." He wriggled down from Noelle's arms and ran to regale the countess with his story.

"Before you start in on me," Carlisle said to Noelle, "no, I don't really think it was a poacher. I didn't want to frighten the boy."

"I know. It was good of you. What happened?"

He shrugged. "We were riding along, Gil on his pony, and there was a gunshot. That unnerved Samson, and he was dancing around a bit, and I was trying to get him under control. The pony acted up, as well, and Gil fell off. I thought..." His mouth tightened, his eyes bleak at the memory.

"You thought he'd been hit."

"Yes. I jumped off. He was lying there, not making a sound, but it turned out the wind had been knocked out of him. Gil wasn't unconscious, no bones broken. There wasn't another shot. I don't know if it was because the fellow ran or if he couldn't get a good shot at us—the horses were between us and the woods by then. But I realized how exposed we were, and if the shooter was still there, he'd had ample time to reload, so I put Gil up in front of me and we rode back to the house."

His simple words were devoid of any drama, but

Noelle had seen their flight. She'd seen the way Carlisle had huddled over her son, shielding him. She reached out, laying her hand on his arm. "Thank you. For protecting him."

His mouth twisted. "I've done a damn poor job of it."

"You brought him home safe. That's what matters."

Gil called to Noelle, and she turned and waved to her son. "I must go."

"Yes. He needs you. We'll talk about this later."

Lady Lockwood, looking much put out, stood on the terrace. Annabeth was beside her, saying, "You see, Grandmother, everything is fine. There's nothing to worry about."

Lady Lockwood harrumphed, thumping her cane against the flagstones. "It's not fine. Any ninny can see that. Carlisle, what the devil is all this fuss about? Maids are atwitter, said the boy was shot." She gazed down critically at Gil. "You don't look shot."

Gil, too excited to be intimidated by his great-grandmother, launched into his account of the incident, which by now had become a thrilling adventure. To Noelle's surprise, Lady Lockwood turned out to be an excellent listener, exclaiming at various points and even letting out a bark of laughter when Gil tried to imitate the way they had flown over the hedge—which had, Noelle noticed, grown much higher in this retelling.

"Well," Lady Lockwood declared. "It sounds as though you had a fine time. Poachers! Filthy lot." She stabbed her cane in Carlisle's direction. "You ought to take care of them. Can't have that sort of person running about, disturbing everyone. Ought to send them to the gallows, I say."

"Mother…" Adeline murmured in the pained voice she often used at the dowager's pronouncements.

"You're too softhearted, Addy. I've always said so."

Lady Lockwood and Annabeth seemed to take the story of the poacher at face value, but Noelle could tell from the worry in Adeline's eyes that she did not believe it.

"I'd best take Gilbert up to the nursery," Noelle said. "I think he's had enough excitement for one day."

"Indeed, I imagine we all have," Adeline agreed and turned to her mother. "You must want a bit of a lie-down, as well."

"It's long past time," Lady Lockwood grumbled and sent her daughter an accusatory look. "One can scarcely get a moment's peace here, what with all these shootings and carryings-on." She turned and started toward the stairs. "Come, Annabeth."

It took some time to get Gil settled down for a nap, as he had to describe his adventure again for Noelle and then for his governess. Finally, Noelle left his room and made her way downstairs, where she found Carlisle and Adeline in the drawing room with Nathan.

"Noelle," Nathan greeted her. "How is Gil?"

"He's fine. He's quite proud of his adventure."

"We've been telling Nathan what happened," Adeline told her.

"Yes, sounds like rather a dustup. I should go. Clearly this isn't the time when you want guests for tea."

"Nonsense," Carlisle countered. "Stay. We need all the help we can get to figure this out."

"Yes," Noelle agreed. "An unbiased opinion would be helpful."

Carlisle raised his eyebrow at the significant glance

she sent him. "Yes, yes, I know. I still hold my idea in reserve. If someone wanted to hurt you, there would be no better way than to harm your son. But I agree it's likely Gil he's after, not you. The question is, who? And why?"

"I suspect that knowing the answer to one would give you the answer to both," Nathan put in.

"It's so mad," the countess said, her fingers worrying at her handkerchief. "Why would anyone want to hurt Gil? He's only a child."

"I thought he would turn out to be someone asking a ransom of you," Noelle said to Carlisle. "But clearly it's not a kidnapper if he tried to kill him."

"Are you certain he was aiming at Gil and not you, Carlisle?" Nathan asked. "Maybe the man was trying to get rid of you so he could take Gil easily."

"If so, he is an extremely poor shot," Carlisle answered. "I was several feet away, and so was the groom. He came within inches of hitting Gil. It's very fortunate that Gil is a small target."

"But who would benefit from Gil's death except his heir?" Noelle asked, turning to Carlisle.

He stiffened. "I assure you it was not I."

"No, of course not. I didn't mean—"

"Even if I were the sort of person who would harm a child," Carlisle plowed on over her words, "*I* am not the heir. No matter how far up the line you go, I'm not related to Gil."

"But the man who *is* his heir would be capable of doing it," Nathan said grimly.

"Oh, no, surely not," Adeline exclaimed. "Marcus is feckless and irresponsible, but he wouldn't do such a thing. He isn't an *evil* man, only weak."

"I wasn't talking about Marcus. I meant his son," Nathan explained. "Sloane would inherit after his father dies."

"Which is probably not far distant, given Marcus's proclivity for drinking," Carlisle interjected. "Still... even Sloane... Gil is just a child." He shook his head doubtfully.

"Who is Sloane?" Noelle asked, looking from Nathan's scowling face, usually so pleasant and friendly, to Carlisle's set expression. "And Marcus? Who are you talking about?"

"Marcus Rutherford is the younger brother of the late earl." Carlisle's voice was clipped. "Sloane is his son—Adam's older cousin."

Noelle frowned. "I can't recall Adam mentioning him."

"He wouldn't have known him well. Sloane and his father were not regular visitors here, and it's been twelve years since Sloane...left."

"Left? Sloane's not in England?" Noelle asked. "Then how could he have done it?"

"Unfortunately, he returned," Nathan said, rising to his feet and walking restlessly to the fireplace, then back.

"Marcus and my Thomas didn't get along well," Adeline said in an aside to Noelle. Noelle squelched the urge to ask who the old earl did get along with, and Adeline went on, "Marcus is... He has a number of bad habits."

"Marcus is a drunkard," Carlisle said in his usual blunt manner. "A gambler and a wastrel. They say he has a charming way about him, but I have never seen him aught but drunk and importuning the earl."

"He *was* charming," Adeline said, smiling faintly

at the memory. "And quite handsome. Some believe he was the best-looking of the Rutherford men, but I always found Thomas much more attractive. They say Sloane takes after Marcus—in looks, I mean. Sloane is decidedly not charming; he's…well, he is not a nice man."

"Not a nice man" was a scathing review for the countess. Noelle looked over at Carlisle, knowing he would not mince words.

"Sloane became a smuggler," Carlisle told her.

"Smuggler?" Nathan snorted. "He's a traitor."

"What?" Noelle's eyes rounded.

"There's no proof of that," Carlisle put in.

"He conspired with the French," Nathan bit out. "Then he helped the French in America plot to free Napoleon. Why do you defend him?"

"I'm not defending Sloane," Carlisle said evenly. "The man is a scoundrel." He turned to Noelle and said carefully, "Sloane hurt someone we are all very fond of."

"Annabeth. Why not say it?" Nathan grated out. "He broke her heart, and then he went off to spy for the French."

"He turned to smuggling, and there were *rumors* that he was in league with the French," Carlisle said in a more restrained manner. "Sloane moved to America afterward, and there were, again, rumors that he was working with the French in the West Indies and Louisiana to free Bonaparte. No one knows exactly what he did, but a year or so ago, he returned to England a wealthy man."

"You can bet that whatever he did to make a fortune, it was immoral, if not illegal." Nathan scowled. "Probably much the same thing as the ventures he's entered into since he returned."

"Yes, well, we needn't go into that." Carlisle cast a cautious eye at Adeline.

"You needn't shelter me, dear," Adeline said. "Mother has kept me well-informed of the things Sloane has been up to." She turned to Noelle. "He owns gambling clubs and taverns, as well as a distillery in Scotland." Adeline sighed and shook her head. "I always felt sorry for the boy. His mother died when he was young, and Marcus was never a good father. I know that doesn't excuse his actions, but…" She shook her head. "This is all so dreadful."

"We don't know that he's behind it," Carlisle told Adeline soothingly. "Don't worry. I'm not bringing charges against him…yet. But I agree with Nathan. Sloane is the likeliest culprit. He never had any honor." He frowned. "He refused to face me again."

"Ha!" Nathan let out a laugh. "You lose one horse race in your entire life and it will haunt you forever."

"He's better at riding than you are?" Noelle raised her eyebrows. It was hard to gauge Carlisle's level of skill when most of the time he was riding at a languorous trot that Gil could keep up with. But she had just seen him ride at a fierce pace, sailing over the hedge with ease.

"He is *not* a better horseman than I am," Carlisle replied firmly. "I had one poor day, and he managed to squeak out a slight win. And then, though he'd been bedeviling me for years to race him, Sloane was suddenly uninterested in another wager."

"That's because he finally got what he wanted. To be the winner. That's all Sloane has ever cared about."

"But that is *not*—" Carlisle cast a repressive look at

Nathan "—why I think we should investigate him. Nathan's right. Sloane is the one who would benefit from getting Gil out of the way. Diggs can look into his businesses in London; clubs and taverns would be likely places for Sloane to find someone to handle such a thing for him. But as for Sloane—I'll talk to him myself."

"I'll go with you," Nathan volunteered.

"You interrogating Sloane Rutherford? I think not. He won't answer, just take jabs at you, and you'll not believe anything he says unless he confesses to it all." When Nathan opened his mouth to protest, Carlisle added, "Besides, I need you here. I could be gone several days. If Sloane isn't in London, I'll have to go to his country house. I can't leave the ladies and Gilbert unprotected."

There was no way Nathan could continue to argue after that. He nodded. "Yes, of course. I will stay here while you're gone."

"Good. Thank you." Carlisle turned to the two women. "I'll leave first thing tomorrow. But you will be perfectly safe. Nathan will be here, and I'm going to put a footman guarding every outside door. Gilbert will have to forego his riding for the meantime, and he should stay out of the garden. He can play in the courtyard in front, with a footman accompanying him. I'd prefer the rest of you keep to the house, as well. I apologize for the restrictions, but I must be certain you're safe."

"Of course, dear, we perfectly understand," Adeline told him.

Carlisle smiled ruefully at the countess. "I am sorry to trap you here with Lady Lockwood."

"Perhaps she'll decide it's too unsafe here and leave,"

Adeline said hopefully. "Don't worry about us. You do what you need to."

"Thank you." He turned to Noelle. "I will do everything I can to find out what's going on and put a stop to it."

"I know you will," Noelle answered. "I am going with you."

"What?" His eyebrows shot up. "No."

"Why not?"

"It's a long trip. It won't be only to London and back. If I have to go to Sloane's estate—it's far away, a great moldering ruin in Dorset that can only be reached by terrible roads."

"Too long a trip? Really?" Noelle crossed her arms. "You're going to claim that I am too delicate to travel all the way to Dorset?"

Carlisle shifted in his seat. "I assure you there is no need."

"*I* need to."

"But to travel all that way alone with a man…" he protested.

"You're saying that my virtue is unsafe with you?"

"Noelle!" Red rose in his cheeks. "Certainly not. But it would look…um…"

"Like it did when you brought me back to London? If that is all it takes to ruin my reputation, it is a lost cause already. Does everyone look askance when you and Lady Drewsbury travel together?"

"No, but that's—it's—I will have to confront Sloane. It could be dangerous."

"No more risky than when Gil and I ran from the man in Barcelona or—"

"I have no intention of exposing you to the kind of

risks you took in the past," he shot back, jumping to his feet. "You are safe here. I have promised you my protection, and—"

"Then I shouldn't be unsafe, as I shall be with you." Noelle rose to face him.

"Gilbert needs you here with him."

"Gilbert will have not only Nathan, but the countess, Annabeth, Lady Lockwood, and his governess to keep an eye on him," Noelle retorted.

"But—"

"I am his mother. I have been protecting him all his life, and I intend to continue to do so. I agreed to live here, *not* to turn over all my obligations and rights as a mother to you. I want to see this man myself. Talk to him. I need to meet him, and you have no right to tell me I cannot. Nor do you have any reason for thinking that I would hinder or slow you down in any way."

Carlisle sighed. "Very well." He sank back down into his seat. "I'm leaving tomorrow morning. At dawn."

She nodded resolutely. "I will be ready to go."

CHAPTER FOURTEEN

CARLISLE SAID NOTHING FURTHER, but the problem of Noelle accompanying him to London nagged at him the rest of the day. He was still searching for a reason for her to remain by the time he went upstairs to his room. He stripped off his suit jacket and jerked impatiently at his cravat, tossing them both onto the chair beside his bed, adding his waistcoat a moment later. He knew he should go to bed; he would be arising early the next morning.

But his mind was too chaotic for sleep. There was a treacherous part of him that was glad he'd lost the argument with Noelle. He looked forward to traveling with her as much as he dreaded it…maybe more. That was the problem: if he had difficulty restraining his feelings here, in a house full of people, how did he expect to do it when it was just the two of them alone?

It was dangerous. Enticing. And it was foolish in the extreme. Everything he did regarding Noelle was foolish, it seemed. He'd finally found her, ended the chase, achieved exactly what he wanted. He should be satisfied. Content. But the bloody woman still had him in a turmoil. She confused him. Worse, she made him confusing to himself. Why the devil had he almost kissed her the other day? It was as if she turned off every rational thought in his head with her mere presence.

The reasons for his distraction were obvious—her petal-soft skin, that plump lower lip that made him ache to kiss it, those deep blue eyes, the neckline that revealed the soft upper curve of her breasts. And her hair—Lord help him, that hair, all golden curls, too short to be subdued into a hairstyle. She decorated it sometimes with a narrow ribbon wound through the curls, and that was even more inviting, for all he could think of was tugging open the bow and sliding the strip of silk from her hair.

Any man would want her unless he was half-dead. But Carlisle was accustomed to being more in control of his urges. He might look at her, think about what it would be like to kiss her, to feel her in his arms, but that didn't mean he would succumb to such stirrings of desire. But standing there so close to her the other day in the library and looking down into her eyes, reason and propriety had had no place in him. He would have kissed her if Adeline hadn't interrupted them.

He had promised Noelle safety and then he'd made advances to her. She held him in little enough esteem already. Would she think that he was like those other men who had tried to take advantage of her? Or would she think that he still assumed she was a woman of loose morals?

With a sinking heart, he realized she probably thought both those things. Today after the shooting was the first time since that moment in the library that they had talked to each other without discomfort and restraint—and despite the circumstances, he had taken pleasure in that. No doubt it said something reprehensible about him.

Carlisle let out a sigh of irritation. He was never

going to sleep at this rate. He went downstairs to his office and poured himself a glass of brandy, then walked down the hall to the library. Noelle spent many of her evenings there, but surely tonight, with them leaving early tomorrow, she would have gone to bed already.

A certain feeling danced in his chest as he made his way to the library, and he suspected that it was more hope of seeing Noelle than fear of it. When he pushed open the large door and found the cavernous room empty, the distinct drop in his energy confirmed his suspicion. But, of course, that was best anyway. Settling at the small table near the globe with his glass and a well-worn copy of Lewis's *The Monk*, he began to read.

By the time he finished his drink, his tension had eased and he was beginning to think he might be able to sleep. That idea shattered when Noelle stepped into the room. Carlisle popped to his feet, suddenly very aware of the fact that he was in his shirtsleeves. He was even more aware that Noelle was clad in a dressing gown, a small V of white cotton visible at the top.

She stopped just inside the door. Her hand went to her hair, which was charmingly mussed, and then to the top of her dressing gown, pulling the lapels a little closer together. "I'm sorry. I didn't realize you were in here. I saw the light and thought I had forgotten to turn off a lamp."

"I was just leaving," Carlisle said quickly. Leaving was the last thing he wanted to do. But it was inappropriate to be here alone with her, clad as they were.

"No. Please don't." Noelle shook her head. "I am the one who has disturbed your peace."

"You haven't," he lied. If only she knew in what way

and how very much she disturbed his peace. "It's always a pleasure to see you."

"I am glad to find you here. Something has been on my mind, and I had trouble sleeping. That's why I came in here, looking for a book." She moved closer, stopping in front of him. "But I'd like to speak to you."

"Yes." He cleared his throat, wondering if he should dread what was coming or hope for it. "Of course. What did you want to discuss?" He must focus, but it was bloody difficult when his eyes kept straying to the smooth column of her throat, so white and soft and utterly inviting. The vulnerable hollow of her throat, which his tongue hungered to taste.

"This afternoon when we were talking about Gil and going to London—"

"Have you changed your mind about going?" His heart dropped.

"No." She looked surprised. "I intend to go. But I did not want you to think…" Noelle paused, as if searching for the right words. "I didn't want you to think that I wished to accompany you because I distrust you. When you jumped to tell me that Gil's heir was not you, I realized that you must believe I still thought you might harm Gil. I wanted you to know that I did not, even for a moment, imagine that you had anything to do with the attempt on Gil's life." She laid a hand on his forearm. "You may very well have saved Gil's life. There is no way I could ever repay you."

"There's no need." Carlisle covered her hand with his. Her touch was so warm. So inviting. "You know I care very much for—for Gil. For this whole family. I would never let any harm come to him."

"I know." Noelle's eyes were large and luminous, shimmering. Surprising him, she reached up on her tiptoes and placed a soft kiss on his cheek. "Thank you, Carlisle."

Hearing his first name on her lips was too much for him to bear. He reached out, his thumb brushing across her cheek. His hand slid back to cup the nape of her neck. She stretched up into his touch, inviting it.

Carlisle bent and kissed her soft mouth. Her lips parted and heat rushed through him. His arms went around her as her mouth responded, and she melted into him. He tightened his embrace, pressing his body into hers. Noelle slid her hands up his chest, her fingers curling in his shirtfront. It felt so good, so right to have Noelle in his arms, her body molded against his. Noelle, Adam's widow. Abruptly, Carlisle released her and stepped back.

"I'm sorry. I didn't mean to… I should not—"

"It's fine," Noelle said quickly, but there was something in her eyes that wasn't there a moment ago. A sadness.

He hated that he had put that sorrow there. Now would she believe he couldn't be trusted? "If you no longer wish to go to London…"

"No," Noelle said firmly, and there was no denying the steel in her blue eyes. "I will see you tomorrow at breakfast."

"Yes. Breakfast. I should, um, go on to bed then." He scooped up his glass and book. There was no way he was reading any more tonight, but perhaps if his hands were full, he'd be less tempted to take her back into his arms and kiss her with an abandon that he wasn't sure he could rein in. "Good night, my lady."

WHEN NOELLE AND Carlisle reached London the next day, Carlisle sent for Diggs and told him about the near shooting with Gil, then set him looking into Sloane Rutherford. "I want to know where he was yesterday, what his businesses are, what unsavory characters he associates with, everything you can discover. But also keep looking for the man who tried to seize Gil here in London. He is our best hope of tying this to Sloane— or proving it was someone else."

As Diggs left with his new orders, Carlisle turned to Noelle. "I am going to call at Sloane's house now. With luck, he'll be there, and it won't necessitate a long journey."

"Very well." Noelle rose to her feet.

"Why don't you remain here and rest? It was a long drive."

She gave him a look. "Don't think you can get rid of me that easily. It was a short drive. I am not tired. And I have no intention of staying behind while you quiz this man about whether he tried to murder my son."

As it turned out, their disagreement didn't matter, for the butler who answered Sloane's door informed them that Mr. Rutherford was not at home. Even with Noelle's best cajoling, the most the servant would say was that Sloane often retired to his estate in Dorset.

They returned to their house, where they found the butler waiting for them as soon as they stepped inside the door. "Mr. Thorne, a visitor is waiting in the drawing room."

"You let him in to wait?" Carlisle asked in surprise.

"I thought it would be what you wished, sir. It's Lady Halder."

"Heaven help me," Carlisle muttered. "Mother?"

CHAPTER FIFTEEN

A TALL WELL-DRESSED woman rose from the sofa to greet them. Carlisle gave his mother a brief nod, and said, "Why are you here?"

"Cannot a mother simply want to visit her son?" Lady Halder turned toward Noelle with a gracious smile, more or less forcing him to introduce them.

Noelle and Lady Halder took a seat on the couch. Lady Halder studied Noelle closely as they exchanged the meaningless sort of questions and answers that constituted polite conversation. Carlisle stood by the mantel, watching his mother as closely as she observed Noelle, his expression vaguely suspicious. It occurred to Noelle that he might be afraid she would make some social slipup with his mother.

Carlisle shifted restlessly and cut into the conversation. "Mother, why are you here?" he said again. "There must be some reason beyond curiosity or a wish to see me."

"Why, Carlisle, not everything I do has an ulterior motive," she said in a wounded tone, but her eyes sparkled with amusement rather than hurt.

"More often than not they do. And how the devil did you know so quickly that I was in town?"

Lady Halder smiled, seemingly pleased by his question. "Surely you've learned by now that I know all the news. Well…if you must go straight to the point, I came to invite you to a small soiree I'm having on Friday. Do say you will come, my lady," she said, turning to Noelle. "And you, too, of course, Carlisle."

"How kind of you to add me to your invitation," Carlisle said dryly. "I take it you want to ensure a large attendance at your party. Scoring political points, I presume."

"It's imperative that Mr. Halder gets the ear of Lord—"

Carlisle held up a hand to stop her. "Much as we would love to be pawns in your political machinations, I am afraid we will be unable to attend."

"Dear, you might want to ask Lady Rutherford before answering for her," his mother pointed out.

"Yes, you might," Noelle agreed, fixing him with a cool stare. In truth, she had no interest in his mother's soiree, but she was not about to let Carlisle arrange her life. "I think it sounds quite nice."

Carlisle snorted. "Clearly you have never been to one of Mother's soirees. If you knew how dull and—"

"What a thing to say!" Lady Halder looked more genuinely insulted than she had at Carlisle's earlier questioning of her motives. "Really, Carlisle. My parties are considered entertaining, and my guests are of the highest order."

Was that it? Noelle's chest suddenly felt tight. Was Carlisle worried that Noelle would be out of place? An embarrassment because Noelle was *not* of the highest order? That she would stumble over names and titles, make some faux pas?

"Doesn't mean they aren't dull," Carlisle retorted. "Anyway, we cannot attend because we won't be in town then. We are leaving for Dorset tomorrow."

"Dorset? Good Lord, why?"

"Because we need to talk to someone who lives there. After that, we are headed back to Stonecliffe."

The woman's set jaw was comically similar to her son's. "Have you thought that this poor girl might not want to be shut away in the country?"

"Why don't we ask her?" Carlisle turned to Noelle with a challenging look. "Perhaps you would like to remain here in London for Mother's party while *I* go to Dorset."

Noelle refrained from rolling her eyes at him. "I am indeed sorry, Lady Halder. I would love to attend your party, but I'm afraid I must accompany Mr. Thorne to Dorset. I hope you will excuse me this time."

"Of course." Lady Halder acceded gracefully. "I hope you will let me know when you return to London, so that I may invite *you* again." The glance she gave Carlisle implied that he was not included in her invitation.

After Lady Halder left, Noelle went up to dress for dinner. The London dressmaker had finished the evening gowns Adeline had ordered for Noelle and had delivered them to the town house. Much as she enjoyed and appreciated the everyday dresses the village seamstress had sewn, Adeline's modiste's creations were clearly a cut above. These were beautiful, elegant gowns. One was a gossamer creation of sea green voile, another a rich, vivid blue satin that did wonderful things for her eyes, and one a delicate pink silk.

Noelle couldn't resist trying them on and modeling them in the mirror. She had spent the last five years striving to be as plain and unnoticeable as she could, and it was wonderful to be able to enhance her looks instead of detract from them. Admiring the delicate, sea green gown, she thought of wearing it down to dinner. Would a spark flare in Carlisle's eyes when he saw her?

She wanted quite badly to see his reaction, to know that the kiss in the library last night was not just a casual, momentary spark. But that was a foolish thing to do. Even though the wealthy dressed up to dine, this dress was too grand for a small simple supper at home. It was appropriate for a ball or some other elegant party—Lady Halder's soiree, for instance. If she swept into supper like this, Carlisle would know she was wearing it for precisely the reason she was tempted to put it on. And the last thing she wanted was for him to think she desired his attention. That she desired...*him*.

She had spent the day wondering if he had kissed her because he thought she was beneath him, not a lady with whom he must follow a strict code of conduct, but someone of a lower class whom he could bed without consequences.

However sincere he had seemed in his apology for his earlier beliefs about her, there was a bedrock of generations of aristocratic privilege in him. The last thing she should do was look as if she were trying to arouse his interest. So, with an inner sigh, she removed the lovely gown and put on one of her usual dresses.

When she went downstairs, she found that they were eating at the small table in the anteroom to the dining room. There was no chandelier here, and the candelabra on the sideboard and table cast a warm glow without chasing away the soft shadows around the edges, creating a soft, intimate atmosphere. The fact that they were alone together enhanced the feeling.

Noelle sat at Carlisle's right hand, so close she could

have reached out and touched his arm. She could see every line of his face, the curve of his lips, the arch of his brow. She couldn't stop thinking about their kiss last night. Even Carlisle appeared on edge, shifting in his seat and glancing now and then at the butler standing ready to serve their dishes. She wondered if he, too, was remembering that moment in the library. She wanted to talk to him; she wanted to ask why he had kissed her, what he thought of her, but she hadn't the courage to do so.

After the meal, they moved to the drawing room for the evening, as they customarily did at Stonecliffe. The difference was that here there was no one besides themselves—no Lady Lockwood or Petunia to distract them, no Adeline or Annabeth to carry the conversation. Noelle took a seat, choosing a chair instead of the sofa, and Carlisle stationed himself beside the fireplace, his elbow resting on the mantel. They had exhausted their supply of commonplace niceties during the meal, and now a heavy silence fell upon them.

Noelle clasped her hands together in her lap, desperately searching for some topic. Carlisle cleared his throat. He toyed with a figurine on the mantel, then set it down and paced a few feet away and came back. "Noelle…"

She looked up at him, and he began to flounder. "I wanted to say, that is, I want you to know that…um, what happened in the library was… I should not have… that is, to say…"

Noelle could no longer contain herself, and she jumped to her feet. "Why did you kiss me last night?"

He stared at her, a flush rising in his cheeks. "I, ah, it was unfortunate."

"Unfortunate?" Noelle echoed. That was how he termed their kiss? He regretted kissing her. Her own cheeks began to heat. "I am sorry that I kissed your cheek. It was impulsive and—brazen of me. I did not mean to—to importune you."

"No." He looked shocked. "I didn't mean you were in any way at fault."

"I fear I seemed exactly who you thought I was. That I was the sort of woman who gave her kisses freely."

"No. Good Gad, Noelle." Frowning, he moved forward, his hand reaching out, then dropping to his side. "I didn't think that at all."

"You didn't kiss me because you thought I was loose? Common? Fair game?"

"I did not," he said indignantly. "And no one could ever find you common."

"Would you have kissed a true lady in the same situation? Would you have kissed Annabeth like that?"

"I certainly would not," he retorted. "I have no desire to kiss Annabeth, but it has nothing to do with her virtue or her station in life. I don't go about kissing women just because I think they'd let me. Noelle, look at me." He tilted her chin up, gazing intently into her face. "I kissed you because I'm cursedly attracted to you. Because I think about you and dream about you. I did it because I couldn't keep myself from kissing you."

"Really?" Her mouth curled up as warmth bloomed in her chest.

"Yes, really. Whenever I'm with you, whenever I see you, I have the damnedest time keeping my hands off you. And trust me, it has nothing to do with your morals. In fact, your morals are bloody inconvenient. When you smile at me like that…" He let out a soft groan and bent to kiss her.

Noelle went up on her toes, meeting his lips. All thought left her head; she was only sensation, carried away by the sound and smell and taste of him. His kiss deepened, his arms tightening around her.

His lips left hers to trail down her neck, soft as a feather against the tender skin. Her name was a broken whisper from his mouth. Noelle shivered, desire lighting her every nerve. She was surrounded by him, and it was a welcome, wonderful feeling to let go, to give herself up to that strength, that warmth. He slid his hands down her body, thumbs brushing the sides of her breasts, caressing her waist and curving over her hips. She could hear his breath, harsh in his throat, could feel the pulse of his flesh against her.

"We shouldn't," he murmured, but his lips continued to travel down her throat and onto the hard line of her collarbone.

A tremor ran through Noelle, desire swarming to life inside her. She wanted to feel his bare skin against hers; her breasts ached to know his touch. There was a soft, low moan, and Noelle realized that it came from her lips. Carlisle's mouth returned to hers, his kiss deep and yearning, and he pressed her hips into him.

Abruptly he pulled back, a soft oath escaping him. "We cannot. Sweet heaven, I've gone mad." He swung away, shoving a hand through his hair. He moved to the fireplace, gripping the mantel so hard his knuckles whitened. "I'm sorry…forgive me."

Noelle, too, stepped back, running a distracted hand over her hair. She started to speak, but her voice came out barely a whisper. She cleared her throat, trying for a firm, detached calm. "Of course. You are right."

"I am a cad to treat you so." He turned back, and Noelle looked away, afraid of what her face might reveal. "I have compounded my wrongs to you. I have acted in a way… I promise I will not do so again. I've given you no reason to believe that, I know, and I cannot blame you if you distrust me. But I swear, I…"

"Stop. Carlisle. I believe you. I have no desire to blame you—I am at fault as much as you. But you're right. We must not…"

"Exactly." His voice was steeped in relief. "I will be more careful. I won't—it was a momentary lapse in judgment."

"Yes." She glanced at him and quickly away. "If you will please excuse me, I, um…"

"Yes, of course."

Noelle hurried to the refuge of her room and closed the door behind her, leaning back against it, as if to block out everything else. Why in the world did passion have to come bursting out of her with this man?

He, of course, had been sensible. Logical. Cool and rational. *He* hadn't been swept away by passion. Carlisle Thorne would never let his emotions or desires impel him to do something impulsive and irresponsible. It was silly for her to feel a sting of hurt, as if he had rejected her. He had been right, and she should be glad that one of them, at least, had enough sense to pull back.

An affair with him would be the worst kind of folly. They lived in the same house. It would impose a terrible strain on them both to hide their secret from everyone. And what happened if—no, *when*, for she must be realistic—the affair turned sour or Carlisle decided to marry someone suitable? That was the way of the aristocracy—one must marry someone of equal lineage and produce an heir. How would she be able to bear living there? Seeing him with another woman?

Noelle had to be sensible. She could not let down her guard again. Carlisle would keep his passion in check—he was, above all, a man who believed in control—and she must do the same. It would be difficult, but she had done far more difficult things, surely.

On these sensible thoughts, Noelle undressed and went to bed. But she could not sleep, only lay awake, listening to the sounds of the house and the faint noises from the street outside. It was late when she heard Carlisle's footsteps on the stairs and in the corridor. His steps did not pause as he walked past her door; she wondered if he even glanced in that direction, and what was in his head if he did.

She thought of the long journey to Dorset ahead of them. They would have to break the journey at an inn tomorrow night. Surely the situation there would be less fraught with the tension that had permeated the air this evening. They would be in a public place; there wouldn't be the enforced intimacy of this evening. And she would be able to ignore these wayward feelings for the last man on earth she should desire.

WHEN THEY SETTLED in at the inn that night, Noelle found, to her dismay, that being alone with Carlisle among strangers made for an even more intimate situation than had existed at the London house. There, the servants had been a constant, inhibiting presence, a reminder of the gossip that would so easily spread. But here Noelle and Carlisle would be gone in the morning, never to see any of the guests or servants again.

Noelle had envisioned having dinner with him in the public room of the inn, realizing too late that aristocrats did not dine with the public. She and Carlisle ate in a private room, the food brought in by the inn's servants and left on the table, with no hovering footman to serve them. They were truly alone in a way they never were at home.

Noelle was all too aware of Carlisle sitting beside her, just as she had been all day long in the carriage. She watched his lean, supple fingers as he carved the roast, and she couldn't help but think of those fingers on her body the day before. The play of muscles beneath his jacket spoke of the strength of his arms pulling her into him. Even his perfect folded neck cloth—and how did he manage to look so tidy and correct after riding in the carriage all day?—made her remember the night in the library, when his throat was bare and she could see the hollow of his throat, somehow vulnerable and enticing.

Noelle tried to concentrate on the food, which was plain but plentiful and good, but she kept glancing over at him. Remembering. Imagining. The moment she finished, she claimed weariness and fled to the safety of her room.

But even there, she could not escape Carlisle's presence. Unlike the Rutherford homes, where their sleeping quarters were separated by several other bedrooms, here Carlisle's room lay next to hers, separated by only a thin wall. She could hear him pacing about and knew when he left the room. From her window, she could see him strolling aimlessly about the yard. She wondered if he, too, was thinking how near she was, how easy it would be to slip into her room, with no one the wiser. And tonight, when she heard his footsteps in the hallway, he paused outside her door for one long, aching moment before he continued to his room.

It was not a situation that was conducive to sleep.

They left early the next morning. Carlisle looked as if he had spent as restless a night as she had, which gave Noelle at least some small measure of satisfaction. She was tired enough that she fell asleep, her head resting against the wall of the carriage, but she came back awake with a start when the vehicle bounced in and out of a rut.

She glanced across the carriage at Carlisle, who was watching her with a faintly amused expression. "I warned you it was a poor road."

"I wonder what Lady Lockwood would have to say about it," Noelle muttered, and he laughed.

The roads grew progressively worse until finally they turned onto a narrow dirt lane that took them rather alarmingly along the edge of a cliff. The stormy gray sea crashed on the rocks below. It seemed a desolate spot, with little vegetation other than a few scraggly bushes and tufts of wild grass. Finally, the carriage pulled to a stop, and Noelle had her first view of Sloane Rutherford's home.

She leaned forward, staring unabashedly. "Oh, my... it really is a great moldering ruin."

CHAPTER SIXTEEN

SITTING ON A cliff above the sea, the house was long and tall and stark, built of blocks of gray stone darkened by lichen and time into a shade just this side of charcoal. It had obviously once been a grand castle, but while the nearest section of the building was still intact, the opposite end of the house was a tumbled mass of stone, the ceiling having caved in to leave partial walls still standing here and there. The remains of a turret thrust up like a jagged spire.

"Why did he buy this?" It was compelling in a bleak way, but Noelle could not imagine wanting to actually live in it.

Carlisle let out a short laugh. "Sloane is known to have a peculiar sense of humor."

"He bought it as a jest?"

Carlisle half shrugged. "I think it was more of a rude gesture. His reputation is dark and ruined, and the house looks like the lair of a wicked count. It's a poke in the ton's eye, so to speak."

"So outrageous it's a kind of defiance." Noelle studied it again. "I can understand that. He's embarrassed, and he wants to show the world that rejects him that he doesn't care…which only proves how much he does care."

"Embarrassed?" Carlisle looked amused. "I'm not

sure Sloane has ever experienced a moment of shame. If he did, he wouldn't have subjected his family to such scandal."

Except for a few wind-shaped trees and scrubby bushes, there was no greenery around the house. Noelle could understand why when she stepped out of the carriage and her bonnet was knocked back by the wind. It was not a setting for growing anything so tender as flowers or vines.

When a servant admitted them into the house, however, they found an interior as elegantly luxurious as the exterior was rough and grim. The entry hall was laid in marble, and an intricately carved Jacobean staircase of dark walnut led upstairs. Matching velvet benches stood on either side of the front door, and a few graceful statues and a narrow table containing more objects of art were scattered about the rest of the area.

The footman led them into the large room that opened off the entry. They were not kept waiting long before a middle-aged man hurried into the room, saying cheerfully, "Carlisle, my boy, it's been an age since I've seen you. What brings you all the way out here?" He leaned in confidingly as he shook Carlisle's hand. "I don't suppose you happened to bring any whiskey with you, did you?"

"No, sir."

"Pity. Ah, well, happy to see you anyway. And who, may I ask, is this lovely woman you've brought with you?" He smiled at Noelle.

This must be Sloane's father, for he was too old to be Sloane. His dark hair was streaked with dramatic swaths of silver at the sides, and lines were thick at the corners of his eyes and mouth. His eyes were a bright, vivid blue, his features even, and his smile just a touch wicked. Even though his jawline was beginning to blur, his flesh softening with age, it was easy to see in him the handsome, charming man Adeline had described.

"Allow me to introduce Noelle, Lady Rutherford," Carlisle said.

"Adam's wife?" His eyes sparkled, his lips curving up, and he bowed smoothly over Noelle's hand. "I am delighted to meet you." His voice turned low and silky. "I knew Adam would have married a beauty, but you are a diamond of the first water, my dear."

Noelle felt Carlisle stiffen beside her and take a half step forward, but this was something she knew how to handle. She gave Marcus a dazzling smile as she deftly slipped her hand from his and stepped back. "I am so pleased to meet Adam's uncle."

"Pleasure is all mine, I assure you." He cast an amused glance at Carlisle. "Don't worry, Carlisle, I shan't do anything inappropriate. Surely an old man is allowed to flirt a bit with a beautiful young woman. Please, sit down, both of you. I would ask you what brought you here, but I enjoy too much the opportunity to chat, so let's save that till later. I told Everson to bring tea. You must be thirsty and tired after such a long journey." He took Noelle's arm, guiding her to the sofa. "My condolences. I was sorry to hear about Adam. I liked the boy—he was the best of that lot."

"He was very talented."

"Yes, indeed. There was *life* in him. I was astonished that he could have sprung from someone as dull as my brother." He cast a glance over at Carlisle. "Now, don't puff up like a partridge over that. I know you were devoted to Thomas. I'm not saying Thomas wasn't a *good* man. He made an excellent earl—certainly better than our father, who was *not* such a good man. I'm simply pointing out that Thomas was boring. Something Adam never was."

"No, he wasn't that," Noelle murmured.

"Tell me about you, dear girl. I was under the impression that Carlisle had managed to misplace you."

Noelle's lips twitched as Carlisle made a noise deep in his throat. "Mr. Thorne and I had, um, a misunderstanding. But my son and I are now living at Stonecliffe with the countess."

"Your son? Ah, yes, Adam had a child. I had forgotten."

"Gilbert inherited the title," Carlisle said, watching the man closely.

The other man gave him an odd look. "Well, yes, naturally."

"Has your son mentioned Gilbert?" Carlisle continued.

"Sloane?" Marcus looked taken aback. "Why would Sloane have mentioned him? I doubt he has any idea that the boy exists."

"We came here hoping to talk to Sloane. Is he here?"

"Oh, no, he's off somewhere; I forget. The boy's always running here or there. He really hasn't any idea how to be a man of leisure, I'm afraid." He sent a twinkling glance Noelle's way. "A skill, as you can see, that I have completely mastered."

"It's too bad he doesn't stay to enjoy his lovely home," Noelle offered.

"He didn't buy this old hulk for himself." Marcus gave a dismissive wave of his hand. "He got it so he could stash me somewhere far away from the lures of

London. I say…" He brightened and turned to Carlisle. "Perhaps you'd fancy a game of whist."

"No, sir, I'm afraid I can't," Carlisle said, his tone tinged with sympathy. "I'm sorry."

Marcus shrugged. "I haven't enough money to make it interesting anyway. Sloane will play it with me for matchsticks," he said scornfully. "Can you imagine? He doesn't understand. It's the risk that makes it fun. I think perhaps the boy is a changeling. The fairies snatched my son from the cradle and replaced him with a book-keeper's child." He tilted his head, studying Carlisle. "Of course, as I remember, you are rather a dull sort, too. Why are you looking for Sloane? The two of you were never friends."

"No, we weren't. It's…something about the estate. How long has Sloane been gone? Do you remember when he left?"

"Oh, Lord, weeks ago. He's usually in London. Did you try there?"

"Yes, we called at his house, but the servant seemed to think he was here."

"No, I fear not. You could write him a note if you'd like. I shan't remember to give it to him, I'm sure, but the butler will. Sloane should return soon. He doesn't like to leave me on my own too long. Afraid I'll pack up and leave. There's not much likelihood of that—not that escaping hasn't crossed my mind. But, sadly, I've reached the age where it seems too much trouble. Sloane would simply track me down, and then there'd be all that tiresome lecturing."

"I'm sorry. Do you mean your son holds you pris-oner here?" Noelle asked.

"Mmm. Pleasant jail cell, isn't it?" The man glanced

around. His gaze returned to her, and he laughed. "No, no, my dear, you needn't look so horrified. Much as I welcome your sympathy, Sloane doesn't *force* me to stay here. He banks on my laziness to win out over a few games of chance. It's why he picked this godforsaken spot. Besides," he added confidingly, "no one will play with me anymore now; they know I haven't a farthing."

There was the sound of the front door opening and a low exchange of voices in the entry hall, ending with a man letting out a loud exclamation. "Who? What the devil is *he* doing here?"

"Ah, that must be Sloane now," Marcus said cheerfully. "How serendipitous."

Boots thudded across the marble floor, and a man strode into the room. He had obviously been riding, his boots splattered with mud and his black hair wind-tossed. He strode to Carlisle's chair, looming over him in intimidation. "Thorne. What do you mean, barging in here and harassing my father?"

Noelle studied him. So this was the man who had broken Annabeth's heart. He certainly looked more than capable of breaking a woman's heart—or any number of things. Tall and whipcord thin, he was fiercely handsome. Though he was not as large a man as Carlisle, he exuded raw power. Lean and sleek and dangerous, he made Noelle think of a great cat, a panther, perhaps. His eyes were a bright blue, in startling contrast to the thick black lashes that rimmed them. His wealth of black hair was shaggier and longer than was fashionable, adding to the aura of wildness that clung to him. It wasn't hard to see the attraction. It was more difficult, however, for her to picture him with the quiet, contained Annabeth.

Carlisle rose to his feet and faced Sloane, ice to the

other man's fire. "Actually, we came here to speak to you."

"Sloane, what a way to greet our guests," Marcus said mildly. "You might have noticed, there is a lady present."

Sloane's eyes flickered over Noelle with indifference. "Excuse me, ma'am." He turned back to Carlisle. "I have nothing to say to you, so you can turn around and go now."

Marcus heaved a sigh. "Really, Sloane, what is the matter with talking to Carlisle?"

"We aren't a part of his family."

"Well, of course not. Carlisle's father wasn't related to us, but my brother was most fond of him."

"I'm quite aware that *he* is accepted by Drewsbury's family. It is you and I who are not; the earl made that abundantly clear years ago."

"He didn't cut Marcus out of the family." Carlisle rose to the earl's defense. "Nor you either. He wanted to pay for your education. You refused his offer."

"Ah, yes, an education so I could serve as his lawyer or maybe his man of business."

"You seem to be a man of business now."

"Of *my* business. Not the earl's lackey."

Carlisle started to retort, but Noelle cut in. "Mr. Rutherford, we are not here to discuss family history. I am Adam Rutherford's widow."

He turned to her with a long, considering look. "I heard he had married…"

"Someone unsuitable. Yes," Noelle finished crisply. "Unlike Mr. Thorne, I have no affection for the late Lord Drewsbury. No one is asking you to either. But I must point out that you are being very childish."

"Childish!" Sloane stared at her in slack-jawed surprise. Carlisle let out a snort of laughter.

"Yes," Noelle went on in the same firm voice she used when correcting her son. "Refusing to talk to us because the earl hurt your feelings is the reaction of a pouting child. Whatever you like to say, we all know that you are a Rutherford, and it is for that reason that we need to talk to you."

Rutherford glanced from her to Carlisle, his anger fading into wariness. "What are you talking about?"

"Adam's son, Gilbert, inherited the title and estate when Lord Drewsbury died since Adam had already passed on," Carlisle began.

Sloane nodded. "And?"

"Your father would be next in line if anything happened to Gilbert." Carlisle looked into Sloane's eyes as he went on, "Someone shot at Gilbert the other day."

"Shot at him? What do you mean? An accident? A poacher?"

"It would be a handy solution," Carlisle said. "But it's a little hard to believe it was an accident since he was also nearly kidnapped in London a month ago. Before that he and his mother were attacked in European cities at least twice."

Sloane stared. "You think someone is trying to kill the boy? But why come here?" He went utterly still. "Are you accusing my father of trying to do away with Adam's son? You can't be serious."

"I wasn't talking about your father."

"Me. You're accusing me of attempted murder." Sloane swung away, letting out a bitter laugh. "Of course. Someone shot off a gun near this child, so naturally *I* am trying to murder him."

"You and your father are the only ones who would profit from his death," Carlisle said flatly. "Where were you on Monday, Sloane?"

"Not shooting at some lad at Stonecliffe, I'll tell you that."

"Odd that you should know it took place at the estate."

"Where the hell else would it be?" Sloane snapped. "I don't know what is going on, but it has nothing to do with me or my father. I don't even know this child. I never heard his name until you said it just now. It may surprise you, but I don't keep up with the doings of the earl's family. I don't give a damn about inheriting the estate, and I have no interest in that bloody title either. I don't expect you to believe my word since you clearly assume I am a man who would murder a child. But have some sense—look around." He swept his arm across the well-appointed room. "I don't need a house. I already have three of them. I don't need Drewsbury's money. I have more of it than he did, I'll wager. Look at my past—a man who cares about his claim to aristocracy doesn't go into smuggling."

"If you've done nothing wrong, why are you so reluctant to tell me where you were when Gil was nearly shot?" Carlisle countered.

"Because I bloody well don't have to answer to you. I owe *nothing* to that family."

"It's your family, too."

"Sadly, I cannot change the fact that I am related. But it doesn't mean I have to have anything to do with them. Much less you. I want you out of my house. Now." He strode out of the room and to the front door, holding it open.

Noelle and Carlisle glanced at each other and followed him. At the door, Noelle stopped and faced Sloane. "Mr. Rutherford. I have no liking for Adam's father. He cut Adam off because he married me."

"He was fond of that sort of thing."

"I am no aristocrat. I don't care about the title or the Rutherford name or the money or any of that. All I care about is keeping my son safe. That is why I am asking for your help. Not as a Rutherford, but as one human being to another."

Sloane sighed and glanced away. Folding his arms, he said, "I've been in Scotland for the past fortnight. I have a fishing lodge there, near Dalguise. I'm sure anyone there can confirm that I was in residence." He turned to Carlisle. "There. You have your information. Now go."

Carlisle nodded brusquely and headed out the door.

"Thank you," Noelle said and followed Carlisle outside.

"My lady..." Sloane emerged from the house after her. When both Noelle and Carlisle turned to him, he went on, "I'd advise you to keep a good eye on your son. I didn't try to harm him, but there are others who would benefit from his death. You might want to look closer to home." His gaze slid to Carlisle. "Why don't you ask Carlisle about the tontine the earl and his friends set up? And what he will gain if he is the last man standing?"

CHAPTER SEVENTEEN

As Noelle and Carlisle stared at Sloane blankly, he whipped around and started back into the house.

"Wait!" Carlisle broke from his momentary paralysis and leaped forward. "What the devil are you talking about?"

Sloane turned a contemptuous gaze on him. "Are you going to pretend you don't know?"

"Tell me," Carlisle growled. "What tontine?"

"The one your father and the earl and the others set up. Dunbridge's father. That whole set. I don't know the exact terms; my father, you see, wasn't allowed in the group."

"I don't know about any tontine."

"If you're telling the truth, then I suggest you find out." Sloane cast a glance at Noelle. "Trust me, my lady, you have more to fear from Thorne than you do from me." He turned away.

"Damn it, Sloane." Carlisle grabbed the other man's arm. "If you know something that would help keep Gilbert safe, tell me!"

Sloane stiffened, his eyes hard as marbles. "I've told you everything I know about it." He jerked his arm from Carlisle's grasp and stalked inside, closing the door behind him with a thud.

Swearing, Carlisle pounded the door knocker against the plate several times. No one responded.

"Carlisle." Noelle moved over to him. "Carlisle." The third time she said it, he finally turned to her. "Enough. He won't open the door."

"That man has always been the most obstinate, arrogant, self-righteous—" Carlisle caught a glance at Noelle's expression and cut off his words. "And don't tell me it's the pot calling the kettle black."

"I wouldn't dream of it," she said dryly. "But this is pointless. He already said he'd told you all he knew."

"Yes, isn't that handy? Information that tells me nothing." He whisked her into the carriage.

"You think it's not true?" Noelle asked as Carlisle settled into the seat beside her. "Why would he make that up?"

"To distract me. To lead my investigation astray."

"But why something so odd? I don't even know what a tontine is. What's he talking about?"

"It's a sort of insurance. A number of people each pay an amount of money on the life of someone, usually a child, who is the beneficiary. The money is pooled together. It's invested. And finally, when the next to last beneficiary dies, the person remaining alive gets all the funds."

Noelle stared at him. "You're inventing this, whole cloth."

"No. I promise you they exist. They were popular a number of years ago and even now some people still use them. The appeal is that one doesn't have to invest much, but if he wins, he receives a large amount."

"So basically, it's gambling. A bet that one particular person will outlive everyone else."

"Well…yes."

"But that's…"

"Mad? Yes, it proved a foolish investment. People saw it as an easy way to leave money to a child or grandchild; that child, if he outlived the others, would be the beneficiary. Businesses sold shares in the tontines to finance large projects. The project would pay the money back to the fund with interest, and in the end the winner would get it all. But there were a number of swindles where everyone lost their money and on other occasions didn't make the amount of money they thought they would."

"Not to mention it sounds like an invitation to murder," she pointed out.

"That is a glaring drawback. At first, when the fund covered many people, it wasn't an issue, but as the group of beneficiaries grew smaller, with fewer people to get rid of, it could prove rather tempting to someone with a criminal nature."

"That's awful."

"I don't know that anyone was actually killed because of it, but there's always that risk."

"And Mr. Rutherford is saying that Gilbert was one of the people with money placed on his life?"

"Presumably." Carlisle nodded. "The thing is, Sloane said that my father, as well as Nathan's father and the earl, were among the people contributing to it. But my father died years and years ago, when Adam was still a child, long before Gilbert was born. How could the earl have placed a bet on him back then? I suppose the group could bet on something more general, like their grandsons, but I wouldn't think it's likely you could put it on someone who isn't even alive yet."

"Yes. You're right." The knot that had been growing in Noelle's chest loosened. "Of course. It couldn't have been about Gilbert."

"If there was a tontine, the beneficiaries would more likely have been the men's children."

"You and Adam and Nathan."

"Yes. And whoever else was in the group. So I'm not sure how a tontine, if it indeed exists, would be the reason for attacking Gilbert. The more I think about it, the more it strikes me as a move to throw us off track."

"You think Mr. Rutherford hopes to lead us astray, send us chasing down this tontine and its members instead of checking to see if he was in Scotland? At the least, it would give him time to pay a witness to affirm his presence there."

"You have a devious mind—I like it." Thorne gave her a smile, the one that never failed to set up a tingling inside Noelle. It was absurd that such a small thing— a faint lifting of his lips, a twinkling of amusement in his eyes—should make her feel at once off balance, yet excited, as well.

Her cheeks warmed and she glanced away, scrambling to pull her mind back from where it strayed. "Do you think Sloane was in Scotland?"

"I don't know. I intend to send Diggs to verify it— immediately, before Sloane has a chance to arrange for a witness. But my guess is that he was there. Sloane wouldn't have tried to shoot Gilbert himself. He'd have hired someone. Actually, the fact that he went to Scotland, giving himself a solid alibi for the time, in itself raises some suspicion."

"The only other suspect is Sloane's father, but I find it hard to imagine him hiring someone to harm Gilbert,"

Noelle said. "It's not only that he doesn't seem wicked enough, but I doubt he would go to such effort. He obviously doesn't like being under his son's thumb, but he doesn't try to leave."

"I agree. I don't think Marcus is a wicked man, just weak. Perhaps he realizes that he can't control himself, so he lets Sloane protect him from his own demons." He shook his head. "Sloane's as hotheaded and stubborn as he ever was, but he's harder now. I wasn't convinced the rumors about him were true. After all, Annabeth found something in him to love. But having seen him, I don't doubt he's capable of any number of misdeeds."

"But he did finally answer us."

"After *you* asked him." Carlisle slanted a look at her. "I suspect that says more about you than it does about Sloane. Even wicked men are susceptible to a beautiful woman."

The spark his smile had lit spread through her abdomen. Noelle couldn't keep her lips from turning up a trifle teasingly, couldn't stop the flashing glance she sent him in return. She saw him swallow, light flaring in his eyes. He was going to kiss her. She desperately hoped he was going to kiss her.

For an instant, it hung in the balance; then he pulled his gaze from her and slid closer to the door. "I…um…" He stopped, seemingly at a loss. "Damn it, but you distract me."

"I don't mean to."

"Don't you?" He huffed out a little laugh. "Then I am an even worse case than I thought." He fixed his gaze on his hands, where he was aimlessly turning a ring around and around one of his fingers. His voice was low as he went on, "Nothing can happen. Tonight at the inn."

Noelle watched the deep flush steal up his neck. "Of course not."

"You are Gilbert's mother."

"I am."

"I have, ah, great regard for you."

"I'm glad." It was doubtless unkind of her to be amused, but she could not help it. There was something intensely appealing about an unsure, even flustered Carlisle Thorne. She could see a younger Carlisle in him now, one who had not yet fully learned to cope and control. And somehow the sight of the firm, cool, implacable Carlisle so obviously ill at ease, unable to put everything into tidy order, aroused her own desire. Or, perhaps more accurately, it stirred her to know that she was the reason for his lack of composure. It was her nearness that unsettled him, the desire to kiss her that had him struggling.

He cast her a dark glance. "You're enjoying this, aren't you?"

"A little." She gave him a slow smile and was rewarded by the subtle slackening in his face.

"You know I'm right." His voice turned husky.

"I do." Noelle crossed her legs, in the process exposing her ankle a bit. His eyes flickered to her and away. Again she thought that she was wrong to tease him, but it had been so long since she had engaged in even the slightest banter with a man, aware that she would be courting danger to flirt. But with Carlisle, she felt…safe.

"I want…" His eyes were dark with passion. "Well, you know what I want. But I cannot. I promised I would not make advances toward you, and I won't. I will not treat you that way."

And that, more than anything, spoke of what he would think of Noelle if she slept with him. She would see in his eyes the loss of his respect for her, no matter how much desire glittered there, too. The things he had thought of her earlier would be confirmed.

She couldn't become his mistress. She could not put her son in that position. Or the countess. If Carlisle refused to look upon her as a loose woman, then surely she should not behave like one. With an inward sigh, Noelle slid over until she was against the opposite wall. "Of course."

Relief—and, perhaps, just a bit of disappointment?—showed in his face. He cleared his throat. "We cannot afford to dismiss Sloane's claim even if it seems unlikely. We must look into it. I'll search the earl's papers—though I cannot imagine how I could have missed something like that before—and speak to his man of business and his attorney. We'll have to remain another day in London, I fear."

"Naturally."

A strained silence fell on the carriage. It was easy enough to say they would not become lovers. It proved far harder not to think about it. In fact, there was little Noelle could think about except the night ahead of them, the intimacy of staying at the inn. Nor could she smother the fire that had started low in her abdomen. Whatever bit of conversation they had, whatever thought she forcibly pulled her mind to, beneath it was that constant physical awareness of Carlisle, the thrum of her own need.

She felt too warm and stifled beneath the heavy material of her carriage dress. The fabric brushed over her skin with every movement of her arms. She rarely noticed such a thing; now she yearned to pull it from her, to have nothing but the touch of air against her flesh. Her pulse thudded too rapidly, her breath came too fast.

Whenever she looked over at Carlisle, it seemed to her that his condition was no better than hers. His color was high; he frequently shifted in his seat, as if he could not get comfortable. He kept glancing at her, then away. He tugged at the lapels of his jacket; he pulled down the cuffs of his shirt. He drummed his fingers on his leg.

Every movement, every restless gesture, every twitch of frustration he made tightened the hunger coiling in her. Noelle wanted out of the carriage, yearned to reach the inn so that she could be released. At the same time, she dreaded arriving, for the inn would offer the real temptation. Here, in the confines of the carriage, she could make a vow of chastity. There, she would actually have to follow through with it.

Evening fell, slowing their progress. The only light inside the vehicle filtered in from the outside carriage lamps, and the darkness made the ride even more intimate, wrapping around them like velvet. Carlisle was a dark form on the other side, his face shadowed.

It would be so easy to slide across the seat to him, to lean into him, her head against his arm. Would he turn and take her in his arms if she did so? Would he pull her into his lap and kiss her lips, his hand gliding seductively down her body? Noelle trembled. It was better not to think this way.

They pulled into the yard of an inn. Carlisle shot out the door, and after turning to give her a polite hand down from the carriage, he went forward to talk to their coachman. Noelle looked around her. It was too dark to see much other than that the place looked tidy but small. It was so quiet she would have thought the inn had closed down except that light glowed through the thick, opaque glass of what she supposed was the public room.

A groom, carrying a paraffin lamp, came forward to help them, and a moment later, the front door opened, revealing a short, heavyset man who beamed at them, waving them forward. "Come in. Come in, sir, ma'am."

Carlisle returned to her side, and as they walked toward the innkeeper, he told her, "Anders said it's another hour to the inn where we stayed yesterday. The horses are tired. If this place is adequate, perhaps we'd better put up here for the night."

She nodded. "It *is* getting rather late." Better, she thought, not to return to the close environs of their coach.

The man at the door bobbed a greeting to them and repeated his invitation. "Come in, come in. Many a traveler tonight. But you're in luck, sir, as we still have a room left for you and the missus."

One room? Noelle felt Carlisle's arm stiffen beneath her hand. "Perhaps we should see it."

"Of course. Of course." The man, who apparently had a preference for saying things twice, led them down the hall. Noelle caught a glimpse of the small tavern, where two men sat, before the innkeeper led them up the stairs. "Will you be wanting supper, then? The private room is free for you and your wife."

Carlisle didn't disabuse him of the notion that they were married, but merely said, "Yes, that would be good even if we decide to travel on tonight."

"I think you'll find the room to your liking." He opened the last door in the hallway. Noelle had been right about the size of the place. There were only four doors along the corridor. "Not what you're accustomed to, I'm sure, but it's comfortable and tidy. My wife's a demon for cleaning."

The room wasn't large, but as the man had said, it was neat and clean, with a washstand, chest, and bed. Noelle looked around the room, not saying a word. Let Carlisle decide this. She sneaked a glance at him. His eyes lingered on the bed. Noelle could see the color beginning to creep up his throat. She pivoted away.

"Yes. This will do," he said at last.

"Excellent, sir. I'll see to your food." He left the room, closing the door behind him.

There was a moment of deeply charged silence after the landlord's departure. Noelle felt as if her heart were bouncing about in her chest. Then Carlisle said in a rush, "I'm sorry. Please don't think—I wasn't—that is to say, you needn't worry. I shall sleep in the carriage. This looks as clean and comfortable a place as we are apt to find anywhere along the road. It seemed the better thing to let him assume we were, um, married. Fewer questions."

"Of course." Noelle nodded. She thought the man might have a great many more questions about her supposed husband sleeping in their carriage, but she decided not to mention it.

"Well…um… I should go down and check about the horses. I'll join you in the dining room."

The room seemed larger and emptier now with Carlisle gone. She glanced toward the bed, thinking of Carlisle's face when he looked at it, and a low, persistent heat deep in her abdomen began to pulse. Carlisle needn't have apologized; she wasn't worried that he wouldn't be in complete control of his desires. It was Noelle herself she wasn't sure of. Despite all her best intentions, she couldn't stop thinking about Carlisle—kissing him, touching him. Sleeping with him.

Shaking free from her thoughts, she went to the bowl and pitcher to wash up. A servant brought up her bag, so she took the time to change out of her road-stained carriage dress into a clean, light sprig muslin and to brush her curls into some semblance of order.

Satisfied that she looked much better—though she reminded herself there was no reason to look her best—she went down the stairs. Carlisle was already in the small dining room when she entered, and the landlord was laying out a repast for them. Carlisle, who was standing by the windows, turned at the sound of her footsteps, and his dark eyes swept over her.

"Noelle." His voice was husky, and he took a step toward her, then stopped, glancing over at the innkeeper. "I hope you have brought an appetite, as our host has laid a feast for us."

The landlord beamed. "There you go, sir. Just ring if you need anything."

Carlisle pulled out a chair for her, and as Noelle sat, his fingers lightly brushed her arm, making her skin tingle. "You look lovely despite the journey."

His words were commonplace, but they warmed her. To cover her reaction, she said lightly, "I think it's the candlelight, but thank you."

"I don't know of any candlelight that could make a woman look like you." Then, as if awakening to his flirtatious tone, Carlisle's face tightened and he took his seat at the table across from her.

He could change his demeanor, but he could not remove the low hum of desire that permeated the air around them. As they ate, Noelle was conscious of his every move. His eyes belied the ordinary words they exchanged, and every glance he sent her way stirred the heat inside her.

When they finished the meal, they lingered at the table, knowing they should leave but unable to do so. Noelle's gaze went to Carlisle's fingers, curled around his glass of port. They were long and agile; she knew well the strength in them. But she knew, too, the gentleness of their touch, the smooth glide of them over her body. His fingers slid down the glass, slow and light, then back up, and Noelle glanced up to see him watching her, his eyes dark and heated. A shiver ran through her.

Was it wrong to want him? Would it be so very bad to seek the pleasure of his touch? She had spent the past five years thinking only of her son, her life consisting of nothing but work and running. Surely, it could not be so terrible a sin to take something for herself, to live, at least for a moment, for no one but herself.

Carlisle must have seen something of her thoughts in her eyes, for he pulled in a shaky breath and said tersely, "We should go to bed." A flush touched the sharp line of his cheekbones. "That is, I mean, we have a long day ahead of us." His voice, usually so sure, stumbled over the words. "If we hope to reach London. You should sleep." He stood up abruptly, shoving his chair back.

The last thing Noelle wanted at this moment was to sleep. But she could not be so bold. She reminded herself that her reputation was more important than one night of passion. Really. It was. *Think of your son. Think of the countess. Think of the future.*

"Yes, of course." Noelle rose, unable to meet his gaze. "Then I shall bid you good-night."

"I'll see you to your room."

They went upstairs, Carlisle walking beside Noelle, carefully not touching her. But he was close enough she could feel the heat of his body, smell the scent of his cologne, her skin so sensitive it was as if he touched her. Noelle's pulse pounded in her ears. She focused her eyes on the polished banister, her hand sliding smoothly up the gleaming wood. Her fingertips tingled. What would Carlisle's flesh feel like beneath her fingers?

And she must stop thinking this way or there was no telling what she would do. She had to maintain her poise, keep her head—no matter how much her mind was telling her that one night would not matter. They were alone and unknown in this rural inn. Who would know? How could her reputation be damaged? She and Carlisle would be the only ones to know, and neither of them would tell anyone.

The countess wasn't here. Gil wasn't here. There was no one to be hurt, except perhaps herself, and at the moment she found it hard to care. It had been so long since she had felt desire, so many years that she had spent untouched, unkissed, her existence as a woman put aside, leaving only a mother.

Noelle loved her son beyond anything. She regretted not a moment of her time with him or the role she had had to take. But he was safe now, protected and cherished by a dozen others.

Noelle sneaked a glance at Carlisle out of the corner

of her eye. His jaw was set, his gaze determinedly focused on the steps in front of them. He, of course, was in control of his animal instincts. But Noelle had tasted his kiss, felt his heat. Lust bubbled beneath his implacable surface. She was certain she could break that control if she wanted. And there was something incredibly enticing about the thought of doing so.

As she reached the top of the stairs, her foot caught on the hem of her dress and she stumbled. She reached out for the railing, but Carlisle's hand was already there to grab her arm and keep her from falling. She could feel the imprint of his fingertips burning into her skin. His hand remained wrapped around her arm. She turned to him. Carlisle stood on the step below her, his face only inches away, his dark eyes locked on hers. It seemed as if all the air around them had been sucked away, leaving her nothing to breathe. The walls closed in on them, leaving her no escape.

They stood poised, silent save for the harsh rasp of their breathing. Finally Carlisle broke their tableau, dropping her arm. "I must go."

"Wait." Noelle's hands went to his shoulders. He said nothing, made no move, his eyes intent on her face. She could feel herself trembling—with trepidation and desire, even a thread of hope. "Don't sleep in the carriage."

He took a short, sharp breath. "Noelle, you don't—" He stopped, clearly unable to find the words.

"I do," she countered simply. "I want you to stay."

In the next instant, he was up the last step, his arms going hard around her, lifting her up and into his kiss.

CHAPTER EIGHTEEN

NOELLE WRAPPED HER arms around Carlisle's neck, meeting his kiss with a hunger of her own. He stepped up into the narrow hallway, his mouth still fused to hers, moving forward blindly until they came up against a wall. There, finally, he raised his head and his arms relaxed around her, letting her slide down his body in a slow and thoroughly erotic manner. He glanced around a trifle dazedly, saying, "Where…"

"Down there," Noelle murmured, making an equally vague gesture to the hall behind her.

He abandoned the topic as he trailed his lips down the side of her neck, his hands gliding down her sides and curving over her buttocks, pulling her hips firmly to him. Noelle pressed into him, eliciting his low groan, and Carlisle's mouth returned to hers, harder, deeper, hungrier.

There was the sound of a door opening along the hall, and Carlisle turned, wrapping his body around Noelle's, shielding her from view. "We should go inside." His husky whisper ruffled her hair.

"Yes." Noelle rubbed her cheek against his chest, soaking up the warmth, the scent, the feel of him, the feel of his heart pounding beneath her ear.

He let out a breathy laugh. "That's not helping."

"Isn't it?" She smiled and slid her arms beneath his jacket and around his waist.

"Nor is that." He nuzzled into her hair.

"I'm sorry." Her hands roamed his back. "Should I stop?" Her fingers spread teasingly down to his hips.

She felt his smile against her hair. "In an hour or so."

Her laugh was low and sultry as she curved her hands down over his buttocks and felt him surge against her. "Is someone still there?"

"At the moment I don't care." But he lifted his head to glance down the corridor. "No. Apparently we shocked them back into their room." He straightened, pulling back a little. "And I would very much like to be back in *our* room now."

"Then we should go there."

"It seems a terribly long distance." He bent to take another kiss before starting down the corridor, his arm around her shoulders, holding her to his side. Halfway along, he stopped to wrap his arms around her and kiss her again.

"We shall never reach it at this rate." Noelle smiled up at him.

"When you smile at me like that, I don't care where I am." He cradled her face between his palms, studying her, then slid his fingers back to tangle in her curls. Heat flared in his eyes. "I can't think of anything except how much I want you. I've been going mad these past days. Weeks. Since the moment I saw you, if I'm honest."

She arched a brow. "You certainly didn't seem enamored of me, I must say." Her fingers went to the buttons of his waistcoat.

He sucked in a shaky breath. "Oh, you were as infuriating as you were desirable. I've never known any woman like you."

"Like me?" She raised a brow.

"So lovely." He bent to place a soft kiss on her forehead. "So strong." He made his way down her face, his lips touching her with each statement. "So determined. So troublesome. So stubborn. So utterly, gut-wrenchingly tempting." His mouth lingered on hers. "And now, I think we must get to the room, or I shall thoroughly disgrace myself right here."

"Well, we can't have that." Noelle pulled back, reaching down to take his hand, and led him to their door.

They had barely stepped inside the room before he pulled Noelle to him, his mouth desperately seeking hers. Noelle trembled, knees suddenly weak, her very core seeming to melt into him. She wanted him with a hunger she could never before remember, flesh and heart aching. His need was raw and fierce, and that doubled her own.

She pressed up into him, moving her body against his. He went to the buttons down the back of her dress, his fingers clumsy with haste and desire. Noelle attacked the buttons of his waistcoat in return and shoved the sides apart, her hands hard and searching through the thin cloth of his shirt. His neck cloth was more troublesome, but she got it unknotted and hanging, then made quick work of the simpler ties of his shirt.

Reaching the last of her buttons, Carlisle hooked his hand inside the neckline of her dress and peeled it down. Stepping back, he shoved off his own unfastened garments. Noelle's dress sagged around her arms and she let it fall to the floor. Noelle grasped the bow that tied her chemise and began to pull, the slender satin strip sliding apart. Carlisle's eyes flared with heat.

"Here," he said hoarsely, taking the delicate ribbon in his fingers. "Let me."

"Very well." Noelle knew how she looked—her hair mussed, eyes lambent and soft, lips red and swollen from his kisses—and she was equally aware of how her appearance affected him. For years she had done her best to downplay her looks, to never show the slightest hint of sexuality. But she wanted now to tease and beckon, to promise him with her eyes and lips…and to know the complete fulfillment of that promise. Her lips curved invitingly. "If you wish."

"Oh, I wish." His voice was deep and rich with anticipation. "I wish very much."

He hooked two fingers in the loosened neckline of her chemise and dragged it downward with aching slowness, across the white globes of her breasts, over the red, hardening buds of her nipples, until it revealed all of her torso. His eyes darkened, his mouth heavy and full, as he reached out and cupped her breasts in his hands, thumbs drifting over her nipples.

She shivered a little under his touch, and he murmured, "Cold?"

"No." Her hands went to the buttons of his trousers, and her eyes glinted as she looked up at him. "Not cold at all."

She felt the press of him against her fingertips, and as he bent to take her mouth again, she slipped her hand beneath the cloth. He made a low sound in his throat, somewhere between a hum and groan. They kissed again and again as they made their way toward the bed, blindly twisting and turning, stopping and start-

ing in a slow dance of passion. Finally, they paused long
enough to rid themselves of the rest of their last imped-
ing garments, then he lifted her up, and she wrapped
her legs tightly around him as he carried her to the bed.

Tumbling onto the soft mattress, his body atop hers,
Noelle remembered that moment only a month or so ago
when they had grappled in the churchyard and she had
felt a traitorous stirring of desire. It was much the same
now—his body heavy on hers, pinning her down—yet
oh, so different. No anger burned in her now, only anticipation.

Digging in her heels, she pushed up into him and
was rewarded by the surge of heat throughout his body.
His lips trailed down her neck, and he made his way
downward with aching slowness until he reached the
soft swell of her breasts. His mouth lingered there, his
hands learning every dip and curve of her body.

Noelle panted, her skin on fire, aching to feel him
inside her, and she rotated her hips impatiently beneath
him. Her movements elicited another soft moan from
him, but he did not satisfy her yet, instead drifting down
her torso, his lips traversing the soft flesh over the bony
ridges of her ribs and onto the tender skin of her belly.
She dug her fingers into his shoulders, whispering his
name, and he slid between her legs. With aching slowness, he pushed into her, stretching and filling her with
such satisfaction that she could not hold back a soft cry.

He moved in a timeless rhythm, passion spiraling
with every stroke. Noelle moved with him, her hands
digging into the sheet beneath her, yearning, reaching, until at last desire exploded inside her, sending
her soaring on a wave of pleasure so intense she could
scarcely breathe. Carlisle shuddered and collapsed, his

breath hoarse and hot against her neck. Noelle wrapped her arms around him, clinging to him in the storm of emotions. She wanted to laugh, to cry, to say any of the thoughts tumbling inside her brain, but it was all too intense, too inchoate to express, and so she simply held on and gave herself up to happiness.

CARLISLE DRIFTED UP from the dark well of sleep, aware of a vague, encompassing sense of well-being. Something soft and warm pressed against him, and his body responded to it instinctively, desire blossoming almost languidly deep inside him. Noelle.

He smiled, nuzzling into the curls that brushed his cheek. It was Noelle's firm, round bottom pressing against him in a most delightful way. And this loose, lazy, thoroughly replete contentment that permeated his body was due entirely to her. He thought about making love to her hours earlier—the taste of her lips, the feel of her satin skin beneath his fingertips, the luscious weight of her breasts in his hand. He thought of sinking into that tight heat, her scent filling his nostrils. The breathless, crashing wonder of coming to climax inside her.

She snuggled closer, her movement setting his nerves afire. Her finger trailed down his arm that lay over her, the touch light as a feather, telling him she was awake… and knew exactly what her motion did to him. He responded to the invitation by softly kissing the side of her neck, and the shiver that ran through her was another silent answer.

"Good morning," he murmured close to her ear and gently nibbled at the lobe.

She turned in his arms to look up at him and smile. "Good morning."

Her voice was soft, her eyes hazy with sleep, her mouth still soft and a little reddened from their kisses. She couldn't have looked more desirable, and his hunger surged. Carlisle hooked a finger under the top of the sheet and inched it down over her breasts, catching slightly on the pebbled nipples before slipping onto the soft plane of her stomach.

He teased his forefinger over her nipples, watching her eyes darken with passion, his own desire ratcheting higher. Bending his head, he kissed each breast, then the hollow of her throat, and finally her mouth, the light touch of his lips becoming deeper.

He raised his head, gazing into her eyes, and said softly, "This is folly, you know. Utter madness."

"I know." Noelle laid her hands on his arms and skimmed them up to his shoulders. Her fingertips traced the hard line of his collarbone, then drifted down the center of his chest.

"We cannot continue this at home."

"Of course not." She nodded, her finger finding and circling his navel.

"Even in town. The servants…" His breath caught in his throat as her fingertips explored lower.

"But we're not there yet." Her eyes gleamed as her hand found him and curled around him.

"No, thank God." He rolled onto his back, taking her with him, her silvery laugh like fingers running up his spine.

Noelle straddled him, going up on her knees and providing him with a breathtaking view of her bare torso. He was already hard as a rock for her, and she wasted no time, taking him into her with a slow, pleasurable, tormenting glide. Carlisle sucked in his breath and he put his hands on her thighs and slid upward to cup her breasts. She felt like heaven, every silken inch of her, and the sight of her face, rapt in pleasure, as she moved on him, filled his chest with an ache so sweet, so piercing, so intense he felt as if he might simply shatter into a thousand pieces.

And when she reached her peak, her body shuddering, he sat up, wrapping his arms around her and crushing her to him as he found his own sweet release.

THE DRIVE TO London was long, so that they arrived at the house after the time for dinner had passed. But Cook was able to come up with a meal of warmed-up meat pie, soup, bread, and pudding, which clearly embarrassed the woman by its plainness but which Carlisle and Noelle found delicious. The butler was horrified at Carlisle's suggestion that they eat at the scarred wooden table in the kitchen, and he insisted on serving them himself at the small table in the dining anteroom.

Carlisle looked across at Noelle and wished the butler would leave them to their own devices. He had enjoyed dining with Noelle alone the past days as they traveled, and he wished he had one more meal to savor in the same relaxed way instead of having to maintain an atmosphere of careful propriety.

He curled his hand around his wineglass to keep from reaching over to touch Noelle's hand. He thought of how easy it had been to take her hand in his as they rode in the carriage today, how natural and satisfying, and he smiled at the further memory of pulling her over onto his lap to kiss her.

What the devil was he going to do? The prospect of living this way, pretending a polite acquaintanceship with Noelle, watching his words, his gestures, even his glances, filled him with dismay. This morning he'd told himself that last night would be enough, that now that his desire had been satisfied, he would no longer hunger for her. That, of course, had been sheer idiocy—or, at least, it would have been if he had actually believed it. One night—ten nights, for that matter—with a woman like Noelle would not be enough to sate one's desire.

With effort he pulled his mind back from where it strayed. Glancing up, he found Noelle watching him, brows raised slightly, and he realized that while his mind was wandering, she had spoken to him and was now awaiting a response. He shifted in his chair, struggling to remember what the devil they'd been talking about. Noelle chuckled, and the look in her eyes was so knowing that it started the familiar coiling deep in his gut.

Noelle cast aside whatever she'd asked and said mildly, "I believe that I shall retire early tonight, if you will excuse me. I find I'm rather tired."

"Yes. No doubt." He thought about Noelle going upstairs to prepare for bed. Undressing, brushing her hair, slipping between the sheets. "Um, rather a long trip." Good Lord, now he could not manage to string together enough words to make a proper sentence.

"I had too little rest last night, I'm afraid," Noelle went on, eyes twinkling.

She was baiting him. It was maddening. And damnably arousing. "Yes, well, country inns…"

"Still, it was a pleasant inn," she went on. "I enjoyed my time there."

He tried to frown at her, but she returned his gaze with an expression so supremely bland that he had to press his lips together to hide a smile. "Did you? I'm so glad. I did my best to find an adequate place." He took a sip of wine, watching her over the rim.

"Oh, it was quite…adequate." She gave him a catlike grin as she tore off a little piece of bread and popped it in her mouth.

He turned his attention to his plate, saying, "One would hope it was somewhat more than adequate."

Noelle chuckled. "It may have been. I would probably have to try it again to be sure."

"Perhaps we could arrange that."

Was it really necessary to stay away from her tonight? Here at the dining table, certainly, they could not display any inappropriate relationship—though at the moment they weren't doing a very good job of that. During the day, it was imperative that they keep their distance and give the servants no grist for the rumor mill. But at night, when the halls were dark and the servants safely upstairs in their beds, there would be no witnesses. It wasn't as if the butler roamed the halls searching out sinners.

If Carlisle waited until the house was silent and the staff asleep, if he went back to his own bed before the servants were up and about—in short, if he was discreet—there would be no harm done. It would be no less wrong, but at this moment, he could not bring himself to care much about right and wrong. Abstinence could wait until they went to Stonecliffe. Tonight he would spend in Noelle's arms.

CHAPTER NINETEEN

CARLISLE WAS GONE when Noelle awakened the next morning. She sighed. Of course he would have to leave her room before the servants were up, but still, it had been so pleasant waking up beside him the day before. She stretched, pleasurably aware of every inch of her body, and turned onto her side, nestling into her pillow and dreamily contemplating the night before. She smiled, thinking of Carlisle's cautious words yesterday morning, which he had completely negated by coming to her bed last night. It would have to be different at Stonecliffe; he had been right about that. But she was very glad that they would have another night here.

He had been right, too, in saying that what they were doing was madness. It was in no way prudent or wise to take Carlisle Thorne into her bed. But she knew, just as she had known the other night when she'd taken the first step, that she was not going to break it off. Whatever might happen, she wanted these few moments of happiness.

When she went downstairs later, she found that Carlisle had already eaten and gone to his study. However, as she ate, he came back into the dining room. His eyes sparkled with devilish good humor as he sat down beside her. "I trust you slept well?"

"Indeed." Noelle wished she could touch his hand

or lay her hand against his cheek. It was so difficult to act as if there was nothing between them.

Carlisle must have felt the same way, for he nodded to the footman attending them and said, "That's all, Forrester." As the man left, Carlisle turned back to her. "I've sent notes to Diggs and to the old earl's lawyer and his man of business, asking them to call on us today. I assume you will want to join me in the interviews."

"I would, yes."

He nodded and fell silent, watching her. After a moment, he leaned in a trifle closer and murmured, "I would like very much to kiss you right now."

Noelle's cheeks warmed, and she smiled a little impishly. "Mr. Thorne! What an improper thing to say. I'm astonished."

"I am a bit amazed, myself." He glanced out into the hall. It was empty, but one of the servants might walk by at any moment. With a sigh, he settled back in his chair. "I suppose I shall have to content myself with looking at you. I find that enjoyable, as well."

"We could converse," Noelle pointed out. "Do you think we will discover anything from Lord Drewsbury's lawyer? Or Diggs?"

He half shrugged. "We'll see what Diggs has turned up about Sloane and his associates. Perhaps it will be helpful. But as for the earl's agent or lawyer telling us anything about the tontine..." He shook his head. "I don't know. They would be the likeliest people to know about the agreement. But if they do, why have they never told me about it? I've been handling the earl's affairs since his death. Frankly, I'm surprised Drewsbury himself didn't tell me; he named me executor, after all. That's one of the reasons I wonder if it's all a hum."

"But what a peculiar thing for Mr. Rutherford to have made up," Noelle pointed out.

He nodded. "Yes, it hardly seems the first thing that would spring to one's mind to offer as proof of one's innocence...or even as a distraction."

Soon Diggs arrived to tell them the results of his investigation. "Mr. Rutherford came back to England rich a few years ago. No one knows exactly how he made his fortune. He owns a shipping company, and there are rumors that he continued his smuggling trade, but he's never been caught."

"Smuggling has begun to die out," Carlisle commented.

"Just so, sir. He's bought a few other businesses. Some, uh..." He cast an uneasy glance toward Noelle. "Begging your pardon, ma'am, he owns a gambling den and a few taverns, as well. A distillery in Scotland. There are rumors of other unsavory things, but I could not confirm them. He has a house in Scotland, one in Dorset, and one here in the city. They say it's a grand thing, used to belong to a duke. He also has a few rental houses in London."

"A man of diverse interests."

"I can't say about that, sir, but he certainly seems to like to own things."

"No signs of debt?"

Diggs shook his head. "Not that I could find. Doesn't gamble himself. He dresses well, buys prime horseflesh, has a curricle and a landau, and probably more vehicles and horses at his other houses. But there's no sign he's living above his means. One of my men talked to some of Rutherford's workers, just friendly like at the local tavern, and they said he was rich as Midas."

"It doesn't mean Sloane's innocent," Carlisle said to Noelle after Diggs left the room.

"No, but it certainly takes away a good deal of motive. He doesn't need to inherit a fortune, which would make the title his only motivation." She sighed. "It makes the tontine seem more important."

Unfortunately, when the earl's solicitor arrived later, he looked at them blankly and said, "A tontine! The earl? I'm sorry, but whoever told you that must have been mistaken. He never said a word to me about any such thing, and I can assure you that if he had, I would have advised against it."

His business agent looked even more appalled, repeating the lawyer's declaration in almost exactly the same words. After the business agent left, Carlisle turned to Noelle. "I fear we aren't getting anywhere with this. I can't think of anyone else to ask."

"There is someone who might know," Noelle said.

"Who? Lady Drewsbury? I doubt it. He never bothered her with business matters."

"No. I was thinking of your mother."

"My mo—oh." He blinked. "Well, yes, if my father was one of the members, he might have discussed it with her."

"And luckily we know where she will be this evening."

"That soiree she invited us to? No." He shook his head firmly. "There's no need for you to subject yourself to that. I'll call on her this afternoon."

"I doubt she will be eager to sit down and talk to you while last-minute preparations for a party are going on. But think how agreeable she would be this evening when you bring her the conversation piece for her party that you said she wanted."

"No. There is no need for you to be exposed to—"

"Carlisle." Noelle leaned forward, placing her hand on his arm. "Tell me truthfully: Will you be embarrassed to arrive at her party with me?"

"No!" His hand closed over hers. "Good Lord, Noelle, no. I swear to you. My only concern is that you will be exposed to their gossip. Perhaps even their snubs."

"I am quite accustomed to being ignored by aristocrats." A little smile took some of the sting from her words. "However, if the stares and whispers will embarrass you, then I shan't force the issue."

Carlisle kept his grip on her hand and took her other one, as well, looking into her eyes. "I will *not* be embarrassed. You are a beautiful, intelligent woman, and no one who spent two minutes in conversation with you would think otherwise. If they are unkind to you, it is from their ignorance alone."

"You may be right. But I must remind you that once your opinion of me was the same scandalous one that the ton will hold."

"Noelle, no..."

"I am not blaming you. I am simply pointing out that even good-willed, reasonable people will believe that...unless they meet me and find out I am not what they thought, just as you did. I have to face the aristocracy sometime for Gil's sake. As you have said, they are his people. I must do whatever I can to make sure he isn't excluded or looked down upon. When Gil enters the ton, *I* will be brought up—my lack of noble blood, our elopement, the rumors about my past—and if I am unknown to them, it will be worse. They will say I am so miserably inappropriate that you and the countess had to keep me hidden all these years. Isn't that true?"

He started to speak, then stopped and, with a sigh, admitted, "Yes. They probably would."

"Then it is better, isn't it, to start here and now? Let them meet me and see that I understand the rules of the ton—how to speak, what topics to avoid, how to address a duchess or a baronet. The butler at Stonecliffe taught me all the niceties—even a good bit of gossip. You wouldn't want me to waste his efforts, now would you?" She gave him a dimpling smile.

"Bennett? Really?"

"Yes. I threw myself on his mercy, and he agreed to tutor me. He's quite kind, really, underneath all that starch. I feel I am well prepared to be entirely unexceptional."

Carlisle chuckled, and the warmth in his eyes heated a little more. "I doubt that you could ever be unexceptional. I also doubt he had to teach you much. I have never seen you depart from proper behavior...well, except when you decided to lead me on a chase through the countryside."

"I promise not to lead anyone on a merry chase," she said wryly and added, "If they meet me now and find me not so very scandalous, perhaps they will over time become accustomed to me. When Gilbert is a young man, they may still whisper about his mother. But it will be much less."

"Yes. You're right. It's better to get it over with." Carlisle sighed, giving in. "And, little as I like it, it's probably better to have you introduced at one of my mother's parties. Halder is influential enough that most will be reluctant to offend his wife. Once they realize how lovely and witty and charming you are, they will spread it about, and your reception at other parties will be easier."

"Good. Then I suppose we should prepare for an evening out."

NOELLE HAD TO admit that she was eager to wear one of the evening gowns that the London modiste had made for her. When she had tried them on the other day, she had wondered what Carlisle's reaction would be, but her imagination could not compare to the expression on his face when she floated down the stairs that evening wearing the confection of sea green gauze and silver lace.

His greeting to her in front of the waiting footman was merely a polite, "How lovely you look tonight, Lady Rutherford." But his eyes said a great deal more, and when he stepped up politely to drape the shimmering sheer wrap around her shoulders, his hands lingered for a moment longer than was strictly proper. "I can see that I shall have to fight off a host of admirers."

"Hardly that." Noelle's eyes danced. No matter how much she did not want to endure the stares and whispers of the ton, there was a certain giddy excitement at the prospect of attending a party on Carlisle's arm.

Her heart quailed a bit when they stepped into the Halders' assembly room, seemingly filled with elegantly dressed, glittering people, and for one panicked moment, she was tempted to turn and flee. Her fingers trembled slightly on Carlisle's arm, and he covered her hand with his. The warm reassurance steadied her, and she was able to paste on a smile for Carlisle's mother.

Lady Halder gaped at them in surprise, but she quickly recovered and swept forward.

"Carlisle. And Lady Rutherford. How delightful." Belinda's eyes glittered as she took Noelle's hand. "I am so pleased you came. I don't doubt you had to drag my son with you. He avoids parties like the plague. Carlisle is the dullest of men." She cast a smile up at him to soften the sting of her words.

"I wouldn't say that," Noelle demurred and cut her eyes toward Carlisle. "I've found he can be quite entertaining."

Carlisle's eyes warmed, and a faint smile touched his lips. His mother looked sharply from him to Noelle and murmured, "Really? Interesting..."

"I need to talk to you, Mother," Carlisle said.

"Ah. I see. So it was not for the pleasure of my company that you attended? Well, of course, dear, we shall talk later. But first you must allow me to introduce Lady Rutherford to my guests. The French ambassador and his wife are here. I believe you have spent much time in Paris?" She guided Noelle toward a knot of people.

Noelle went with her, Carlisle following with a resigned air. Lady Halder began the introductions, and all eyes turned to Noelle. Some were bright with interest, others more avid; a few glittered maliciously. Noelle could feel her palms sweating inside her gloves. She reminded herself that her dress could compare to any of theirs and that Carlisle was there to support her. Maintaining a measured smile, she exchanged greetings and chatted for a moment. It was a relief, actually, to slip into French with the ambassador's wife, who spoke little English and was delighted at the chance for a conversation.

"Mother, we wanted to talk to you," Carlisle said as they left the first knot of guests, but by that time, they had reached the next group Lady Halder sought, and there was another round of introductions and pleasantries. Before she could lead them to yet another cluster of guests, Carlisle took his mother's arm and steered her toward an empty spot by a palm. "We need to talk."

"But dearest," Lady Halder protested, "I cannot simply disappear from my own party." She used her folded fan to indicate the rest of the room. "I must see to my guests. There are several more people whom Noelle should meet. We are doing well, though it would help if you wouldn't glower at everyone so. But it will quite cement Noelle's place in the ton to make friends of the Chesters."

"No doubt. And I'm certain the Chesters can't wait to tell us about their seven spaniels—"

"Carlisle! You know they only have five, and I didn't raise you to be rude."

Noelle wanted to tell Lady Halder that it didn't sound as if she did much raising of her son at all, but she held her tongue.

"Either way, Noelle and I have more important concerns than establishing her in society."

Lady Halder's look conveyed her disbelief that anything could be more important, but she sighed and said, "Very well, I can see that I won't be able to attend to my duties until you're satisfied. Why do you 'need' to talk to me?"

"Did you ever know anything about my father buying into a tontine?"

His mother stared at him blankly. "A what?"

"A tontine. It's an insurance contract." He started to explain, but Lady Halder interrupted him.

"Yes, I do remember the concept. Vaguely. What an odd thing to be asking about."

"Did Father take part in one?"

"I wouldn't think so." She frowned. "Surely you would know more about that than I. Drewsbury handled all that after Horace died; he must have told you about his financial affairs."

"Yes, he did, but he said nothing about a tontine. I went through many of Father's old papers after I came of age, and there was no mention of a tontine. However, Sloane told me—"

"Sloane? Sloane Rutherford? Carlisle, whyever are you talking to that man?" Lady Halder's brows knitted. "He's thoroughly disreputable. You cannot be friends with him—it would not reflect well on Lord Halder—" Carlisle cocked an expressive eyebrow, and she grimaced. "Yes, I know, you don't care how it would look for my husband, but you should have some care for your own reputation. And Lady Rutherford's, not to mention her son's."

"Mother… I am not friends with Sloane Rutherford. Far from it. But he told me my father entered into a tontine with Lord Drewsbury and Nathan's father."

"Well, it sounds like exactly the sort of foolish scheme Nathan's father would have gotten into. George Dunbridge was always trying to recoup his fortune in one idiotic fashion or another." Her mouth twitched in irritation. "And if Drewsbury asked your father to join it, no doubt he would have. Horace would do anything Drewsbury wanted, no matter how nonsensical it might be." She sniffed disdainfully. "But if George Dunbridge was involved, I am sure it was a failure and they lost all their money."

"I suppose that could be why there was no record of it among Father's papers," he mused. "Still, I must look into it."

"Good...now if that is all..." Lady Halder turned to Noelle. "You really must meet the Chesters."

Noelle nodded and braced herself, but Carlisle, with a swift glance at Noelle, intervened. "No, Mother, she does not really need to meet the Chesters." He took Noelle's arm. "I think Lady Rutherford has furthered your agenda quite enough already. I am sure she must be tired."

"My goodness, Carlisle, you are the rudest man alive. Sometimes I wonder how you could be my son. Lady Rutherford might wish to remain for a while. *Some* people actually enjoy parties." She turned to Noelle. "Please stay. Carlisle can leave if he wants, and I'll have the carriage take you home later."

"Thank you; you're very kind, but I fear I do have a bit of a headache." Noelle smiled. "And we are returning to Stonecliffe tomorrow, so we shouldn't stay too long."

"Of course," Lady Halder acquiesced gracefully. "I do hope you will come again, though. Carlisle, why don't you fetch Lady Rutherford's wrap? I'll walk her to the door."

"Mother..." He frowned.

"Don't look so suspicious. I shan't bite her." Lady Halder linked her arm through Noelle's and started toward the front door, giving her son little choice but to do as she bid. She sighed, glancing back at Carlisle as he strode away. "I fear he will never forgive me for remarrying."

"I'm sure he understands," Noelle replied soothingly.

The other woman shot her a sardonic look. "Please... I do hope we aren't going to start out lying to one another. I know Carlisle has been angry at me. He thinks I'm disloyal to his father's memory and callous because I let Drewsbury and the countess raise him. I won't pretend that I didn't want my own life, my own enjoyment, but I also knew that Carlisle would be happy with them and miserable with me and the life I chose. Indeed, I think that he *was* happier, but..." She gave a little shrug. "Still he resents me."

"I...um, Carli—Mr. Thorne hasn't discussed it with me." Noelle fumbled for something to say. She could not imagine turning over her son to another to raise, no matter what, but she couldn't help but feel a little sorry for the woman.

"Of course not. He's tight as a clam about things. Just like his father, who—while I loved him dearly, you understand—was rather rigid. Loyal to a fault, a man of honor and courage, Horace was—" She cut off her words, her eyes glimmering with moisture. Then, swallowing, she continued, "He was a wonderful man. But he saw everything in absolutes—up and down, black and white, right and wrong. There was no room for mistakes, for actions or feelings that were not clearcut. Carlisle worshipped him. Horace and Drewsbury were cut from the same cloth. I did my best in raising Carlisle to leaven that with tolerance. I'm unsure how well I succeeded."

"Mr. Thorne has been most considerate with me."

"No doubt that is why you remained abroad all these years." Lady Halder cut her a teasing glance. "No need to tell me; it's clear there must have been an estrangement between you and the family. It couldn't have been on the countess's part; Adeline is the easiest woman to get along with. I know my son, and my guess is that Carlisle was sharp, absolutely certain of his beliefs, and probably a bit arrogant."

Noelle had to smile. "A rather accurate guess."

"I was pleased you and he reached a rapprochement. If for no other reason, I am fond of Adeline. And now, making your acquaintance, I feel quite hopeful. You've been a good influence on my son."

"Me? Oh, I don't—I fear I have no influence on Mr. Thorne."

"I suspect you have more than you think. Carlisle seems different, and I can attribute it to nothing else. Why, he came to this party tonight, and that is most unlike him. He has always preferred a quiet—dare I say boring—life. Reading or totting up numbers or puttering around in the garden, tending to those fish of his father's. I'll warrant you were the one who persuaded him to come to the party tonight."

What was she getting at? The longer they talked, the more Noelle feared that Carlisle's mother had guessed the relationship between Noelle and Carlisle. But Lady Halder appeared pleased at the idea, which was such an out-of-the-ordinary notion that it made Noelle vaguely uneasy.

"Don't worry." Lady Halder patted her arm. "I have no expectations that you two will be attending my parties. I just wanted to ask you to…be patient with Carlisle. He can be blunt and stubborn and dictatorial, but he is a good man at heart. And though he will hide it, he can be badly hurt." She sighed. "I know."

They had reached the entryway, and Noelle was relieved to see Carlisle striding toward them, effectively putting an end to their conversation. As Carlisle draped Noelle's sheer wrap of silver voile around her shoulders, Noelle turned to make her polite farewell to Lady Halder.

"Goodbye, my dear." Carlisle's mother reached out and took her hand, giving it a little squeeze. "Do call on me when you are in the city again. And, please... think about what I said."

Noelle was not surprised when Carlisle's first words after they settled into the carriage were, "What does she want you to think about? There is no necessity to do anything she asked. I won't let her bully you into furthering her schemes."

"She wasn't trying to lure me into any scheme. No, really," she added when he looked skeptical. "She was perfectly pleasant, and I am grateful for her help tonight. The presence of the French ambassador was a stroke of luck. I think she made my entry into society as easy as it could possibly have been."

He gave a noncommittal grunt. "She is good at that. But she'll want something in return, I have no doubt."

"Carlisle...aren't you being a trifle harsh? I think she loves you and wanted to help you by doing this."

He cocked an eyebrow. "Was that her reason for that little tête-à-tête? She was enlisting your aid and sympathy? Explaining that I am not a dutiful son?"

"No. She said nothing about that." Noelle wasn't

about to tell him his mother's comments on Noelle's relationship with Carlisle.

"Then what?"

She lifted her brows. "Do you mean to interrogate me all the way home? It was a private conversation."

Carlisle scowled. "Why are you being so secretive? Whatever she said, I can assure you that it was carefully sculpted to help her somehow."

"Oh, for goodness' sake, you are a most exasperating man. Very well. She wanted to assure me that you were a good man underneath your rigidity and pride. That you were loyal, honest, and kind, just like your father, despite your tendency to see everything as good or bad, with no allowance for the in-between. There." She crossed her arms. "Does that satisfy you?"

He gaped at her. "*That* is what she wants you to remember? That I'm not quite as bad as I seem?" Carlisle laughed.

"Yes. And doubtless I will have ample opportunity to remind myself of that." Noelle grinned.

"I think it's rather too late to inform you of my flaws," he said, taking her hand, his thumb tracing caressing circles on her palm. "I think you've seen the worst side of me already."

"If that is your worst, then I'm not worried."

"I shall endeavor to make sure you see nothing but the better part of me from now on."

"I see you as you are, I think, and that is who I want."

"Do you?" He raised a teasing eyebrow, lifting her hand to his lips to place a soft kiss on it.

"Yes." She scooted closer to him. "There is only one thing I have to say."

"And what is that?"

"That tonight is our last night here." Noelle's lips curved up invitingly. "And I don't want to spend it talking about your mother."

"We'll not say another word." He reached out and pulled her over into his lap. "About anything." He bent to kiss her.

CHAPTER TWENTY

THE RIDE BACK to the town house was filled with heated kisses and seemed impossibly short. When they pulled up in front, they separated hastily, doing their best to adopt a look of composure. Grateful for the darkness that hid her face, Noelle slipped out of the carriage and hurried into the house, not waiting for Carlisle. If he was beside her, she feared it would be all too clear how they had spent their time on the ride home. She heard Carlisle enter the house behind her, unnecessarily announcing that he was going to have a brandy in his office.

Noelle spent the next hour in a fever of anticipation, hurrying about her tasks of getting ready for bed, all the while listening for the sounds of Carlisle's footsteps in the hallway. How long would he stay in his study with his drink? Would Carlisle come straight to her room? Or would he go to his own chamber first, allowing more time to pass? Should she get in bed? Remain up? Either way seemed presumptuous somehow, as if she expected him to come to her. She did, of course, but...

At that moment, with the faintest of knocks, the door eased open and Carlisle slipped inside. She went into his arms, all questions and doubts fleeing her head. They came together in a storm of passion, lit by their kisses in the carriage and fanned into fire by the long wait since. With swift, jerky movements, they shed their garments, kissing and caressing as they moved toward the bed. Noelle felt as if her very skin was afire, her body yearning for completion, and when he thrust into her, she caught her breath in a short, sharp gasp, the satisfaction so sweet, so deep, so all-encompassing it was almost unbearable.

Afterward, they lay wrapped together, her head resting on his chest, still idly stroking, touching one another, as if unable to end the moment. Noelle felt his lips brush her hair, his hand slide down her arm. She smoothed her own fingers over his chest, following the hard ridges of his ribs. *The last time*, she thought. Tomorrow they would be at Stonecliffe, and everything would change.

But, oh, the prospect seemed far harder now than she had dreamed a few days ago. Their nights together had been too brief; they had only increased her thirst, not slaked it. She had not foreseen how deeply Carlisle's lovemaking would affect her, how utterly pleasurable it would be. Now she only wanted more and more. Unfortunately, wishes did not change the fact that the end of the affair was inevitable. She let out an unconscious sigh.

Carlisle caressed her hair. "Perhaps we could return to London soon or…well, I'll think of something."

"Don't worry about it. I will be fine." She raised her head to let him see her smile. "And there are many more hours tonight." Noelle slid up to kiss him.

CARLISLE GAZED OUT the carriage window at the buildings of the village without really seeing them. In another two miles, they would reach the lane leading up to Stonecliffe. For perhaps the first time in his life, Carlisle found himself uneager to see it.

The sight of the house rising in the distance, which usually made his heart lift, now aroused only reluctance and a twitchy impatience at the thought of the occupants of the house who would greet them—Nathan, Annabeth, Gil, the countess and her obstreperous mother, the servants. Lord, it was like living in an anthill. Even though the place was enormous, there were too many people always about.

He glanced over at Noelle, who sat looking out the opposite window. He could see only the side of her face—the soft skin, the little tilt of the chin that was becoming so familiar, the curve of a delicate eyebrow—but it was easy to conjure up the image of her smile, the mischievous light that gleamed in her eyes when she teased him, the creamy white complexion, tinged faintly with pink.

A throb of hunger started deep within him, and Carlisle turned resolutely away. He could no longer be her lover; he must become only the guardian of her child, a friend and protector. It had seemed easy enough when she invited him into her room. He could handle it; he would ease the hunger, and then it would be over. Simple.

If only that were the case.

His desire for her was not quenched—far from it. Now that he knew the delights of her body, he wanted more. He should not have been so rash, so thoughtless. But the truth was, presented with the same situation, he would make the same choice. Take the same consequences. Giving up what he had felt the past few days was unthinkable.

"What is it?" Noelle turned to him. "Is something amiss?"

He realized that he had let out a sigh. "No, nothing. Just a trifle restless—we're almost home." Carlisle forced a reassuring smile. He would act as he should, do what was expected of him. He'd always been able to manage his life. It might take a few days of discomfort, but his desire would die down. Everything would return to normal. He would make sure of it.

NOELLE WAS EAGER to see Gil again, and there was even a part of her that was beginning to feel as if Stonecliffe was her home, but beneath those emotions lurked regret, even sorrow, at the thought that this would be the end of her time alone with Carlisle.

Both Lady Drewsbury and Nathan were waiting for them in the entryway when Noelle and Carlisle entered the house. Adeline swept forward to take Noelle's hands and kiss her cheek. "Welcome home. I know you want to see Gil first thing, but he is taking a nap—he quite wore himself out bouncing up and down and running to the window for a sight of your carriage."

"Oh. Well, then I shan't wake him." Noelle thought of going upstairs to take a peek at her sleeping son, but she knew how likely that was to awaken him.

Adeline lowered her voice and cast a cautious glance up the staircase, as though speaking of her might bring Lady Lockwood out. "Mother is napping, too. It's a perfect opportunity for us to sit down and chat."

"Yes," Nathan said as he shook Carlisle's hand and offered Noelle a perfect bow. "I want to hear what Sloane said. I suspect he didn't confess on the spot."

"Far from it," Carlisle agreed as the four of them

walked into the drawing room. He went on to describe their meeting with first Marcus, then Sloane himself. "Sloane was furious that we were talking to his father."

"Probably because Marcus knew something about Sloane's plans."

"I doubt it." Carlisle shook his head. "Marcus was pleased to see us, happy to talk, and not suspicious in the least about why we were there."

"He seemed quite sincere," Noelle agreed.

"Marcus isn't good at lying," Adeline said. "It's one of the reasons he was always such a terrible gambler."

"I'll believe Marcus had nothing to do with it, but that doesn't absolve his son," Nathan pointed out. "I'm sure *he* is adept at lying."

"Probably, though his denial seemed real enough," Carlisle said. "He has an alibi. He was at his fishing lodge in Scotland."

"Fishing in Scotland!" Nathan scoffed. "That sounds unlikely. Is there any proof? Besides, it doesn't matter if he was in Scotland or Constantinople. Sloane doubtlessly sent someone else to actually shoot Gilbert—you know he has a raft of disreputable characters to choose from."

"I know," Carlisle agreed. "Diggs has sent a man to Scotland to find out if he was really there. And he's looking into who Sloane might have hired. But what I can't get past is a motive for him. Sloane doesn't need the money. His home is filled with valuable art and furniture. He owns several houses, including the lodge in Scotland. I saw his carriage in the stable yard as we left." Carlisle's eyes took on a gleam. "You should have seen the horses, Nate. Four prime bays, completely matching."

"He was always showy."

"Yes, but it takes some gold to make that kind of show. Diggs confirmed that he's well set up—shipping company, real estate, a distillery in Scotland. He doesn't need Gil's money."

"The title," Nathan pointed out.

"Would he murder a child to become an earl? He never seemed to give a whit about the title."

Nathan sighed, clearly reluctant to let go of his theory. "I don't know. But who else could it be?"

Noelle spoke up. "Mr. Rutherford suggested an alternative theory."

"Sloane told Noelle that she should watch out," Carlisle explained. "He said the motive was more likely the tontine." He was greeted with blank stares from both his listeners.

"What on earth are you talking about?" Nathan asked. "What's a tontine?"

Carlisle turned to the countess. "Do you know anything about a tontine the earl and his friends might have set up?"

"My dear, I have no more idea what a tontine is than Nathan."

Carlisle explained, though neither Nathan nor the countess looked terribly enlightened. "Lady Adeline, did Drewsbury ever talk about such a thing with you?"

"Goodness, no, dear. Thomas didn't talk business with me."

"It had to have happened before my father died. Sloane intimated that my father and Nathan's father were in on it, along with others. He said they excluded Marcus because of his lack of funds—Sloane was bitter about that fact, which makes me more inclined to believe that he's telling the truth."

"Pretty handy thing to come up with, I must say, since it takes the blame off him and puts it on you and me," Nathan pointed out. "I wouldn't believe anything out of Sloane's mouth."

"Carlisle, wouldn't Drewsbury have told you about it?" Adeline asked. "He must have kept some sort of record if he put money into this thing."

"One would think. But he didn't. Nor did my mother know anything about it."

"You went to see Belinda?" Adeline asked in surprise. "Well, Horace would have told her, I suppose. She was always much cleverer than I about such things."

"I'm not sure. She said Father would have known she wouldn't like it. He might have hidden it from her. What about your father, Nate?" Carlisle asked. "Did he ever say anything? Maybe he didn't use the word *tontine*. Could it have been among his papers?"

"No." Nathan shook his head. "I'm not the dab hand at finances that you are, but I would have noticed anything that odd. Thompkins, Father's lawyer, is dead now, but his son Cato still has the office, and he handles all the family affairs. I'm sure he would have Thompkins's old files. I planned to talk to him while I was home anyway; I just haven't had the time yet. I'll send him a note. He's in Seven Oaks, not far."

"This is all very perplexing." Adeline frowned. "What are you going to do, dear?"

"Look through the earl's old papers again, I suppose. Ask the estate manager—though I don't imagine he would have been privy to that sort of information. We already talked to the earl's lawyer and his agent."

"There's nothing to it. Sloane's trying to waste your time." Nathan looked up at the sound of steps and saw Annabeth in the doorway. He colored. "I beg your pardon, Anna."

"It's perfectly all right." Annabeth smiled at him fondly and shook her head. "You can speak his name; I won't go into a swoon. That was ages ago."

"What was ages ago?" Lady Lockwood demanded, thumping into the room after her granddaughter and heading for a chair. "I say, Addy, must you have these little stools scattered about everywhere?" She poked the small footrest in front of the chair with her cane, knocking it off-kilter. "They're a hazard. Always at one's feet."

"I'm sorry, Mother." Adeline smiled tightly.

"Grandmother, it's your favorite chair," Annabeth reminded her, helping the old woman ease down into the seat.

"I know it's my favorite chair. Only one that's comfortable." She cast a disapproving look around at the rest of the furniture.

"And the chair is more comfortable with your feet on the footstool," Annabeth went on.

"Of course it is," Lady Lockwood agreed. "Chair's too high—made for Thomas, no doubt. I always held that he was too tall." She glanced around. "What have you done with the dog? Petunia? Ah, there she is."

Petunia's nails clicked on the wood floor as she trotted into the room. Catching sight of Carlisle, the animal bounded forward. With a sigh, Carlisle removed the dog from his ankle and placed her in Lady Lockwood's lap.

"There's my girl." Lady Lockwood patted the pug and put her feet up on the stool, settling back in the chair. "Now..." She pinned Nathan with her gaze. "What was ages ago? Who's going to send Annabeth into a swoon?"

"Um, well..." Nathan cast an apologetic look at Annabeth. "It was really nothing."

"He was talking about Sloane Rutherford, Grandmother," Annabeth told her.

"Good heavens!" Lady Lockwood scowled at Nathan. "Why did you bring up that rogue?"

"I didn't—I mean—"

Noelle took pity on Nathan and said, "Mr. Thorne and I were the ones who brought up the subject. We went to see Mr. Rutherford three days ago."

"I told you, Mother," Adeline put in. "They went because someone shot at Gilbert."

"Yes, yes, I know. I'm not in my dotage yet." She focused her eagle eye on Carlisle. "Well, what did you find out?"

"Sloane told us he was in Scotland when it happened and that Noelle should be wary of Nathan and me because of a tontine our fathers set up."

"That idiotic tontine!" Lady Lockwood shook her head in irritation, and everyone else in the room fell silent, gaping at her.

"You know about it, ma'am?" Carlisle sat forward in his chair.

"'Course I do. Adeline's brother was part of it, too."

"Sterling?" Adeline said in astonished tones.

"Yes, Sterling. How many brothers do you have? Annabeth's father, as well. Well, the whole silly lot of them."

"The whole lot of whom, ma'am?" Noelle asked patiently.

"The group of men who hung about at that club—you remember, Adeline, Thomas and Horace were the ones who made it fashionable, and then of course everyone came, so after a time they quit the place."

"Frobisher's?"

"Yes, exactly. Frobisher's."

"Lady Lockwood, do you remember the names of the men in the tontine?" Carlisle asked eagerly. "How many there were?"

"Oh. Well… I'm not sure about that." She paused, thinking. "Drewsbury, Thorne, and Dunbridge—" Lady Lockwood nodded at Nathan. "I'm referring to your father, of course, not you. Those three were the core of that group. Marcus went to Frobisher's sometimes, but the gaming was too tame for him. Sterling, of course, and Annabeth's father, too—you know how Hunter was, he would always do whatever Sterling did. Probably Freddie Penrose. Let me see, I believe Lord Haverstock was around a good bit. There were probably ten or twelve young men who were part of that set, but I don't know that they all participated in this scheme. Sterling called it a trust, but it was clearly a tontine. And so I told him."

"Trust or tontine, there must have been a document laying out the terms," Carlisle said grimly. "Why have Nathan and I never seen it? Or heard of it? It wasn't to be found in Lord Drewsbury's estate papers. I'm certain; I went through them all again when we were in London."

The old lady shrugged. "They kept it very sub rosa. It's the sort of thing that it's best the recipients don't know about."

"So they won't try to murder each other to get the prize," Carlisle said sardonically.

"Yes. They trusted each other, but one never knows how one's children might turn out." She shrugged. "So they agreed not to tell anyone."

"But you knew about it," Carlisle pointed out.

"Sterling told *me*, of course."

"Of course," Adeline murmured.

"Do you know what the terms were, Lady Lockwood?" Noelle asked.

"Not in detail… Sterling gave me the gist of it. It came out of some silly conversation they had—you and Thomas were newlyweds, Adeline, and Nathan's father was engaged. Horace and Belinda had been married a year or two. They were chatting about how they were settling down and having children and that sort of thing, and for some reason they thought up this scheme to create an endowment for their descendants."

"Even the men who didn't have children yet?"

"Yes—well, some of the other men may have already had children. Anyway, the idea was that it was to end on some certain date, I'm not sure when, and the money would be divided among their last living male offspring."

"Only the boys?" Noelle asked. "That hardly seems fair."

"It rarely is, is it?" Lady Lockwood replied.

"This seems a most peculiar arrangement," Carlisle said.

"Well, they had been drinking all evening."

"But they went through with it? You're certain they set up a trust?"

"Yes. I told Sterling it sounded like a fool's game and

he shouldn't throw his money away on it, and he said it had already been done."

"Who drew it up? I spoke with Lord Drewsbury's lawyer, and he knew nothing about it."

"No. I imagine Drewsbury's solicitor would have tried to talk him out of it. They must have used one of the other men's lawyers."

"So Sloane is maintaining that one of the other beneficiaries of this trust is trying to kill Gil so he can claim the money?" Nathan grimaced. "What nonsense! Lady Lockwood just said there were ten or twelve men in that group. Those men had offspring, some of them probably several. It beggars belief that this chap is working his way through all of the descendants, killing them off one by one. No one's taken a potshot at me. What about you, Carlisle?"

"No." Carlisle shook his head.

"A child would be easier to do away with than a grown man," Annabeth pointed out. "Besides, Gil is younger and therefore likely to outlive the rest of you. He could be seen as a greater threat."

"That would make sense," Carlisle agreed. "But there's another problem. How does this person know about the tontine if the thing was kept so secret?"

"Grandmother knew about it," Annabeth responded. "Perhaps one of the other men told his son. Or his wife or a friend. Who's to say that they were all as dedicated to following the rules as your fathers?"

"Annabeth…" Carlisle said carefully. "I know you don't want the villain to be Sloane, but—"

"And you and Nathan *want* it to be him," Annabeth snapped back.

"No. We don't. My only desire is to stop whoever it

is. I intend to look into every possibility, no matter how likely or unlikely."

"Of course." Annabeth lowered her eyes to the needlework in her hands.

"Good." Carlisle settled back in his seat.

Noelle, watching Annabeth thrust her needle into the cloth and yank it through, had the suspicion that Annabeth was not as satisfied with Carlisle's answer as he seemed to think. She decided that she would talk to the other woman about the matter when neither of the men were around.

Just at that moment, there was the sound of running feet in the hall, and Noelle jumped to her feet, all other thoughts fleeing her head. "Gil!"

She hurried out of the room and held out her arms to her son, her heart swelling in her chest.

"Mama! You're home!" Gil threw himself at her, and Noelle wrapped her arms around him, kissing his head as she squeezed him to her. Whoever the villain was, she promised herself, she would find him. No one was going to hurt Gil.

CHAPTER TWENTY-ONE

NOELLE SPENT THE rest of the day with Gil, playing with him in the courtyard garden, laughing at his antics, and listening to his chatter. She ate early with him in the nursery rather than joining the family for supper and followed that by reading to him until bedtime. It was almost as it had been in the past, just the two of them, and she didn't think of Carlisle at all...well, at least not more than once or twice.

But when she went to her room and faced the emptiness of her bed, loneliness and yearning claimed her. She told herself it was absurd to miss Carlisle. They had been alone together only a few days, not long enough to develop a strong attachment. And, in any case, it wasn't as if he was gone from her life. He was right down the hall.

But that was part of the problem—his nearness was a temptation. It would be so easy to slip down the hall to see him, talk to him. Kiss him. Which she absolutely must not do.

Still, when she went down to breakfast the next morning, anticipation rose in her at the thought of seeing Carlisle. They might even be alone at the meal. Nathan had returned to his home the day before, and the countess was not an early riser.

Unfortunately, when she walked into the dining room,

Noelle found that Carlisle had already eaten, and only Lady Lockwood and Annabeth were there. Lady Lockwood was in a particularly obstreperous mood, so much so that Noelle took pity on Annabeth and remained with the two women as they withdrew to the sitting room. Annabeth threw her a grateful look; they both knew Noelle would divert some of the old woman's ire onto herself.

Carlisle joined them not long afterward, his eyes going first to Noelle. "Ah, I thought I heard voices in here. May I join you?"

Annabeth and Noelle chorused agreement as Lady Lockwood harrumphed and said, "We all know whose voice impelled you to visit."

"Grandmother…" Annabeth murmured.

"Surely, Lady Lockwood, you must know I am always drawn by your dulcet tones," Carlisle replied.

Lady Lockwood let out a sharp laugh. "Drawn to leave the house, I'd say."

The butler appeared in the doorway, interrupting their acerbic banter, to say, "Lady Lockwood. Mr. Thorne. Mr. Dunbridge to see you, with a guest."

He stepped aside to usher in Nathan and a tall, pale, very thin young man. The man hung back a bit behind Nathan, looking uncomfortable. Aside from his slenderness and his waxy, almost translucent skin, he was unremarkable in looks. His bespectacled face was serious, his dark suit plain and businesslike. Noelle took him to be a clerk of some sort.

"You're back already, Dunbridge?" Lady Lockwood asked. "I must say, you might as well take up residence here."

Nathan's eyes twinkled, but he swept Annabeth's

grandmother a formal bow and said, "Please forgive me for intruding, ma'am. But I sent a note to my lawyer yesterday, asking him to meet with us regarding the tontine, and he was, as you can see, gratifyingly prompt. Ladies, Thorne, allow me to introduce Mr. Cato Thompkins."

Lady Lockwood turned her piercing gaze on the man, who visibly wilted. "I can't imagine why you thought he could tell us anything. He's far too young to know your fathers' legal affairs."

"His father was my father's attorney, ma'am," Nathan explained. "You might say I inherited him. He is privy to all his father's files and quite familiar with the family business."

"You know about the tontine?" Thorne asked, his eyes brightening.

"Well…that is to say…no, sir." Thompkins tugged a little at his cravat. "When I received Mr. Dunbridge's request yesterday, I went to my father's old files. I looked through them for any documents or even notes of such a thing, but there were none."

Looking at him more closely, Noelle decided that the man's awkward manner made him appear younger than he was. He must have some degree of experience and confidence, which made his lack of knowledge of the tontine more disheartening.

"No correspondence?" Carlisle asked, though his voice held no hope.

"No, sir. I'm sorry," Thompkins replied apologetically. He glanced around at the group. "I wish I could have been of more help."

"Not your fault, Thompkins," Nathan assured him, clapping him on the shoulder and walking with him toward the door. "It was good of you to come all the way from Seven Oaks."

"It was nothing, sir. Happy to do it." Thompkins bowed to the room at large and made his escape.

Nathan turned back to the others. "Sorry. He could have just sent me a note saying that, but he's almost frighteningly conscientious."

"At least we know that your father's lawyer is another dead end," Thorne replied. "Come, join us."

Nathan happily did so, sitting near Annabeth. Noelle imagined that Nathan bringing his lawyer to talk to them had more to do with seeing Annabeth than a need to deliver such paltry news.

"I'm going to write Mr. Penrose to see if he was part of this tontine," Carlisle said after Nathan had settled in with a cup of tea. "Lord Haverstock, as well. I don't know who else I could ask."

"It is unfortunate that so many of those men have passed on." Lady Lockwood frowned as if their deaths were a personal affront. "Even my poor Sterling. Of course, the men in our family have never had strong constitutions." There was a moment of silence as there so often was after one of Lady Lockwood's statements. "I doubt you'll discover much from Freddie Penrose. Haverstock seems a better choice for answers, though they say he's sadly diminished. It seems very careless for Thomas and Horace to have left no information. Surely they realized that they were all going to die."

"I imagine that none of them expected to do so when they did. My father wasn't yet forty," Carlisle pointed out.

"Doesn't it strike you as peculiar that so many of them are already gone?" Annabeth asked. "My father and Uncle Sterling were both in their fifties when they passed."

"My father was only a few years older than they," Nathan added. "Though his health was never particularly good, so none of us thought much of it."

"Are you saying that there was something suspicious about their deaths?" Lady Lockwood glared so hard at Nathan that he finally mumbled, "No, ma'am," and turned his attention to his teacup. Lady Lockwood turned her stare on Annabeth. "You two are both being absurd. Who has ever heard of such a thing? A Lockwood? Murdered?"

Noelle had never thought of homicide as a social solecism before. She made the mistake of meeting Carlisle's gaze, and she had to struggle to suppress a giggle.

Annabeth, accustomed to her grandmother, said, "We weren't saying they were murdered. But it seems odd, and given what's been happening…well, doesn't it make you wonder?"

"You read too much," Lady Lockwood told her. "Gives you peculiar ideas."

"It does seem unusual," Noelle said to Annabeth.

"There was nothing suspicious about your father's death," Lady Lockwood told her granddaughter.

"No, but—"

Lady Lockwood plowed on. "And my poor Sterling died from a fever; he always had a weak chest. As for your father…" She turned to Carlisle. "He tried to take a fence he shouldn't have. Nathan, your father drank himself to death and we all know it. No point beating about the bush or calling it bad health."

Nathan, who had been midsip as Lady Lockwood turned her blunt words on him, coughed into his teacup.

"My heavens, Dunbridge, mind your manners," Lady Lockwood admonished him. "It's excessively common to spit into one's cup. There are ladies present. You should ring for the serving girl to bring you a fresh cup."

"Yes, ma'am." Nathan set the tea down and coughed into his handkerchief.

Noelle clamped her teeth tightly together. This was no time to be laughing. Even in the face of Lady Lockwood's own lack of manners.

"Yes, ma'am, and the earl suffered a heart attack," Carlisle cut in, obviously trying to take her attention off Nathan. "I agree that it's a trifle strange, but I think it was only a twist of fate. For all we know, the rest of the men are still alive. I intend to find out everything I can about the tontine and what happened to the men. I am going to look through the earl's papers again, and, if need be, I'll go back to my house and search it for any clue my father might have left." He glanced at Annabeth with a touch of sympathy. "But we can't ignore that the simplest, likeliest suspect is Sloane. I'm sorry."

"What nonsense," Lady Lockwood said. "Marcus may be a wastrel and his son's a scoundrel, but they are still Rutherfords."

Family status seemed to be Lady Lockwood's standard for determining everyone's guilt or innocence.

"Well, it has to be someone," Carlisle retorted. Noelle thought she actually could hear his teeth grinding.

"It was just a poacher," Lady Lockwood decreed. "Sort of thing happens all the time. Or…if it wasn't some silly accident, the far more likely answer is right here." She wagged her spoon at Noelle. "Any woman who looks like her is bound to have a disappointed swain or two running about. And she's been living among suspicious sorts of people—Frenchmen and Italians and such."

This time Noelle couldn't restrain a bark of laughter. Quickly turning it into a cough, she pressed her napkin to her mouth to smother it.

"Grandmother!" Annabeth exclaimed. "You're being very rude."

"I'm being rude?" Lady Lockwood gestured between Nathan and Noelle with her spoon. "These two are the ones coughing madly. You'd think the whole room suddenly caught consumption. Now, don't you start, too," she went on as Annabeth clapped her hand to her own mouth. "Besides, it's not rude; it's simply the truth. No need to be mealymouthed about it. We're all family."

"We are not all family," Carlisle snapped. "I, for one, am no relation to any of you. And Noelle doesn't have any 'swains' running about. I certainly hope you don't intend to put it out that Noelle's past is anything but respectable."

Lady Lockwood gaped at him. "Whatever is the matter with you? Of course I'm not going to say anything in public. The boy's my great-grandson. But one has to consider the facts."

"The facts are clear," Carlisle retorted, his jaw set. "Diggs has found no threat from anyone from the Continent. The miscreant is right here, and I daresay he's English."

As the two of them glared at each other, Annabeth said, "I'm sure Grandmother didn't mean anything unkind about Lady Rutherford."

"No," Noelle agreed, clearing her throat. "Lady Lockwood would never say anything that would harm the family. Thank you for your support, Mr. Thorne, but I imagine some would say her line of reasoning is a valid possibility." Her last words held a sardonic twist.

Carlisle turned a sharp gaze her way, then grimaced, murmuring, "Point taken." Visibly relaxing his shoulders, he nodded to Lady Lockwood. "I apologize if I have given you any offense, Lady Lockwood. I fear my temper is a bit on edge these days."

"Of course." Lady Lockwood swept the matter away with a flick of her hand. "Your father always looked just so when he was being mulish."

Noelle finished her tea quickly and escaped before laughter could overtake her again. She heard footsteps hurrying after her, and Carlisle said, "Noelle. Please wait."

She stopped and turned as he came up to join her.

"I'm sorry."

Noelle smiled. "No need to be. I have become well enough acquainted with Lady Lockwood to expect the sort of thing she says."

He shrugged a shoulder. "Yes, but… I mean about what I said in the past, too. I didn't—it wasn't—"

Noelle raised her eyebrows, her voice teasing. "Yes? I do hope you aren't about to tell me again what you had mistaken me for in the past."

He let out a groan. "I suppose you'll never let me forget that."

"Probably not," she agreed lightly as she started down the hall, Carlisle strolling along beside her. "But I long ago decided that you aren't to blame for your aristocratic ignorance."

"You're too kind," he said sardonically.

"You probably shouldn't have hurried after me like that. It might make Lady Lockwood suspicious."

"Fortunately, Lady Lockwood has so many suspicions, no one takes them seriously." He sighed. "But I suppose you're right. I shouldn't…it's just…I didn't see you last night at dinner."

"No. I ate with Gil and put him to bed. I was rather tired so I went to sleep early myself." That was something of a lie, as she had spent a good bit of time tossing and turning first, but she saw no reason to let him know that.

"I missed you. I mean, it was odd," he backtracked quickly. "Not seeing you. We'd been together so much the past few days."

"Yes."

"I wish…well, it doesn't matter." He shoved his hands into his pockets and stopped. "Yes. Well. I should get to work." He made no move to leave. "What are your plans for the day?"

"I thought I'd work in the library this morning while Gil is at his studies."

"I'm sure you missed him a great deal."

"Yes. It was wonderful to be with him again." She beamed.

"I wish…" Carlisle glanced away, his jaw clenching. "I should get to writing those letters."

He nodded to her and turned away. She watched him stride off down the hall, wondering what he had been about to say.

NOELLE WAS ON the upper walkway of the library later when a woman's voice interrupted her cataloging. "Excuse me."

Noelle turned to see Annabeth standing in the doorway below. "Miss Winfield."

"Please, call me Annabeth."

"Of course. Annabeth." Noelle set aside her pad and pencil and started down the winding staircase to the floor below. "Please come in. May I help you?"

Annabeth walked forward to meet her, glancing around the room as she did so. "Aunt Adeline said you were working in here. I hope I'm not disturbing you."

"Not at all. It's a task that will take me years, so a few minutes scarcely matters."

"What are you doing?" Annabeth asked curiously.

"Cataloging the library."

"Oh, my."

Noelle chuckled. "Yes. It's an even larger task than I envisioned. I suppose I should say that I am *attempting* to catalog it."

"I'm sure you're doing an excellent job. I should be happy to help you...that is, if you'd like some assistance."

"Of course. You're more than welcome. But I fear most people would find it rather boring."

"It's certain to be more enjoyable than listening to Grandmother snipe at poor Aunt Adeline."

"I would imagine so." Noelle relaxed into a smile. She wasn't quite sure what to make of Annabeth. The woman was so uncomplaining and patient with her grandmother that Noelle was tempted to think of her as meek, but there were flashes of humor, even tartness, that made Noelle wonder what was hidden beneath the woman's surface. "I, um, would you like me to show you what I'm doing?"

"That would be nice, but, first, I want to talk to you." Annabeth drew a breath and began. "I know Nathan and

Carlisle are convinced that Sloane is behind the attack on Gil, but I am certain it's not so."

"Oh. Well…I…we must consider everyone who might benefit," Noelle replied carefully. Annabeth must still have feelings for the man, however poorly he had treated her.

"No. I see what you are thinking—that I'm an empty-headed girl still in love with a scoundrel, that I am blind to his faults. But that's not true. I'm not in love with Sloane any longer. Once perhaps I would have argued that he could do no wrong. I was so mad about him that even his faults seemed endearing. But that was many years ago, and I have come to accept that I was foolish. That he did not return the feelings I had for him. However, all those girlish hopes and dreams aside, the fact is that I have known him all my life—long before I fell in love with him. We grew up not far from each other, and I was with him more often than either Nathan or Carlisle were. They don't know him as I did. I am certain that Sloane isn't the one who tried to hurt your son."

"I hope you are right."

"I am. I swear to you. I have no idea if the people in that tontine scheme are the ones who are threatening Gil. But I *am* sure that looking for evidence against Sloane is a waste of time. I fear that Carlisle won't look at anyone else because he and Nathan are positive that it's Sloane even though they haven't any proof. Nathan and Carlisle aren't rational where Sloane is concerned. And while they concentrate on Sloane, they won't be hunting for the person who really did try to harm your son. It leaves Gilbert in danger."

Her words knotted Noelle's stomach. Carlisle said he was going to look into all the possibilities, but what if Annabeth was right? What if he was too fixed on the man he already disliked to really consider anyone else? "Why are you so certain Sloane didn't do it? Do you know something that proves it?"

"I know Sloane." Annabeth gazed earnestly into Noelle's eyes. "He isn't an easy man, and his temper burns hot. He is quick to take offense and very sensitive about his father. He always had a great deal of anger toward the earl. But he would not harm a child. He simply would not."

"If it helps you any, I'm not convinced Mr. Rutherford is the culprit either," Noelle told her.

"Truly?"

Noelle nodded. "He was belligerent and sarcastic, and I have little doubt that he is a hard man, but I thought his surprise seemed very real when Carlisle brought up the attacks on Gil. He wasn't secretive; he was quite open about his dislike for the Rutherford family and his disinterest in the title. I have no idea whether he would hesitate to get rid of a child who stood in the way of something he wanted, but, truthfully, he didn't seem to want it very much."

Annabeth nodded. "He was always scornful about the succession and the title." She reached out and took Noelle's hand, squeezing it a little. "Thank you."

"I have not entirely ruled him out," Noelle cautioned. "But I certainly intend to keep looking at all other possibilities." She shrugged. "The problem, unfortunately, is that at the moment, none of the possibilities seem very likely."

"Could Grandmother be right that it was just a poacher? An accident?"

"I suppose, but Carlisle clearly doesn't think it was."

"Carlisle is a very cautious man." Annabeth's mouth quirked up. "But, irritatingly, he's usually correct."

"Yes."

"Thank you for listening," Annabeth said, then straightened her shoulders a little and glanced around. "Now…if you could show me what to do, I would be happy to help you."

Noelle was quick to take her up on her offer, handing Annabeth a pencil and paper and assigning her the bookcase next to the one she was herself recording, and for the next couple of hours, they made their way through the shelves, chatting as they worked.

They talked mostly of the past. Noelle was intrigued by Annabeth's stories from her childhood with Carlisle and Nathan, and, somewhat to her surprise, the other woman seemed equally interested in hearing about Noelle's growing up in her father's easygoing, even lax, care. Annabeth told her stories in a light and amusing way, with that wry twist of humor that Noelle had glimpsed in her now and then. She was friendly and likable, with none of the haughtiness that Noelle had seen in many of the women at Lady Halder's party, and she listened with a bright and focused interest.

Noelle began to think that perhaps she had found a friend, or at least the potential for one, in this new life. Still, she could not help but notice that, however pleasant a companion Annabeth was, she did not show much of herself in her conversation. There was something very contained about her—not so much aloofness as a sort of separation, an unseen barrier between her and the rest of the world.

They worked together in the days that followed, and Noelle quickly grew to trust the woman, which made

Noelle doubt Sloane's guilt even more. But she had no other suspects. Carlisle had promised to keep her informed on anything he learned—which, so far, had been absolutely nothing of consequence.

It created a sense of incompleteness and constant anxiety in Noelle. Late at night, though, she had to admit to herself that her inner turmoil and yearning also sprang from her diminished time with Carlisle. Even the time they were together was spoiled by the other people around. She had to constantly stay on guard to keep herself from gazing at him for too long or speaking to him too informally—she had to squelch every urge to touch his hand or face. It was exhausting. And even more disheartening, it seemed as if Carlisle, so absorbed with his task, wasn't struggling as she was to keep their distance. Her only hope was that it was his aristocratic upbringing that allowed him to hide his emotions from her—and not that he didn't feel them.

CARLISLE STOOD LOOKING out the window of his study, aware of the same restlessness that had swirled inside him since they returned to Stonecliffe two weeks ago. The fortnight had seemed twice as long as that. He'd written to Lord Haverstock and Penrose, but neither had written back to him.

In the meantime, Carlisle had had ample things to occupy him, not only the usual matters of business around Gil's estate or dealing with his own agent, but also a thorough search of all the earl's old records. It was painstaking work, dull and unrewarding, but that wasn't what made him restless. No, his disquiet was caused by one thing only, and that was Noelle—or, rather, the absence of Noelle.

She wasn't gone, of course. That was the problem. Noelle was right there in the house every day, all day. He saw her at meals and in the evening; he ran into her in the halls—especially since he had taken to roaming through the house aimlessly at various times through the day. He knew that he had only to go into the library or the drawing room and he would see her. He knew that every afternoon she spent time in the courtyard garden with her son. He could easily join them, could sit on a bench beside her and talk as they watched Gil play.

He also knew that doing any of those things would draw attention to them and cause speculation. Lady Lockwood had eyes like an eagle and a suspicious mind...not to mention an acerbic tongue.

If they didn't live in the same house, this thrumming lust inside him would surely die down. He wouldn't spend his nights tossing and turning if he didn't see her every day. If he didn't smell a trace of her perfume in the air or hear her voice. If he did not see her smile.

He could, he knew, resolve the problem by returning to his own home, at least for a while. He had a convenient excuse—he needed to look through his father's papers again for some mention of the tontine. Yet day after day he dawdled and procrastinated.

He thought of asking Noelle to accompany him to his estate to help him with his father's papers. The thought conjured up visions of days spent with her, nights in her bed. But that excuse was the thinnest of reasons and might arouse suspicions. Besides, it would be beyond foolish to take Noelle to his home. He needed to end the affair, not continue it.

Of course, it didn't have to be an affair. There was marriage. But surely that would be an even greater folly.

Carlisle barely knew Noelle, really. Marriage required more than passion, and that was all they had between them. It was, admittedly, a more intense attraction than he had ever felt for any woman, but he didn't love her. He *wanted* her. Yes, she had a quick wit and could hold her own in conversation. She was strong and loyal and fierce. He looked forward to seeing her each day. He hungered after her, dreamed of her at night. But none of those things were love. Were they?

"There must be something terribly fascinating out in the garden."

"What?" Carlisle turned to see Nathan lounging in the doorway, one shoulder resting against the frame. "Sorry. Just thinking. I didn't realize you were there."

"So I noticed." Nathan strolled into the room and dropped into one of the chairs, stretching his long legs out in front of him. "What occupies your thoughts so?"

"Nothing." Carlisle shrugged a shoulder. "Nathan, what do you want in a wife?"

Nathan stared. "I beg your pardon? Are you wife shopping?"

"No. 'Course not. Just an idle thought."

Nathan narrowed his eyes but said only, "Love might be a consideration."

"I mean beyond that. Something more substantial. Trust, don't you think?"

"Well, not the first thing that comes to mind, but, yes, one would want to be able to trust one's wife. You know the woman I would choose. But, since Anna-beth won't have me… I suppose it would be someone I wouldn't mind spending the rest of my life with. So far I haven't found someone that I could put up with for longer than a week." He paused, then said, "What brings this on?"

"Oh…nothing in particular. This matter of the tontine, I guess, got me thinking about the future. Marriage and heirs and all that."

"Ah, the duty of producing heirs. Are you considering bloodlines, then? I hear that Benningfield's daughter is out of mourning now. Her mother's line goes back to the Conquest, but I wouldn't think it's worth it."

"God, no. I don't really care about her family."

"What do you care about?"

"I'm not entirely sure." Carlisle smiled and shook his head. "Enough of this nonsense. I suggest we seek out the ladies. Their conversation's bound to be more interesting."

They found Adeline and Noelle in the drawing room with Gilbert, who was playing on the floor between them, tiny tin soldiers spread around him. "You found the toy soldiers," Nathan said and settled down on the floor beside the boy, picking up a red-jacketed figure. "I always loved these. Remember when I'd bring over my set, Carlisle, and we'd have massive battles?"

"*I* certainly do," Adeline said, chuckling. "I remember when Thomas stepped on one of them in his stockinged feet."

"You're very kind, Nathan, but you'll get your clothes dusty," Noelle protested.

"Ha! Bennett would never allow a speck of dirt to linger on one of his floors. And Gil and I have become fast friends these past few days, haven't we?"

Gil nodded. "We caught butterflies while you were gone, and we went up into the attic one day."

"The attic?" Noelle cast a laughing look at Nathan. "My, you are a friend indeed."

"Yes, and they came down looking like chimney sweeps, both of them." Adeline smiled fondly. "The boys always loved exploring up there. I cannot imagine why."

"It's a world of mystery and wonder," Carlisle told her, coming over and squatting down to look at the toys.

Gilbert's head went up and he looked toward the window. "Somebody's coming."

He jumped up and ran to the window that faced the courtyard garden. "It's a man."

Carlisle joined the boy at the window just as a thunderous knock sounded at the front door. "Good Lord." He turned around, his face grim. "It's Sloane."

CHAPTER TWENTY-TWO

"WHAT THE DEVIL!" Nathan rose to his feet, his hands knotting at his sides. "Where is Annabeth?"

"Where is Mother is the better question." Adeline's eyes grew round. "She's the one who's likely to stab him with her knitting needles."

"I wouldn't stop her," Nathan retorted.

Noelle started to say that she had seen Annabeth going out to the back garden to pick flowers, but at that moment Sloane Rutherford strode into the room with somewhat less fury than the last entrance Noelle had seen him make, but looking no less antagonistic. The butler trailed after him, saying, "Mr. Rutherford, please. If you'll just allow me to introduce you."

"I think they know me," Sloane replied dryly, stopping just inside the room. "Thorne." His gaze slid over to Nathan, the corner of his mouth curling up in a sneer. "Dunbridge. Of course you would be here." He glanced down at the tiny army scattered around Nathan's feet, and his eyes glinted mockingly. "Still playing with tin soldiers?"

Gil studied their guest with interest. "Hello."

Sloane blinked, whatever he was about to say dying on his lips, and his face softened slightly. "Hello. You must be the Earl of Drewsbury."

Gil laughed. "That's silly. I'm only five." He went

up to Sloane, offering the polite bow Noelle had been trying to drum into him. "How do you do?"

"I'm well, thank you." Sloane's lips curved faintly, though it could hardly be said to be a smile, and he reached down to shake the boy's hand. "I am your cousin, Sloane."

"My cousin," Gil said wonderingly. "I didn't know I had a cousin."

"I am the family member they like to hide." This time the quirk of his lips was actually a smile, albeit a small one.

"Mama and I used to hide, too," Gil offered in a comforting way. "But then Uncle Carlisle found us, and we don't have to now. Maybe he can help you."

Rutherford let out a short, quiet laugh. "I wouldn't count on that. The fact is, I have come to help *him*."

"Gilbert," Adeline said, rising, "I believe Mr. Rutherford and Mr. Thorne need to talk. Why don't you and I go see if Cook has any of those tarts left?"

Gil jumped on this idea eagerly, taking the older woman's hand and leaving the room. A silence fell as Noelle, Carlisle, and Nathan watched Sloane. He turned back, looking a bit distracted, as if the moment with Gil had thrown him off stride. He straightened, setting his jaw, but he could not quite regain the bellicose attitude with which he had entered the house.

"My father wanted me to bring you this," he said abruptly, reaching inside his jacket and pulling out a folded piece of notepaper. "I told him about your reason for calling on him. He had me write down the names of the group who set up the tontine."

"Really?" Carlisle's eyebrows rose in surprise.

"Yes, really. Do you think I rode all this way on a lark?" Sloane scowled.

"No. I was just…surprised." Carlisle reached out to take the note and unfold it.

"It's not like you to go out of your way to help someone," Nathan commented. His arms were crossed, his expression fierce.

Sloane looked at him for a long, cool moment. "I'd say I have a vested interest in providing the names of possible murderers other than myself."

He turned and walked out the door.

"Well, you two were certainly rude enough." Noelle sent Nathan and Carlisle exasperated looks and started after Sloane, calling out, "Mr. Rutherford! Wait. Please."

Sloane stopped in the hallway and turned, waiting expressionlessly as Noelle hurried toward him. She heard the other two men following her, but she didn't glance back as she extended her hand to Sloane. "I wanted to tell you how much I appreciate this. It was very good of you to come all this way."

It didn't surprise her when he shrugged off her thanks, saying, "I had to return to London anyway—it's only a trifle farther." But a ghost of the smile he had shown her son touched his face as he bowed politely over her hand.

"Yes, thank you, Sloane," Carlisle added, coming up behind Noelle. "I am grateful."

Sloane cast him a sardonic look. "I'm sure."

As he began to turn away again, a sharp gasp came from down the hall. Sloane turned, his gaze going to the door at the end of the corridor, where Annabeth stood as if rooted to the spot. The basket of flowers she carried slid from her grasp, spilling irises and hollyhocks across the floor. Sloane's hands clenched at his side, and for a short, charged moment, the two of them stared at each other in silence. Then Sloane whirled and strode out the front door.

Annabeth broke from her momentary paralysis. She reached down to retrieve the basket, her movements stiff and jerky. Nathan let out a low curse and started down the hall toward her, but she shook her head and backed up, not looking at him, and he stopped, his face a study in frustration.

Noelle laid a hand on his arm. "No, let me. You and Carlisle go back to the drawing room."

Nathan hesitated for a moment, then did as she said, and Noelle walked over to Annabeth. The other woman's eyes were filled with tears and her face was bone white, but she continued to pick up the flowers. Without a word, Noelle began to help her.

Annabeth set the basket down on the hall table with a thump. "They're ruined."

"There are plenty more in the garden," Noelle responded, dumping the stems she had gathered into the basket. "Annabeth…"

The other woman shook her head, wiping away the tears that had spilled onto her cheeks. "Silly of me— for an instant I thought that he had come to see me."

Noelle took her arm. "Why don't we go sit in the garden?"

"You're very kind." Annabeth summoned up a smile. "But I'm fine. You needn't worry. I don't know why I reacted so foolishly. It's been years and years. I don't go about moping over him. Really. Or even think about him. I gave up loving him long ago. It was just… I don't know, seeing him unexpectedly like that. He looks so different…and so much the same."

"Years dull the hurt," Noelle said. "But I think it hangs about in one's heart, just waiting to pop up again."

"Do you still miss Adam?" Annabeth looked at her. "Is it still so painful?"

"Sometimes, when Gil smiles in a certain way or I see one of Adam's paintings."

Annabeth nodded. "I'm sorry. I think I'll go up to my room and rest a bit. Would you reassure Nathan that I'm all right? He worries so."

"He cares for you."

"I know. I care for him, as well." Annabeth sighed. "I just wish that I cared for him in the same way." She started toward the stairs, then turned and looked back. "Why was Sloane here?"

"He brought us a list of the men in the tontine."

Annabeth smiled faintly. "So he helped you. I knew he couldn't have tried to hurt Gil."

"No. I think you were right." Noelle swung around and went to the drawing room, where she found the two men engrossed in studying Sloane's note.

Carlisle looked up at her entrance. "There are ten names."

"Do you know them?" She went over to stand beside him and look at the scrawled list of names.

"Some. They're our fathers' age; a good number of them are dead."

"What about their sons? Lady Lockwood said it was based on a male heir who would still be alive by a certain date."

"It's only the original participants, but we can find

their sons' names. This gives us a place to start looking."

"We have to consider the fact that this could all be a hum," Nathan pointed out. "Something Sloane made up to throw us off his trail."

"I don't think he's guilty," Noelle said.

"Neither do I," Adeline said from the doorway. She walked over to join them.

"Just because Sloane brought this list, it doesn't mean he's innocent. I think we have to continue to suspect him," Carlisle said.

"You can suspect him all you want, but it doesn't make him guilty," Noelle retorted a little acerbically. "Whatever else he may have done, I don't think he tried to kill my son—not after I saw him with Gil."

"She's right," Adeline agreed. "The way he looked at the boy, the way he spoke to him. Smiled at him."

"It could be a pretense," Nathan said stubbornly.

"I think you want him to be guilty." Noelle crossed her arms and looked from one man to the other. "Both of you. Nothing he has done or said indicates that he tried to murder Gil. Just the opposite."

Carlisle let out a reluctant sigh. "I think they're right, Nathan. Much as I hate to admit it, it's hard to believe Sloane's behind this. He doesn't need the money. And would he really murder a child to get a title?"

"I don't know." Nathan scowled. "But it seems unlikely that anyone would kill Gil in order to win the tontine money either. There are ten men listed here." He waved at the sheet. "A number of them are bound to have sons and grandsons. One would have to kill an inordinate number of people."

"That's certainly a point," Carlisle admitted. "I have no intention of clearing Sloane yet. Diggs is still looking into Sloane's unsavory connections, as well as his Scottish alibi. However, these men must be investigated, too. Let's make note of all the possibilities, the signers and the heirs."

Noelle went to the countess's dainty secretary against the wall and pulled out a piece of paper. "I'll write down the names."

"Nathan's father and mine are both deceased, as is the earl." Carlisle started at the top. "That leaves Nathan and me. Well, Gilbert, too, of course, but I think we can ignore him."

"I believe so." Noelle uncorked the inkwell and settled down to write.

"Lady Drewsbury's brother, Sterling Lockwood, who passed away two years ago," Carlisle began. "Annabeth's father, Hunter Winfield, died a few years ago." He glanced over at the countess, who was dabbing at the corner of her eye with a handkerchief. "I'm sorry, ma'am. I don't mean to distress you. Perhaps we should talk about this somewhere else."

"No, it's all right. They've been gone for some time; it's just sad, thinking about them all together like that. But this is important." She straightened her shoulders. "None of my brother's or sister's heirs would inherit. They're all girls."

"Since females are barred from the contest, that eliminates several already," Noelle pointed out.

"Yes, we must be grateful for their lack of fairness." Carlisle sent her a sardonic look and went on, "Vinson Brookwell. Is he still alive?"

"I've no idea," Adeline said. "He had several children, as I remember. I'm sure some of them were sons."

"Yes, Milton was my age. But he died at Waterloo." Carlisle looked at Nathan. "What was the other one's name?"

"John," Nathan supplied. "I've seen him at the club every now and then." He shrugged. "You know, the sort of person whom you nod and smile when you see each other, but never really converse. I don't know anything about him."

"Lord Haverstock is still alive, though I understand he has retired to their estate," Lady Adeline supplied. "His eldest boy, Sprague, died last year in a boating accident. His other son, Timothy, has always been a sickly lad. His other child was a girl—I believe Annabeth was somewhat friends with her when they were younger."

"So Haverstock has only one son remaining, and he is unlikely to outlive anyone." Carlisle frowned. "Our number of possible villains is shrinking by the moment. What about—" He stopped, raising his head, as a voice trumpeted down the hallway.

"Adeline!"

The countess sagged. "Oh, dear. Mother is up from her nap." Her words were confirmed by the sound of Lady Lockwood's distinctive shuffle, punctuated by the thump of her cane, though it moved at a faster pace than usual.

"Actually, she would be a great help," Nathan pointed out. "She knows everything about everyone."

Adeline brightened. "That's true. Mother doesn't get out much, but all the gossip comes to her."

"What is going on here?" Lady Lockwood steamed into the room. "Annabeth won't answer my knock. And her door is locked. I need her to carry my things. She knows I always come downstairs at this time."

"I'm sure she's fine, Mother," Adeline said soothingly. "I'll send one of the maids up to get your things."

"Humph. She already is." She motioned toward the door, where a harassed-looking maid stood, her hands full of Lady Lockwood's knitting bag and other necessities. "No doubt she's left something behind. Annabeth knows just what I need." As Adeline steered her mother toward her usual chair, Noelle took the old lady's possessions from the maid and settled them beside Lady Lockwood. "What's the matter with Annabeth? That's what I want to know."

"I'm sure she's fine," Adeline repeated. Not having witnessed the earlier scene in the hallway, she sent a worried look toward Noelle and murmured, "She didn't see—"

Noelle nodded, but said only, "It's nothing to worry about, Lady Lockwood. Annabeth's just taking a bit of a rest."

"A rest. Annabeth? Is she ill?" Lady Lockwood swung on her daughter. "What do you mean, 'she didn't see'? See what? What's going on?"

"Sloane Rutherford was here, ma'am," Carlisle told her.

"Here?" Lady Lockwood slammed her cane down on the floor. "That man! Did he come to bother Annabeth? I trust you sent him away with a bee in his bonnet, Thorne."

"Actually, he brought us a list of the men who were in the tontine with the earl. And we could certainly use your help in studying it. Lady Drewsbury and I are unsure about them and their children."

His words satisfactorily distracted Lady Lockwood. Her gaze sharpened and she rapped her cane on the floor. "Well? Get on with it, boy, who are they?"

"Mr. Penrose."

"Freddie Penrose," Lady Lockwood said in a disgusted tone. "I can tell you right now, he had nothing but girls, so I'm certain there's no danger from one of his children. As for Freddie himself...pfft." She flicked her fingers. "That man is lucky to find his way home; he couldn't possibly plan a murder."

"Richard Snowden and Sir Basil Cunningham," Carlisle said, listing the members they had not yet examined.

"Basil Cunningham never married. Snowden... hmm," Lady Lockwood mused. "Oh, I remember. He married one of those French émigrés. Bit of a dustup. His father was not pleased. Now, what's their son's name?"

"But why was the family upset?" Nathan asked. "I thought Lady Snowden was an aristocrat; that's why they fled Paris."

"Yes, of course." Lady Lockwood waved away the objection. "But they're French. And they hadn't a penny to their name; they escaped with the clothes on their backs and that's all."

"Oh!" Noelle looked up in surprise. "I met her." She turned to Carlisle. "She was at Lady Halder's party. I remember the French ambassador's wife introduced me to Lady Snowden because I could speak French. I'm certain she said something about her son. Gaspard?"

"Of course." Lady Lockwood emphasized her words with a thump of her cane. "Damned silly name."

"I believe it's French, Mother."

"But why saddle an English lad with a French name?" Lady Lockwood retorted. "They had another boy, too, now that I think of it. Another foolish name. Filbert or something."

"Fulbert," Noelle said, giving it the French pronunciation. "But I believe Madame Blanchard—the ambassador's wife—told me he died several years ago. He was climbing a tor and fell to his death when he was sixteen. He was the older of the two."

"So, another deceased heir," Carlisle summed up. "That leaves rather few people—Nathan, me, Brookwell's younger son, Haverstock's younger son, and this Gaspard fellow."

"That's also a great many deaths," Nathan put in grimly. "Six of the original signers. Four of their heirs."

There was a long moment of silence, then Adeline said, "But, Nathan, surely someone didn't do away with that many people?"

"That's ridiculous," her mother said. "Brookwell's boy died in the war. Some boys died as children; Sprague Haverstock drowned in a boating accident. All the others who died were old men."

"And several of the original signers are still alive," Adeline added. "Lord Haverstock and Sir Basil, Freddie Penrose, Mr. Snowden, Mr. Brookwell."

"No, Vinson Brookwell died some years ago," Lady Lockwood corrected. "Accident while he was cleaning his gun, they said. But I suspect that was a kind lie. More likely killed himself. He was never the same after Milton died at Waterloo."

"I have to point out that the large number of deaths also means a rather small number of suspects," Carlisle said. "One of those remaining is Gil, who is the intended victim, and two of them are Nathan and me, who I would hope we can assume are not the perpetrators."

"Which leaves only John Brookwell and Gaspard Snowden," Noelle said. "Unless one thinks the Haverstock who is in poor health is doing it."

"Yes, I suppose we can't leave him out," Carlisle agreed.

"What about the creators of the trust who are still alive?" Nathan asked. "You said there were four of them, correct? I can imagine that the men who had no children or had all daughters might resent the fact that they have no hope of winning the prize. Does it have to be an heir who receives it? Could it be one of the original men if they outlived everyone else?"

"Or possibly it reverts to them if all the heirs die," Carlisle mused. "If so, would they split it among them? That would be a larger amount than they put into it, depending on whether the fund has grown. We have no idea how it's distributed. Or when it terminates. Or how much money is in the trust." A heavy silence fell on the room as they looked at each other in frustration.

"Then we had best get started." Noelle rose from her chair. "We need to find that agreement. It will answer most of our questions. And we have to talk to these men. Lord Haverstock, Mr. Snowden, Sir Basil, Mr. Penrose." She turned to Carlisle, her eyebrows raised in question.

"Yes. Hopefully one of them has it. Or, at least, they can direct us to the lawyer who drew it up. I'd like to speak with the surviving sons, too. John Brookwell and Snowden. The younger Haverstock son." Carlisle paused, thinking. "Haverstock's place is in Sussex, isn't it? We can travel to my home and look through my father's papers, then go on to Haverstock's to speak to him." He stopped abruptly and turned to Noelle. "That is, if you wish to accompany me."

"Yes, of course." Noelle's pulse picked up a little at the thought. She and Carlisle would be alone again. It was terrible, she knew, that her mind went to that thought when there was such a serious matter at stake. "I'm Gil's mother. I must help. And two people to observe are better than one." It occurred to her that she was giving too many explanations. Last time, she had simply, forcefully, said she would go. Last time, before Carlisle and she had made love. Before she felt guilty.

Belatedly, she turned to Adeline. "If you do not mind being in charge of Gil for a few days."

"Nonsense." Lady Drewsbury beamed. "I'm happy to look after him. And dear Nathan, I'm sure, could be persuaded to join us again." She cast a smile at Carlisle's friend.

"I would never pass up the opportunity to be with three charming ladies." Nathan added with a grin, "And frankly, I sorely miss Mrs. Demson's cooking when I am at my own estate."

"Luckily for your appetite, that is a rare occasion," Lady Lockwood said pointedly.

"I'm going to send Diggs a message to come here, as well," Carlisle told him.

Nathan raised his brow. "Are you suggesting I won't be able to protect Gil?"

"No, of course not. But I want to have someone to patrol the grounds as well as you watching over Gil inside the house. I don't want to leave it to just the gardeners and grooms. And Diggs will be far more useful here than he is in London, looking for something to point to Rutherford. He'll be under your direction, naturally."

Nathan nodded. "Yes. I see. Perhaps he will be able to dig up some local information about who shot at Gil, as well."

"Good. It's settled then." Carlisle nodded. "The only question now is where we should go from Haverstock's?"

"The Snowdens are in London," Noelle offered. "Or, at least, they were when we were there."

"I am sure Freddie Penrose lives in the city. They always have some daughter or other making her come-out," Lady Lockwood said. "And I cannot imagine Sir Basil anyplace but London. Who else?"

"Actually, that's all the original signers who are still alive. But I'd like to see the heirs, as well; they're our suspects. Timothy will be at the country house with his father. If you see Brookwell at your club, Nathan, then he must live in London, as well."

"Yes, I believe so. Though I can't remember last time I saw him."

"If we're lucky, Snowden's son lives in London, too."

"No, I believe the Snowden boy lives in Yorkshire." Lady Lockwood frowned. "Can't imagine why."

"Then I suggest we leave him until last," Carlisle said. He looked again at Noelle. "Is tomorrow too soon?"

"No." Noelle had to press her lips together to keep from smiling. It wouldn't do to reveal any of the excitement she felt at the prospect of spending several days alone with Carlisle. "It won't take me long to get ready."

"Excellent." Carlisle smiled no more than Noelle did, but the look he sent her told her that he was looking forward to the trip as much as she was.

"I'll start immediately." Noelle turned and left the

room, her steps light and her heart buoyant as she hurried up the stairs. Tomorrow, she thought, tomorrow she wouldn't have to wait or dissemble. Tomorrow she could be with Carlisle.

CHAPTER TWENTY-THREE

NOELLE PACKED QUICKLY, though she found she lingered over decisions of wardrobe far longer than she had in the past. Afterward, she spent the remainder of the day with Gil. The extra time was, she knew, more for her than for Gil, who seemed to have no worries about her being away. Indeed, he seemed delighted at the prospect of again being left under the doting eye of his grandmother.

After he had eaten and she'd put him to bed, Noelle returned to her room, but there was nothing left to do. She decided to say her farewells to Adeline, for they would be leaving early the next morning, long before Adeline normally arose.

She was almost to the door of Adeline's chamber when the sound of Lady Lockwood's stentorian tones stopped her. Perhaps she should come back later, after Adeline's mother had left. Hand raised to knock, Noelle hung there for a moment in indecision.

Lady Lockwood went on, "I cannot understand how you could let him leave with that woman."

Noelle stiffened. "That woman" was undoubtedly Noelle. She knew she should turn and go, but curiosity made her linger for another moment.

Inside the room, Adeline replied mildly, "I can hardly tell Carlisle what to do, Mother. He's a grown man."

"Grown men could benefit from being told what to do," her mother retorted. "I would talk to him about it myself, but he won't listen to me. He would, however, listen to you."

"But why would I want him not to take Noelle with him? She has every right to go; she's Gil's mother. It can only help to have her along. Carlisle listens to her, as well."

The old lady let out an indecipherable noise of disgust and banged her cane on the floor. "Of course he does. That's the problem."

"I can't see how. Noelle is very levelheaded, I've found, and quite smart. I vow, sometimes when she starts talking about books, I have no idea—"

"Don't be a ninny, Adeline. I'm not talking about her intelligence. I'm talking about the fact that Carlisle is smitten with her."

Noelle glanced up and down the hallway. She should not eavesdrop. It would be most embarrassing to be caught lurking outside Lady Drewsbury's door. But she could not pull herself away, not when they were discussing her and Carlisle. She took a soft step closer.

"Do you think so?" Adeline sounded pleased. "I have wondered about it, but I couldn't be sure. Carlisle hasn't said anything, but sometimes there is this look in his eyes. And he smiles more than he used to. It's much nicer this way. You know, at the beginning, they did not get along at all."

"Well, I am happy you think it's 'nice,'" her mother replied acidly. "I hope you'll find it just as 'nice' when they drag the family into a scandal."

"Mother! What a thing to say. They've done nothing

to cause a scandal. I just told you, they've been most circumspect."

"It won't remain that way long if they keep jaunting off alone together. I doubt he will be so 'circumspect' when there's no one around to see. I don't care how far away we are from London, word will get out that Thorne and your grandson's mother are having an affair!"

"You don't know—" Adeline began, but her mother rode roughshod over her words.

"It will be a horrid scandal. That woman has already caused one stain on the family name by eloping with Adam. She has no name, no breeding—"

"Mother!" Adeline's voice rose. "She has a very good name—Rutherford. She has as good a manners and speech as any lady I know, and she knows a good deal more than most. Noelle is a wonderful mother, and she has been nothing but good to me. I quite enjoy her company."

Noelle's chest warmed at Adeline's praise. More surprising, however, were Lady Lockwood's next words. "I enjoy her company, too. She brightens up the dinner table, even if I find her conversation too bookish at times. And, thank heavens, she's neither bold nor a mouse. But what does that matter? I'm talking about gossip. How do you think it will affect Gilbert's standing among his peers?"

"He's only five years old, Mother."

"People have long memories. What about *your* reputation? How can you countenance Carlisle keeping his mistress under the same roof as you?"

"That's enough!" Adeline said in a far sharper tone than Noelle had ever heard her use with Lady Lock-

wood. "I won't allow you to slander Carlisle and Noelle. I told you that they have done nothing untoward.
If they love each other, they will marry. There won't
be any scandal."

"Love!" Lady Lockwood said scornfully. "Carlisle
won't marry for love. You should know him better than
to spout that pap. He will marry for sound reasons—
family, name, breeding—yes, breeding, because, whatever you say, that is much more than good manners or
proper grammar. It's knowledge that is bred in the bone,
an understanding of what it means to be a lady, a realization of one's place in the world and the responsibili-
ties that are required of her position. Carlisle will marry
someone who is like him, like us. Someone who has
aristocratic bearing and is related to important people.
Most especially, he will not marry anyone attached to
scandal. You know how he feels about his mother's re-
marriage so quickly after his father's death. He felt the
sting of the gossip; he realized the inappropriateness
of her behavior. Carlisle never acts impulsively or out
of emotion. And he will not marry some shop-owner's
daughter because of 'love.'"

"Her father was a professor," Adeline replied heatedly, "and Carlisle would marry her if she—"

"If she managed to get with child?"

"Well, yes, but not just that. He would marry to protect her from gossip and scandal. If they were in fact
swept away into improper behavior, he would not keep
Noelle as a mistress. He would marry her."

Lady Lockwood grunted. "I will give you that—he
probably would tie himself to her just to keep a scandal from entangling you and Gilbert. But that is exactly
why you must tell him to go on this quest by himself. It

is your duty to keep him from the temptation. To stop the scandal before it starts."

Noelle turned away, her stomach churning, and went back to her room; she could not face Adeline right now. However pleasant it was to hear Adeline's approval, Noelle had learned about life in a far harsher school than the countess. She knew that Lady Lockwood was right. Carlisle would marry someone more appropriate.

As Lady Lockwood had said, he would marry her if she became pregnant; he was honorable above all else. But the last thing Noelle wanted was to trap him in a forced marriage, where whatever affection he had for her would be worn away daily by his resentment and regret.

She reminded herself that she had gone into this with eyes wide open. She had told herself she didn't love Carlisle any more than he loved her. But she could no longer fool herself that she was teetering on the edge of falling in love with Carlisle. The truth was that she had already tumbled into that dangerous chasm.

How could she continue an affair with him, knowing that he would never be truly hers? Could she live like this, hiding her feelings, grabbing little bits of time with him, all the while knowing he would marry someone else? Her pride, her heart told her no.

But neither, she thought bleakly, could she give him up.

CARLISLE AND NOELLE departed early the next morning and arrived at Carlisle's home late in the afternoon. His house was built of red brick, with one wall covered by climbing ivy. It was not as grand as Rutherford Hall, but it was warm and inviting.

"Do you like it?" Carlisle asked Noelle as they started toward the door, his voice unaccustomedly hesitant.

"Yes, it's lovely," Noelle said. "It's...welcoming. You must be very happy to see it again."

"I am. And I am very happy to show it to you."

It took only a few minutes to introduce Noelle to the small staff. Jamison, his butler, apologized profusely for not having prepared a bedchamber for Noelle.

"Perfectly all right, Jamison. It's hard to be prepared when I gave you no warning of my arrival. Just make up, um, the blue chamber for her, and I shall take Lady Rutherford for a tour of the house while you're doing that."

His home was a comfortable place, with furniture built more for comfort than fashion and long windows in every room to let in light. In the rear of the house was a glassed-in conservatory filled with greenery. Noelle let out a little gasp of delight. It was a light and airy space, lush with small palms and ferns and flowering plants she couldn't identify. Waxy-leafed orange trees that would perfume the air when they bloomed. This, Noelle thought, would be her favorite room if she lived here.

But she must not think that way. It didn't matter that she could picture Gil romping with a dog through these hallways or herself in a chair in this sunny room; it was foolish to dream about.

Later, they ambled through the garden, meandering along the twisting paths until the one they were following ended in a small arbor. Graceful trellises on three sides created a small enclosure, surrounded by red and white roses tangling together and perfuming the air.

It was lovely and secluded, and they were utterly

alone. Noelle looked up at Carlisle. Somewhere along the way, he had taken her hand; it had felt so good, so right, that it had scarcely registered with her. In the shadow of the arbor, his eyes were deep and dark, intent on her face. Without thinking, she took a step closer, and his arms closed around her, pulling her up into him.

He kissed her, heat surging between them. She pressed against him, her lips answering his. Every thought, every doubt, every sensible hesitation fled from her instantly. All that existed was this moment, this kiss, this almost unbearable pleasure. Carlisle made a noise deep in his throat, and his hands moved over her, stroking her back, her hips, her buttocks.

Desire teased through her, a delicious yearning that was certain it would be satisfied. Noelle had thought she remembered how this felt—how her flesh tingled, the way her blood heated, the coiling hunger deep within her. But the reality was so much more than her memory, every part of her alive. She slid her arms beneath his coat, her hands roaming over his chest and back.

His clothes were an impediment, so she began to unbutton his waistcoat, then the shirt beneath it. At last her fingers were on his skin, warm and smooth and now familiar in a delightful way. His lips left her mouth and worked their way down her neck, seductive and slow, while his hand slipped beneath the neckline of her dress and curved around her breast.

It wasn't enough. She wanted more. Noelle reached behind and began to undo the hooks and eyes that fastened her dress. Carlisle quickly moved to help her, and she reached for the waistband of his trousers. He groaned and bent to kiss the flesh exposed by her sagging dress. They continued to undress in the same haphazard manner, their clothes pulled off and dropped beneath them between kisses and caresses.

Spreading his jacket atop their discarded clothing, Carlisle pulled Noelle down with him and covered her with his body. Fallen rose petals lay all around them, their scent drugging, pulling Noelle ever more deeply into the blind thrall of passion. Need rose in her, insistent and powerful, and she dug her fingers into Carlisle's back, murmuring, "Now."

He thrust into her, satisfying her physical need as well as something far deeper inside her. They moved together, each thrust and retreat adding flame to the fire, knotting the desire ever tighter until at last it exploded, sweeping them into a cataclysm of pleasure.

For a time, Noelle simply lay there, languid and limber and at peace, Carlisle's body warm against her, and gazed up through the tangle of roses above her.

The roses. The garden. "Carlisle!"

"Mmm-hmm," he mumbled against her neck.

"We're outside!"

"I know."

She shoved at his shoulders. "For goodness' sake, get up. What if someone came along and saw us?"

"They won't." A laugh rumbled through his chest, and he sat up, but moved no farther, gazing down at her. "There's no one around except the servants and they won't come looking for us. I'm the only one here to see you." His hand moved slowly down her body. "And I like what I see very much."

Noelle rolled her eyes at his words, but she made no move to push his hand away. She loved his touch and the way he looked at her. Reaching up, she caressed his cheek, brushing back a strand of his hair. If only it could always be like this. Words of love pushed up through her throat, and she pressed her lips together tightly to hold them inside.

She turned her head, lest what she felt showed in her eyes, and glanced around them. "I cannot believe we just tore off our clothes and…"

"Oh, I can," he responded. "I'd been thinking about doing exactly that all day."

"You planned it!" Noelle laughed. "I might have known. I wondered what had you in such a deep study. Deep thoughts, I assumed…and all along, you were just planning to seduce me in the arbor."

He chuckled. "Oh, I wasn't thinking just about that." He rose to his feet. "I laid out a great many plans." Grinning, he reached down to pull her up. "And I intend to show you every one of them."

CHAPTER TWENTY-FOUR

CARLISLE KEPT HIS PROMISE. They made love that night in his bed, first slowly and gently, and then, waking in the night, again with a fierce, urgent passion. Noelle fell asleep in his arms, warm and content.

Unfortunately, they slept too deeply, and Noelle popped awake suddenly the next morning at the sound of the door handle turning. The maid! The handle rattled, not turning, for Carlisle had had the foresight to lock the door. But the maid would go to Noelle's room next to clean out the ashes and set the fire to burn off the morning chill.

Noelle jumped out of bed and threw on her shift, frantically turning to grab her clothes that were strewn about. Carlisle slipped out of bed after her, going to the wall between their rooms. Reaching behind the bookcase, he pulled a lever, and a small, door-sized section of the wall swung open, leading into her bedchamber.

Her bedroom was still empty. Noelle darted through the door as Carlisle tossed her pile of clothes in after her and closed the connecting door. She jumped into bed and yanked the covers up to her neck just as the hallway door opened quietly. Noelle kept her eyes closed, keeping her breath as slow and even as her shaken nerves allowed.

She listened to the soft sounds of the maid working at

the fireplace, her entire body tense until the door closed again. Letting out a breath of relief, Noelle opened her eyes and sat up, glancing around the room. Her clothes lay in a heap on the floor. She wondered what the maid had thought of that. Hopefully she assumed Noelle was a careless aristocrat who never gave a thought to tidying up after herself.

Noelle brushed her hands across her face, holding them against her flushed cheeks. She wondered if the maid knew about the door into Carlisle's room. There was little to indicate it was there, only a very thin line separating it from the rest of the wall. But surely the butler had known the opening was there, which cast a different light on Carlisle's placing her in this room. Did Jamison assume she would be sleeping in Carlisle's bed? Was it a habit of Carlisle's to bring home female guests to stay in the connecting room?

Firmly she pulled her mind away. She was not going to let such thoughts spoil the day. She was going to enjoy this time as the gift it was. And after that…well, she wasn't sure.

"WHAT DO YOU suppose we will find out here?" Noelle asked that afternoon as they climbed out of the carriage in front of the Haverstock house.

"Really, at this point, I no longer have any idea what to expect. It all seems so…"

"Fantastical?"

Carlisle nodded. "Yes, I suppose. But what's happened to you and Gil is very real, and I sincerely hope Lord Haverstock can make it clearer."

The door was answered by a tall, thin footman who took Carlisle's card and disappeared, returning a few minutes later to lead them down a long hall. They emerged at last into a pleasant sitting room, where a low fire burned in the fireplace despite the summer warmth.

A young man of slight stature sat in a wheeled bath chair beside the fireplace, a crocheted throw across his legs. A woman some years older stood beside him. Their kinship was immediately apparent in the light brown of their hair and the smattering of freckles across their cheeks. There the resemblance ended, for the woman was tall and her cheeks filled with color, whereas the man was small and slender to the point of frailty, and his face was pale and sallow.

"Mr. Thorne. Lady Rutherford." The young man nodded to them. "Timothy Haverstock. Pray forgive me for not getting up." The young man gave a ghost of a smile, gesturing toward his covered legs in silent explanation. "Allow me to introduce my sister, Lady Priscilla Haverstock."

"I'm pleased to meet you." Priscilla came forward to shake their hands briskly. There was a competent, no-nonsense air about her.

They spent the next few minutes politely chatting, neither of the Haverstocks betraying a hint of the curiosity they must be feeling at the unexpected visit.

"It's rather some distance from Stonecliffe," Priscilla commented finally. "Would you like some tea? You must be tired from your journey."

"That's very kind of you, but no. The trip was only three hours. We're staying at my estate."

Priscilla's brow rose a little in surprise. "Alone?"

"Lady Rutherford's son and his governess are with us, of course," Carlisle lied smoothly, then went on, "I am sorry to intrude, but we would very much like to speak to Lord Haverstock. I wrote him about a rather important matter and have received no answer. Time is of the essence, I'm afraid."

"My father is somewhat disinclined to receive visitors," Priscilla replied. "Perhaps my brother or I could help you."

"That's very kind of you, but it regards a business arrangement Lord Haverstock had with my father and Lord Drewsbury many years ago. I myself have only recently become aware of it."

"My brother has taken over much of our father's business matters," Priscilla countered.

Timothy chuckled. "I fear my sister exaggerates my share of the estate business. Priscilla does most of the work. She's always been ahead of me in math. Even Sprague—" He broke off and turned his head away. Priscilla's eyes were suddenly moist, though she blinked it away immediately.

Noelle felt a wave of sympathy for them; clearly their brother's death still affected them. She said gently, "I am so sorry for your loss. We don't mean to disturb you or your father. But I fear this business is separate from anything in your estate."

"It has been, well, rather secret," Carlisle said. "I discovered its existence only a few days ago. And it is rather important. I promise we will not bother Lord Haverstock for long."

Priscilla's eyes were curious, and Noelle suspected that it was more than their pleas that made her say, "Yes, all right. I'll take you to my father."

She led them down the hall and into another short corridor, stopped at a closed door and knocked, saying,

"It is I, Papa." Without waiting for a reply, she opened the door and stepped inside. "You have visitors."

Noelle and Carlisle followed her into the room. It was dim, with heavy brocade curtains pulled across the windows, the only light coming from a candelabra placed on a desk. A man with the same unmistakable Haverstock freckles, though slightly faded, in a fleshy, dissipated face sat in a wingback chair, a glass of light brown liquid beside him. From the rather strong smell and the blurred look in Haverstock's eyes, Noelle suspected that the liquid was alcohol.

He made a faint motion as if to rise, then sank back into the chair. Noelle and Carlisle went closer. His daughter closed the door and sat down in a chair beside it, so quiet and unobtrusive that one could almost forget she was there. Noelle wondered if Priscilla already knew about the trust or if she would be hearing it for the first time today.

"Lord Haverstock, I apologize for the intrusion." Carlisle bowed politely and introduced himself and Noelle.

"Lady Rutherford…" The old man repeated, frowning at Noelle. "Who—"

"I am Adam Rutherford's widow," Noelle explained. The man looked worse close up. His face was flushed and puffy, the shadows beneath his eyes almost purplish, deep grooves running down from his mouth. She thought of Lady Lockwood's words about him—"he's sadly diminished." He was diminished indeed.

"He's gone, too." The old man shook his head. "All our sons. Poor Adam. Poor Sprague." He turned toward Carlisle. "Not you. You're Horace's boy? Yes, I can see it in your eyes. Come. Sit. Sit." He took a large gulp and lifted his glass to Carlisle. "Join me, won't you? Cabinet's over there." He waved vaguely. "You'll excuse me if I don't get up—it seems I'm a mite unsteady."

"Thank you, sir, I'm fine." Carlisle and Noelle sat down across from him.

Haverstock turned his eyes to Noelle. "Easy to see why Drewsbury's son chose you. Did you know my son? Sprague?"

"No, sir, I'm afraid not." She noted that he did not mention his other son.

"I knew Sprague a bit, sir," Carlisle put in. "He was a year or two behind me at school. I'm sorry for your loss."

The old man nodded. "Been a year now. A year and a month."

"It must have been very hard for you," Noelle said. She wondered if the man had always been like this, sitting alone drinking in a gloomy room in the middle of the day, or if Sprague's death had sent him on a downward spiral.

"Sprague was..." Lord Haverstock shook his head, swallowing hard. "No matter. He's gone now. Nothing can bring him back." He straightened a little. "What did you want to ask me?"

"It's about an agreement made by my father, Drewsbury, Nathan Dunbridge's father, and several other men about thirty years ago. Lady Lockwood said—"

"Good Gad, do you mean she's still alive?" He let out a little grunt. "Don't know why I'm surprised. She'll be here long after all the rest of us are gone, no doubt."

"Probably." Carlisle gave him a faint smile and returned to the subject. "Lady Lockwood told us that you were a member of that group. You used to meet at Frobisher's."

"Oh, yes. We were the cock o' the walk back then. At least, we thought we were."

"I was hoping that you could tell me about this agreement—you invested money, with the idea that it would be inher—"

"Agreement!" Haverstock almost spat the word. "Damned curse, that's what it was. It's killed us and our sons."

"I'm sorry, Lord Haverstock, but what do you mean? What's 'killed' you?"

"Not me yet, but it won't be long." He leaned his head back. "Thomas and Horace. Sterling. Dunbridge. Winfield. Brookwell—he couldn't stand it, you see, when his boy was killed at Waterloo. Put a gun to his head himself." He looked intently at Carlisle. "You'd better watch out for yourself. It's after our sons, too."

"What is, sir? What's 'after' us?"

The older man waved his hand in a vague circle. "Fate. Destiny. The curse. We shouldn't have done that, you know. It's tempting fate, gambling with your children's lives. I'd understand if it was just us. Cruel to take our children, too. Brookwell's boy was the latest."

"Brookwell, sir? You mean Milton?"

"No, no, Milton was killed at Waterloo, I just told you." He frowned at Carlisle. "The younger one. James. John. Something like that."

"John Brookwell died?" Carlisle glanced over at Noelle.

Haverstock nodded. "Couple of months ago. Disturbed a robber, you see, and they bashed him over the head with a fireplace poker."

"I'm sorry to hear that."

Noelle wondered how Carlisle could be so calm. Her own heart was hammering inside her ribs. Another of the heirs dead? This went far beyond coincidence.

"All I have left is my Timothy, and it's clear he'll be gone soon enough. Frail—always has been. We nearly lost him last winter. The least thing can carry him off." He stared moodily down into his glass, adding, "Bloody Freddie."

"Freddie Penrose?" Noelle asked. She remembered Lady Lockwood's slighting reference to the man yesterday.

"Aye." Haverstock's mouth twisted. "It was his idea, well, his lawyer's, I suppose. Freddie's not the sort to have ideas."

"Mr. Penrose's solicitor drew up the agreement?" At the old man's nod, Carlisle went on, "Do you have a copy of it, sir? Nathan Dunbridge and I have found nothing of it in any of our fathers' papers."

"Drewsbury always thought it was a bunch of rot. I think he went along with it just because Dunbridge wanted it. Everyone knew Dunny's lands were mortgaged to the hilt. They're a pleasant lot, you understand, but money has always slipped through the Dunbridges' fingers."

"This document, sir," Carlisle said, bringing the conversation back to his question. "Do you have a copy of it?"

"No." The old man waved his hand. "All very hush-hush, you know. I think that was part of the fun. Freddie's man kept it. He took care of the money. Invested it." He sighed. "It was a bit of lark, you see. A gamble. One might have only girls, as Freddie did. Sir Basil turned out to have no children at all. Bloody stupid idea…like rolling dice on your children's lives. It's why we're cursed." He looked into Carlisle's eyes intently. "You understand, don't you? It's not natural for sons to die before their fathers."

"No, sir, it's not." Carlisle paused. "I—I'm trying to understand…do you remember the main terms? Could you tell us when it was supposed to end?"

"Ah, well… I don't remember exactly. It went down to all the heirs, grandsons and so on. Ends a few years from now—we had to set a date, because it couldn't run on forever. Some legal thing."

"But surely there might be more than one of the men's heirs alive when it ends," Noelle pointed out. "What would happen then?"

"Split it up among them evenly."

"Just the heirs? Not the men who originally set it up, too?"

He shook his head. "No. It was for the future, you see. Doubt any of us will still be alive then anyway."

"But what if none of the heirs outlived it? What would happen then?"

"Goes to some charity. A foundling home." He sighed, settling deeper into his chair, his words slurred. "You should talk to Freddie. Not that he'll know much, but he'll send you to his solicitor."

They took their leave of Lord Haverstock, nodding a goodbye to Priscilla. As they made their way toward the entrance, Noelle murmured, "Another son dead? How many does that make now?"

"Far too many for my liking," Carlisle answered. The footman opened the front door and they walked out, but just as he started to close the door, there was the clicking of rapid heels on the floor of the hall behind them, and Priscilla called, "Wait. Mr. Thorne. Lady Rutherford."

They turned, and Priscilla joined them outside, closing the door behind her. "I'm sorry. I wanted to say— that is, I needed to speak in private with you." She stopped, her hands clenched together in front of her. "I've never heard about this trust you mentioned."

"Neither had we," Carlisle assured her. "It was quite by accident we found out."

"Of course, girls were excluded," she said, with a bitter twist of her mouth. "I don't suppose it really matters; I doubt Timothy will live to see that day. The thing is— well, I thought you ought to know that Timothy and I don't believe that Sprague died in a boating accident."

"I'm not sure I understand." Noelle couldn't think of a delicate way to phrase her question. Was she saying he died in a different manner? That he wasn't really dead? As strange as all this was turning out to be, she wouldn't have been surprised by anything.

"I mean that it wasn't an accident. Sprague was an excellent sailor. He'd done it all his life."

"I remember that he and Sloane used to go sailing," Carlisle said.

"Yes." She nodded emphatically. "He wouldn't have made a mistake. The weather was perfect that day. Papa has decided to believe all this nonsense about our being doomed, though I didn't understand till now why he believed he was cursed. He needs some reason for Sprague's death, some explanation for fate's cruelties. Some way to justify his own...retreat from the world. He cannot accept, as Timothy and I believe, that Sprague was murdered."

"Murdered?" Carlisle said carefully. "Are you certain? Sometimes even the best of sailors can make a mistake."

"No. Sprague was often foolish, but never when it came to his boat. He—there was blood and a lump on his head; they said he'd probably hit his head on something as he went over. And there were bruises all around his throat. He was wearing a scarf I knitted for him." Tears filled her eyes, but she plowed ahead. "They say it probably caught on a hook and he hung there for a while before slipping on down into the sea and drowning."

"I see your concern."

"Excuses!" She dashed away the tears, her voice vibrating with anger. "They're all excuses. My aunt and uncle want to cover it up to prevent a scandal, and Papa chooses to believe it's a terrible stroke of fate. Timothy says they probably believe Sprague committed suicide, that he wanted to die at sea. But he didn't! I know he didn't! Sprague wouldn't have left us. He wouldn't have left Timothy. Or me. He'd always looked out for us." She stopped, swallowing hard. "But what you said to Father—so many of those people have died. Do you think someone is doing away with them all? Sprague and John and Adam and I don't know who else?"

"We don't know. A few suspicious things have happened. That's why we want to talk to all the men involved."

"Will you tell me?" Priscilla gripped Carlisle's arm, her eyes intent on his. "If you find out anything about Sprague? About who—did this thing?"

"I will let you know," Carlisle promised. "If we discover anything, we will write you."

"Good. Good." She relaxed, letting her hand fall

from his arm and taking a step back. "Thank you. Both of you. Thank you."

Noelle watched the other woman walk back into her house. "Poor woman." She looked up at Carlisle. "If she is right…"

"Someone really is trying to kill his way to this money," Carlisle finished for her.

CHAPTER TWENTY-FIVE

THEY DROVE TO the inn in the village to eat an overdue luncheon and discuss what they had learned at Lord Haverstock's. Noelle opened her reticule and pulled out the notes she had made the other day, jotting down the new information.

"Several of the original signers have died," she said. "It's a trifle odd, but they were growing older, and the deaths have reasonable explanations."

"Besides, they can't get the money, so there's no reason for anyone to do away with them," Carlisle added.

"There weren't a large number of male children to begin with. Milton Brookwell died in battle; clearly his death wasn't planned. Nor was Adam's."

"Are you sure?" Carlisle asked carefully. "Could someone have arranged for him to fall off that bridge?"

"I can't see how." She frowned, thinking. "He was out drinking with his friends. We'd..." She sighed. "We had argued about the money he spent; he'd bought me more useless jewelry. So he stormed out and went carousing with his friends. He drank too much and was 'larking about,' his friends said. He was walking along the stone wall of the bridge, and he lost his footing and fell. His friends saw it happen. They would have noticed if someone had given him a push. Besides, how could a killer have known that he would be out that particular night, drink too much, and decide to walk along the edge of the bridge?"

He nodded. "I think it's safe to say it was an accident. Nathan and I are alive, and there have been no attacks on either of us. Or Timothy, I assume."

"But he's in poor health, everyone knows that. They would have only to wait a short while for him to die," Noelle pointed out. "The only ones who could have been victims are Sprague and John Brookwell. And Gil." They were silent for a moment, then Noelle said, "Carlisle…we are rapidly running out of suspects."

"I know. With Brookwell gone, we are down to only Gaspard Snowden and Timothy Haverstock. I suppose it's possible Lord Haverstock could be behind the killings, so that Timothy gets the inheritance before he dies. Though I cannot imagine him doing away with Sprague."

"No, I cannot either." Noelle leaned back against the cushioned seat back. "You know…" She sat up straighter, turning to Carlisle. "There's another person who would like for Timothy to inherit—his sister."

"Priscilla?" Carlisle's eyes widened. "No, surely not."

"Why not? She was understandably bitter about the fact that females were excluded from the agreement. She's very protective of her brother and father, and she's stronger and more forceful than either of the two men. Let's say she wants Timothy to get this prize and knows he won't last many more years, so she decides to help the thing along. And—" She held up a forefinger to make her final point. "I would venture to guess that whatever fortune her brother has when he dies will go to her. So she will get the money in spite of the terms of the agreement."

He stared at her for a moment, then his gaze turned thoughtful. "I can see your argument, but do you really think she would have killed her older brother?"

"No," Noelle admitted. "And it would make no sense for her to raise suspicion about Sprague's death if she were the one who did away with him. Still...perhaps her conclusion of foul play about her brother's death gave her the idea. She realized then that Timothy could win the thing if only she got rid of a few others. That would leave her with having to kill only Mr. Brookwell, Mr. Snowden, and my son."

"And Nathan and me."

"That's true." Noelle sighed. "It's a great many people for anyone to contemplate murdering." She sighed. "Oh, Carlisle...perhaps she was wrong about Sprague and he did commit suicide. Or perhaps his death, like Adam's, was simply an accident. Brookwell's house could have been robbed. What if we are on entirely the wrong trail?"

"This is the only trail we have. You can't think of anyone from your past who would want to kill Gilbert. You don't believe it's Sloane. I cannot imagine how anyone else would benefit. Yet someone has tried to abduct Gil, repeatedly, and someone fired at him that day on our ride."

"And we have this oddity of several men dying at young ages," Noelle added.

"Didn't Gaspard Snowden have an older brother who died when he was young?" Carlisle said thoughtfully.

"Yes, in a climbing accident. Are you suggesting that Gaspard started out by doing away with his own brother?"

"It made him heir to the title," Carlisle pointed out. "Maybe it gave him the inspiration for the rest of it."

Noelle nodded. "He does seem the likeliest suspect. Indeed, he looks like the only suspect left. Where does he live—was it Yorkshire? Shall we go there?"

"Yes, but first, I think, to London. It's time we talked to Freddie Penrose."

NOELLE WOKE UP before dawn. Carlisle's arm was around her, enfolding her in his warmth. It was so sweet, so good, to lie here like this with him. In this moment, feeling his breath against her hair, his heart beating in a slow, steady rhythm beneath her head, she could pretend that this happiness would endure, that Carlisle loved her and they would be together, that she would not in a few days have to return to her role as a friend—or not even that, really, merely someone whom he was obligated to protect and help, the mother of his ward.

She had slept little tonight, awakening more than once, her mind churning, her chest aching. How was it possible to feel the sorrow of the future mingling with the pleasure and sweetness of this moment? She wanted to smile and snuggle closer to him; at the same time, she thought she might start to cry.

Around the edges of the drapes, the dark was turning lighter. It was almost dawn. She should go back to her room now, before the arrival of the maid sent her scurrying as it had yesterday. Her throat tightened. Softly, she pressed her lips against Carlisle's skin, then slipped out of bed and put on her dressing gown. At least she had been better prepared tonight.

"Noelle?" Carlisle's voice, rough with sleep, came from the bed. "What is it?"

"Nothing. Go back to sleep. I'm returning to my room."

But he had already slipped out of bed and was pulling on his trousers. He came to her and wrapped his arms around her from behind, kissing the top of her head. "There's still time. Come back to bed."

Noelle shook her head, her throat tightening, and after a moment, he said, "What is it? What's wrong?"

"Carlisle... I can't do this anymore."

"Do what?" he asked carefully, his body going utterly still behind her.

"This." She swept her hand out in a vague, encompassing gesture. "Creeping back to my bed so I won't be found out. Deceiving everyone, pretending—I cannot do it. No matter how much I want you, this is wrong. I feel...dirty. I am being the sort of woman you thought I was when you met me."

"Noelle, no." He stepped back, putting his hands on her shoulders and turning her to look at him. "I don't think that. I was wrong to ever assume it. I was arrogant and hard and stubborn. But now, I—"

"I'm not accusing you of still believing I'm a loose woman. But you know that others among your peers believe I am. I cannot afford to give them any further reason to think so. You saw Priscilla's face yesterday when you said we were staying at your estate; you had to lie, pretend that there were chaperones with us."

"I made them think Gil wasn't at Stonecliffe to protect him in case they might be the ones behind this."

"That's all very well, but we both know that that was not the reason you said it."

He frowned. "All right. Yes, I lied to her because I

will not let anyone think ill of you. There is nothing wrong with that."

"I thank you for doing so. But it is wrong because it goes against your nature. You cannot continue to do so, if for no other reason than that someone will recognize the lie. Word will get out. Blast Lady Lockwood for being right!"

"Lady Lockwood! What the devil does she have to do with it?"

"I heard her talking to Adeline. She's afraid that you and I will cause a scandal. And she's right—she already suspects, or at least she is afraid of what you and I will do. If she does, so will others. Servants will talk. There will be gossip. It will hurt Lady Drewsbury's reputation and more, it will hurt her that I deceived her. And Gil—I can't allow his good name to be tarnished because of his mother's indiscretions." She stepped back, drawing a breath to steady herself. "We have to end this."

"There would be no scandal if you married me," Carlisle said quietly.

"No!" she cried out, whirling away. It was just as Lady Lockwood had said: Carlisle would marry her, no matter how little he wanted to, in order to prevent a scandal. He would sacrifice his future because of his sense of honor. "That is the last thing I want. Marriage should be about love, not the opinions of others. I believed that when I eloped with Adam, and I believe it still. I will not marry for anything but love."

Carlisle looked at her for a long moment, his eyes dark, his face immobile. "I see." He stepped back. "As you wish." He turned away and picked up his shirt from where it lay on the chair. He pulled it on and began doing up the buttons, his eyes fixed on his task.

Noelle watched him, her heart breaking. If only he would say something. Some secret part of her had hoped that he would deny her words, that he would say he loved her and wanted her to be his wife for no other reason than love. Instead he had simply accepted it, as cool and calm as ever, and gone on to the next task.

"No doubt you are right," he said now. "Do you wish to go on to London with me? Or would you prefer to return to Stonecliffe?"

"I would like to continue the investigation." It would be hard, being with him, having to see him, talk to him, knowing he was lost to her, but she might as well begin now. It would not get any easier by fleeing to refuge. There were many more years of this ahead of her. "I'll go to London."

Carlisle nodded, and Noelle's spirits sank lower than she'd thought possible. She knew she would dissolve into tears if she stayed in this suddenly cold and suffocating room a moment longer, and she could not risk that. She would never be able to recapture their friendship if Carlisle thought her helplessly in love with him. He would probably stay away from her entirely if he thought his presence caused Noelle to suffer. And losing him entirely was the last thing she wanted.

She took a deep breath to steady her voice. "I'll get ready for our trip, then." She averted her eyes to hide her tears and hurried to the door to her bedroom. Though she needn't have bothered—she glanced back as she shut the door and saw that Carlisle was not even watching her, but had turned away.

WELL, THAT HAD certainly not been what he expected. Carlisle sat down, bracing his elbows on his knees and dropping his head into his hands. In all his tangled thoughts about marrying Noelle, he had not considered that she would turn him down.

He'd thought she might worry and fuss a bit about scandal, and he would have to reassure her that any scandal would die down, and anyway he didn't care what other people thought of him. It had never entered his mind that she would tell him she didn't love him.

He had awakened this morning, happy with the world and looking forward to another day alone with Noelle. He'd even gotten out of bed with the goal of enticing her back into it. Now his world was turned upside down.

Damn Lady Lockwood. He should have guessed she would find a way to spoil everything. He should have pursued that point, reminding Noelle that Adeline's mother delighted in ruining things, and she shouldn't let the harridan ruin their happiness. He should have made reasoned arguments or kissed and cajoled her into changing her mind or…well, just about anything except suggesting marriage.

The words had jumped out of him without thinking. He'd been impulsive, as he never was, and it had clearly been a mistake. That look on her face—anger? horror?—would haunt him. And the way she had so flatly declared that marrying him was the last thing she wanted!

The last thing. The words kept resounding in his head. It shouldn't have come as a surprise, he supposed. He knew Noelle was romantic. She would never marry for practical reasons or for affection or passion, the sort of things he felt. Only a glorious love would do for her. The kind of love she had had with Adam.

Did she feel so little for him? He wasn't asking for her to love him madly. He knew he was not the kind of man to inspire grand passion. He was too dull, too staid and unemotional. But surely she had some spark of feeling for him. There was so much love in her—for Adam, for Gil, even, he thought, for Adeline now. Was there nothing there for him?

He ached to go after her, to throw himself at her feet and tell her how much he could not bear to lose her. To beg her to stay with him, love him, marry him. But of course that was foolish. He could not force Noelle to love him, and it was pointless and cruel to make her feel guilty about hurting him.

He had to accept her decision. It was the way of the world, and Carlisle had long known it. People left, one way or another; one couldn't hold on to other people, and it was pointless to cling. His only choice was to resume the shell of the relationship they had or go away. Carlisle wasn't about to do that.

He would accept it. He would adjust. It might be difficult to regain his footing, but surely he could recapture the easy, friendly way that had existed before he ruined it with his desire.

THE CARRIAGE RIDE was dreadful, filled first with an empty silence and later with awkward conversation. Carlisle was remote and formal, and several times Noelle had to struggle to hold back tears. She had burst into sobs after she left Carlisle's room, pressing her hand to her mouth to keep him from hearing. She refused to cry in front of him, but throughout the day, the ache in her chest seemed to expand, as if the effort to hide her sorrow was forcing it deeper into her body. It filled her up like ice in her soul until she wondered if she would ever be warm again.

It was a relief to reach London and be able to escape to her room. She did not go to dinner, sending down one of the maids with a note saying she was not hungry and, being tired from the long journey, she was retiring early. Carlisle sent up a tray of food for her, and his silent consideration brought the all-too-ready tears to her eyes.

Noelle barely picked at her food. She had been telling the truth about her lack of hunger. Nor had she lied about being tired, though she thought it was more heartsickness than weariness that weighed her down. However, sleep eluded her. She tossed and turned, her brain unwilling to shut down. She hadn't thought it would hurt this much. More than once, she heard Carlisle's footsteps down the hall, and she wanted to get up and go to him, tell him she'd been silly and wrong and hold him until her chest didn't hurt anymore. But she restrained herself. She couldn't go back. She had done the right thing.

The next morning, her sleepless, unhappy night showed in her face. Her eyes were puffy and red-rimmed, her skin pale and dull, and her expression was desolate. It would not do. She must face up to the future and learn to live with Carlisle without either intimacy or their recent forced formality.

Pinching her cheeks to bring back a little color and setting her face into a determinedly pleasant expression, she went downstairs to breakfast. It cost her a pang to see Carlisle sitting there at the table, so much like always, but she managed a smile. They exchanged a few commonplace niceties. He made a wry remark, and Noelle chuckled. They would manage, she thought, no matter how heavy her chest was.

"I sent a note round to Freddie Penrose," Carlisle told her. "He replied that he would see us this afternoon."

"That long away?"

"Yes, it seems our Mr. Penrose is a late riser and takes a few hours to be presentable."

The word *presentable*, Noelle realized a few hours later when Penrose sauntered forward to greet them, had a different meaning for the man than it did for her. Though he was presumably the age of Lord Drewsbury and the other original signers, his hair was a gold so bright it glinted under the lights, without a hint of gray, and he was dressed like a foppish young man, with collar points so high he could not completely turn his head, and a lavender jacket over a paisley-patterned waistcoat. His watch chain was weighed down by fobs and seals, and a gigantic posy adorned his lapel. From his stiff posture, Noelle suspected he had a girdle wrapped around his middle to control a burgeoning stomach.

He came forward with an amiable smile, saying, "So you're Horace's boy, eh? Imagine that. Come in. Sit, sit." He waved them toward chairs. "Haven't thought of Horace in years. 'Course I was never the chum with him that Drewsbury was. Too brainy by half for me. I didn't attend their parties—always thought Belinda was a handsome woman, but I didn't understand half of what she said. How is your mother, by the way?" Without waiting for a reply, he went on cheerfully, "But enough of that, you don't want to hear an old man tell old stories, do you? Did you come about the horses?"

"Horses?" Carlisle repeated blankly. Noelle was beginning to understand why Lady Lockwood had called Freddie Penrose a "rattle."

"The pair I have for sale. Thought you were here about them. Fine pair, matched grays. Bought 'em from Jeremy Harefield two years ago; you know what an eye he has for horseflesh. But…" He sighed, giving a shrug. "What's one to do? Bought a new landau, you see, yellow, and, well, they just don't make the show with it that they did with the black one. Pity."

"Mr. Penrose," Carlisle jumped in as the man paused for a breath. "We came because we spoke with Lord Haverstock, and—"

"Haverstock. Poor chap." Penrose looked grave. "I hear he's taken to the bottle since his son died last year. Terrible thing, that."

"It is indeed. We were discussing the trust agreement you set up years ago with my father and the others."

The other man's eyebrows flew up. "The trust? Oh, you mean that tontine thing! My, I hadn't thought about that in years. No reason to—never thought I'd have five girls, but there you are… Too bad, really. I understand the thing's made a fortune."

"It has?" Carlisle glanced over at Noelle.

"Oh, yes, indeed. A few years back. Some venture or other in India. Or was it Barbados? I'm not sure. Never pay much attention to things like that."

"I was interested in the terms of the agreement. Do you by any chance have a copy of it?"

"Good Gad, no." Penrose looked faintly offended. "A lot of legal gibberish. I leave that up to my solicitor."

"Your lawyer was the one who drew it up?"

"Oh, yes. Well, the old man is dead now. His son's the one who handles my business."

"I'd very much like to speak to him about it," Carlisle said. "If you could give me his name…"

"Of course!" He looked relieved. "He'll be ever so much better at explaining it to you. Thompkins and Thompkins. Well, now it's only the one Thompkins because his father died, but—"

"Thompkins!" Carlisle looked thunderstruck. "Cato Thompkins? Dunbridge's solicitor?"

"Why, yes!" He beamed. "Do you know him? Yes, he was Dunnie's solicitor, too. Not Cato, you understand, but his father—can't remember his name, but it wasn't *odd* like Cato—named after some Roman, if you can believe that. We were the ones, Dunnie and I, who were keen on the idea."

"Thank you, Mr. Penrose," Carlisle said abruptly. "We very much appreciate your help."

"Anytime, old chap! Never mind talking about the old days." For the first time, the cheerful look fell from his face. "Not many left to talk about them anymore."

Noelle almost had to trot to keep up with Carlisle's rapid strides as they left Freddie Penrose's house. "Carlisle! Slow down. I'd prefer not to have to chase you down the street."

"Sorry." He slowed down, turning to look at her. "Damn that man! Nathan's solicitor lied to us. Stood right there and barefaced lied to us."

"I know. I was there."

"All that time, he had the agreement. He knew exactly what it said—he's been administering it, for heaven's sake!"

"Why did he lie? I know it was supposed to be kept

secret, but doesn't that seem extreme—keeping all knowledge of it from the beneficiaries? Especially since yours and Nathan's fathers are both gone and you two inherited everything."

"I don't know. But I am bloody well going to find out. We're going to pay that lawyer a visit. I am damned tired of their secrecy and games. Cato Thompkins is going to give me straight answers. Now."

CHAPTER TWENTY-SIX

IT WAS ALMOST dusk when their carriage pulled into Seven Oaks. They found Cato Thompkins locking the door of his office. He looked around at the sound of their carriage, and his eyes widened as Carlisle fairly vaulted out of the vehicle and strode toward him. He took a half step back.

"Sir. Mr. Thorne. This is quite a surprise." Thompkins's words came out in a rush. "I was just closing up. Perhaps tomorrow—"

"Right now," Carlisle said, cutting him off. "We can go back inside or have this conversation in public view. It's your choice. But one way or another, you are going to give me that agreement."

"But, sir…" Thompkins's hand shook as he unlocked the door and started back inside. "I've told you…"

"A pack of lies, that's what you've told me." Carlisle strode in on the other man's heels, Noelle right behind him. "Your father was the attorney who drew up that trust." As Thompkins drew breath to speak, Carlisle held up a hand. "Don't bother to deny it. I've just spoken with Freddie Penrose, and he told me that your father was Dunbridge's attorney as well as his. He wrote the bloody thing. Not only that, he told me that you had been administering the trust yourself since your father's death. Yet you stood there and told all of us that you knew nothing about it. What the devil kind of game are you playing?"

"Ah, I—well, that is…" Thompkins's eyes darted around the room, as though help might suddenly appear. "I didn't want to. I wouldn't have kept it secret if— that is—" Breaking off this confused speech, he thrust his fingers back into his hair, avoiding Carlisle's eyes.

"I don't give a damn about your excuses." Carlisle took a long step forward, looming over the man. "I want to see that agreement, and I want it now."

Thompkins nodded and whirled around, heading into his inner office. He pulled out a drawer and began to thumb through the papers inside. "There!" He seized a folded, blue-backed document and thrust it toward Carlisle.

Carlisle snatched it from him and opened it, scanning the document.

"Why did you keep it a secret, if you didn't want to?" Noelle asked, knowing it was useless to try to look at the document while Carlisle was reading it.

"Why, because he told me not to. And he was my client, so I felt I should obey his wishes."

"Mr. Penrose?" Noelle asked in astonishment. "But why would he do that? He's the one who told us you had it."

"No, not Mr. Penrose. Mr. Dunbridge."

"Nathan's father? But—"

"No, no. Nathan Dunbridge."

Carlisle's head snapped up at that statement. "What? Nathan! What the devil are you talking about? Nathan was standing right there with us when you said you had no idea about the tontine."

The other man swallowed, straightening his cuffs

and lapels and touching his watch chain. "Yes, but, well, you see, he already knew. His father told him, I believe; he and I have discussed it once or twice."

"You're lying." Carlisle's voice was deadly quiet.

"It's the truth," Thompkins shot back indignantly. "When he took me over to Stonecliffe that day to talk to all of you, he told me to pretend to know nothing about it. It seemed a bit odd, but I assumed it must be a surprise or possibly a prank of some sort. I didn't like deceiving you, I assure you, but since he had instructed me to do so, I withheld the information." As Carlisle continued to glare at Cato, he went on, "I am an honest man, but I could hardly go against my client's instructions."

Noelle felt almost as dumbstruck as Carlisle looked. Nathan knew? Why had he not told them? But, of course, the answer to that question was right in front of her; it was just that she didn't want to believe it. Nathan knew and hid it because he was the one who was behind the killings. She whirled to face Carlisle. "Gil! We left Gil with him! We must go!"

Noelle ran for the door and Carlisle followed, leaving the attorney spluttering, "But, sir, the document... you still have...sir..."

Carlisle wasted no time, just lifted Noelle up into the carriage and jumped in behind her. His first words were, "It isn't Nathan. It can't be."

"I don't want to believe it either." Noelle knotted her hands together in her lap, wishing the carriage would move faster. "But what else can it mean? Why would Nathan not tell us about it? Why would he tell the lawyer not to give you the information?"

"I don't know," he replied grimly. "But I've known

Nathan all my life, and he's never been anything but trustworthy and honest. He's my *friend*." He made a fist, bringing it down on his leg. "There has to be some other explanation."

"There are…well, it would fit with some of the things Nathan has said," Noelle said slowly. "He was terribly insistent on the idea that it was Sloane who was behind the killings."

"That's just his resentment of Sloane; it's to do with Annabeth, not this. He wasn't even there when someone shot at Gil."

"But he was. He and Annabeth and Lady Lockwood had already arrived. He came to call not long after you carried Gil in."

"That doesn't prove he did it. And he certainly wasn't running about Europe trying to take Gil from you."

"No, but we've already surmised that whoever is behind this hired people in Europe; he didn't do it himself." She paused, then added, "He said he was badly in need of money."

"All he has to do to get money is marry an heiress, as his aunt is always urging him to. He needn't go about killing off the other heirs." He looked at her. "You know Nathan. Can you honestly believe that he would do such a thing?"

"No. But our choices are becoming limited. He knew about the trust and didn't tell you. He lied to you. He brought in his attorney to lie to all of us. Why would he try to conceal it? His actions reek of guilt."

"I know." Carlisle sighed. "And I intend to question him, believe me. But I think there must be a good explanation." He reached over and took her hand. "Try not to worry. I know it's difficult, but I don't believe

Gil is in any danger. Even if I'm wrong and it is Nathan who's doing this, Diggs is there, too. He will be watching Gil carefully."

"I know." It was logical, but Noelle found that logic did little to ease her fears.

The drive to Stonecliffe seemed to take an eternity. Noelle spent it staring out into the darkness, willing the carriage to go faster. Carlisle, too, was quiet, frowning moodily down at the folded document he still held in his hand.

"I was so sure this would show us the answer." He slapped the paper against his thigh.

"It didn't?"

"No. Unless I am simply too blind to see it. The men who signed are exactly the ones on the list Sloane brought us, and the terms are just as Lord Haverstock said. It will come to an end twelve years from now and it goes to the male heir still living, to be shared equally if there are more than one. If none are alive at the time, it goes to a charity."

"I don't understand why whoever is doing this is doing it *now*," Noelle said, glad to have something to divert her thoughts. "Even if he kills everyone else, he can't get the money for twelve more years. And it's possible some of the men might die naturally during that time."

Carlisle shook his head. "You're right, there isn't a rush. I suppose he must reason that if he spreads it out over a number of years, no one will suspect any wrongdoing. Or perhaps he is targeting the younger heirs—Sprague and Brookwell are both younger than Nathan and I are. And obviously Gil is the youngest. He might hope that Nathan and I will oblige him by dying in the meantime."

A shiver ran down Noelle's spine, and she said rather snappishly, "Well, I sincerely hope you will not be that obliging."

He smiled faintly. "I won't. And I won't let him hurt Gil either."

"Even if it turns out to be Nathan?"

His face was grim. "Even if it is Nathan."

WHEN THEY ARRIVED at the house, it was ablaze with lights. Noelle turned to Carlisle, her heart suddenly pounding. "Something's happened."

They were out of the carriage as soon as it stopped in front of the house. The gates to the courtyard were locked, as they always were these days, and it seemed to take the coachman forever to get down from the high seat of the vehicle and unlock them. Flinging the gate open, Noelle and Carlisle ran across the courtyard. No footman opened the door to greet them, and when they rushed inside, they found the entryway empty. From the drawing room came a babble of voices, with Lady Lockwood's trumpeting over all the others. "Silence! Having hysterics won't remedy the situation."

"No...oh, Gil," Noelle moaned.

"Steady on." Carlisle took her arm, and they hurried down the hall into the drawing room.

Adeline and her mother, as well as the butler and three footmen, were clustered around the chaise longue. Diggs, looking rather pale, stood beside the mantel, and several other servants huddled together on the far side of the room, whispering.

When Noelle and Carlisle entered the room, everyone swung around.

"Carlisle!" Adeline cried with relief and started toward them.

The crowd around the chaise longue parted, and Noelle saw that Nathan lay on it, his eyes closed and his shirtfront stained red with blood. Annabeth knelt beside him, pressing a wad of cloth to his chest.

"Carlisle!" Echoing Adeline's cry, Annabeth jumped to her feet and turned to face him. "Thank God you're here. Nathan's been shot!"

"What the devil!" Carlisle strode across the room to her.

Noelle glanced around. "Where's Gil? Is Gil all right?"

"He's fine," Adeline reassured her, taking Noelle's hand. "Nothing happened to him. He's in bed, asleep."

"Thank God." Suddenly Noelle's knees went weak, and she sat down hastily.

Carlisle had gone down on one knee beside Annabeth. "Is Nathan—"

"He's alive," Annabeth told him. "We sent to the stables for one of the grooms to ride for Dr. Havers."

"I'll go. My horse is fastest, and none of them can ride him." Carlisle turned to the footman. "You. Potter. Run to the stables and tell them to saddle Samson. I'll be there in a minute." As the footman hurried off, Carlisle lifted the cloth from Nathan's chest to inspect the wound. "Did the ball go through him?"

Annabeth shook her head. Tears shone in her eyes. "He'll have to pull it out. Oh, Carlisle, is he going to live? I cannot bear it!"

"Of course." He nodded reassuringly. "You're doing well. Just keep pressing the bandage to him." He rose and swung around to face the rest of the room. "Someone tell me what the devil happened here. Who shot Nathan?"

Diggs straightened and stepped forward manfully. "That was me, sir."

CHAPTER TWENTY-SEVEN

"You!" CARLISLE GAPED at Diggs. "How—what—"

"I had to, sir. I didn't know what else to do. I was guarding the lad, and I must have dozed in my seat because I woke up, sudden-like, and there Mister Dunbridge was, holding a pillow over the boy's face. I shouted and grabbed my gun, but Mr. Dunbridge swung around and aimed his pistol at me. So I fired. I knew I was a dead man if I didn't, and if he did me in, he'd kill young Master Gilbert. I'm sorry, sir. I didn't even realize who he was until he fell and I went over to him. It—well, I didn't see what else I could have done."

"Are you certain he was smothering Gil?" Carlisle asked. "Couldn't he have been merely checking on the boy?"

Diggs shook his head. "No, sir. He had the pillow across the boy's face and was holding it down with both hands. I wasn't certain the lad was alive until I pulled the pillow away. And there is Mr. Dunbridge's pistol on the mantelpiece. I picked it up from the floor where he dropped it. I'm sorry, sir. I shouldn't have fallen asleep. He wouldn't have been able to do it if I had been awake; he wouldn't have tried."

"No, it's not your fault. I can't blame you." Carlisle's face was set in weary lines. He looked over at Noelle, and she had to fight the urge to take him in her arms to comfort him. She felt saddened and betrayed by what Nathan had done; she could only imagine how deep Carlisle's feelings must run. But, of course, she could do nothing to ease his pain.

"I'll return as quickly as possible." He walked past Noelle, his hand brushing her arm in a gesture of silent reassurance that warmed her heart.

Diggs followed him down the hall, the two men talking in an undertone. Noelle watched them go, then turned back to Adeline. Everything inside her wanted only to run up the stairs to Gil; despite Adeline's assurance that Gil was unharmed, she could not feel better until she saw him for herself. Yet she felt that she should say something, do something to help Annabeth and Adeline.

Fortunately, Adeline seemed to sense what Noelle was feeling, and she reached out to pat Noelle's arm. "Go see Gil. I know you must want to, and that is where you belong. We will do well enough here. There's little to be done other than pray Carlisle returns with the doctor before..." Her voice trailed off and tears filled her eyes as she looked back at the chaise where Nathan lay, still and silent.

Noelle wasted no time in taking her advice, rushing out of the room and up the stairs. The hallway lay in gloom, the sconces on the wall providing only a little light. As she hurried down it, Noelle couldn't help but think of the servants carrying Nathan, wounded and bleeding, along this shadowy corridor to the stairs, and the image sent a shiver through her.

It was all so unbelievable, so utterly wrong. How could that pleasant demeanor, that easy smile and warm, candid face have hidden such wickedness? She scarcely knew whether she was more filled with rage at Nathan for trying to hurt her son or pity and sorrow for Carlisle and the others who had known and loved him all his life. How could Nathan have done this?

She slipped into Gil's room. A low-burning lamp on the dresser dimly lit the room. Gil was asleep, turned on his side, his cheek upon his hand. She crossed the room to him, queasily sidestepping the bloodstain on the rug. She laid a hand on the boy's forehead, smoothing back his hair. How could Gil have slept through all that? She could not imagine him sleeping through the sound of gunfire, but it seemed equally unlikely that he'd awakened then gone placidly back to sleep.

Leaning down, she kissed his forehead. Still, he didn't stir. Growing more uneasy by the moment, she said his name. She didn't want to awaken him, but his continued sleeping seemed abnormal. She repeated his name, louder this time, then reached down to shake his shoulder. What was the matter with him? Had Nathan's attempt to smother Gil sent him into a coma?

There were footsteps in the hall, and she turned to see Diggs step through the doorway. He checked at seeing her, then said, "Beg pardon, ma'am. I didn't know you were here."

"I can't awaken Gil," she said, fighting to control the panic that welled in her chest.

Diggs nodded. "I think Mr. Dunbridge must have put something in his food or drink tonight. So Master Gilbert wouldn't wake up when he came into his room. Easier, you know, to…" His voice trailed off.

"Yes. No doubt you're right." The thought eased her mind a trifle, though she could not help but worry that Nathan might have given Gil too much.

"I'm sure he'll be fine," Diggs reassured her. "His color's good; so's his breathing."

"I'm sorry, I should have thanked you already for saving my son," Noelle told him.

"I'm just glad I woke up in time. I'm sorry I fell asleep like that."

"I'm sure you were tired. You should get some rest now that the danger is over. I plan to spend the night with Gil."

"Well, that's the thing, ma'am." Diggs shifted uncomfortably, twisting his cap between his hands. Why had he brought his cap into Gil's bedroom?

"What is?"

"Mr. Thorne told me to take the boy someplace else. For his safety, you see."

"But why? Nathan's no threat to him now." She frowned. "Carlisle doesn't still think Nathan is innocent, does he? I mean, you caught him."

"No, he realizes that. It's just—he said as how there might have been someone working with Mr. Dunbridge. An accomplice, you see. It doesn't seem likely that he would have done all those things by himself."

"But surely someone he hired would not continue after Nathan was found out."

"I don't know, ma'am." Diggs shrugged. "Mayhap he doesn't know what's happened. Mr. Thorne is a cautious man."

Noelle knew that was certainly true. "He wants us to leave tonight?"

Diggs nodded. "I know it's sudden-like, but that's what Mr. Thorne wants. I'll take good care of the boy; you don't have to worry."

"I won't worry. I'm coming with you."

"Oh. Well, he didn't say anything about that." Diggs looked doubtful. "You won't want to be tromping through the woods at night."

"Not particularly," Noelle admitted. "But there is no way I am letting Gil out of my sight after what happened tonight. Don't worry. I'll make it clear to Mr. Thorne that I insisted on accompanying Gil. He won't blame you."

"No, ma'am." He nodded. "Well, um…we'd best get going."

He edged around Noelle and picked up Gil. Gil stirred, then turned his cheek against the man's shoulder and continued to sleep. Diggs led Noelle down the back stairs and through the kitchen, deserted at this time of night.

"We should tell Lady Drewsbury that we're leaving," Noelle said, glancing toward the hallway leading to the front of the house.

"Mr. Thorne will tell them," Diggs said. "He said I must hurry."

It felt very odd to be slipping out of the house this way without telling Adeline they were leaving. It was almost as if Carlisle suspected someone else in the house, too. But surely not. She could not imagine any of the women here trying to hurt Gil. She wondered if perhaps Carlisle thought one of the servants was in Nathan's employ. Of course, knowing Carlisle, he would err on the side of caution, just as Diggs had said.

She followed the man as he led her out the door and through the garden. A pony cart awaited them at the end, and Diggs laid Gil down in the cart. He started off along the path, leading the pony, and Noelle brought up the rear. Even with the moonlight, the path was dark, and before long, Diggs left the trail, striking out through the trees. Diggs lit a lantern as they trudged along a barely discernible track.

"Where are we going?" Noelle asked.

"It's a cottage on the estate," Diggs answered. "No one lives there now; not many people even know about it."

Bushes snagged Noelle's skirts, and she stumbled once or twice on the uneven ground. It had been a busy day, and the numerous emotional jolts she had received added to her weariness. She was beginning to think she might have to ask Diggs to stop for a rest when he said, "There it is. Just up ahead."

She could make out a vague, dark form in the small clearing in front of them, and as they drew nearer, the shape resolved itself into a bare and bleak little cottage. The windows were shuttered, and when Diggs pushed open the door, the hinges screeched. The light of Diggs's lantern left shadowy corners in the room. Noelle shivered and wished she had paused to get a wrap before they left the Hall.

"There's a bed in here, ma'am, such as it is." Diggs led the way into a smaller room and laid Gil down on the narrow cot. Gil sighed in his sleep and turned onto his side. Diggs turned toward the door. "I'll, um, let you get some rest."

He left, taking the lantern with him and closing the door. The room was pitch-black, and Noelle thought for a moment of calling Diggs back and searching for a candle, but it seemed too much effort. Better just to go to sleep.

Noelle sat down on the foot of the bed and leaned back against the wall, closing her eyes. It was the first moment of peace and quiet she had experienced, the first chance to think over the tumultuous and confusing events of the day.

How could she have been so wrong about Nathan? How could all of them have been so wrong? Adeline was a loving and generous soul, someone who saw the best in everyone, so it was not surprising that she had not caught on to the flaws in Nathan's character. But Carlisle and Annabeth, both sensible, levelheaded people, had been friends with him their entire lives, yet they, too, had had no suspicion of what lay beneath his facade.

She shivered, thinking of how close Gil had come to death. It had been horribly wrong to leave Gil in Nathan's care. No matter how pleasant and well-liked he was, she shouldn't have entrusted her son to a man she had known for such a short time. Yes, she had gone with Carlisle to investigate the matter because her son was in danger, but if she was honest, she would admit that Carlisle could have done it just as well without her. Guiltily, she knew that part of the reason she had been so determined to talk to Sloane and the others was because it gave her a chance to be alone with Carlisle.

She was very lucky that Nathan had not tried to harm Gil earlier, when Diggs hadn't been there to intervene. Why, she wondered, had he not done so at the first opportunity, when she and Carlisle traveled to Sloane's house? He couldn't have been certain that he would have another chance. Perhaps he had thought it would appear too obvious for Gil to die while under his care.

But if so, why had he decided to kill Gil tonight? And with Diggs sitting guard? Surely he had realized the possibility of Diggs waking up and discovering him. He could have slipped something into Diggs's food, as well, to make him sleep. But then why had Diggs awakened so quickly? Gil was still sound asleep. He was smaller than Diggs, but still, it seemed peculiar. She would have to discuss it with Carlisle when he arrived.

Gil stirred, mumbling in his sleep. It reassured her somewhat that he was merely in a drugged sleep, not irreversibly harmed by the sleeping draught Nathan had given him. She stretched out beside her son, one hand laid protectively on him.

Noelle was almost asleep when a clatter outside brought her wide awake. She waited, muscles tensed. There was some rustling and a man's curse, followed by the neigh of a horse. The pony. Of course. Diggs must have pulled the pony cart around back and taken the horse from his harness. She doubted that Diggs, a city man, was well versed in unhitching a pony from its cart.

She relaxed and once more settled in to sleep, but before she could, Gil began to squirm, mumbling again. "Don't wanna. No, I won't."

Noelle went up on her elbow, peering down at him. "Gil? Love, you're having a nightmare. Wake up. Gil?"

"No!" he said clearly, flinging his arm out and hitting her shoulder. "Stop… *Maman! À moi!*"

His weak panicky whisper was like a knife to Noelle's heart. "I'm here, love. I'm right here. It's all right. You're safe." She took him in her arms, caressing his back soothingly and murmuring words of reassurance.

"Mama?" He stilled and his eyes flew open. "Mama?" Gil threw his arms around her neck and clung to her.

"Yes, I'm here. You're safe."

"Good." His arms relaxed and he snuggled into her.

"Darling, do you remember? Did Mr. Dunbridge make you drink something?"

"Nuh-uh." He yawned enormously and his eyes drifted closed. "Was Diggs."

CHAPTER TWENTY-EIGHT

DIGGS? NOELLE STIFFENED. Her heart began to race, and any thought she had entertained of going to sleep vanished. "Diggs did it?" She shook him gently. "Gil, wake up. Tell me. Did Diggs make you drink something?"

He nodded. "Mmm-hmm."

For a moment Noelle was too stunned to think. Then her mind began to race. Why had the pony cart been waiting for them at the bottom of the garden? She hadn't really questioned it at the time. She'd been too tired, too fearful for Gil to even consider it odd.

When had Diggs hitched up the cart and positioned it there? When she left the room to go to Gil, Diggs had still been talking with Carlisle. Only a few minutes later he had walked into Gil's room. How could he have gone out to the stables, hitched up the pony cart, taken it to the edge of the garden, and still made it to Gil's room in that amount of time?

He could have requested that the pony cart be brought to the garden, but that would have entailed him telling a footman to tell a groom and thereby revealing his plans to two servants—when Diggs had told her not to tell anyone they were leaving. The only thing that made sense was that Diggs had placed the pony cart at the edge of the garden earlier that evening. Before he shot Nathan.

Why would Diggs have been planning to take Gil away? Carlisle wouldn't have given his man such instructions before he and Noelle left on their trip.

No, Diggs had been acting on his own, and he had intended to take Gil away all along. It was difficult to think of any reason for his doing so that wasn't nefarious. Diggs fit as the villain—it was he, after all, who had found out where she was every time in Europe. Carlisle believed Diggs told his men only to ask her to return to live at Stonecliffe, but that didn't mean Diggs had actually done so. That night when the ruffian had grabbed Gil in Seven Dials, Diggs would have known where his guard was sitting, keeping an eye on the millinery shop; he could have put the sleeping draught in his employee's drink and sent a different man after her and Gil.

But why? Diggs wasn't an heir. But he could have been paid by some man who *would* benefit. Had he been working for Nathan? But then why would he have shot him? No, it seemed more likely that Nathan had discovered Diggs kidnapping Gil, and that had caused the altercation. So Nathan was not the villain. But then why had Nathan lied to them about the tontine?

None of that mattered at the moment. The reality now was that Noelle had unwittingly delivered her son to the very man who wanted to harm him. She could not understand why Diggs had not already killed them, since he had them alone and vulnerable.

Her first thought was to barricade the door with the bed and wait for help. However, she doubted that the bed would prove much of an impediment to her captor, and besides—who would be coming to her aid? On Diggs's instructions, she had not told the others what she was doing. Carlisle hadn't told him to take them here; that had to have been a lie. So Carlisle would have as little idea where she was as everyone else.

She was entirely on her own, just as she had been all those years. She had kept Gil safe then, and she would do so again. Noelle glanced around the room. It was utterly dark since Diggs had taken their only light with him. However, she remembered seeing a window in the back wall. If it was large enough, they could climb through it and escape. The darkness was a hindrance, but fortunately, the room was so small that she could easily find her way to the window by simply following the wall.

Putting her fingertips on the wall, she walked slowly forward, turning at the corner, and in another few steps, the wall suddenly vanished. She extended her hand farther and it came up against wood. The window didn't have glass; it was simply open to the shutters. No wonder the sounds of Diggs unharnessing the pony had been so clear. Carefully, she felt her way around the perimeter of the window. It wasn't large, and it was a little high, but it was big enough she and Gil would be able to climb through it.

She pushed against the shutters. They didn't move so she pushed harder, and the shutters opened with a screech similar to the front door's. She stopped, heart pounding. When there was no sound of footsteps rushing toward their room, she opened the shutters wider. She could make out the darker outline of the pony standing beneath a tree. Going on her toes, she peered at the ground beneath the window and was glad to see that Diggs had left the cart there, which would make it easier for them to climb down, especially Gil.

Noelle turned and looked at Gil, who was once again

soundly asleep. How were they to run with him in this condition? She could carry him, but that would slow her down; Diggs would be bound to catch up before she could get far. There was the pony cart, but it would make a great deal of noise, alerting Diggs to their escape. Not to mention that she had no idea how to harness the pony to the cart. The pony was her best option. She could put Gil up on its back, and they would be able to at least move along at a brisk walk.

First, she needed to reconnoiter a bit and find out exactly what she was dealing with. With the faint light the open shutter provided, she walked quietly across the floor and eased open the door a crack. She could see only a slice of the room, but it was enough to see Diggs's feet propped up casually on a stool.

What was he waiting for? For his employer to arrive? Further instructions? In any case, Diggs wasn't watchful. For a moment she toyed with the idea of finding something in the room that she could use to hit him over the head. But that was a risky proposition. She might not have the chance to hit him before he saw her or she wouldn't be able to hit him hard enough to knock him out. It would be better to leave quietly and get as far away as they could. If she was lucky, Diggs might not miss them for hours, thinking them securely asleep in the bedroom.

She eased the door closed again and returned to the bed. Then she set out to awaken Gil. It wasn't easy, but after a time, he opened his eyes, scowling and whining, "Maman…"

"Sh." Noelle hastily covered his mouth with her hand and leaned down to speak in his ear. "Gil, love, you mustn't say anything. Diggs is right outside and he might hear you. We have to get away. Quickly and quietly. Do you understand?"

He blinked owlishly at her. She couldn't see his expression well enough in the dark to judge how fully conscious he was, so she continued to whisper. "Diggs is a bad man. You remember he gave you the nasty drink?" Gil nodded. "He's the man who's been chasing us. We just didn't know. He lied to me and I believed him, trusted him. So now we must run."

"But Uncle Carlisle…" Gil whispered back.

"Carlisle isn't here. He doesn't know where we are. So we have to find our way back to the house. To Carlisle."

Gil nodded his understanding. Noelle let out a breath of relief. Gil was awake enough that he would be able to follow instructions. She led Gil to the window and lifted him up and out the window into the cart. It was a more difficult task to pull herself up and out the window, given its size, but she managed to scramble out, holding on to the shutters for support.

The pony, watching their movements, gave a little whicker and walked over to them, bumping Noelle's arm. Noelle saw that Diggs had not bothered to tether him; the placid pony had simply remained, munching on the grass. He seemed amiable enough that she wouldn't even need a lead for him, but she unbuckled a strap of leather from the harness and fastened it around the pony's neck to give Gil something to hold on to.

The cottage lay in the middle of a clearing, which they would have to cross in full view of the house in order to reach the path back to the Hall. For a moment she thought of heading into the woods behind them, where Diggs couldn't see them leave, but she had no idea where she was, and it wouldn't help if she and Gil became hopelessly lost in the woods. No, the best course was to return home as quickly as she could.

Noelle drew a breath, and, heart pounding, started across the clearing. The docile pony ambled along at its own pace, setting her nerves jangling. Gil was nodding off on his back. Noelle grasped the back of his nightshirt to keep him upright and hooked her other hand around the makeshift collar, tugging to move the pony forward more quickly.

They were almost to the path leading into the trees when she heard a shout in the house behind them. She began to run, pulling the pony. "Wake up, Gil! Hold on!"

Gil obeyed her, groggily opening his eyes and curling both hands around the pony's collar. He bounced along on the pony, which was shaking his head, clearly disliking Noelle's insistence on running. Behind them, Noelle heard the door of the cottage slamming open and Diggs running after them. He carried a lantern, and the light swung crazily over the clearing as he ran.

Frightened even more, the pony jumped and twisted, pulling his head from Noelle's grasp. Gil clung to the leather strap, but began to slide to the side. "Mama!"

Noelle grabbed Gil as he came off the horse, staggering under the weight of him. The pony thundered off down the path. Noelle swerved and ran into the trees. If she could just lose Diggs in the woods…

It was a vain hope. Diggs was on her in seconds. He grabbed her arm and jerked her to a stop. She twisted away. Knowing she couldn't escape, she let Gil slide to the ground and bent to grab up a fallen branch.

"Run!" she screamed to Gil as she came up swinging at Diggs.

CHAPTER TWENTY-NINE

CARLISLE STRODE INTO the house, the doctor following on his heels. They had not yet reached the door of the drawing room when Annabeth came running toward them.

"Carlisle! Dr. Havers! Thank God."

"Nathan?" Carlisle asked, his stomach clenching. Whatever had happened, however damning it looked for Nathan, Carlisle could not bear for his lifelong friend to die.

"He's still alive. Doctor, this way."

Carlisle followed the others into the drawing room. The doctor went down on one knee beside Nathan and began to examine his wound.

"Where is Noelle?" Carlisle asked, glancing around the room. It had been emptied of the crowd that had been in here before, leaving only Annabeth and two footmen.

"She went upstairs to Gil," Annabeth told him. "Aunt Adeline took Grandmother to her room, thank goodness."

"Has he awakened?"

"Once." Annabeth's voice quavered. "Potter and Bennett had to hold him down. He was so agitated that Bennett made him drink some brandy. He went back to sleep, but he's been very restless."

"I have to take the ball out," the doctor said, rising to his feet. "We must move him to a table with more light."

"The dining room," Carlisle said. "Annabeth, go tell Bennett. Potter, you and Hargrove, help me lift him. Gently, men, gently."

Carlisle took Nathan's head and shoulders, wincing as Nathan let out a groan when they lifted him from the couch. They proceeded as carefully as they could out the door and down the hall, but it was impossible not to jar their patient. Nathan's eyes fluttered open and he looked up at Carlisle. Carlisle felt him relax. "You're here. Thank God."

"Yes. I'm here. You're going to be all right."

"Diggs. He—"

"Shot you. Yes, I know. Nathan, save your energy; there's no need to talk."

"Gil—"

"He's fine. Don't worry."

"No." Nathan shook his head weakly. "Hurt him. I didn't—I'm sorry. I tried…stop him."

Carlisle stopped instantly at his words, going cold all over. Nathan let out a hiss of pain at the jerky movement. "Who, Nathan? You tried to stop whom?"

"Diggs. Help Gil."

"Gil's safe," Carlisle assured him, his mind racing. "He's fine."

They had reached the dining room at last, and the men lay Nathan down on the table. The two footmen stepped back, but Carlisle leaned over the table to gaze into his friend's face. "Nathan, why did Diggs shoot you?"

"Caught him…" Nathan's gaze wavered, eyelids fluttering closed.

"No. Stay with me. Nathan..."

The doctor came up beside Carlisle, edging him aside. "Mr. Thorne... I must operate."

"Yes. Of course." Carlisle stepped back from the table and walked over to Annabeth, standing in the doorway. "Where's Diggs?"

Annabeth shook her head. "I've no idea. What was Nathan saying? He kept muttering in his sleep all the while you were gone."

"What did he say?"

"He said your name or Gil's over and over, and sometimes he said he was sorry." Tears glinted in her eyes. "Oh, Carlisle, Nathan didn't try to hurt Gil, did he? He couldn't have."

"I've no idea what's going on. I can't imagine Nathan doing that either. He just told me—he seemed to be saying that he tried to stop Diggs, that he caught him. He told me to help Gil. Was the situation the exact opposite of what Diggs told us?"

"What!" Annabeth stiffened. "I *knew* Nathan couldn't have tried to hurt Gil."

"I've never felt so at sea in my life. I must see Noelle. And Gil." Carlisle took her arm, giving it a gentle squeeze. "Stay with Nathan, will you? I have to go."

"Of course. I'll be right here."

He started toward the door, gesturing at one of the footmen to follow. "Potter. Where's Diggs?"

"I don't know, sir."

"Find him. I want to talk to him."

Carlisle took the stairs two at a time. Was Nathan delirious? Had Carlisle misunderstood what he said? Perhaps Nathan was a cold-blooded liar, trying to clear himself of wrongdoing. But a lifetime of friendship with the man would not let Carlisle believe that.

But Diggs? Diggs, who had worked for him so long, been so reliable? Could Diggs have lied? Could he have tried to harm Gil and shot Nathan because Nathan saw what Diggs was doing? It seemed absurd—what reason would Diggs have to hurt the boy? Perhaps it had all been a dreadful mistake. Had the two men both somehow misinterpreted the other's actions?

He must talk to Diggs. But first he had to see Noelle. He felt so strange, so torn and confused and on edge, so uncertain. He wanted—he needed—to hold her, to know she was safe and secure in his arms.

The door to Gil's room was closed. Opening it, he stepped into the dark room. The light from the hallway was enough to show that the small bed was empty. Nor was anyone sitting in the nearby chair. "Noelle?" His heart sped up. "Gil?"

He walked to the center of the room, turning around to look in every corner. It was a small room and clearly empty. He hurried back out and down the hallway to Noelle's room. Gil would have been frightened, and Noelle had probably taken the boy back to her bed to sleep.

The door to Noelle's room stood open, the bedchamber dark. Grabbing a candle from the hall table, he carried it inside, but the room was just as clearly empty. Where was she? For one awful moment, he thought that she had fled from him again, had taken Gil and run as far away as she could. God knows, he could hardly blame her, given how poorly he had managed to protect her and her son.

But no. Noelle wouldn't have done that. Not now. She knew him; she trusted him. She wouldn't simply leave without talking to him first. Anyway, the room was tidy; there was no sign of a hasty departure.

Adeline. Of course. He was swept with relief. Noelle and Gil must be with Adeline and Lady Lockwood. He hurried out the door and turned toward the cozy sitting room Adeline preferred. Before he reached it, Adeline appeared in the doorway, looking apprehensive.

"Carlisle! What is it? Why are you running all about? Is—is Nathan—"

"No. I'm sorry, ma'am, for worrying you." He tried to will calm into his voice. "The doctor is with Nathan now. When I left, he was about to operate. Annabeth will let us know if…" He let his voice trail off, unwilling to say the words. "I was looking for Noelle and Gil. I realized they must be with you." He followed her into the sitting room. There was only Lady Lockwood there, staring at him balefully.

"Noelle and Gil?" Adeline said, turning to him with a puzzled face. "But they are in Gil's room. Didn't anyone tell you? She went up there when you left."

"She's not there. Neither of them is." The knot was back in his chest, tighter than before. "Have you talked to her? Did she say anything?"

"No, the door was closed when we came up, and I didn't want to wake Gil if he was asleep." Adeline frowned. "Have you checked her room?"

Lady Lockwood thumped her cane against the floor. "What the devil is going on *now*?"

"I've no idea," Carlisle said shortly. "They're not in her room either. I've already checked. Where's Diggs? Have you seen him?"

"No. Do you think he's with them?" Adeline's face

regained a little of its lost color. "That would be good. At least they'll have someone to protect them."

Carlisle didn't tell her the awful theory that had taken lodging in his brain. He jerked on the bellpull. "Surely someone must have seen them if they left. Tell Bennett to question the servants and set them to looking for Noelle. They are to search everywhere. No matter how unlikely it might seem. And Diggs. I want him found."

"Yes, of course, but—" Adeline began, but Carlisle was already out the door.

He ran down the hallway, flinging open every door and sticking his head inside, calling her name. He ran to the governess's room, startling that woman by pounding on her door and demanding to know if she'd seen Gil and Noelle. He went through the servants' hall. By now, maids and footmen were scurrying all around, looking in each room, just as he was.

The library. That was her refuge. It seemed a bizarre place to take Gil to at this time of night, but it was where Noelle spent the most time. He ran to the library, even though in his heart he knew it would prove futile. He was more and more certain that Nathan's warning was right. Diggs had tried to murder Gil, and now he and Gil and Noelle had all gone missing.

Annabeth, looking pale and drawn, was leaving the dining room as Carlisle strode back from the empty library, and he stopped. "Annabeth. What's happened? Is Nathan—"

"He's still alive," she said hastily.

"Here. Sit down." He led her toward a bench against the wall. "You look exhausted."

She offered up a faint smile. "I am." She sat down,

letting out a sigh. "When the doctor finished, I just… melted. Before that I was holding on, but…"

"It's understandable. Did the doctor say anything?"

"Only that it was in God's hands now, which is not exactly what one wishes to hear."

"Nathan's young and healthy. He'll recover." He wished he was as sure of that as he tried to sound.

"They're setting up a bed in one of the rooms down here so they won't have to carry him up the stairs. I'll sit with him."

"I'm sure Adeline would be happy to take your place for a bit. You should rest."

"I couldn't. Not while he's still…so uncertain."

He nodded and started to turn away, but Annabeth put her hand on his arm. "Wait. What's going on? I heard everyone running about, and you look…"

"Noelle is gone." He'd been trying to preserve a false front of confidence for Annabeth's sake, but he couldn't keep himself from blurting out, "I can't find Gil and Noelle. Or Diggs. I have no idea where they are."

Annabeth sucked in a breath. "Carlisle!"

"I have everyone combing the house and grounds for them. I must find her. But I don't know what to do. Where else to go." He sank onto the bench beside her. His insides were churning; he'd never felt so helpless. "Annabeth, what if Diggs has killed them? What will I do? I love her. And I never even told her."

"I imagine she knows. *I* could see it in your eyes every time you looked at her." Annabeth gave a little chuckle at his surprised glance. "I know both of you did your best to hide it, but I was certain anyway. I just wasn't sure whether *you* had realized it yet." She laid her hand on his arm. "Noelle's not dead. Nor Gil. And you will find her."

"I *have* to find her." He jumped to his feet, shoving his hands into his pockets, and began to pace. "Where the devil would Diggs have gone? Why did he take her? Why did he not wait and try again in secret instead of doing something so obvious? Everyone believed him; we thought Nathan did it."

"Nathan is going to recover," Annabeth said fiercely. "Maybe Diggs realized that he hadn't killed him and decided he'd better leave before Nathan could tell you what really happened. Or perhaps he made another attempt and Noelle caught him. Maybe he did or said something that made her realize the truth, and he knew that—"

"That he had to kill them," Carlisle finished harshly.

"No! He knew that he had to get them away so they couldn't tell you. But there's nothing to say he killed them. Surely Diggs must be aware that he cannot escape after kidnapping them. Eventually he'll be caught, and it will only go worse for him if he's murdered them. He could have decided to use them as hostages so that you'd let him go free, maybe even pay him a ransom."

"I don't understand how he could have done this. Or why. What could he hope to gain? He gets nothing from the trust." He shook his head. "Someone else must be paying him; that's the only explanation I can see, the only profit there could be for him. And they must be paying him damn well to be worth losing my business."

"He wouldn't lose it if you never knew he was the one doing it," Annabeth pointed out. "And he would be receiving payment from two sources. In the beginning, he might even have thought you'd be happy to have Noelle out of your life. She was, as I remember, something of a thorn in your side."

"She was indeed." For a moment, a faint smile touched his lips, but it quickly fell away. "I'm going to search the cellar." As he turned away, Potter ran toward him from the back of the house.

"Sir!"

"Did you find Diggs?" Carlisle went forward to meet him, hope and fear surging in him in equal measure.

The footman shook his head as he drew in a breath. "No, sir, but I found—I went to the stables to ask if they'd seen him, and Grisham said he—Diggs, I mean—came in earlier this evening and took the pony cart. He's gone, sir."

"The pony cart?" Carlisle stared. "Not a horse?"

Annabeth came up beside him. "A pony cart would be a handy thing for carrying a child."

"It would. When was this, Potter? When did he leave?"

"That's the thing, sir. He took the cart hours ago. Before everything happened."

"I see." Carlisle let out a long breath, his eyes suddenly so cold and fierce that the footman took an involuntary step backward. "He'd already made plans to take Gil away, and Nathan must have interrupted him. Where did he go with this cart? Show me," Carlisle said to Potter.

"I don't know, sir. I came straight back to tell you. But," he added hastily, "I told Grisham to try to follow the cart's tracks. He's out there now with a lantern."

Carlisle ran, throwing open the door and taking the shallow steps in a single leap. He raced to the stables. They had never seemed so far away before.

The head groom was waiting for him, lantern in hand. "My head lad followed the tracks. They went that direction, to the back of the garden."

"Give me your lantern."

The groom blinked as Carlisle grabbed the lantern and started off. "But, sir...don't you—"

Carlisle paid no attention, intent on following the trail before him. Thank God it had rained recently. When he reached the back entrance into the garden, he saw the ruts were a little deeper, and he paused to examine the area. The cart had obviously sat here for a time; the pony had left several droppings. There were also a number of footprints, some of a man's shoe and others the smaller indentations of a woman's feet.

His shoulders relaxed fractionally. Noelle was with Diggs, but clearly she was walking, so he had not yet killed or drugged her, and there weren't any signs of a struggle. Gil had doubtless been carried and was riding in the pony cart—why else take the thing? The tracks of the vehicle, now with footprints added, ran straight ahead toward the woods. Of course. Diggs had taken them into the trees, where tracks could easily be lost and hiding places abounded.

Carlisle's heart squeezed in his chest. He took off at a run toward the woods.

CHAPTER THIRTY

THE BRANCH NOELLE wielded hit Diggs with a satisfying crack, but he had managed to throw up his arm to protect his head. She pulled back to strike again, but before she could swing, Diggs plowed into her, driving her to the ground. He reared up astride her and Noelle brought her knee up with all the force she could muster. Diggs let out a screech, clutching at his privates. From the side, Gil threw himself against Diggs, and the man toppled over.

"Gil, run!" Noelle shouted as she dragged herself out from beneath Diggs and scrambled to retrieve her makeshift weapon.

Diggs rolled over and grabbed her ankle. Frantically she tried to pull away, but he clung to her tenaciously. Gil jumped on the man's back, drumming his fists against him. With a roar, the man let go of her as he surged to his feet, and Noelle grabbed the branch. She swung back to face him, her arm raised, and saw that Diggs held Gil against his chest, one hand firmly around her son's throat.

Noelle froze. Diggs nodded, a grim smile curving his lips. "Aye, that's right. I have him. Drop that stick."

Noelle did as he said. "Don't hurt him. Please. He's just a child."

"I won't if you do what I tell you."

"I will."

He nodded toward the clearing. "Go back to the house. And don't try nothing. I can see everything you do."

Noelle nodded and started walking back, her mind racing. Diggs could have killed Gil right there and then. For that matter, he could have done it far earlier. Why had he not? Was it possible that when he was faced with actually killing a child, he hadn't been able to make himself do it?

Seizing on that thought, she said, "Killing a man is one thing, but killing a child? You know Gil. You watched over him that day in the park. Surely you must hesitate at the thought of murdering him. Doing this will haunt you the rest of your life."

"Shut up."

Noelle ignored his words. "Think of what will happen to you. There is no way you can conceal this. Everyone will know. When they find Gil and me gone, and you, as well, they'll know. What do you think Carlisle will do when he discovers your treachery? He'll hunt you down; you know he will."

"Enough! Shut up, I tell you, or I'll do it right here and now."

Noelle stopped and swung around to face him. She saw that Diggs had shifted Gil, who was still struggling, and now held him under his arm like a package, pinning the boy's arms to his sides and making it more difficult for Gil's kicking feet to reach Diggs. Now that his hand was no longer around Gil's neck, perhaps she could rush him, and he would release Gil. Diggs was not a large man, and right now, in her fear and fury, she felt as if she could level a stone wall to save Gil.

"Move on," he said gruffly, but Noelle stood her ground, waiting for him to come closer, tensing to spring. He stopped, his face red with anger, and began to curse. "Go on, I tell you!"

He raised his hand, gesturing toward the house, exposing his side, and Noelle launched herself at him. He half turned, so that she hit only his side, but that was enough to make him stagger backward, feet slipping on the dirt path, arms windmilling. He lost his hold on Gil, who tumbled to the ground. Noelle was knocked off her feet by the collision, and her skirts impeded her as she tried to stand.

Diggs grabbed her arm, pulling her up, his face contorted with fury. He drew back his arm to hit her. Suddenly there was a loud crack, and red burst across his temple. Noelle gaped at Diggs, stunned, as he crumpled to the ground, his hand falling away from her arm.

"Mama!" Gil ran to throw himself against her, wrapping his arms around her legs.

Carlisle, Noelle thought, her heart leaping inside her chest. Carlisle had found them. She whirled to look behind her. A man stood at the edge of the clearing, but it was not Carlisle. In her shock, it took her a moment to realize who he was and another instant to remember his name.

"Mr. Thompkins!" The lawyer! Nathan's lawyer. What was he doing here? "What—I—" She glanced down at Diggs's lifeless body on the ground, then back to Thompkins.

"Oh, my. Oh, dear." The man ran forward and stopped short, staring down at Diggs. "Is he—oh, dear."

"Yes, he's dead." Noelle took his arm, thinking that he might be about to swoon.

But Thompkins only blinked a time or two, then turned to her. "I didn't really—I mean, he was about to—I'm so sorry." His gaze was pulled back to Diggs.

"Why are you here?" Noelle asked, turning him away from the body. "Not that I'm not eternally grateful, but I don't understand." Gently prying Gil from her leg, she picked him up and began to walk toward the cottage.

Beside her, Mr. Thompkins, his hands twisting aimlessly around the pistol, began his explanation. "I, well, when I realized, I had to come. I mean, of course, first I went to Stonecliffe, or else I would have been here sooner. When Mr. Thorne wasn't there, well, I didn't know where to go. But then I remembered about the nurse's cottage. It's empty, and I realized that would be the place. Mr. Adam Rutherford's nurse, of course, but Mr. Thorne had great regard for her, and now, naturally, she's gone, but no one else…well, thank heavens I was right. I wasn't sure… I couldn't believe, I mean, not really, that it was he. But still, of course, I had to act."

He babbled on in this manner all the way to the cottage, but Noelle didn't try to stem the flow or make sense of what he was saying. She was too shaken herself to put things into order. The important thing was taking care of Gil, who was clinging to her, his head on her shoulder. Noelle rubbed his back, murmuring words of reassurance to him.

For a long time Gil was silent, but when she carried him into the bedroom and set him down on the bed, he said, "Why did Diggs do that?"

His lower lip trembled slightly, and his eyes welled with tears. Noelle smoothed her hand over his head. "I'm not sure, dearest." She bent and kissed his forehead. "I think someone must have paid him."

"Where's Uncle Carlisle?"

"I don't know that either. I'm going to talk to Mr. Thompkins and see what I can find out."

"He talks silly."

"Mmm. A bit. I think he was very shaken by what happened."

"I was scared."

"I know, sweetheart; so was I. But you were a very brave boy. I'm proud of you." She smiled, thinking of how ferociously he had attacked Diggs. He should have run as she'd told him, but she could not but love his loyalty and courage.

Gil hugged her tightly for a moment, then flopped back down onto the bed, yawning widely. "I'm tired."

"I should think so."

She watched him as he yawned again and struggled to keep his eyes open. No doubt he was still groggy from the sleeping draught Diggs had given him. In his excitement he had managed to fight it off, but now that he was exhausted from struggling with Diggs, the drug was pulling him back to sleep.

Noelle stroked his forehead as his eyes fluttered closed. She stayed for a few more minutes to make sure he was fast asleep. She didn't want him to wake up and find her gone, but she had to talk to Mr. Thompkins and make some sense of what had happened.

Rising, she tiptoed across the room, pausing to give a last look back at Gil, then slipped out the door, closing it softly behind her. She found the lawyer sitting on a stool at the rough wooden table in the outer room. He had apparently recovered his composure, for he was reloading his pistol. A matching pistol lay on the table before him. It surprised her that he had brought a pistol, let alone two.

But, then, perhaps he was well accustomed to guns; his shot at Diggs had been on target. She had assumed it was more luck than anything else, but perhaps he was an excellent marksman. Clearly, she had an inaccurate image of the man.

He saw her and immediately rose to his feet. "My lady. Pardon me—I—it seemed it might be wise to be prepared." He gestured toward the pistols lying on the table. "Please, come, sit down. You must be quite shaken after such an ordeal."

She smiled faintly. "I am, thank you." She took the chair he offered. "Mr. Thompkins, I'm afraid I still don't understand exactly why you're here. How did you know Diggs had taken us? You said you went to Stonecliffe?"

"Yes. After you left, I could not stop thinking about what Mr. Thorne had said. I couldn't understand why Mr. Dunbridge had asked me not to reveal it to Mr. Thorne. I could see that the two of you thought Mr. Dunbridge had done something wrong. And the way you rushed out of there…well, it made wonder. So I looked at the other copy of the trust, and I realized that there was, well, a very disturbing pattern of deaths among the descendants of the trust's creators. There are only a few of them still alive, and that seemed very long odds, given their ages."

"Yes, I know. That is why Mr. Thorne and I have been looking into the matter. It was clear that my son was the next target. I must say, it would have been helpful if you had told Carlisle the truth when he asked you."

"I know. Obviously I should have. It's no wonder you are upset. But I had no idea what was going on. And Mr. Dunbridge had explicitly told me not to tell

Mr. Thorne. Tonight I realized that you must think it was Mr. Dunbridge who had done away with all the others." He shook his head. "But that was such a ludicrous idea—I've known Nathan Dunbridge for years, and I cannot imagine that he could do such a thing. Then when I learned that he had been killed—"

Noelle gasped. "He's dead?"

"That man Diggs shot him. Did you not know?"

"Yes, I know, but he was still alive when we left. Carlisle had gone for the doctor."

"I doubt he would have tried very hard to find him," Thompkins said bitterly.

"What?" Noelle's eyebrows soared. "What do you mean by that?"

"It is Carlisle Thorne who's behind all this, not Mr. Dunbridge."

"No. You're mistaken."

His face softened with sympathy. "No, my lady, I'm afraid I'm not. I suspected very strongly that it was Mr. Thorne, not Mr. Dunbridge; that's why I went to Stonecliffe. I felt I must warn you and Mr. Dunbridge—although I suppose Mr. Dunbridge must have already had some idea of the danger. That must have been why he told me not to reveal the truth to Mr. Thorne."

"That's nonsense. How can you think that Carlisle was behind it?"

"Because he clearly lied to you, to me, to everyone. He pretended that he didn't know about the trust, but he had talked to my father about it. I looked at my father's records. He took meticulous notes of every meeting. Mr. Thorne came to see him about it after the earl died. They discussed it in full. I know it's hard for you to accept, but it's the truth."

Noelle gaped at him, stunned. It was more than hard for her to believe it; it was impossible. "No. That can't be true. When we get back to the house, Carlisle will explain it all."

"How can there be any other explanation? Why would Thorne have lied about the trust all this time if he were not guilty?" Thompkins asked reasonably.

"I don't know, but—"

"There's only Mr. Snowden and Gilbert left in his way now. Who else would benefit?"

"Snowden. Or it really was Nathan, but he was killed in the process." She frowned. "No, that wouldn't work. But—"

There was a noise outside, and Noelle jumped to her feet, turning toward the door. An instant later, the door crashed open.

"Carlisle!"

CHAPTER THIRTY-ONE

CARLISLE FOUND IT slow going through the woods, where he had to stop several times to make sure he was still following the right trail. When the path began to widen, he broke into a trot. He was beginning to suspect that their destination must be the abandoned cottage Adam's old nurse had lived in after she retired. He couldn't understand why Diggs would take Noelle and Gil there, but then there was very little in this whole affair that he did understand.

He emerged in the clearing. A body lay between him and the cottage. He ran to it, his heart in his throat, but as he drew nearer, he realized that it was Diggs who lay sprawled across the grass, blood soaking the ground beneath him. He had been shot. Had Noelle managed to take his gun away and shoot him? But no, there was Diggs's pistol, shoved into the back of his waistband.

A horse nickered from across the clearing and Carlisle glanced up. Someone else was here. That's why Diggs had taken them here; he was giving them to the man who had hired him. Doubtless it was that man who had shot Diggs, and now he had Noelle and Gil in the cottage.

These thoughts flashed through Carlisle's mind in an instant, and he started to run to the cottage, but he was caught up short by the realization that, in his anxiety, he had run after Noelle without even stopping to pick up a weapon. He yanked the pistol from Diggs's dead body and charged toward the cottage. Carlisle took the two steps up to the porch in one leap and slammed open the door.

The first thing he saw was Noelle, standing by a small table. Her face lit up when she saw him, and he nearly sagged with relief. Then his gaze went to the man standing beside her, who held a pistol aimed straight at Carlisle's chest.

Cato Thompkins.

Suddenly it all made sense. "It was you…"

Thompkins snorted. "It is I who is going to stop your murderous career."

"Excellent line; you've rehearsed it well." Staring down the barrel of the other man's pistol, it occurred to Carlisle that his own weapon might not be loaded. If so, all he had as a weapon was a bluff. He'd better make it good. He kept his hand steady, his face cold; there was no need to fake the murder in his eyes.

"You can sneer all you want," Thompkins began, his eyes glinting. "But I—"

"Mr. Thompkins, please. Carlisle." Noelle started toward Carlisle.

"Noelle, stand back," Carlisle told her. "Don't get in his line of fire." Clearly Noelle was not aware of the man's villainy. She took a step aside at Carlisle's request, no longer directly in his line of fire, but she was still too close to Thompkins. The man could reach her in only a stride and take her hostage. A threat to Noelle would make Carlisle do almost anything.

"It's all right. Mr. Thompkins saved me from Diggs, Carlisle," Noelle explained.

"Yes, I saw the body. Got rid of your accomplice, eh, Cato? Neat and tidy, I must say. No need to pay him. No one who could tell everyone the truth." Carlisle kept his gaze riveted on the lawyer, not daring to take his attention from the man to even glance at Noelle. Chillingly, he saw that Thompkins held a second pistol in his other hand, hanging by his side. He wouldn't have to stop to reload. He could shoot both Carlisle and Noelle in seconds.

"Please, the two of you, stop this," Noelle said in an exasperated voice and took another step toward Carlisle. Silently he willed her closer. If he could just get her behind him, she'd be protected from Thompkins's shot.

"My lady, stop!" Thompkins exclaimed. "Don't take another step. He's dangerous."

Noelle sighed and turned to Thompkins. "Mr. Thompkins, please, Carlisle is no danger. If you would just listen to him, I'm sure he can explain why he didn't tell us about the trust."

"What?" Her words shocked him so much Carlisle turned to her, then hastily returned his gaze to Thompkins. "Noelle, I don't know what this fellow has been telling you, but I am certain it is all lies. You cannot trust him. He is the one who's been doing all this. Come—"

"No, please, my lady! Don't!" Thompkins's voice cracked. Carlisle could see that his hand was shaking slightly. "*He* is the liar. Thorne's trying to deceive you again. It's him; he is the only one who could profit. Not me. Diggs is *his* man. Diggs killed Nathan. He kidnapped you and the boy and tried to kill you both. Diggs did it because Thorne ordered it."

Noelle looked at Thompkins, then back at Carlisle,

her face thoughtful. Could she actually believe that Carlisle had tried to hurt Gil? Hurt her? Did she still carry a distrust for him deep inside her?

"Who chased the two of you all those years?" Thompkins pressed his point. "No doubt he claimed it was someone else, but who? Diggs was the one who tracked you all those times, who sent men after you. It was on Thorne's orders. You know it must have been. Diggs would not have betrayed Thorne; he was his faithful servant. His confidant."

"Noelle, come here." Carlisle's voice was clipped, the knot in his chest too hard and cold to say anything else. She doubted him. He could see it in the way she turned her head toward Thompkins consideringly. Despite everything that had happened between them, she didn't trust him.

Noelle turned and, casting a last sharp look at Carlisle over her shoulder, she walked toward Thompkins.

"Noelle, no!"

Gazing up at Thompkins, Noelle clasped her hands together at her waist. "You will protect me, won't you?"

Carlisle tensed. That sounded nothing like Noelle. And the look she had given him...

Thompkins glanced at her. "Lady—"

Noelle slammed her joined fists up into Cato's arm, and his pistol went flying, his shot hitting the ceiling. Thompkins raised his other pistol, but Carlisle was already on him, crashing into him and sending them both to the floor. The impact of the fall knocked the second pistol from Cato's hand, and Noelle darted around the men to grab it. The men rolled across the floor, punching and wrestling. But Carlisle was clearly the stronger of the two, and he soon ended it, smashing his fist into the other man's jaw. Thompkins went limp.

Carlisle jumped up and pulled Noelle into his arms. She wrapped her arms around his neck as he squeezed her close. "Noelle. My love." He broke off and kissed her.

When at last he raised his head, he said, "You frightened the life out of me. I thought you believed him."

Noelle pulled back sharply, giving him a not-so-gentle slap on the arm. "You thought I swallowed his story? How could you? Honestly, Carlisle, you have so little faith in me?"

"It wasn't that!" he protested. "I was scared that you still harbored a distrust of me. Because of what I did in the past. That you—"

"What utter nonsense!" She planted her fists on her hips and glared at him. "If I were not so insanely happy to see you, I would give you a tremendous scold. To think that I would take the word of a stranger over that of the man I love!"

Her words shot straight through him, filling him with such a strange, hot, sweet emotion that it was almost painful. He couldn't speak, his mind so numbed by this final revelation coming on top of a day filled with confusion and fear that he could scarcely think.

Noelle turned away quickly. "We should tie him up. I don't want him waking up and shooting us while we stand about chatting."

"No. I—yes, of course." He took a step closer. "Noelle…"

"But what will we use to tie him?" Noelle ignored Carlisle, surveying the room. "There's nothing here.

I haven't even a ribbon in my hair. I could tear off a ruffle."

Carlisle frowned, starting to speak again, then stopped. She was right; this was not the moment for this discussion. They would talk later. Right now was a time for practicality. "No, I'll use my neck cloth." He began to unwind the once elegant knot.

Rolling the unconscious man over, he pulled Thompkins's hands behind him and securely tied his wrists, tying the other end of the cloth around the leg of the table. Noelle in the meantime ripped off the ruffle of her petticoat to tie the man's feet together, as well.

"That should hold him for a while," Carlisle said, rising to look down at his handiwork. "As soon as we get back to the Hall, I'll send someone around to take him to the constable." He looked around, frowning. "Where is Gil? Is he not with you?"

"In the bedroom, asleep."

"Asleep?" His brows shot up. "Through all this?"

"Diggs drugged him. I managed to wake him up to escape, but then I thought we were safe—" She cast a dark look at the bound Thompkins. "And I put him back to bed."

She led Carlisle into the other room, where Gil still lay, asleep. When Carlisle picked him up to carry him out, Gil's eyelids fluttered and opened. "Uncle Carlisle." The boy smiled sleepily and laid his head against Carlisle's chest. "I knew you would come. Didn't you, Mama?"

"Yes." Noelle smoothed a piece of hair back from Gil's forehead. "I knew he would."

THEY FOUND THAT the pony, which had bolted when Diggs attacked them, had returned to the cottage and was placidly munching grass in the clearing. Carlisle harnessed him once more to the cart, and they started back down the trail toward home. Gil, now wide awake, was happily ensconced in the cart and enjoying the ride. Carlisle led the pony, and Noelle walked beside him, relating everything that had happened to her and Gil since they left Stonecliffe with Diggs.

"I would never have guessed that Diggs was working against me the whole time," Carlisle said. "It's still a shock. He must have been the one who hired the ruffians who pursued you, and he was in a perfect position to slip something into his agent's drink and send another man to kidnap Gil."

Noelle, breathing a little sigh of relief that he hadn't asked her again about her declaration of love earlier, continued this safer line of conversation. "Do you think it was Diggs who shot at Gil that day?"

"I presume it must have been. Though Thompkins certainly seemed to have excellent aim to drop Diggs like that." He looked over at Noelle. "I am so enormously sorry, Noelle."

"It's hardly your fault."

"It is, though. I am the one who bungled everything from the moment I first met you and then compounded my sins by hiring Diggs to search for you. I doubt Thompkins would have ever thought to hire Diggs if I had not already set him to the task. I paid him and never once was wise enough to doubt him. How could I have been so blind?"

"It is, I think, easier to deceive people who are honest and forthright. Devious people distrust others from the beginning," Noelle told him. "Besides, you had no reason to suspect him. I imagine when he began, he probably was just trying to find us and talk to me, as you hired him to. Later he decided he could get even more money by betraying you. How could you have known that? Who would have thought Thompkins would have hired Diggs—or that Thompkins would have had such a mad plot to begin with? Speaking of which, why in the world *did* Thompkins hire him? Why did he want to kill all those people?"

"I finally understood it when I saw him there with you. The answer was right before me in the document. I read it, but with everything that happened afterward, I didn't really think about it. Freddie Penrose said that the fund had made a great deal of money the past few years. Thompkins the son was apparently good at investing. He must have started thinking, 'Why should some aristocratic descendant get all this money? I'm the one who's doing the work. I deserve the benefits.' Or maybe he was simply greedy and evil from the start."

"Whichever he was, I don't see how it benefited him. He wasn't one of the possible beneficiaries."

"Ah, but he did benefit from it—if *all* the heirs died before the trust ended. In that case, the fund would have gone to a charity, also overseen by Thompkins. He killed the others and was planning to lay the blame on me or Nathan, whichever worked out the best. My guess is when we look at the fund's books, we will find that he has been siphoning off cash ever since he took over from his father. It would have been easy. I doubt he had any supervision, at least not after Lord Drewsbury died. Haverstock and Freddie clearly paid no attention to the workings of it. Nor would Nathan's father, and the others were gone."

"So he could transfer the funds to the charity and continue to embezzle from it."

"Exactly."

"What a cold-blooded man." Noelle shuddered. "To decide to kill all those people..."

"We don't know that he killed them all. Unless he confesses, we are certain only that he tried to kill Gil and Nathan and frame me. And I don't know that he planned it from the start. He may have simply realized one day how few of the founders had sons who grew to manhood. Maybe he began to think how convenient it would be if they *all* died."

"So he decided to help them along."

Carlisle nodded. "Sprague Haverstock's and John Brookwell's murders may be hard to prove, but it's my opinion he either killed them or paid Diggs to do it."

"They were the most recent deaths. He began much earlier with Gil, but, then, Gil would have been the most danger to him, being so young."

"Yes. He might not have been bent on killing Gil at first, just kidnapping him and making sure we didn't know where he was. But once Gil was here at home, Thompkins must have realized he had to do away with him entirely. Or he discovered, after Haverstock and Brookwell, that killing someone didn't bother him all that much. Maybe he even enjoyed it."

"What I don't understand is why he shot Diggs. Diggs worked for him."

"To keep from having to share the money with him. That's my guess. And Diggs knew much too much about him and his crimes. If Diggs were caught, he would probably have given up Thompkins, hoping for leniency. Diggs's knowledge also made Thompkins ripe for blackmail. Diggs could demand money in return for not revealing what Thompkins had done. Year after year, for the rest of his life."

"But if Thompkins shot Diggs, he'd look like a hero, as well as relieving himself of a threat. It played into his scheme, too," she added. "When he was trying to convince me that you had orchestrated the killings, one of his main arguments was that Diggs worked for you. Someone had hired Diggs, and the obvious person would be you."

"Yes, that would have looked bad for me." He glanced over at her. "I'm very glad you didn't believe him."

"No one would have." They were on dangerous territory again. Noelle wished she hadn't blurted out that she loved him; in the midst of her relief and joy, she hadn't paused to think. Carlisle must already know it, of course, but as long as it wasn't said out loud, it would be easier to remain friends.

Noelle hurried on. "There were a number of things that didn't make sense. If I hadn't been so stunned and confused, I think I would have already realized that there was something decidedly off about his story. How did he know that Gil and I would be at this cottage? And it wasn't necessary that he shoot Diggs. Diggs wasn't trying to strangle me or shoot me. He might have done so later, but at the moment Thompkins fired, he had only grabbed my arm and was about to hit me."

At this revelation, Carlisle's face contorted with fury. "It's probably a good thing Cato shot him—I would have made Diggs pay dearly if he had landed that blow."

Noelle couldn't help but smile at the fierceness with which he reacted. "What I'm saying is: threatening Diggs with his gun would have been enough to make him stop. Later, when Thompkins started telling me that you were behind the plot, his story was unbelievable. I knew you would never do such a thing, and if you had, you certainly would have done a better job of it."

"Thank you. I think."

She gave him a half smile. "You know what I mean—the whole thing's been very haphazard, hasn't it? Everything this evening was impulsive. He hadn't planned well for it, hadn't prepared."

"And I am never impulsive." Carlisle shrugged and gave a rueful smile. "Except tonight, when I came running after you without thinking to pick up a weapon. Thank God I found one on Diggs."

Noelle instinctively reached out to squeeze his hand. "I am very glad you came to rescue us, weapon or no. Thank you."

"Of course I came after you. I always will." He stopped, his fingers interlacing with hers, and cast a frustrated glance back at Gil, who was watching them with great interest. "I must talk to you."

"Carlisle, there is no need."

"There definitely *is* a need. I don't—"

"Look!" Gil yelled. His face was stamped with excitement as he pointed ahead.

There was a light through the trees, bobbing a little. No, several lights, she saw now. "Rescuers?"

At that moment, a familiar voice trumpeted, "For pity's sake, man, can't you go any faster? We'll never reach them at this rate."

"Lady Lockwood?" Noelle and Carlisle glanced at each other in surprise, then hurried forward. Even the pony picked up his pace. Soon they saw men carrying torches or lanterns, and in the rear was a dark figure on horseback.

"Grisham!" Carlisle called out to the head groom, hurrying forward. "You followed us!"

"Sir! Thank God we found you." Grisham glanced back over his shoulder at the figure on the horse.

The rider came forward, men jumping out of the way. Now in the torchlight, Noelle could see that the rider was Lady Lockwood dressed in riding habit and boots, crop in hand.

"Lady Lockwood! It's you. On horseback." Carlisle stared.

"Yes, of course it is I," she snapped back. "What a foolish thing to say. How else do you think I'd make my way up this trail? Hobble along on my cane?"

"No, it's just—I'm surprised you joined the search party."

"Joined! Hah! Who do you think organized it? This lot was completely useless, running to tell us instead of going after you. It was obvious I couldn't send them off without someone competent along to advise them."

Noelle hid a smile. From the look on Grisham's face, it was clear that Adeline's mother had "advised" them all along the way.

"Who else was there?" Lady Lockwood went on. "My daughter would have been of no help, and Annabeth was occupied hovering over the boy."

"Nathan?" Carlisle seized on her words. "How is he? Is he—"

"Still alive when we left." Lady Lockwood turned her gaze to Noelle and then to the pony cart, where Gil was gazing at her with his usual fascination. "Well, boy, I'm glad to see that you are all right." She nodded at him and turned her mount. "Come, come. No point in standing about here. Grisham, get out in front with the torches. What are you thinking? It's dark as Hades out here."

The groom scurried out in front, and the other men fell in meekly behind her.

Carlisle shook his head and, taking Noelle's hand, he followed, as well. "Only Lady Lockwood could make one regret seeing a rescue party."

CHAPTER THIRTY-TWO

By THE TIME they reached Stonecliffe, it was approaching dawn. Adeline met them with cries of joy, and Annabeth, hearing the noise, came rushing out, all smiles. For the next few moments, it was a pandemonium of exclamations, hugs, and kisses.

"Tell us everything," Adeline said. "I'll have Cook make up a midnight supper. You must be starving after your ordeal."

"Yes, what the devil happened?" Lady Lockwood demanded, apparently none the worse for wear after a sleepless night and a horseback ride. "First Nathan's shot, then Noelle disappears, and Carlisle takes off like a scalded cat, and no one seems to know anything at all."

"I beg your pardon, Lady Lockwood. We'll explain everything," Carlisle said, then turned and took Annabeth's arm, looking intently down at her. "But first, I have to know, how is Nathan?"

A smile broke across Annabeth's tired face. "He's better. He hasn't developed a fever, and the doctor says that's a good sign. He even woke up once and asked for you. He was agitated, though I assured him that you were here and everything was all right. So the doctor gave him a little laudanum, and he's been asleep ever since. The doctor's still here, but he's sleeping, too. Do you want to talk to him?"

Carlisle shook his head. "Later. I'll look in on Nathan in a bit."

Carlisle sent some of the men to get Thompkins at the cottage, then joined the others at the dining table, where he and Noelle tried to explain the entire story as everyone dug into the array of cold meats, bread, and cheeses the cook had laid out. Unsurprisingly, it took some time, as people kept interrupting with questions.

"One might have known Penrose and Dunbridge would set up a trust with a criminally inclined lawyer," Lady Lockwood said when they reached the end of the tale.

"To be fair, Mother, it was his son who was of a criminal bent," Adeline pointed out.

"Doesn't matter," Lady Lockwood said, pushing back her chair with a screech and rising to her feet. "All of this nonsense has kept me from my bed far too long. It'll be a wonder if I don't fall ill." She cast an accusatory eye all around the table before turning and walking to the door. There she paused and looked back at the table. "Well, Adeline?" She jerked her head toward the corridor. "Someone must carry my things. Annabeth is no doubt going to continue her vigil, though I must say, I can't see the point. The doctor is here, and the boy is asleep anyway."

With a sigh, Adeline followed her. Annabeth also excused herself, returning to Nathan's bedside. Noelle, too, stood up. "I should put Gil down for a rest."

"Mama!" Gil protested. "I've been asleep *forever*."

"I'm sure his governess can take care of Gil now,"

Carlisle said, coming around the table. "I want to talk to you, Noelle."

"I—um—I'm very tired. I think I shall lie down. If you'll excuse me…" She was certain Carlisle still wanted to talk to her about her revelation that she loved him; he was like a dog with a bone once he got hold of a subject. But she couldn't face dealing with him right now. She was drained, her brain muzzy, and she was all too likely to say something else she'd want to have back.

Carlisle looked as if he might protest, but at that moment, the butler appeared in the door, saying, "Mr. Thorne. They've brought Mr. Thompkins here, sir. I've sent for the constable, but I thought you might wish to speak with him."

"I certainly would," Carlisle replied grimly, and followed him out of the room, turning around to say, "I still want to talk to you."

At least she had a reprieve. She didn't understand why Carlisle was so insistent about this. She couldn't imagine that he didn't already know she loved him, and she would have thought that he would be as glad as she to pretend she hadn't told him so. Perhaps he thought she might have expectations that he would marry her or that she would be weepy and whining about it. Or maybe that she might leave, taking Gil with her, so that she wouldn't have to face the heartache of being around Carlisle. She would have to make it clear she would not do any of those things, and right now, given how exhausted she was, she was afraid she would start to cry, which would put the lie to all her assurances.

She handed Gil off to his governess, relieved that he seemed to have no qualms about leaving Noelle and was instead happy to relate to someone else all the things that had happened to him. Going back to her room, she fell on the bed, too tired to even unlace her half boots, and fell asleep.

A knock on the door woke her up, and she sat up groggily. Without waiting for an answer, Carlisle opened the door and came inside. Closing the door behind him, he strode across to the bed and sat down beside her.

"Carlisle! What are you doing? You shouldn't be in here. Everyone will talk."

"I don't give a damn. You keep slipping away, and I want to talk to you."

"Well, I don't want to talk to you," Noelle replied crossly. "You might have noticed by the fact that I keep slipping away."

"Yes, you've made it abundantly clear. What I don't understand is why. Blast it, Noelle, just answer my question and I will leave you alone."

"All right!" Noelle scooted back until her back was against the headboard and crossed her arms, glaring at him. "Ask your question."

But now that he'd got what he wanted, he seemed curiously reluctant to speak. He looked down, then stood up and turned around to face her. "Last night…you said—did you mean what you said?"

"That I love you?" Clearly there was nothing for it but to admit it. "Yes. I meant it."

"Then why the devil did you turn down my proposal?" he said, his voice rising.

"Proposal?" She stared at him. "What proposal?"

"At my home, when you told me you couldn't—"

"Proposal! You call saying 'perhaps we should

marry' a proposal?" Noelle swung off the bed to face him, hands on hips.

"That's why you turned me down? Because I didn't ask you properly?"

"You didn't *ask* me at all."

"You told me that marrying me was the last thing you wanted!"

"Carlisle, you're shouting. Everyone will hear you."

"I don't care!" he thundered, swinging his arms wide, hitting a bottle on the dresser and knocking it to the floor, where it shattered. "Oh, bloody hell."

The next moment the door swung open and a maid stuck her head in. "Ma'am? Are you all—" She stopped abruptly at the sight of Carlisle. "Beg pardon. I, uh…"

Carlisle turned to scowl at her. "Go away."

With a squeak, she pulled the door to and fled.

"It's a good thing you don't care about people talking," Noelle commented.

He turned back to her and with a visible effort said more calmly, "You said that you would marry only for love. You said that was why you wouldn't marry me."

"That's right. I have no desire to marry because it would prevent a scandal or because you don't want to offend Adeline or because it's the honorable thing to do. I want *love*, Carlisle, but it has to be love on both sides. It's not enough that I love you. I don't want to spend a lifetime loving you, wishing that you felt the same, wanting more, my heart dying a bit at a time while you came to resent me because you had to marry me instead of some 'proper' lady with good breeding and—"

"Good breeding! Where in the hell did that come from? There is no 'proper lady' I want to marry."

"Not at the moment, but Lady Lockwo—"

"Do not—" He jabbed his finger toward her for emphasis. "*Do not*—bring bloody Lady Lockwood into this."

"It's not just her. It's society. The aristocracy—your people. Whatever you say, you care what others think; you want to do the right thing, you want—"

"I don't give a damn about society. What I *want* is to marry you."

Noelle went still, staring at him, a strange, light feeling beginning to bubble up in her chest. "Why?"

"Because I love you, that's why," he said in a goaded tone. "I thought I'd go mad last night when I realized you were in danger. I didn't think; I didn't measure or plan. I didn't even have enough forethought to grab a weapon. All I could do was run after you, try to find you and pray that he hadn't hurt you already." He stepped forward, raising a hand to caress her cheek. "I told myself not to be impulsive; I told myself it was infatuation and it would go away. But it hasn't. It won't. My life would be barren without you. I don't know what I'd do. I want to marry you. I want to be with you always. Please, tell me you will marry me."

Noelle gazed up at him, her eyes glowing. "Now *that* is what I call a proposal," she said and went up on her tiptoes to kiss him.

"Is that a yes?" Carlisle pulled back and looked at her seriously.

"Yes, you silly man." Noelle laughed. "Yes, it is very much a yes."

* * * * *

ACKNOWLEDGMENTS

A special thanks to Anastasia Hopcus. The best thing about writing *An Affair at Stonecliffe* was getting to include my daughter. We had fun all the way through, but the highlight was sending little notes back and forth about our favorite Lady Lockwood moments!

As always, this book would not be here without the efforts of a large number of people: my wonderful agent, Maria Carvainis; my editor, Brittany Lavery; and the whole team at HQN, who make the beautiful covers, correct my errors, and get my books out to the readers. You all are the best!

AUTHOR BIO

Candace Camp is the *New York Times* bestselling author of over seventy novels, including *A Momentary Marriage* and the popular Mad Morelands series, which now encompasses a not-so-small portion of that seventy.

Candace wrote her first novel while in law school. The experience taught her two things. One, she can write even surrounded by towers of textbooks tall enough to crush her to death if there were an earthquake. Two, the only kind of tort she has any interest in is the kind that comes after the word *chocolate* and has an *e* on the end.

So after Candace sold her first book, she happily gave up lawyer-ing to pursue her lifelong dream of writing. She lives in Austin, Texas, with her husband, Pete Hopcus. Her daughter is author Anastasia Hopcus.

To join Candace's newsletter for exclusive content and monthly prizes go to her website: candace-camp.com.

You can also find her on social media.
BookBub: Bookbub.com/Authors/Candace-Camp
Facebook: Facebook.com/CandaceCampauthor/
Twitter: Twitter.com/CampCandace
Amazon: bit.ly/CCampAmazon
Goodreads: bit.ly/CCampGoodreads
Instagram: bit.ly/CCampInsta